DANGEROUS GAMES

Dangerous Games

Julian Rathbone

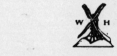

HEINEMANN : LONDON

William Heinemann Ltd
Michelin House, 81 Fulham Road, London SW3 6RB
LONDON   MELBOURNE   AUCKLAND

First published 1991
Copyright © Julian Rathbone 1991

A CIP catalogue record for this book
is held by the British Library
ISBN 0 434 62393 8

Phototypeset by CentraCet, Cambridge
Printed in Great Britain
by Clays Ltd, St Ives plc

PROLOGUE

The office was panelled in pale oak against which gilt-framed oil paintings of nineteenth century battles glowed with heroic realism. The furniture was solid and large, gave an impression of stability and robust old age, though in fact it was modern and functional – very comfortable black leather chairs, a big desk, deep carpets. The lighting was indirect, apart from a reading lamp on the desk, and bright. A tall sash window with velvet drapes in an old gold that nicely matched the panelling looked down from the first floor on to one of the wider streets between Bond Street and Grosvenor Square. In the centre of the desk was a small nineteenth-century bronze representing the last moments of a wolf with an Irish Wolf-hound at its neck. Over the years Wolf-hound had gone steadily up-market.

So too had its owner – Colonel Finchley-Camden. Even his legitimate business, providing individualised security packages tailored to suit a firm's particular needs, was making profits which the Inland Revenue could concede matched a life-style that was restrained but unsurpassable: the Jacobean farmhouse with additions in the Cotswolds, the racing yacht at Cowes, the one built for comfortable cruising at Ajaccio, three 'chasers in training . . .

The Colonel himself, now just fifty years old, was the very picture of health and prosperity. Tall, his figure had indeed begun to thicken a little, but without losing proportion, his hair was perhaps a little thinner than it had been but remained a fine mane of corrugated silver like the curlicues on the edge of the small silver salver his secretary used for calling cards and

1

personal mail. He no longer affected the military look that had seemed right when he started – his suit was impeccably cut, but the slightly waisted jacket with longer than usual skirts, the tapering trousers, recalled times when even middle-aged men of substance were allowed to cut a dash. His only visible concession to *fugaces anni* was a pair of half-moon gold-framed spectacles, which he played with more than he realised.

'Up shit-creek sans un paddle, eh?' He leant back in his big chair, swung his spectacles between thumb and forefinger. 'How bad is it?'

His effortless superiority was a bitter cup which the younger man in front of him had to swallow – if he were to get what he wanted.

'Not good, Nuncle.'

'Sam Dorf, I know, has given you your marching orders. I take it it's no worse than that – no question of Mr Plod fingering your collar? What were you up to? Let me guess. You traded copper with someone else's money, the market deserted you, you "borrowed" to take up a new position, and that went wrong too. It could be the slammer. Post-Guinness no one's safe. Certainly not a tuppenny-ha'panny trader on the Metal Exchange.'

This was meant to rile, and it did.

'If you knew, why ask?'

'Dear boy. I just wanted confirmation that it's as bad as I'd been told. And it is. So what do you want?'

'Work.'

'That's a relief. I thought you might be looking for a loan. What makes you think I might have work for you?'

But before his nephew could answer a polite buzz cut him off. The Colonel flipped a switch. His secretary's voice came as a discreet but audible murmur.

'Mr Herz from Zürich is on the white phone.'

The Colonel closed the switch, picked up the white phone.

'Heinrich. How are you? Good to speak. Yes. Fine. Right away. I'll get back to you right away.' He replaced the white phone, picked up the red, and paused, fingers poised over the buttons.

'Really, you know, if you're asking me what I think you're asking me, you should be talking to Mr Herz.'

He pressed the buttons on the second handset. Thus prompted, the younger man listened. The sound of a fly tap-dancing. 010 for International. 41 for Switzerland. 1 for Zürich. He was sure of the next four, fairly sure of the last two. Sure enough.

'Heinrich. Look. I've gone over your proposal very carefully. And at this point in time I have to say the whole business has . . . dimensions, I think that is the word I want, which I'm not at all confident . . .'

Mr Herz of Zürich had a lot to say to this which the Colonel had no particular need to hear. Hand over the mouthpiece he returned to his nephew.

'I have got a job you could do. Spot of minding for the Emir of . . . Heinrich, that's still an offer I could just about refuse. But certainly not without giving it some serious thought. Give me a week or so, and I'll see if I can get back to you on it. Bye for now. Take care.'

He replaced the phone, opened the switch back to the outer office.

'Gwendolyn, I'm out to Heinrich Herz for the next fortnight.' He closed the switch, leant back, picked up his spectacles, gave them a twirl. 'Won't touch that with a bargepole. Where was I? The Emir of Kamar wants a minder on his plane to Hamburg day after tomorrow . . .'

'I don't want to be a minder. And certainly not to some wog Arab – '

'He's paying over the odds. And with good reason. Two good reasons. One. The fundamentals have a contract out on him – an eternity of houris in paradise to the nutter who pulls it off. More than I can promise anyone who labours in the vineyard on my account, eh? And, two, he has a distant cousin here in

England, illegally, and they want to get him out before the lads at Wapping hear about it – '

'Nuncle. I don't want to be a minder. I can function on the other side of the fence, which I imagine pays better. I know how. I'm an expert.'

'Of course, dear boy. But the trouble is your distinguished expertise is very much on public record. So. Not for me, not for Wolf-hound. Now. The Emir has a private DC9 parked at Luton . . .'

PART I

1

North Germany, an autobahn, dusk, a thunderstorm. The southbound lanes took a slow curve towards the West. Flashing gleams of eye-piercing yellow light skipped off the wet surface – scything star knives hurled by a Ninja prince. The Woman blinked away, pulled down the sun visor, tightened her grip on the wheel as a Volvo container truck, klaxons bellowing, thundered by in the middle lane. It sucked wind that made her 1975 VW camper rock towards it, sliced oily water over the Greenpeace decals, snatched curtains of mud across her windscreen as it lurched into the slot she'd left in front of her.

'Bastard.'

Then she grinned, enjoying the drama of the traffic and the storm. She rummaged the cassette holder, uncased and planted without looking, turned the volume up. Brrm, b-b-brm b-b-brrm brrm . . . Schubert's 'Wanderer Fantasy', fierily played by Bolet, she sang along like a Valkyrie, determined not to be put out of sorts in the first hours of her long summer break.

Lights on gantries, huge road signs bright like cinema screens against the back-drop of stacked black cloud, a slip way to Hanover airport. She could see the control tower over to her right, the terminal, the avenue of runway lights arrowing almost to a point on the flat horizon. Warehouses, hangars, workshops intervened behind high fences topped with razor wire, and then the tall, dark firs closed in on both sides. The autobahn became a river of light through the forest.

The storm clouds prowled in from the north, wolves circling for the kill. Lightning forked, and thunder rolled unheard beneath the black noise of the traffic. Out of it, lights flashing on its nose and wing tips and under its belly, a DC9 dipped against the band of stark yellow light beneath the cloud, banked and came on, its flight-path aimed obliquely to cross the autobahn a kilometre further west.

'Surely that must be too low.'

Brrm, b-b-brrm, b-b-brrm, brrm.

Cranmer peered through the rain-streaked window, looked at his watch, and then at the warning sign suspended above the dividing curtain five files of seats in front of him. It was lit – fasten your seat belts, no smoking. But beyond the tartan curtain they weren't bothered. He could hear voices in a language he could not understand, laughter, was aware of people still moving about. He shrugged: it wasn't his business to tell the Emir what to do. He fastened his own seat belt.

The rear of the DC9 had been left as it was when the Emir bought it – ordinary passenger seats with economy class spacing, British Caledonian livery. But the front had been converted into a state-room with black leather chairs, tables rimmed with padded black leather, fancy lamp-shades made from Venetian glass, silver spigots dispensing iced water, lemon sherbet, spiced buttermilk. On this trip it was full, over-crowded – the Emir, three wives, seven children, and five advisers. Throughout the flight, Luton to Hamburg, the three male children had been free to do as they pleased, including flying the thing right into the storm's turbulence as they crossed the North Sea coast.

Then came the Captain's announcement, passed to the rear by word of mouth, not broadcast over a PA system. In ten minutes they would land. But not at Hamburg where the freak storm had flooded the runway, Hanover instead. And that meant a long drive back up the motorway, riding shotgun in the first of the limos that would be hired for them, all the way to the Ramada Renaissance Hotel where he'd hand over the package to a German equivalent, and catch the next flight back. Club-class.

8

The aircraft banked, spilled pine forest on to the ovoid dish of his window. An autobahn of light, white headlights on one side red taillights on the other, snaked lazily through it. Presently, he reckoned, they'd cross it.

On the other side of the narrow gangway the only other person in the rear section suddenly shifted, pocketed the worry beads that had threaded the names of Allah through his fingers again and again since take-off over an hour earlier, scratched his armpits, and pushed his face across the space. Grey, a sheen of sweat, squashed nose, pock-marks. The Illegal. Was he worried about his documentation? Had he a routine lined up that would work in Hamburg, but not Hanover?

'Are we nearly there?'

There was sour uncooked garlic on his breath. Gold glimmered in his mouth.

'Yes. Five minutes. At the most.'

The Illegal shifted again in his seat, then stood, manoeuvring the joints of his body round the arm rest, unfolding and straightening his legs in the gangway. He turned his back on the Minder, reached up into the luggage locker above his seat, struggled with the catch and let the plastic casing drop. That close to his backside Cranmer caught gases other than garlic and sweat. They triggered memories nine and four years old.

The Illegal looked down over his shoulder. Near black cheap suit, white shirt, no tie.

'I have a gift for the Emir. The Emir is a great and good man, a true father to all his nation. I must seize this moment to make a humble gesture of gratitude.'

He lifted down a square parcel, gift wrapped in metallic silver paper, swathed with a scarlet ribbon and a bow, sealed with a big stick-on label, gold on scarlet.

'Sweetmeats. *Mille feuilles* with honey and almonds. It's not much but the children will enjoy them.'

He was The Illegal because, according to the Emir's chargé d'affaires in London, the Emir wanted him taken out of the UK where he had no business to be, whose immigration laws he had broken. And he happened to be a remote cousin of the Emir's, but not so remote that the British Press would not make a meal of it if he was arrested. The Minder had slipped five hundred pounds, not his own, to a passport official at Luton. The official was thus encouraged to blink as he counted the crew and passengers onto the DC9. Twenty-two people were on board. The manifest said twenty-one.

The Minder watched The Illegal carrying the square silver and scarlet box, bouncing light off its crinkled surfaces like the boxes placed on the moon a quarter of a century earlier, up to the tartan curtain. The Illegal had carried no luggage when he came on board, so the parcel of sweetmeats had been put in the locker ahead of him. He went through the curtain, was gone. Shouts from the children, audible even above the scream of jets reversed for landing. The smells remained. They reminded Cranmer of a shepherd's hut above Goose Green and the Duke of Wellington pub in Belfast: they were the smells that come off people who know they are about to die.

He moved – not forwards, it was too late for that – but to the rear of the plane, just up in front of the tail unit. There, in the tiny galley those Caledonian girls had used so many years before, the safety straps were still in place. He parked himself on the narrow fold-down seat which was only just too low for him, fastened the straps, and waited. He had time to wonder what would be said if, after landing, the Emir's children, whose fingers and lips would be smeared with honey, almond chips and flaky pastry, found his minder thus ignominiously at the other end of the plane. But it wouldn't come to that. He had time to experience a star-burst of ecstacy, to ride like a surfer the wave of euphoria that followed. It had always been like this in moments of extreme danger. Then the blast came, just as he knew it would.

Lean, long fingers with rings embellished with amethyst and topaz tightened on the wheel as the Woman saw the forepart of the DC9's passenger pod grow swiftly incandescent with white heat and then burst. She stamped the brake and the big high bus behind, from the airport perhaps, klaxoned her eardrum, herded her on. The aircraft dipped in a slewing slide. It was now almost above the autobahn. For a moment she thought it would drop on to it no more than four hundred metres ahead. Stricken, it spewed flaming debris, shards and the curling skin, and suddenly the red lights in front of her, blurred through the mud and grime that the wipers hardly cleared before the next slurp came, boxed up on each other then froze and zoomed in on her. She swung to the right on to the hard shoulder. Braked on the wet greasy surface, the camper slewed, swung back to the carriageway, but she steered into the skid and out of it. The onside fender crunched against the crash barrier almost touching the back of the BMW in front of her. She let her forehead drop on to knuckles that seemed permanently welded to the steering wheel and pulled in a sigh of gratitude that she was alive, and then another because she was not hurt.

Hail followed the lightning strike of less than a minute before, curtained down the frozen stream of traffic in front of her, rattled across the still intact windscreen inches in front of her face. She lifted her head, and over to her right out of the forest a great fireball rose, red and yellow, shedding whirling metal sheeting, flaring plastic, fragments of aircraft and people into the now black air above. Across the space between, the roar of it came, punctuated by smaller explosions as fuel lines and tanks exploded, and then the tops of trees. Showers of multi-coloured incandescence danced down through the hail and rain, turned to ashes before they settled.

Moments before impact the tail unit separated, crashed into and through the tops of the firs, already whittled by the passage of the front part of the aircraft, including the scything wings, and settled no more than four metres above the floor of the forest. Like the rest it burned, though less ferociously now that the tunnel of burning air funnelled down the passenger tube had been separated from it.

The blast had blown out the rear door. A man stood for a moment in the space, black against the inferno behind him. The suit on his back ignited. Arms and legs spread he hurled himself out and on to the forest floor. He rolled forward, again and again, away from the wreck, through the rain, the sodden fir needles, until the clothes on his back stopped burning and merely smouldered. He tore them off, stripping them off like peel, and screamed with the agony as his scorched skin came too. When he was completely naked he yielded for a moment, arms raised in triumph at being alive, to the blessing of the rain and hail. Then he stumbled away out of the heat and into the dark of the forest.

The Woman stayed in the driving seat of her camper. Not trusting her old battery she turned off the in-car stereo and sat in darkness. With a BMW in front, an ERF truck behind she didn't feel she was running any risk of being shunted. And it wasn't dark in any real sense either. Police bikes and cars first, then fire-engines and ambulances – blue and orange lights swirling, sirens wailing or yelping like a race of giant guinea-pigs – swung shadows across her face, across the empty seat beside her. She lit a cigarette with a small gold Zippo and tried not to think of people blasted to bits, of people on fire. Presently from the blacker shade of the forest she was seen and watched.

A polizei bike, white green and red, wing lights flashing, swung by, twin exhausts spinning vapour into the rain and spray. It circled, almost lazily, came back, halted. The rider put heavy armed boots to the blacktop, spoke into a microphone on a short coiled lead, then swung himself clear. From panniers behind him he took two batons with circular reflective discs like giant lolly-pops, used them to command the silver grey BMW in front to pull out into the fast lane, move on. Then, with goggles framed in yellow against the white helmet and buttoned up leather, reflector belts like barbaric jewellery, he came through the silver rain and waved his lolly-pops at her.

The Woman stubbed her cigarette in the black plastic dashboard ashtray, turned the ignition key to *fahrt*, so her lights came back on, gave the key another nudge, tapped the throttle with her toe, engaged first gear, let out the clutch. She felt how the camper heaved for a moment against the barrier, then the engine died. The policeman waved again, irritated now, quick jabs in the air with his ridiculous lolly-pops. She tried reverse, heard wheelspin, felt again the vehicle that she loved as if it were a horse or a mule strain in ways that must hurt it. This time she killed the engine herself.

The traffic cop turned his goggles full on her. She shrugged, largely, expressively, wondered how well he could see her. He got the message, came up to her, passed her, ignoring her now as someone or something that had become irrelevant, stood level with her rear fender but out in the middle lane – she could see his back in her wing mirror – and she watched while he signalled out the ERF truck behind her. Then, still ignoring her, he stamped back, swung his fat bottom into the wide leather saddle, kick-started, and smoothly, solidly idled past, back down to the next vehicle that could move, and the next, and the next. The Woman lit another cigarette.

There was a high fence, chain-link with razor, between the forest and the motorway, built on top of a low narrow rampart of earth. A fox had been there before the Man, and dug a passage for itself through the rampart. Chest, belly, genitals, knees pressed into the wet cold earth he managed to wriggle under. Four yards of sloping rubble, the crash barrier, buckled but not broken where the camper had hit it, and the sliding door on the side. He grasped the handle, knowing it would be locked, and pulled.

The noise, to those who know it, is unmistakable – the side door of a VW van, pre-1980, trundling open. For a moment he perched, one bare foot up on the barrier, the other seeking to cross it, then he tumbled off the barrier, forward and in. He could see she was lean, and tall, that already she was hoisting herself through the gap between the front seats towards him,

13

that she was holding a large heavy spanner. He could hear her voice. High, peremptory, like a bugle.

'*Rauss*! Get out. Get right out, right now. Come on, shift yourself. *Rauss*.'

Inside his head he had held on to something that allowed him to make the pain a problem for his body but not for him. Now, in the still warm darkness, out of the rain, with some sort of thin but gentle carpet under his knees instead of the grit, gravel and pine needles, he let it go and the pain crashed over him like a wave. Through it he still heard her voice and felt her brush past him, her three-quarter length skirt brushing his arm and shoulder.

'Jesus. You need help. An ambulance, hospital.'

His German was better than good, he understood, and sensed rather than saw that she was heading for the open space he had come through. Blindly he caught her arm, and held it, remembered to answer in the language she had used.

'*Kein krankenwagen. Bitte. Kein krankenwagen.*'

He shifted his grip to her wrist, tightened it – it was, she said later, like a sprung trap – until he felt her relax. Then the door trundled and clunked as she closed it and the rumble of vehicles moving, of engines starting and the nearer hiss of the rain were cut off, and the warmth folded more certainly round him.

She had more or less passed him to get to the open door. Already on his knees but still upright, he now began to sink backwards, his body turned a little more as it sagged, and she sank to her knees too, behind him, letting his back and shoulders sink into her lap and her chest, his head loll on to her shoulder. He hung there for a moment and she felt his weight go dead, realised that strong though she was she might have difficulty shifting him once he lost consciousness. She got her hands into his armpits.

'Come on. Come . . . on. On to the seat. Please.'

2

The Woman straightened as far as the unraised roof of the camper would let her, pushed long dark hair, a little grey at the temples, back over her ears, let her hands smooth it down and press it into the nape of her long neck. She was far from sure that she was doing the right thing. Even in the broken darkness, lit by sweeping headlamps and flashing blue she could see he was in a bad way. His front had been streaked with blood, rain and mud, and that had been bad, but now she could see his shoulders and back, see the bright fierce magenta of burn marks in four distinct places, each the size of a hand or bigger, and smaller islands around them. He surely needed help more expert than she could provide. But at that moment three clanging thumps shook the camper. It was as if it had been attacked, beaten. A yard from her face but below it and separated by rainstreaked glass, the patrolman, or his clone, loomed up at her.

'Come on. Move. Out. Now.' And the three thuds from a hand gloved heavily enough to make it a weapon, came again.

'I can't. I'm stuck. I told you. Can't you see.'

She was angry, let herself be heard to be angry.

She watched him move on, down the motorway.

'Fat pig.'

Her mind made up she began to bustle, briskly but carefully, knowing exactly what to do, exactly what to do next, drawing on knowledge and skills she had been at pains to learn following an accident some years before.

She released clips where the roof met the sides, pushed, secured the clips again so through most of the van she could now move without stooping. She drew all the curtains – not the standard ones provided by the conversion people, but lapis blue with peacock green and shards of lemon woven in. Then she lit a paraffin lamp that gave a light good enough to read by. From a cupboard above the side windows she took a wooden box, her first aid and medical kit. In the tiny kitchen area between the side door and the raised area at the back above the engine she cranked a chrome lever and drew water into a small plastic bowl. Then she put all this on the floor of the narrow gangway below the bed-length seat the Man was now stretched on. Lastly she took off her rings, topaz and amethyst, and dropped them in a drawer next to chunky necklaces and gold chains. Then she knelt, began to clean him up.

She soon realised that the analgesic antiseptic aerosol spray she used before touching each lesion was not enough. He flinched, sometimes uttered sharp little cries at every dab, however gentle. She shifted, moved her face closer to his.

'Can you hear me?'

He moved his head. If he had been sitting up it would have been a nod.

'I've got pain-killers. Tablets.'

DF–118, dihydrocodeine, in an English bottle. She had an English friend whose doctor prescribed them for migraine. She broke out four tablets, poured Spa water into a tumbler.

'Come on. You must sit up and take these. If you don't I'll drive you straight to the nearest hospital.' The medical lore, she had been taught, came back to her. 'You should drink as much as you can. Dehydration can be a problem after burns.'

He took the tablets, drank some water, but gagged when she urged more. Fearing he'd lose the tablets she let it be. She thought: they'll need time to work. She floated the light duvet she used herself over him, wound the wick on the lamp down to a reddish glow and clambered back into the driving seat, lit a cigarette.

Outside there was less movement than there had been. Orange plastic bollards and fluttering plastic tape fenced off the inside lane, and her camper in it. A hundred metres ahead they included the middle lane too. Orange and blue lights flashed demonically above a fire engine and at least three ambulances; men in uniforms, silhouetted occasionally by the electric blue flame of metal cutting equipment, worked round the shattered and impacted wrecks of the Volvo container and the airport bus. Occasionally a freighted ambulance wailed away into the night towards Hanover. Over to her right the forest still burned and lights flashed there too.

She'd been lucky, and that pleased her, more than pleased her. Though one side of her mind struggled with the thought of bodies torn and burnt the other side sang a paeon of praise to life. She was, she realised, high on it, high on being alive. And . . . there was the adventure too. A man, hurt but presumably not vitally hurt, had come into her camper – naked, but almost ritually painted with blood, water and earth, out of the forest, out of the fire, and into her life.

Not vitally hurt? Clearly no bones broken, no serious bleeding. The advanced first aid course she had taken had taught her to differentiate first degree burns from second and third, and she was sure that most of his were first degree and would heal within days. But what about the trauma, the shock? They were the real killers in such cases. So what if he did die on her, what then? A cold mean anxiety momentarily cramped her heart – but she rejected it precisely for its meanness. Nevertheless she twisted in her seat, looked down at him. Stretched on the bench on the opposite side of the camper his head was close to her. If she stretched her right hand out behind the passenger seat she could touch it. The gasping and occasional moans had stopped, his breathing now was even and deep. No. He wasn't going to die.

Why, though, had she accepted him, not handed him over to the professionals? Because he had asked her not to, and very fundamentally she believed in the right of people to make their own decisions – she had suffered too much in the first half of her life from decisions taken by others on her behalf. Because, at just the right moment the patrolman had banged on the side

17

of the van, a potent symbol of 'them', the 'them' she would in some sense at least be handing him back to. They would clothe him, find a name for him, a place to be, the slot in the machine he had dropped from. Let him find his own way when he was ready – it was no business of hers to do it for him.

She snuffed the cigarette, climbed over the gear lever and hand-brake into the rear, turned up the lamp and knelt beside him. She lifted the duvet away and began again to bathe and soothe his shoulders and his back, but now she was slower about it, less urgent. The burns looked raw, horrible, the surface skin black and creased in places where it had not burned away above the red beneath. She used cold water, then cream which was antiseptic and which would mask them from the air. The instructions recommended no dressing unless the burns were third degree and the skin more or less completely destroyed. She knew this was not the case.

She drew more water to wash the rest of his back, his buttocks and his legs. She wondered – should she warm it? but recalled that so long as a burned person is not in deep shock, he was best allowed to remain cool, that heat aggravated the burns. Anyway, the water from the container beneath the tiny sink was not all that cold. From her own washing things she took a sponge and a travelling tube of shower gel, and gently she washed away the mud, grit and pine needles.

Unbothered now by the burns, there were almost none below his shoulder blades, she became aware of the interplay of muscle, skin, and bone beneath her palms. It was almost as if she were, in a gender reversal of the Pygmalion and Galatea legend, moulding, modelling him into something new. Although the sculptures she now made were welded constructions of steel, she had in the past used clay, had made life-size figures and the very last finishing moments had been like this. But what she made then remained cold and could only recall the beauty that breathed beneath her fingers now.

He stirred as she padded him dry with a towel and she used the moment to ease him on to his side, facing her. She felt he

18

should not lie on his back, put the pressure of his weight on the burns. She thought for a moment that he was going to wake, but he didn't, or not properly, though it seemed to her as she began to wash his front that some of the anguish and stress that had clamped the muscles on his face was leaking away and that something not that far from a smile was hovering on his mouth.

And what sort of face was it? Dark hair cut short but stylishly, with some curl in it, dark eye-brows, clean-shaven but would need a shave by morning. A strong nose with a hint of curve to it, but not enough to be called a beak, between deep sunk and rather narrowly spaced eyes. What colour? She would have to wait and see. Thin lips, and the most marked sign of ageing he had – the lines that came from the corners. They spoke of disappointment or worse. How old? Thirty? Ten years younger than her. So let's say thirty-five. A strong face, even handsome. But even now in troubled sleep aloof, distant. She sensed reservation, withdrawal.

But his body, even with the blood and muck that was already drying on it, was magnificent. A slight and probably permanent tan, compact but not stocky, tough but not overdeveloped, it was the body of somebody who trained, kept fit, not disproportionately so for a specific skill or sport, but in an all round way. Not unblemished. In his front right side, just below his ribs and above his pelvis there was a star-shaped deep indentation, as big as a five mark piece, of puckered skin. It was too uneven to be a bullet wound and there was no exit wound in his back.

When she came to his sex, uncircumcised and not one of the silly ones, it stirred and leaked a little urine, dark, almost orange. Again she thought – dehydration is a danger, I must get him to drink.

His legs had hair, tight dark curls and the muscles were like marble for hardness, like coiled springs for wound-up strength.

She had, she thought, finished. She pulled the duvet back over him but as she did so he stirred, and opened his hands, which he had kept clenched and which she had ignored. The burns in the palms were bad. Yes, she realised, his clothes were

19

on fire, he had to beat out the flames and drag them off. This time she found lint and bandages and dressed them neatly. He came to a little – sort of half sat up. When she had finished he murmured: 'You did that well. You knew what to do.'

She stood now, looked down at him. His eyes were grey or blue. She found later that the depth of blue varied according to the light.

'You should drink more.' She turned, poured more Spa, handed him the plastic camping mug.

He drank half, offered back the mug.

'All of it.' She was firm.

His eyes narrowed a fraction, the line corners of his mouth seemed to deepen. But he drank it. When he looked up again there was, at last, a hint of a smile – but not one she liked. It was ironical, very nearly a sneer. She found later that he hardly ever said thank you, or indeed anything which implied reliance or debt. And if he did the offering was always compromised, even poisoned by this smile.

'You gave me pills. They were very effective.'

'Yes. Do you want more?'

'No, not yet. What were they?'

'Dihydrocodeine.'

'You'll make a junkie of me. But I think I could sleep. Can I sleep here?'

'Of course.'

Carefully he got his body flat again, on his side. She reached to adjust the duvet, but he pulled it up himself. After a moment she turned the lamp down and off.

3

The codeine, in one of its clinically stronger forms, distanced the pain, induced euphoria as well as sleep. Broken fantasies came and went. He was a child in a cot in which he had laid a neat coil of shit of which he was inordinately proud. He had got his pyjama trousers off in time, pushed back the covers, and there it was, on the bottom sheet, with rubber beneath. Lovely job. He stood at the cot rail and crowed. A woman came and praised him, kissed him.

A blonde girl, plump and pink as if from a bath, offered him her nipples. The odd thing was that though her breasts were firm and round the nipples (small pink pimples, shaped like the grease nipples in a car engine) were on the lowest curve of her breasts, pointing straight down. Without entirely waking he became aware of his erection and the sweet longing that went with it, but found the palm that went to hold it was coarse cotton not skin. And it hurt. Badly.

After that the dreams were all bad. The erect penis he was holding belonged to someone called The Major. They were sitting behind a gorse bush on coarse grass, and an evil cold wind buffeted his ears, made them hurt. The Major wore a long plain rain-coat with pockets that had an inside vent as well as an outer one. If you put your hand through the outer one, and then the inner one, you came to his penis, which was wet, fat and hard. And then he gave you one of the new fifty pence coins. This was not the bad part. The bad part was what followed. Inquisition in front of the Head Master's desk. When Did You Last See Your Father?

Good question. Actually he was fucking Nanny, who was the Woman, and I blew his head off just as I blew the heads off those Argies with their own M60 machine gun. Only joking. About Daddy, I mean, not the Argies. They were real enough.

He stirred on the bunk, and pain lacerated his back, a moment of panic, real panic, then he remembered and the euphoria flooded back – it could work out. It could work out very well indeed. And the Woman . . . well, she was something else. She could yet turn out to be a problem, but so far she was a plus, a definite plus.

He could hear traffic, solid, loud, slow. He could smell smoke, roasted dark tobacco, but not too heavy, longed for a cigarette himself. But not yet. Warily he opened one eye, then the other one. She was sitting in the driving seat, he could see her arm, a shoulder, a lock of dark hair almost black but with amber richness in it. A soft woollen cardigan, dark but with colour in it, he remembered the softness of it, a long woollen skirt, and cheap black Chinese slippers: she was dressed as she had been when he first saw her coming at him with a spanner. His lips creased in his mean smile – he liked that, she had guts, was tough. And a looker as well. Maybe they'd get on fucking terms. It would be a battle if they did, but he'd win. He always did. His prick thickened a little at the idea of it, but no point in touching it – not with the bandages and the pain behind them.

He shifted a little, but carefully, took in what he could see of the rest of the interior. On the other side a cushioned bench like the one he was lying on, but shorter, because of the sliding door he'd come in through. Why had it not been locked? Forgetfulness. But the Woman was not a slob, not careless. Was she a truster then? Someone who expected not to be robbed, ripped off, exploited? May be. People like that tended to be good, even do-gooders. He'd have to watch out for that, go carefully until he'd sussed her out thoroughly.

A tiny kitchenette with a single spigot for water, a pair of gas rings mounted on an enamelled hob. Cupboards beneath, and a tiny fridge or cold box. More cupboards at the back and above the small bench opposite, but not above his. All in all, as far as he could tell, a conventional conversion, certainly not a de luxe job, but there were touches of individuality – the woven curtains, dark blue but with lights in them, postcards blu-tacked to the cupboard doors, all of them as far as he could see of modern sculpture, except for an A5 size poster for Firenze with Donatello's David, louche and sexy.

She shifted, stubbed out her cigarette, murmured, but forcefully:

'Bastards.'

Time to let her know he was no longer asleep.

'Who?'

'You're awake are you? Them. Outside. We're stuck on the crash barrier and they're all too busy to give me a hand.'

Carefully he put his feet on the floor. No real pain. Straightened and looked over the back of the passenger seat. Dark grey plastic moulded to simulate material. Grey blustery dawn, the tarmac still wet. Orange cones and flickering red and white plastic tape. Men in orange and yellow overalls, flashing lights, and a hundred metres away big mobile plant, lifting gear and a transporter coping with the airline bus and the Volvo container truck. A slow line of heavy traffic in the fast lane rumbled by at cortège speed.

'If you've got anything I can wear, I'll have a look at it.'

'Do you think you're up to it?'

'I can try.'

She climbed into the back, and he was suddenly very aware of her closeness, her physical presence – the warmth of her clothes, womanly fragrances, the cigarette smell. From a cupboard opposite the kitchen bit she pulled a mono, a blue all-in-one overall made out of strong cotton. It was clean and pressed but there were splashes of paint and plaster of Paris that had not come out in the wash.

'You should be able to get into this. You're not much bigger than me and I like them loose.'

She was right. The arms and legs were an inch or so short, no more.

23

'That's OK then. Shoes might be a problem, but I've got long feet.'

He thought: like your hands. She found a pair of leather flip-flop sandals with a twisted thong toe-hold, but he rejected them. Then she came up with blue canvas espadrilles. They cramped his toes but she managed to ease the backs over his heels. Again in the narrow space he felt a surge of strange joy, close to panic, at her presence, at the luxury of her hair as she bent over his feet. She pulled open the side door, and the cool air that fell over them was a balm he was beginning to feel he needed. The cloth of the mono was like a hair-shirt on his back, and his hands were a steady scream of pain now he had had to move about a bit, but he forced himself on.

He climbed out over the buckled crash barrier, could see immediately what the trouble was. The onside wrap-round on the front fender had ridden up on to the barrier. His hands rebelled at the thought of the rigid inflexibility of the meshed girders, but his brain worked briskly enough. There was a litter of broken building blocks between the barrier and the forest fence he had crawled under – he could see the foxy tunnel he'd used – and he soon found one that he reckoned would do, a broken rectangle of concrete conglomerate. It was quite heavy, and because of the closeness of the barrier, and the overhang at the front of the van, awkward to get into place behind the front onside wheel but he managed. He straightened, went round to her window.

She spoke first.

'You look awful. Are you all right?'

'I will be. Start the engine. Put it in reverse, slip the clutch slowly, steer slightly out, that's left hand down.'

She did it perfectly. The wheel rode up on the building block, with a slight wrench and a squeal the fender came clear, the wheel thudded back on to the road surface. He shifted three of the cones that still fenced them in from the funeral procession in the fast lane. He got back in, pulled the side door shut, found he was facing her.

'I shouldn't have let you do that. That really knocked you up.'

He swayed towards her, pulled back.

'Yes. Mainly it's the pain. Especially my hands. You gave me pills last night. They worked.'

'I'll get them. Then I think you should sleep again.'

'Yes. I think so.'

She moved to the back of the van. He pulled off the mono, sat naked again on the bunk. She came back with tablets and Spa.

'You did a good job on me.'

'You did a good job getting us unstuck. Lord knows what it would have cost in breakdown fees if I'd called someone out. Are you hungry?'

He thought about that.

'No. Not exactly. Not yet.'

'Nor me. Right. Come on. Back to bed.'

She pulled the duvet over him again, climbed into the driving seat.

'Where are you going? Where do you want to go?'

'Anywhere. It doesn't matter.'

'You really mean that, don't you? But you must have been going somewhere last night. I mean you were in one of the cars that crashed?'

'No.'

'You were on the plane? The plane that crashed? Shit. People don't survive crashes like that.'

She re-started the engine, waited for a driver courteous enough to let her into the traffic flow.

'You speak very good German but you aren't German, are you? Danish? Dutch?'

Still no answer. It bothered her. Other things too.

'Why won't you go to hospital, get proper treatment? You're not on the run are you? I mean wanted by the police or something?'

'No.'

They passed the wrecked airport bus and the Volvo container

25

truck. Machinery roared, sliced metal screamed. Eventually the road spread out into its normal three lanes. A thought freighted with horror occurred to her.

'You didn't make the crash happen?'

A small laugh, bitter.

'Indeed not. I was there to make sure something of that sort didn't happen. Rather cocked it up, wouldn't you say? Christ I'm tired. Your pills. Why do you carry junk like that?'

'I live on my own. I travel a lot in this old crate. I can't stand pain so I keep them just in case something happens . . . the same sort of thing that happened to you. I used them once – for a tooth abscess. Used. Not abused.'

She drove on, past a nuclear power station plumed with steam from its cooling tower. She muttered her private ritual curse at it.

'And you know about treating burns. Why? Are you a nurse?'

'No.' She paused, remembered an acetylene gas flame on the end of a tube that danced uncontrollably like a snake, near her face, her hands. 'It's a long story. But to keep it short . . . I make metal sculptures, I use metal cutting equipment, and I weld. Once I nearly had a very nasty accident so I took the trouble to learn what to do for myself if it happened again.'

Then: 'You should sleep, you know? I shan't kick you out until you're ready to go.'

She picked up the signs for Frankfurt, drove on through the busy, rich heartland of the new Reich. Presently she turned on the stereo player. The slower middle section of the 'Wanderer Fantasy'. The Man slept.

4

She drove for six hours without stopping, kept to the autobahns, came to a frontier at half eleven in the morning. He hadn't stirred. She took a chance, reached out her left hand, pulled the duvet over his head. There was a huge queue, three lanes of it, but it hardly stopped at all. The first week of July, and much of the north of Europe was moving to the south of Europe. No problem getting out of Germany, but on the French side a policeman waved her down, made her stop.

She passed her Euro ID through the window.

'Alone?'

She shrugged, smiled.

'So far.'

That made him grin, as she knew it would. The exchange meant: If you weren't tied up here I could take you with me . . . He fell for it and waved her through.

She turned on the radio, got an old Jacques Brel number, sang along to it: Les Flam, Les Flam, Les Flamandes. The Man came awake with a shout.

'Christ! I had my head under that thing, I thought I was suffocating, in my coffin or something.'

She glanced at him, then back at the autoroute. He looked better, she thought, a little flushed from being under the cover, but the awful pallor that came over his face after moving the building block had gone.

'How do you feel now?'

'Better. In fact a whole lot better. Very little pain now. Sorry if I gave you a fright. I just had no idea where I was.'

'It's possible that is the case.'

'What do you mean?'

27

He pulled himself up, looked over the back of the passenger seat. Big autoroute signs pre-warning a major junction: A4 Paris 243kms, A31 Metz et Nancy . . .

'Hey. We're in France.'

'That's right. Do you mind?'

'Not at all. But the frontier . . .'

'Not a problem. Nowadays they hardly ever bother you. Especially not at busy times.'

'But if they had . . . I, we could have been in the shit.'

'But they didn't and you aren't.'

She caught the movement behind her in the rearview mirror. He was pulling the mono back on, the espadrilles. Presently he climbed over into the front seat, arriving there just as she took the spur for Metz and the A31 south. He helped himself to a Gauloise Light from her pack, lit it, offered it to her and she took it. Then he lit one for himself.

'I'm hungry and I could do with a wee.'

'Me too. We'll stop at the next service station. And don't worry – no more borders. I'm heading for the other end of France, but it is in France.'

'What's in France?'

'Where we . . . where I'm going. I've got a farmhouse in the Pyrenees, but not far from the Atlantic. I go there every summer.'

'Holiday home?'

'Not exactly. You'll see when we get there. That is . . . if you want to come with me that far.'

'Why not?'

It was a statement, not a question. She glanced at him again, serious, questioning. He met her eyes for a moment, his as expressionless as hers, then his lips pouted wryly and he gave a tiny shrug.

'Why not, indeed?' he repeated. He read the next sign aloud. 'Services à Atton, 5kms. That should do nicely.'

She felt a tiny frisson of annoyance at the ease with which he took charge, but concealed it.

*

He spotted a slot for her, *quite* close to the restaurant, even though the carpark was quite full. She drove past it, engaged reverse, backed. A horn, three notes in thirds, blasted behind them, and a large white Jaguar cut into the space. The Man leaped down with a lithe agility she had not yet seen, but had suspected was his natural way of moving.

He was pale again, this time with anger. He banged on the roof of the Jaguar with the side of his hand, careful not to use the palm. Because he did not want her to know English was his mother tongue he spoke German.

'Come on, out. This lady had the space before you. Out.'

The driver of the Jaguar let himself out of his car, but slowly, arrogantly. He was large, nearly fat, red-faced, yellow hair, no older than the Man. He was wearing a pale linen suit, had a beer gut beneath a brightly-coloured kipper tie. In his left hand he held a cigar. With his right, he locked the door. He spoke slowly, loudly, in bad German, the way English people of his class do when speaking to foreigners.

'I was here first. The fact my car is where it is proves it. There's plenty of room back there, and back there is where a vehicle like that belongs.'

The Man gathered the bright silk tie into his fist, spoke quietly in English, with an accent and emphasis that claimed status beyond that of a mere Jaguar owner.

'You are a fat wet fart with the manners of a drunk Irishman. And I have a mind to kick the shit out of you.'

However, he turned on his heel and got back into the camper.

The headlines screamed across the counter of the newstand. While he was in the toilets the Woman bought two: *Süddeutscher Zeitung*, and *Le Monde*. They joined the queue in the self-service area.

'They've started serving full hot meals. It's not what I want really.'

'Nor me.'

She went for the salad bowl, as much as you can get on a

29

plate for forty francs. She avoided the pastas and potato based dishes, went mainly for crudités. He took a made-up salad with thin-cut very red slices of beef. They both had coffees, large and black. When they got to the cash-out the Man was in front. He turned to the Woman, held out his bandaged hand.

'I'll pay, if you give me the money.' His eyes were cold and she sensed his determination, resented it, but she handed over a one-hundred-franc note, new and crisp from her handbag. There wasn't much change and without asking her he dropped it in the saucer that had been left for tips. I can, she said to herself, get rid of him whenever I want to. The moment, and the feeling passed.

They had to go close to the fat Englishman. Already he was wading into steak and frites, with a half bottle of Beaune at his elbow. He grinned at his plate as they went by. They found a small table in a corner which they would not have to share with anyone else, unpacked their trays, sat opposite each other. The Woman put the newspapers at her elbow, read aloud, between small forkfuls of grated carrot and coleslaw. The Man ate slowly and carefully, listened intently.

'Luton to Hamburg. Re-routed to Hanover because the Hamburg runway was flooded in a cloud-burst. The Emir of Kamar. All his closest family. That's awful. Four children on board. That's terrible. No survivors. One of the crew was alive when the emergency services arrived, but he died on the way to hospital. So. No survivors. Twenty-one dead all together, from the plane, another sixteen on the autobahn.'

'Twenty-one? Twenty-one bodies?'

'That's what it says.' She checked back, folded the paper to an inner page for more detail. 'The four nearest the explosion including the Emir himself were so badly blasted and burned that individual identification is likely to be impossible . . . it really is very horrible . . . But the German authorities are sure that all on board are accounted for, and all are dead. Is something the matter?'

He had stopped eating, was staring at his plate. Then he picked up his coffee cup and as he lifted it his eyes smiled but not for her. They were fixed on some inner space filled with the triumph of realised expectation. She shuddered, went back to the paper and then looked up again.

'But that can't be right, can it? I mean, with you as well, there should have been twenty-two on board.'

'There was an illegal passenger. Smuggled on. Not on the manifest. A cousin of the Emir's.'

She took her time, ran it through as if it were an equation whose answer had been too easy to work out, needed checking.

'They'll take it for granted that one of the unidentifiable corpses is you. The police. Your family. Everyone.'

'Yes.'

'You're dead.'

'Yes.'

The next bit was even more difficult to take. She heard the incredulity, wonder in her own voice.

'That's why you wouldn't let me get an ambulance. You'd thought it out . . . in the middle of all that horror and pain, you knew . . . You walked away from it all hoping it would turn out like this.'

The smile told her she was right. Presently he said he'd have to use the toilets again. Would she wait for him?

A row of urinals faced a row of wash-basins across a narrow passage. At the end of the passage a right-angle turn lead to a row of WC cubicles in such a way that all but the first of the cubicles were hidden from most of the urinals and basins. When Charles Churchill, the fat Englishman, came in the Man was using a hot-air hand dryer placed at the end of the basins next to the cubicles and at the far end from the entrance. The only other man using the urinals was on his way out. Churchill came down the passage between the urinals and the basins and found he was face to face with the Man who had threatened to kick the shit out of him. People like Churchill are never embarrassed, and never admit mistakes. However, they are cowards too, and it was probably fear that prompted him.

31

'Hallo again. I say, if I'd known you were a Brit I would have let you have that space. But you were in a Kraut car, with Kraut licence plates . . .'

He found he was looking at very close quarters into a face that was a white mask. He blundered on. Saloon bar *bonhomie*, wink, wink, nudge, nudge, say no more.

'Anyway. No hard feelings? Nice bint you've got with you.' He put his hand on the Man's shoulder, squeezed. 'Good-looker. And all the better for being a shade long in the tooth. At that age they know what it's all about, eh?'

He slapped the shoulder, and perhaps a corner of what passed for his mind wondered why the Man winced – and squeezed past round the corner of the L-shaped area to the cubicles. He tried the first cubicle door, found it locked, moved down the row out of sight of all but the very end urinal and wash-basin. The Man looked down the unused urinals and followed Churchill round the corner. As Churchill was about to enter the third cubicle in, the Man pushed him from behind, and followed, kicking the door shut behind him. With his left arm he locked Churchill's neck, with his right hand and arm he broke it. He lowered him to the floor and locked the door. He found Churchill's wallet, extracted two large folds of paper money, some coins and replaced it. Then he pulled the flush, heaved the body half upright and against the door. He squeezed round it and out, letting the weight of the body close the door behind him. Two men came into the urinal area as the Man left. They ignored him. On the way out the Man dropped a coin in the saucer of the ancient Gardienne who sat at the door and sold toilet paper. It was an English twenty pence piece. Too late he realised. But either she hadn't noticed, or didn't care.

'No name. Nothing. You've lost it all. I envy you that. Sloughing it all off, like a snake in Spring, shedding its old skin.'

She glanced at him. He was leaning into the corner that the back of the seat and door made, looking at her, watching her profile while she drove and talked. It was, she knew, a good

32

profile. Long straight nose, strong chin which might look witchy when she was seventy, but looked all right now. Presently though he began to undo the bandages on his right hand.

'Are you sure they're ready.'

'I think so.' He examined the palm, held it so she could see it. It looked very raw, and somehow sort of naked. She was reminded of the skin in the hand of a very new baby, in the first half hour of its life.

'Doesn't it hurt.'

'A bit. If I put heavy pressure on it. But it's more a very sharp tingling sensation than actual pain. I think the newly exposed layer needs to get to know what the world is like.'

He was far more relaxed now, not opiate relaxed, properly relaxed, looked almost healthy – which, she guessed, was normal for him. In spite of the one or two moments when he had bothered her, mainly by male assertiveness, she was beginning to feel more confident with him, more at ease.

'Perhaps the scales of a snake in its new skin feel like that. Slipping away across the stones and into the grass leaving the old constricting skin behind. What have you left behind? I don't want to know, please believe me. But I can guess what sort of thing. I guess . . .' She glanced at him, 'that you hate to be bored. You don't tolerate boredom, do you? I guess if this hadn't happened you might have been driven to break out in an even more dramatic way . . . breaking out, smashing your way out. Probably, no, certainly, it's better like this. And now you're free. Really free. That must be wonderful.'

She was much taken with this, and briefly grasped his knee, not sexily, but expressing her excitement at his situation. She was naturally free with physical contact, touched, hugged, kissed easily. For a moment she looked fully at him, and he at her. Their eyes were full of knowledge, and serene with it.

'I wonder how you will use your freedom. I wonder what your first really free act will be.'

*

33

Back at the Atton service station the men's toilets were busier than they had been. The ancient Gardienne struggled with bucket, squeegy-mop, cloths and a bottle of cleaning fluid, waddled between the lines of men at the urinals and wash-basins, round the corner, searched for the cubicle they had complained about. Two empty, one apparently locked. She pushed on it, moved it a few centimetres but couldn't open it. A toilet flushed and a Hell's Angel, over forty, beer gut, leather gear, big beard, hair in a pony-tail, came out.

'Can't you do something about the fucking smell in here? Some punter's shat himself.'

'I'm trying to. But the door's stuck. Give us a hand.'

The Hell's Angel put his huge shoulder to the door and heaved. Inside Churchill's body, slumped against the door, was pushed up and sideways, until it slipped round the side of the door, fell backwards and outwards with twisted neck and head, contorted face.

5

Brightly lit gantries bridged the blackness of the night, the three lanes multiplied to six, red lights, island kiosks, PÉAGE – illuminated white on blue.

'*Vorwärts – eine gebürenpflichtige Autostrasse.*'

Always they spoke German. She'd tried him with English, which she was now pretty certain was his mother tongue since the DC9 had been flying from Luton. All she got was the cold stare that both annoyed and frightened her. Now she hoisted herself up from the bunk behind the passenger seat, looked over it.

'Oh Christ. Where's my bag?' She fumbled in the near darkness. 'How much?'

'Twenty-five francs.'

She put coins into his right hand, he slowed, lowered his window. He passed the money to his left hand, tossed it into a small metal hopper. A machine spewed a ticket, the light turned green, the automatic metal barrier in the road in front clanged flat, he accelerated through.

White on blue – A10, Poitiers 74.

'It's possible we'll have to pay again at Poitiers. To stay on for Bordeaux. I'll leave my bag on the seat in case I'm asleep.'

She turned on to her back, hoisted pillows up behind her head, lit a cigarette, passed it forward, lit one for herself.

'You've no idea how I envy you. I've tried for the sort of freedom you have now. But I could never get there.'

'Why not?'

'When I was eighteen I thought I had it. Art college, in the early seventies, you know? Do as you like time. Demos. Vietnam. RAF. Dope, sex, and no AIDS. But the parents were still there, always looking over your shoulder. Train as a teacher too, just in case. That sort of thing. So of course I ended up a teacher. I hated teaching, at first. I don't mind it now. But then along came Mr Wonderful – the way out. Next thing I knew I wasn't even a teacher any more. And certainly not the sculptor I always meant to be. I was a housewife and mother.'

'There are worse things to be.'

There he goes again. *Kinder, Küche, Kirche.*

'Not many. Coal miner. Soldier . . .' She sensed his reaction. For sure he had never hewn coal – so had he been a soldier? 'Better to give life than take it.'

She pulled on the mild version of Gauloise, went on: 'Anyway, the point is, it wasn't what I had chosen. It's what other people thought ought to happen.'

Lights. The slipway for Chatellerault Nord.

'Are you still married?'

She considered the question. Well, OK, you have to get that

one out of the way. But he's not going to answer the same question if I put it to him. But then I don't want to, do I? He's new, fresh, reborn, I don't want to know what happened before.

'No. After six years I booted Mr Wonderful out. But I was still stuck with Laura.'

Those hands – with the skin of a new-born baby.

'Laura?'

'My daughter. A mess.' Not a subject she wanted to pursue. She put out her cigarette. 'Christ, I'm tired. Are you sure you're all right to go on driving.'

'Fine.'

'That's great. We should be there by dawn. A whole extra day for me.' She yawned, partly to conceal the touch of dread that fell on her now whenever she asked a question that he might resent. 'No Man, you can call me Inger. Inger Mahler. I have no name for you and I don't want to have one. But what shall I call you?'

'Just that.'

'Niemand? Mr Niemand?'

'Herr Niemand.'

A good dawn. High sky, almost cloudless to the west and north, the few tufts of grey cloud turning luminous and gold, mist in the sharp, narrow valleys to the south, a smudge of snow here and there still to be seen high up in the peaks, on these north facing slopes. Everything fresh and clean, a little dew, not much. Dry stone walls enclosed an untended meadow on a hillside. A gate, tubular steel painted black, a sweet chestnut overhanging it. Moon daisies, chamomile, scabious in the meadow, apple trees and pears with fruit beginning to ripen, an apricot and a cherry whose fruit had been scavenged by birds and small boys. A dry white stony track led through it up to a stone farmhouse and barn.

Cranmer, back in the passenger seat, dropped down, opened the gate. Inger drove through, he closed it behind her, climbed back in. She drove slowly now, relishing her return. Her sculptures were waiting. Some welcomed her, some ignored her. It was always the way. They stood in the grass and flowers and the better ones played Grandmother's Footsteps – you felt they might move if you turned your back, had perhaps moved in the moment or two before you looked at them. The bad ones were junk, litter. Most were made out of combinations of twisted metal plates, each one cut and shaped to resemble a leaf, a petal, a feather, a flame, a plough-share or a blade – those sorts of shapes.

The barn had a high double door, high enough for a hay cart. Between the barn and the house there was an enclosed area covered with vines and geraniums creating a patio. The vines were heavy with green grapes, the geraniums needed water but looked as if they might survive. There was a side door into the house. The front of the house had three small but widely spaced shuttered windows on the ground floor, climbing white roses in bloom between them, and a porched front door made out of oak boards, studded with bolt-heads. There was a second floor with four small dormered windows, also shuttered. Inger parked the van in front of the front door, put her hand on Cranmer's knee.

'Here we are then. What do you think?'

'It's fine. Splendid.'

He depressed the inset door-handle, swung his legs out, dropped down, walked to the rear of the van, looked out over and down the valley – woods, meadows, more farmhouses. Sun from the east touched the high peaks and slopes on the west side of the valley, but the mountains behind and the farmhouse itself remained in cold shadow. She came round the other side, joined him.

'It's far too big. But it suits me, suits what I want to do here.'

He looked at the nearest sculpture. It could be a giant insect, it could be a man, or woman, enclosed in a contraption of wings which he or she hoped would get her off the ground.

'I can see that.'

A bird began to sing from the bough of the apricot tree, high and low notes, tee-roo, tee-roo. It had a black cap, and a bright yellow eye.

'That sounds almost like a nightingale.'

'Orphean warbler. Well. No Man. What are you going to do now?'

He shrugged. She turned away, behind him, her hands clasping her upper arms. She made her voice as flat as possible – she did not want to pressure him or show eagerness.

'You can stay if you like. Until you know better what you want to do. I could use you – there's lots of work needs doing that I really need a man for.'

'Really?' He knew she couldn't see the smile. 'Yes. I'd like that. For a time anyway.'

She turned, touched his arm, allowed herself and him a very different sort of smile.

'Well that's settled then. Come on, I'll show you around.'

She took his elbow, and steered him onto the patio: a table, benches, the vines, the geraniums, and, now he was inside and could see it, a purple bougainvillea too.

'The patio. Easy to waste time here after lunch.'

She lifted three large flat stones from the raised flower-bed that ran along the wall of the barn and the rear wall too, and found a large old-fashioned key. She took it back to the heavy front door, unlocked it, pushed. Immediately behind there was a velvet curtain, faded maroon.

'Cuts down the draughts.'

To the left a door into what he soon discovered was a large sitting-room that was not much used when the weather was hot, ahead a flight of narrow wooden stairs between whitewashed walls, to the right another door.

'The kitchen. Easy to waste time here before lunch. Ugh. Cobwebs and dust everywhere, but it really doesn't take long to clean.'

He had a brief sight of a large airy room, white walls, stone-flagged floor that would be light as well once the shutters were opened, of a big scrubbed wooden table, with a saucer-shaped declivity at the end where several generations of cooks had done their chopping and slicing, of rush-seated chairs, of French cooking implements on the walls, saucepans, racks for cooking knives, a cleaver, and so on, dusty bottles in a rack. Then she screamed, and slammed shut the cupboard door she had just opened.

'Oh damn, oh hell!'

'What is it?'

'Rats. Family of them. Oh shit, I hate them. Every year it's the same.'

'I'll deal with them. You go back into the van.'

She did as she was told, glad this time to do so. She sat in the driver's seat, smoked. In spite of the thick stone walls she was close enough to hear: smart cracks, metal on stone, metal on wood, often muffled. They became more intermittent – she guessed there were one or two less easy to catch than the rest. She felt an irritating twinge of guilt, which she suppressed, and no pity at all.

At last he came out. In one hand a large plastic carrier bag, filled and weighty, in the other the meat cleaver. She would not use it again, although he washed it carefully and hung it back on its hook. He passed round the front of the barn, dropped the bag on the far side, came back.

'I'll bury them later.'

'Every year I put down poison. Bastards just thrive on it.'

'I'll check out the rest of the house.'

He walked briskly back in. Sunlight marched briskly down the meadow and filled the camper with light and warmth. Suddenly her house looked a good place to be after all. She realised she didn't want him to have his first sight of it all without her there as guide. She chucked the cigarette and followed him.

As she went through the front door, he was coming out of the living-room.

'The door was well shut, and there's no sign of them.'

He began to climb the stairs. Two in the middle creaked. A skylight lit the stairwell and the landing. Four doors. He opened the first into a large bedroom over the kitchen. She followed him in, opened the window and the shutters. He lifted the tassles of a white heavy woven cotton bedspread, the sort African princes hawk on southern beaches, looked under the big bed with its four short, obelisk posts, straightened and took in the rest of the room: white walls, some pictures, heavy French peasant furniture. There was a portable stereo radio cassette player on a table by the bed. He opened the wardrobe, ran his hand along the floor beneath her cotton dresses, over old tennis shoes, sniffed the mothball odour and found nothing else.

The bathroom was modern but small and simple, faced a steep hill at the back that climbed to beech woods. The mountains rose beyond. When Inger opened the rear-facing window above the small bath they both heard goat bells and the rustling chatter of a mountain stream.

The second bedroom was smaller than the first, was sited over the front door. There was a single bed beneath a sloping roof, a dormer window, filled now with light. A poster – a late Picasso of a pigeon loft with the Mediterranean beyond – advertised the Museu Picasso, Carrer de Montcada, Barcelona. It kept uneasy company with Michael Jackson moon-walking, Clint Eastwood as the Man with No Name, and three surfers coming down an improbably large curler. On the pillow, instead of an old teddy-bear, a glove puppet with a Michael Jackson head.

'All clear? This is Laura's room.'

'I guessed as much.'

'I thought . . . you could use it.'

'She's not around then.'

'No. At the moment she hangs out with surfers in Biarritz and drops by when she needs money. Thank you for dealing with our foul friends.'

He turned out of the room, tried the fourth door. It was locked.

'It's the old part of the house. I've never really been in it properly, it's just stacked with old furniture I had to take on board when I came. There may be mice, but I doubt if there are any rats.'

He turned away, descended the narrow stairs, leaving her to follow him.

'You knew they'd be here. What do you usually do about them?'

'Get in a neighbour. He has terriers.'

'But this time . . .?'

'I thought – if they are here, No Man will cope.'

'The kitchen is still not a very pretty sight.' He paused with his hand on the door.

'I don't mind blood. We'll clean it up together.'

'And my back. After all that it's playing up. And I don't want any more junk.'

'Oh Christ. You're so good about all that. I forget. And your poor hands.'

She seized his right wrist, prised open his fingers, and very gently licked the palm with the skin like a new born baby's. It tasted of medication but salt too, and the sweetness of a mild infection.

He slept through most of the rest of the day. She cleaned and unpacked, made a short trip to the nearest village for supplies. They ate well, if simply off hard Pyreneean sheep's cheese, *pain intégral*, peaches and Madiran wine. That night both most carefully avoided any suggestion they should sleep together, even though she spent some time on cleaning up his back as well as his hands before they went to their separate beds. The burns were healing, or at any rate sealing very quickly, the underlayers of skin drying out, hardening in crinkly patches, the inflamation slowly fading.

6

Two mornings later, over coffee and chocolatines in the patio, he insisted, with the wry, slightly sour humour which was the nearest to real warmth that he seemed capable of, she should give him work to do.

'As you promised. You know I haven't a bean in the world. But it's part of the creed that the . . . No Mans have adhered to since time immemorial, that they should pay their way.'

She thought: this has more to do with machismo than anything else, but let that be.

He could have repaired fences, rebuilt dry stone walls, looked at the roof of the house, but she wanted him near her. And not just because she liked his company, cool and laid back though it was, and was now very desperately attracted to his lithe, fit but mature body, but also because she didn't quite trust him about the place unobserved. She didn't think he would steal. Almost she knew that he wouldn't. But he might rummage and explore, find things he might later turn against her. And so she set him to repairing a broken pane in the skylight of her barn. Which, of course, was no longer a barn, but her studio.

The big high, double doors were open. Inside, the sun, filtered by cobwebs, barred by cross-beams, filled the large space with cool light. The floor was filled with metal: mainly sheeting for car bodies, and rods, bought as bankrupt stock but by no means cheap, neatly stacked. She had welding equipment, oxy-acety-lene burners that could slice the sheets into the shapes she wanted, ratcheted levers that could twist it, a metal lathe and other tools and machinery for cutting, shaping, and polishing metal. Cranmer was high above it all up an old, long, narrow, wooden ladder whose top rested against one of the beams.

Outside house martins twittered as they fed their second broods of the season in nests beneath the eaves.

Having put him there, she then had to find something to do. She had had plans, sketches too, ready, created through a winter of peripatetic teaching in the very most northern part of Germany, but these now seemed stale, irrelevant. Instead of working them up, putting together the armature for the sculpture they were meant to become, she sat beneath him, looked up, sketched him in quick, fluent charcoal strokes, on an A3 size pad of good but fine paper. She moved quickly through it, only stopping to spray fixative on each unfinished drawing before moving on to the next. She was using the poses he got into, silhouetted against the light, to create fast semi-abstract studies of a man twisting and turning in space.

Without pausing, she asked: 'How's it going?'

'All right. Fine really.'

'The hands OK? Not bothering you?'

'No. The palms are still sore but at the moment I'm not putting any real pressure on them.'

They both worked on. Presently: 'What's it like up there?'

'Well, I'll have to knock out the old glass and putty first.'

'No. I mean, what is it like? I've never been up there.'

'Lot of cobwebs. There's a fair bit of woodworm.'

'I had it treated when I bought the place. Cost a fortune. So there shouldn't be any fresh holes.'

'I think you're right. There'd be new dust in the cobwebs if the little buggers were still at it. There's a big bit of glass just about to come away. It won't fall near you, but watch out anyway.'

A triangle, the hypotenuse an uneven curve following the line of a crack, slipped from his hand a moment before he wanted it to, so it hit a cross-beam on the way down, shattered into flame-shaped shards that caught a dust-laden sunbeam between her and him as they fell.

'Jesus.'

'Sorry, didn't mean it to do that.'

'No, no, it wasn't . . . It's just I think I know now what I'm doing.'

'Always a help.'

The charcoal flashed across the page more quickly now. She smudged it in places, on purpose, blew off excess, hardened and softened tones.

'Yes. But it's not something you can force. You have to let it happen. Or rather you have to let it creep up behind you and pounce. Like a tiger. The Tigers of Wrath are wiser than the Horses of Instruction.'

He paused, looked down at her.

'What was that?'

'Blake. An English poet. The Tigers of Wrath are wiser . . .'

But at that moment the ladder began to fall apart. First a rung exploded in a burst of woodworm dust, then as his foot slipped it began to telescope. Just in time he abandoned it, and grabbed, like a trapeze artist, the beam it was leaning against. She felt the pain in his hands. For a moment or two he swung, his eyes searching for a space in the litter of metal and sculpture beneath. There was one, near the woman, and he swung himself over dropping into it and rolling forward, head over heels to break the fall. He came out of the roll, almost into her arms. Her hands caught his shoulders, braced and steadied them both, prevented them from tumbling backwards. She was breathless with excitement, with expected calamity forestalled. A sudden pallor disappeared beneath an equally sudden flush that made her seem radiant.

'Oh Jesus, how the hell did you manage to do that? What are you? A circus performer? Well, for sure you could earn a living in a circus if you wanted to. Oh, I'm sorry. I really am sorry. That bastard ladder could have killed you, but you're all right. You're really all right . . .'

She held him at arm's length for a moment looking at him with large eyes that sparkled, then pulled herself into him, let her head rest on his shoulder, felt the coarse warmth of the mono he still wore, smelled the dust of the place he'd been

44

working in, watched the dust of his fall settling in the sunbeam, felt his sex stir, and a responding wave of lust deep in herself.

'I'm all right, I'm fine. I really am.'

He broke back and for a moment they looked at each other, faces pale again with the sudden sexual tension. Then she shuddered, turned away, picked up her pad. On it, abstracted or formalised but clear enough, a naked man dropped through space with flames streaming behind him. Cranmer drew near again, and she let him see it.

'It's you. Breaking free out of that crash. On fire. But into something new and free and lovely. Will you help me to make it?'

She felt him near again, almost touching, a penumbra of heat coming off him, got a grip on herself. Not here, not now, and certainly not a mad dash upstairs ripping our clothes off as we go like the soft porn bit in a Hollywood romance. She turned quickly, moved out into the sunlight. Her voice was very firm.

'I think we should go to town and get a new ladder, a metal one, and we need food too. Really we should go to Pau.'

7

He sat on Laura's bed, and the posters of mythic heroes looked down at him. If he glanced up, his own face looked back at him from a narrow but full-length mirror screwed to the back of the door. It said things about Laura: that she should have this mirror so placed that if she lay on the bed facing it, she'd see herself, as much as she wanted of herself, either in foreshortened perspective or, if she sat on the end of the bed or stood in front of it in any other aspect of herself she desired.

He looked back at the wad of notes in his hand, Churchill's, *loads of money*. English and French banknotes, one hundred and fifty-five pounds, one thousand eight hundred and twenty francs, a very tolerable haul. Trouble was – he couldn't spend it, any of it, couldn't let Inger (he was learning to think of her as Inger, not The Woman) couldn't let Inger know he had it. Nevertheless he peeled off two one hundred franc notes, slipped them into the back pocket of the mono.

She called from the kitchen or the bottom of the stairs.

'Are you coming then? We want to get there before the market closes down.'

He hid the rest of the money in the head of the Michael Jackson glove puppet.

The immediate approaches to Pau were dismal: Jurançon with its fake Swiss chalet-style drive-in *dégustation* for the over-priced local white wine (the red Madiran had, however, been reasonably drinkable), the Chaume cheese factory, and the inevitable French ribbon development of low grey houses, workshops promising to repair your windscreens, change your tyres or sell you, at knock-down prices, exceptional bric à brac. On a hill above the town a brutal water tower lorded it with far more menace than Henri Quatre's pretty château.

Inger, glad to be out of Schleswig, away from her aged, semi-crippled and complaining mother and her routine of adult education classes, saw only the beauties she had missed. She wanted him to see them too, took a chance, and made for the Boulevard des Pyrénées where she had no right to expect a parking place, but found one. She fed change into the meter, while he locked up the camper, including the side door.

'Why are you doing that? There's nothing in it worth stealing and you need the right key to drive it away. Listen. And look.' She took his arm made him cross the wide road to the parapet. 'Isn't it heavenly? Start at the back. There's still some snow, a tiny bit. That one, like a broken canine tooth is the Pic du Midi d'Ossau. You can drive into Spain on a road right below it. Then . . .'

Then this, and then that, right down to the refurbished

funicular, a tiny affair, that used to bring *les Anglais* up from the railway station below to stay in the grand hotels that line the Boulevard. Except that now they are all converted into apartments or into spaces, like gaps left by drawn teeth, where higher apartment blocks will be built.

'And the trees in front of us are mimosa. Heavenly in March. If you can get here then.'

No one is so possessive about a place as he or she who has bought a second home in a foreign land.

She ordered a ladder at a shop specialising in anything a smallholding peasant might desire, delivery promised the next day, then took him to the markets, the same complex contained all three. First the enclosed municipal market, a big modern hangar split into malls of small shops but filled with good food of every sort imaginable. She bought a sea-bass, more bread, *beurre en motte* – butter cut off a big patted lump – , a bottle of good claret, huge tomatoes, fennel, flat-leaved parsley, the list went on and soon he was bored. Then through a big high hall where small holders could make their pitches with their surplus produce, including roses and gladioli, she bought an arm full of each, a chicken 'for tomorrow', yellow from the corn it had been fed on, and tiny goat cheeses mounted on little rafts of woven straw.

Then she took him out into the open-air market where covered stalls sold Korean toys, Taiwanese spanners, Romanian batteries, and denims that had Levi or Wrangler labels.

'Come on. I'm going to buy you some proper clothes.' She pulled a denim jacket off a hanger, held it against him.

'No.'

'You can't go on wearing my things. OK it's all right round the house, but in town . . .'

'No, I'm not having you buying me clothes. I'll pay for them.'

'But you can't, you haven't . . .'

'I haven't any bloody money.'

'I'll pay you for the work you've been doing for me. Will do

47

for me.' She turned back to the stall-holder, spoke French. 'How much for this jacket?'

He simulated an anger he part felt, turned on his heel, and walked away. Almost immediately he knew she was not following, and that pleased him. He wanted, needed to be away.

He walked briskly to make sure of it, into the medieval alleys near the castle – boutiques, camera shops, shops selling tins of *confits du canard* and *foie gras*. A mistake? He began to think so, but there was at last, close to the castle, a shop selling postcards, dolls representing Henri Quatre, and tobacco. Which meant it also sold *Télécartes*, phone-cards.

There was a phone box in the corner of the cobbled, irregular square in front of the castle entrance. 010? No. We're in France now. But it's still 41 for Suisse, and 1 for Zürich, and . . . he had the remaining six digits right.

'*Darf ich bitte mit Herrn Herz sprechen.*' There was a wait. He checked she hadn't after all followed him. But he didn't think she would. Above all she had her pride. 'Herrn Herz? Wolfhound asked me to contact you. In connection with some work you wanted done. Yes, that's right. OK. Right. We have our procedures too. From now on you make no contact with Wolfhound at all. If you do then the deal terminates. From now on you deal with me direct. Is that clear? No. No. I don't give you my number. I ring you. Tomorrow. Tomorrow morning, ten o'clock.'

He thought: will he nevertheless check back to Nuncle? Yes. Does it matter? No. Why not? Because Nuncle said to his secretary: 'I'm out to Herz for the next two weeks,' and there are still eight days of those to run. It will work. It might work. It's worth a try. He walked slowly back to the Boulevard des Pyrénées, but took his time. On the way a poster caught his eye.

Inger wasn't in the camper. He looked around, expecting her not to be too far away. He was right. She was sitting at a table in a terrace café separated from the road by a low stone wall.

She was drinking coffee. He put his hands on the wall, looked up at her.

'I'm sorry. That was stupid of me.'

'Yes. It was. Stupid of me too, perhaps.'

'Will you buy me a beer?'

'Of course.'

He climbed over the wall, ignoring the proper entrance ten metres away, damaging a petunia or two as he did so. Inger ordered the beer, but still looked angry, unhappy. He played his card.

'How far away is Morlàas?'

'Not far. Fifteen kilometres. Why?'

'There's a fête there today. Do you like fêtes?'

'*J'adore les fêtes*.' She forgave him. 'Shall we go? Will you take me?'

The waiter brought the beer. He drank, wiped his mouth, put his hand on hers.

'Of course. But only if you first lend me enough money to buy some clothes. On the poster it said something about bull-fights, something of the sort, can that be right?'

'Of course I'll lend you the money.' Emphasis on 'lend' – she was not to pay him or make a gift of it. 'As for the bull-fights that'll be *Course Landaise* and may be the *cocarde* too. They have lively heifers, same breed as fighting bulls. The *Course Landaise* can be a bit boring but the *cocarde* is great fun. They put paper roses between their horns, and all the young men have to try to get them off without being hurt. It's all very macho, a way of showing off to their girl-friends. Hey. I'm so pleased. Lots of people think fêtes are silly, for children, but I really do love them. And they're not something a woman can go to on her own.'

They bought the clothes he wanted – a close knit navy sweater, smart denim jacket and jeans, three pairs of briefs, three pairs of socks, and a pair of stylish but functional shoes. He was particular about them, that they should be flexible, light yet tough, and have soles that would never slip. It came to a lot of francs – she paid with Visa. He said that by the time the bill came in he'd have money of his own to settle with. Finally he asked for a thousand francs, also a loan, but so he could pay the expenses of the fête, and have some pocket money he could call his own. Ironically, wryly, she accepted his demands and the mood between them remained good as they drove north into the lush Béarnaise countryside.

They found the village, still largely medieval, boasting on its welcome sign that once it was the tenth century capital of Béarn, and that the Romanesque portal of its church was *exceptionel*. The streets were lined with the big high narrow stalls that magically appear at every fête and fiesta selling nougat, cheap dolls, crêpes, waffles, and merguèz – spicy thin sausages. Loudspeakers blasted the appalling music the French have used for celebrations since the Thirties, occasionally interrupted by coy interchanges from an *animateur* and an *animatrice* which always contrived to end with a plug for a local shop or restaurant. There were plastic flags everywhere, mainly the tricoleur but also the Royalist *fleur du lys*, and the bear of Béarn. With dry aplomb Cranmer scored the maximium possible on a .22 rifle shooting range – he offered the prize, a giant panda, to Inger, who shook her head, so he gave it to a little girl.

For an hour they watched the *Course Landaise* but the succession of *équipes* performing apparently identical routines of *écarts* and *sauts*, swerves and leaps to avoid charging but tethered heifers soon palled after the first excitement. Cranmer was disappointed that the sharps on the heifers' horns were masked by leather balls as big as large oranges, that their charges were controlled by ropes so no sudden dramatic twist or swerve was possible. The course was a competition of agility and grace, with the element of danger reduced to a minimum.

'There's still the *cocarde*,' Inger remarked, as they left their places on a temporary stand beneath the plane trees of the public park, 'Let's find where they're doing that.'

At the other end of the village they found a small mobile

corral made of stout plank palings bolted together. There were plank seats on scaffolding above it, already nearly full. They found places high up at the back. A silver bugle call announced the first heifer, a wise old peasant in a black felt hat pulled up a trap and in she came. Again the sharps were protected but the balls were small, made of *gutta percha* or cork. Certainly they could still deliver a very nasty blow, even cause internal injury, though not presumably an actual goring. Between them a small red rosette was attached to her black forehead.

In the first minute she caught a youth in the stomach, felled him, and continued to worry him until yanked away by three more pulling on her tail. They scattered as she turned. The crowd screamed, cheered, or surrendered to gales of laughter for twenty minutes, a small silver band played paso dobles and she charged, swerved, tossed, kept her *cocarde*, and caught two more youths before the organisers withdrew her on the grounds she was tiring. The bugle again and in came the second.

Cranmer stood up. Inger caught his arm.

'Oh no you don't. It's much too dangerous if you don't know what you're doing.

'But I do know.'

He ran smoothly down a division in the seating, leapt into the ring. Shouts and screams from the crowd. Two of the youths already there gathered round him, clearly tried to persuade him to get out, at the same time looking anxiously back over their shoulders. The heifer saw the group and charged. The group scattered, the heifer turned, only Cranmer was now in her vision. Her head went down, she charged again. Cranmer, arms above his head, span on the balls of his feet, leaned ever so slightly out and the curve of her horn brushed the back of his leg. The crowd screamed and cheered. She turned, came back, and this time as she went by and her head came up he reached backwards, plucked the *cocarde*. The crowd went wild. Youths used their coats as capes to distract her while he walked across the ring holding the rosette above his head. He looked, Inger realised, very pleased with himself, but the smile, the nearest

51

thing to a grin she had seen on his face, evaporated when the photo flashes went off around him. Quickly he tossed the rosette up towards her, the man in front of her caught it and passed it on, then he vaulted the palings and trotted back up the steps to rejoin her.

'Come on, let's go. I could do with a beer.'

But they wouldn't let him. Still scowling he was made to return to the ring to receive a garlanded bottle of champagne, and a new barrage of flashes.

8

From the gate they could see it – an old 2CV with formalised, cartoon-type paintings of curlers on its panels and mudguards, grotesque monsters surfing down them.

Cranmer closed the gate behind the camper, got back in.

Inger said: 'Shit.'

'Why? Who is it?'

'Laura for certain. Maybe her boyfriend as well. Listen, No Man. She's very beautiful, but she's also definitely bad news. Very bad news. All right?'

She took off the hand-brake, let out the clutch.

Up in her bedroom Laura heard the camper arrive.

'At last, Michael,' she was speaking to the glove puppet on her left hand, 'We're going to find out who's been sleeping in our bed. You know of course, but you wouldn't tell me, would you?'

She slipped the puppet off her hand, put it back not where she had left it, on her pillow, but in the small bedside locker where she had found it. She put the money, pound notes and francs, into the battered white soft leather shoulder bag she habitually carried, stood in front of the mirror, head on one side, smoothed her short sun-bleached blonde hair off her temples, adjusted the loose fitting short blue cotton top so it sat just right over her wide spaced nipples, gave her short shorts a tug to make sure her navel showed properly, twisted, looked at her tight but not skinny buttocks. Then she blew herself a kiss, headed for the stairs.

She came through the front door just as Inger and the man were getting out of the van. The man was holding a bottle of champagne with a red ribbon and the *cocarde* round its neck. He hung back while Inger and her daughter exchanged perfunctory kisses. She was, he saw, even more beautiful than her mother and in a very different way. The provocative top, frayed shorts, gold chain with fetichist, surfing pendant, gold bangles to set off her tan. It all added up to an aggressive sexiness, but there were flaws. The polished nails were chipped, there were shadows round her eyes, he was soon to discover that in repose her natural expression was mean, sulky. She was also younger than he had first thought – probably not yet nineteen.

'Hi, Mum.'

'Laura. Hallo.'

They broke from the swift, cold embrace.

'No need to ask why you're here. I'm sure it's not just a social visit. You'd better come in.' Inger moved towards the door. 'Is that awful boy with you?'

'No. I just borrowed his wheels.' Her eyes, lit with a questioning half smile, remained on the man. 'I don't see why it shouldn't become a social visit. Aren't you going to introduce me?'

But Inger had already gone through the door and into the kitchen. She went straight to the gas oven which she was already lighting when the other two came in behind her.

Without looking up she said: 'You'd better go through to the patio. I'll be with you in a moment. Do you want a beer?'

'I'd rather have a vodka martini.'

53

The man undid the inside bolts to the door between the kitchen and the patio.

'No Man?'

'Beer, please.'

He followed the girl into the patio. She sat in the cane armchair at the head of the table, he set down the champagne bottle, sat on the bench at the other end.

'No Man? What sort of a name is that? Is that your first name, or should I call you Herr No Man? I'm Laura. Madam's daughter. Hi.'

'Hi.'

He remained composed, his face almost expressionless, yet nevertheless appreciative of Laura's attractions. She was more overtly aware of him. She was also a touch embarrassed that the wad of money in her bag was presumably his. Nevertheless she spoke quickly, attempting to secure the bridgehead she had gained, trying to ensure that she would be invited to stay.

'No, really. I mean I can't call you No Man, can I?'

'You don't have to call me anything.'

'I suppose not. Let me guess. Champagne with a ribbon round it. Have you just come from the fête at Morlàas? Mum's a mug for fêtes. How did you win the champers? Let me guess again. Shooting on one of those rifle ranges?'

'No. I got it for winning that.' He touched the *cocarde*.

'From between the heifer's horns? Golly. I am impressed. What else can you do?'

Inger came in, carrying a vodka martini for Laura, a beer for Cranmer. She heard the question, answered it herself.

'Ski extrème, free-fall parachuting, hang-gliding. He kills rats with his teeth, and badmen with two fingers . . .' Unable to resist showing off to her daughter she stabbed the air, in imitation of a martial arts expert. 'The lot. Here are your drinks. Oh dear. The fish is in the oven, but the champagne is not in the fridge.'

She scooped up the champagne bottle and went back to the kitchen.

Laura fluttered eye lashes, vamped.

'Wow, and what else? I bet you're a whizz in bed. No wonder Mum likes you. Cheers.' She drank, grimaced, sighed. 'That's better.'

Her mother returned with a vodka martini for herself, sat opposite Cranmer.

Laura went on: 'If you can afford to do all that, you must be rich.'

Inger reacted – an amused pout and eyebrows raised, but away from Laura, sharing the joke with Cranmer. He remained cool.

'Actually, I haven't a bean. Not a *sou*.'

'I don't believe you.' But she did. She had his money in the battered soft leather bag on the table beside her. Then, with malice: 'You're much the nicest boy-friend she's had for ages. Have you known her long?'

Her mother had had enough, was sharp.

'None of your business. Right, Laura. How much?'

A big, black carpenter bee buzzed in from the meadow, headed for a beam supporting the vine, bumbled for a moment trying to remember where its hole was. Then it squeezed in – a perfect fit.

Laura looked at her glass, already almost empty, then up at her mother – with hate.

'Two thousand. My share of the month's rent.'

'I'll get it.'

When she was gone her daughter leaned as close to Cranmer as she could.

'I mean where did she find you? Usually her lovers are either weedy arty types or boys my age. Sometimes both. I mean she was such a lousy mother to me, she's got lots of maternal instinct left unused.'

But her mother was already back with a two thousand franc note.

'Here you are. Don't smoke it, or pop pills with it. Pay the rent. Right?'

55

'Thanks, Mum. The rent. Right. Can I stay for supper?'

'No.'

'Why not? I'll go when we've finished.'

'The fish is only big enough for two, and there's only one bottle of champagne.'

Laura grinned, gathered up her bag which she clutched to her chest, between her breasts.

'I can see I'm really not wanted. Yet. See you. Both? OK.'

She went, and presently they heard the 2CV engine cough, turn, pick up.

Cranmer offered his near-grin.

'Thank the Lord. I thought for a moment we were going to have to give her a push start.'

A three-quarter moon rolled slowly up the line of the mountain to the south, its cold beams fingered their way through the vine and bougainvillea, made love with the warm candle-light on the table. Fish bones and peach stones, No Man and Inger. Outside a dog fox sniffed at the patch of earth where the rats were buried and loped on, nose in the air, questing. A little owl, Athene Noctua, gave her squawk, swooped away from the telephone pole it had perched on unnoticed for most of the day. Inger smoked, they both drank brandy.

'I know I was a lousy mother. And she's never forgiven me.'

'But why? What for?'

'Neglect. Not physical, emotional. She knew I was never really that interested. She knew she was something that had happened to me that I had not chosen.'

'But you were always there.'

'Yes.

'I don't think she had such a bad deal.'

Inger thought about that, about the coldness with which he had said it.

'You had a worse deal?'

'I'd say so.'

Inger put briskness into her voice.

'Well, that's something I don't want to know about. Remember, No Man – I'm your present, not your past. I don't want to know about your past.' She sat back again, sipped brandy. 'But she really has been a pain. Last year she was in Barcelona, got hooked on junk. I had to go there, find her, get her off it. It wasn't easy. When she was a kid I gave her dancing lessons, then diving and swimming. She got to be very good. I thought she might do something. But . . .' she shrugged, dabbed out her cigarette.

'Forget her for now. Leave it be.'

'Yes, you're right.' She covered his hand with hers. 'No Man. My daughter thinks we're lovers.'

'I know.'

'Why aren't we? Why aren't we lovers?'

With the moon they needed neither light nor darkness. With the warmth of a southern July they needed no covers. Her daughter, with malice, was wrong. Inger did not want young men to mother – at least not actually in bed. In bed she wanted a male god – a body hard with healthy muscle, a chin that felt coarse if not bristly, a prick as solid as oak. She wanted a man who could make her feel like a goddess, a young goddess, above all that: young again.

With skill that was neither knowing nor harsh Cranmer achieved all that: no doubt she was very ready, met him more than half way, was making him as far as she could into what she wanted him to be – and was finding it easier to do that now in bed than she had in the day and night-time busy-ness of their journey and arrival. Where, outside, she had resented at times his assertiveness, had been irritated by his coldness, she now welcomed the assurance with which he took control.

When the moment came, she gladly let him scoop her up, his hands firmly clasping her buttocks, his arched body, bent like a bow away from her, above her, so there was almost no contact between them above their waists. For a moment she felt, as the spasms came, that she actually was flying with him, that he was carrying her upwards on wings spread behind his back. Then they faded and the moment was past, her body went limp, or tried to, but he still held her, his prick was still oak-hard inside her.

She half murmured, half moaned: 'I came, I came. Please, please, you too. Oh my darling, please, please let yourself go.'

It was a plea, not untouched with despair. She sensed a ruthlessness in the way he had held on until he had possessed her.

'Please . . .!'

He released her buttocks, put his arms on either side of her head lifted his head and torso even further from her than before. Then he began to thrust into her, slowly, purposefully, no doubt relishing the warm moist relaxed place he was penetrating, but making it very clear that he was now doing it to himself, using her, not allowing her in any way to do it to him.

'Yes, yes. Go on my darling, yes.'

She began to moan a little, twist a little, and he moved again, putting his hands on her shoulders, suddenly letting her feel his weight, like chains. She fell quiet, waited, and he came.

He placed himself on his back beside her. It was some time before she dared to speak.

'No Man. You make love very well.'

She waited. When he spoke his voice had no colour, no appeal or apology.

'I know how to fuck. I can't make love.'

'Why not?

'I was taught . . . not to.'

Later, not much later, he began slowly and carefully to explore her body with his mouth and fingers. She suspected he was consciously, self-consciously enjoying its femaleness: the exposed vulnerability of her throat, the roundness of her shoulders, the softness of her breasts, the gentle firmness of her nipples. She welcomed this, and with some trepidation returned the caresses.

'No. Let me.'

She bit back any retort, let him go on, forced herself to submit to it, made herself remain open for him. She was ready when he penetrated her again, welcomed that too – but she could not come again, nor did he seem to want her too. But he did. And again once more, when the sparrows began their chirping in the vine below, and the dog fox trotted back through the dewy meadow, past her sculptures, irrelevant in the mist, with a neighbour's chicken in his mouth.

9

At half past eight in the morning she felt him leaving the bed, five minutes later she heard the engine of her camper fire, and then the ticking chug-chug of its rear-mounted engine. The noise receded, altered tone. Without getting out of bed she could visualise him at the gate, getting out to open it beneath the sweet chestnut, driving through, closing it behind him. Why should he close it behind him, when already he had offended by borrowing the vehicle without asking? Borrowing? She might never see it again! But borrowing or stealing he would close the gate behind him, of that she was certain. There were some things she knew about No Man and one was that what he did, good or bad, he did properly. She pulled the duvet over her shoulders and allowed herself more sleep. That at least was one thing sex did for you – even his sort of sex: it granted deeper warmer sleep than any dull opiate and it was a delight, the sleep that is, she too rarely had.

But by eleven she had had her coffee and warmed over rolls with *beurre en motte* and was in the barn leafing through the sketches she had made the previous day. She felt inspired, no other word. Not with excitement, but knowledge. She knew she knew enough about him, about herself, and about what the figure twisting out of space leaving a trail of flame behind it meant to her, to make a go of it, a sculpture that would be a delight to make, and, who knows, a delight to behold. That knowledge made her happy – it was the form of happiness she most revelled in: beyond sex, relationships, the blessing of good weather . . . anything. She drank from a glass of icy white wine – toasted herself and the work she was about to begin.

Then came the double rhythm, the ticking magneto against the more commonplace drumming of the engine, up the hill, stop at the gate, start again. He parked the camper, jumped down, moved towards the front door. She called: 'Just in time. I really need your help now. But did you get what you went for?'

'Yes. Yes, I did.' There was a new elation in his voice too, something she had not heard before. She was wise enough not to believe that it had anything to do with the night they had spent together.

He added: 'Hang on a moment. I'll be right with you.'

Inside the farmhouse he ran up the stairs, swung into Laura's bedroom, opened the bedside locker, thrust his hand into the Michael Jackson puppet. It was on the tip of his tongue to say something like 'Up yours, Michael,' but the void he found killed the joke.

'Shit.'

Stunned he slumped back on to the bed, looked around. Was this some sort of trick one of them had played? Would he find the money if he looked for it, Hunt the Slipper? No. That wasn't Inger's style. She made a fetish out of privacy, out of respecting other people's space and expecting them to respect hers in return. But the daughter? There'd be no game there either: anything she could take easy – she'd take.

'The cunt,' he whispered – in his own language. 'The fucking cunt.'

*

60

For five hours he worked for Inger like a navvy. Together they sliced sheeting, twisted it, bent and twisted rods, welded them. The barn filled with the stink of burning metal, of caustic fluxes. He was – she had expected it – experienced in the techniques, and unquestioningly obedient. That surprised her rather more: it occurred to her that the effortless way he assumed authority in most areas was not merely or only sexist: anything he had applied himself to, he expected to have mastered. However, he respected people, regardless of sex, who showed similar mastery, and allowed himself to serve when he recognised he was being asked to operate in areas – like sheer creativity – where he knew he knew nothing.

A figure in metal began to emerge and she felt deeply pleased with it, the beginning of an elation that only artists, perhaps some scientists on the frontiers of knowledge, can experience. But he kept pushing up his face shield, looking at the new watch on his wrist.

'That's the third time you've looked at your new watch in an hour. Do you have an appointment to keep? Or is it just that you're so pleased with it? I remember how pleased I was with my first watch.'

He put down the welding equipment, turned back the blue flame, reached a hand to the cylinder, killed the flow of fuel, lifted the visored helmet off his head.

'Look. I'm sorry. But I do have to go.'

She had not properly heard him, stood back, admired the way the figure was emerging.

'OK. It's a good moment to stop. You know, that would have taken a week on my own.'

'It's finished?' Incredulity in his voice.

'Oh no. There's a lot of work still to do. If this were clay I'd say we had the armature I want. But the rest is basically filling in, finishing, polishing, even colouring. So. Go to your appointment. Where is it? Sorry, don't answer that. But how long will you be?'

61

'Can you drive me to Tarbes? To the airport? The evening plane for Paris leaves in two hours.'

Carefully she put the steel sheet she was holding, a leaf or flame shape – the ambiguity was deliberate – on the work table she used for cutting out paper templates.

'You . . . what? Christ.' She resisted, but it had become suddenly more difficult so she had to find reserves of will which drew their strength from principle rather than feeling, she resisted the temptation to ask him what it was all about. 'You're going away. Are you coming back?'

'I don't know. But listen. I'm sorry, but I had some money in the house. I'm not going to tell you where I got it from or how. That's not your business. But yesterday evening Laura stole it. Before we got back.'

She was almost overcome with fury and distress, almost all of it directed at her daughter. Not because she had stolen money, Inger had had to cope with that before – but in part at least because Laura had turned Inger's relationship with No Man on its head. Now Inger was the debtor, now she was the one who owed. She stormed out of the barn, paced back and forward with fists clenched, head in the air and shaking. Eventually she got herself under control, came back, stood in front of him.

'How much? How much did the little bitch take? How much do you want?'

Two different questions, with different answers. He chose the right one, gave an honest answer.

'A single air fare. Tarbes to Paris. Scheduled flight I'm afraid, no reductions. And a bit over for the Metro at the other end, and so on. A mille should do.'

It was less than a third of what he had taken from Churchill's body, of what Laura had stolen from him.

She drove him to Tarbes airport, she didn't mess about, didn't want to have on her hands the responsibility if he missed the plane. And it is not an easy drive: even with modern improvements the road still has some nasty bends, especially before and after Lourdes whose pilgrims numbered in millions per year are the reason for there being an airport at Tarbes at all. In the late afternoon light the northern crags of the Pyrenees were grey and menacing although the weather held up. There were a lot of campers and caravans about as well as endless coaches streaming to and from St Bernadette's Grotto. In seven minutes less than she had ever taken over the trip before, and less than thirty-five minutes later, she slotted the camper into a place in the car park.

Still clutching the steering wheel as if it might be dangerous to let go, and staring sightlessly in front, she said, carefully placing words she had prepared: 'I've tried really hard not to ask any questions, but I find there are two. I have to ask them. Again.'

He said nothing. Waited.

'Are you coming back? If you are, then when? Listen. Before you answer, get this straight. A very strong part of me doesn't really give a wet fart. Three, four days ago I didn't know you, and I was happy a lot of the time, and the spaces where I wasn't happy had nothing to do with . . . any gap you might have filled. They related to Laura and to my mother. In three weeks' time you'll be a memory. On the whole a good one. Because while even if I'm now pretty sure you're a Grade A bastard, it is at least Grade A. And I admire people who are Grade A anything. But we had good times too, so I can live with whatever answer you give, or with no answser at all.'

This was all more or less as she wanted it to be. He took his time and, looking at his new watch, he estimated he had time.

'I may not come back. If I do . . . it should be within . . . four weeks? Give me four weeks.'

He reached behind for the small hold-all he had bought or found. Inger grabbed his wrist, held it, squeezed, let go.

She said, almost as if it were a curse: 'Ciao.'

'Ciao.'

He got out, walked away across the black top, passed in front of hexagonal concrete tubs filled with fulsome petunias, pastel pinks and blue.

Inger watched him, then she started the engine, set the Volkswagen camper moving in a slow turn away from him, so it was impossible for either to see if the other waved. Neither did.

'Bastard. Grade A. But a bastard.'

The anger was a dressing for a hurt that burned.

10

He had a messy couple of days in Paris before everything was settled, or rather properly begun. There were problems with his documentation, photographs had to be taken, that sort of thing, and of course he had not taken as much money from Inger to replace what he had lost as he should have done. He was tempted to use his new freedom and steal, but thought better of it. No need to complicate matters. He slept rough on the Gare du Nord – until he had documentation a hotel was out of the question. The second week of July and the place was littered with backpackers. A couple of days eating tuna sandwiches from materials bought in a supermarket were no real hardship and on the third morning he was given precise instructions for meeting the man who would be his control.

The arrangements were efficient, even clever. At precisely ten in the morning he was to take the funicular from Place St Pierre to the Sacré Coeur on top of Montmartre. He'd be met on the belvedere beneath the main entrance to the church, and when the meeting was over he was to take the funicular back down. The point of it all was clear to him. Once he was in the funicular his control, and anyone else who was there watching him, could leave the rendezvous with no fear that he might follow them. He might of course have had an accomplice who could pick up the trail – but he knew he had been under surveillance ever since he made contact on arrival, and he had been scrupulously careful not to do anything that might arouse suspicion. No telephone calls except the scheduled ones to them, no sudden moves or attempts to shake them off.

North European weather remained bad. He stood at the rear of the cabin as it ratcheted its way up over the terraced gardens, and Paris slowly exposed herself beneath him. Banks of low cloud rolled in from the west on a warm breeze. Squalls rinsed the huge blocks on the skyline towards Orly, while in the other direction the same breeze shafted golden sunbeams across the wooded hills around Versailles. He was the last to leave the station at the top, took his time, looked up and around. The church with its white domes and deep recesses looked like a stack of skulls – hominoid if not human. There were plenty of tourists, a couple of bus-loads of them, prey for ice-cream vendors and sellers of religious gew-gaws. He walked up the steps and on to the belvedere, leaned on the rail and looked down between the pollarded acacias, already in pod after their brief flowering a month before. The Seine snaked her way through the metropolis below, he picked up the landmarks. Notre Dame. The Pompidou Centre. The other way the Eiffel Tower, the Bois de Boulogne. Up to them now, let them come to him.

Up in the main portico to the church two men watched him. They made an ill-matched couple. Heinrich Herz of AlterLog was about fifty, stocky, medium height, fit, with short-cropped grey-hair, smartly dressed in a three-quarter length camel coat, over a smart business suit. Willi Weise, his chief gofer, was twenty years younger, fat, untidy, wore a black Tina Turner Foreign Affair European Tour (1990) T-shirt, beneath a black leather jacket, and jeans that were too small for him – beneath the silver buckle of a broad, worn leather belt, the top button was undone. The buckle itself was formed by two hands clasping two naked buttocks which Willi thought was very droll.

65

Presently Herz gave him the nod and, clutching a document case in one hand an unlit cigarette in the other he trotted down the steps. Herz watched as he approached the man they already knew as Herr Biedermann, asked him for a light.

The meeting was short, the conversation brief. Cranmer lit Willi's cigarette, they chatted for a moment or two, and it seemed the most natural thing in the world that at the end of it Cranmer should take Willi's document case in exchange for lighting his cigarette. He turned, walked down the steps again to the funicular station. Willi waited at the railings until Cranmer was safely in the cabin, and the cabin was safely dropping back down to the boulevards below. He bought an ice-cream and peeled the paper off the cone as Herz came down to meet him.

'Well? What do you think?'

Willi bit into the crust of chocolate and chopped almond, a podgy finger wiped cream from the corner of his small mouth.

'I think he's for real.' His voice was high, fluting, as if it had never broken.

'Nationality?'

'I'm pretty sure he's British.'

'Professional? Track record?'

'I'd say so.' He gave a high little laugh, a sort of giggle. 'He didn't like the Makarov, so he knows something about it all.'

'But he will use it?' Herz allowed himself a tiny hint of anxiety.

'He says he will. I told him there was no deal if he didn't.'

They began to walk back down to the belvedere.

'He did give a sort of explanation of why the passport and driving permit were so important to him.'

'Yes?'

'He reckons he's dead, officially dead. Recorded killed in a disaster. So each contract he does he takes on a new identity, and the employer has to find the documents. That's his routine. He says it works well. One thing's for sure. Hans Biedermann is not his real name.'

66

They were back at the rail, just about where Willi and Cranmer had talked. Willi crunched through barquette biscuit, pushed the end in after, wiped his fingers on his jeans.

'He reckons dead person status confers immunity, makes him invulnerable. I have to say I liked that. That impressed me.'

The older man gave it some thought, then nodded.

'Yes. I can go along with that. Not easy to pin a murder on a dead man.'

Cranmer walked the short distance down the Rue de Dunkerque back to the Gare du Nord, clutching the flat document case upright in front of his chest. He went into the toilets, put a franc in the Gardienne's saucer, took a leaf or two of toilet paper. Sitting on the pedestal, in what was, for France, a very reasonably clean and well-appointed public loo, he sat on the pedestal, turned the little brass wheels to the numbers Willi Weise had given him, lifted the lid. The bottom was nicely lined with thin bundles of notes, each with an owl and a cowslip on one side, and a Renaissance gent (the man who drew them?) on the other. Predominantly a soft shade of olive green, they were the perfect background for the black automatic pistol held in place by the diagonal straps of the case and the thin booklet with its scarlet cover and white cross. There would be, he was sure, one hundred and twenty of them – six thousand Swiss Francs, roundabout two thousand two hundred pounds in the currency he most naturally thought in. He might check later, more important to him right now was the passport.

He had no real means of checking how good it was – it was something he would simply have to take on trust. The brief details it gave of his physical appearance were accurate: height 175 cms, eyes blue, hair dark brown. The picture on the page three recto was him all right – he had sat in a booth for it thirty-six hours earlier – but now the corners had been scalloped and overlaid top left, bottom right with an embossing stamp – the Swiss cross and the letters around it 'Ambassade Suisse, Paris'. The paper looked good, greyish-brown with intricate banknote

67

style engraving based on lozenges which just possibly suggested formalised mountain peaks. His name was Biedermann, his *prénom* was Hans. His date of birth was 6 January 1958. There was only one fault he could find: it had been issued just a year ago, in July 1990, but looked too new, too unused. The same was true of the grey driving permit in its transparent plastic envelope.

The gun was less satisfactory. To begin with, at under one and a half pounds, it was too light. Secondly he had no real way of knowing where it or the seven rounds he now spilled from the magazine into his still raw palm had come from. Czechoslovakia would do nicely, Russia was all right, China a liability. In any case, he suffered from an ineradicable prejudice against all things from the east – he just did not believe they worked. The five pointed star on the butt was for him an evil talisman.

In the lid of the case was a simple manila brown folder. He unclipped the straps, opened it on his knee. On the inside just one sheet of good quality, grey A4. A passport photograph pasted at the top showed an elderly man with glasses, wearing a tweed outdoor, countrified hat with a feather. He was looking at the camera with angry alarm. Underneath, immaculately laser-printed, a name for heading – Herrn Dr Otto Schumacher, an address in Vienna, with a brief account of his habits and way of life that was strictly factual, made no judgements, offered no background. Attended the Staat Opera and the Burg Theatre during the season, but shopped in his suburb, rarely on the Ring. Liked country walking in good weather. On Sundays frequented the Prater with his grand-children, went coarse fishing on his own in the Danube once a fortnight or so and so on. The account filled less than three quarters of the sheet, and was, Cranmer judged, the product of a reasonably competent private detective. Except that there should have been no look of surprise, and certainly no anger on the photograph.

He took two sheafs of ten notes each, put them in the inside pocket of his denim jacket together with the passport. The gun was a problem without a holster – for the time being he left it in the case which he now carefully relocked. Later he bought a roll of sticky medicated tape and taped it to his body in his left arm-pit. In the Gare du Nord concourse branch of the BNP he changed the twenty bank notes into French francs and the passport survived its first scrutiny. Then he walked the short distance down Dunkerque and Alsace to the Gare de l'Est and booked himself a couchette on the Arlberg Express, leaving that evening at 2240, arriving at Wien Westbahnhof at 2000 the following evening.

He had eleven hours to waste. He bought some more cheap clothes and a cheap suitcase big enough to hold the document case as well. He went to one of the big restaurants opposite the station, had a dozen oysters, a plate of steak tartar, and a bottle of blanc de blanc de Limoux. Fifteen years earlier he had been to Limoux with a Cambridge college Rugby football team, and after the match they had nearly drowned in the stuff. He chose it because he remembered the name out of the twenty or so on offer. The remaining hours he spent in the station's round-the-clock soft porn cinema, seeing the programme two and a half times. The action portrayed was less intense and rather more jolly than the sort of thing he had experienced three nights before with Inger.

The Donauinsul is a long thin island in the Danube. At the end of the second week in July 1991 it was the scene of extensive public works – the town hall was turning it into parks and pleasure-grounds. Consequently much of it was in an untidy, unfinished state. There are several links to the banks of the great river, but the most notable is the Reichsbrücke, a modern but elegant bridge carrying four road lanes, two U-bahn tracks, and a separate facility for pedestrians.

On the Saturday afternoon, at about one thirty, Otto Schumacher got off the train and walked down the steep ramp onto the island. Already he was glancing through the thick mesh fencing at the river below. It was a pale grey gun metal sort of colour and there were not, as far as he could see, any anglers there ahead of him.

He was a very fit, jolly old man, wearing a belted jacket, plus-fours and a hat with a feather, and under it Walkman ear-phones. The Walkman was attached to the belt of his jacket. He was carrying fishing gear: a rod, a keep-net, a small collapsible stool, a bag, and so on.

He came off the ramp and on to blacktop, looked around. High fences cut off the building sites, concrete climbed in ziggurats behind it, cranes stood immobile for the weekend, their buckets loaded with the wheelbarrows and tools that might otherwise be filched. He moved on a bit. Sad saplings struggled out of concrete hexagons, it would be a decade before they came to anything, way beyond the life-span he expected. A hundred metres or so more brought him to undisturbed wasteland – that is to say scrub, weeds and small trees that had grown there unbothered for twenty years or more. This was his favourite spot. Willow and a willow-like tree with silver spear-shaped leaves, very delicate, and tiny yellow flowers, grew above spikes of willow-herb, the tops seeding fluff but with delicate pinks and mauves still robust below. Warblers and finches raised their second broods and swallows murdered the gnats and their allies above the wide deep river.

He unfolded a tiny camping stool and began carefully, and in the right order, to deploy and adjust the paraphernalia he had brought with him. This was not so easy. At seventy-seven years old Dr Schumacher, who had taught philosophy at various eminent European universities, and had also suffered unspeak-ably in Dachau, had finally refined his speculations to the point where he could say with confidence that a happy person was a person who was enjoying as many of the simple, healthy pleasures available to us as he can, preferably all at the same time. Thus he came to the Donauinsul to smoke his pipe (he was old enough not to believe this was unhealthy), to fish for pike-perch, to watch the swift flow of the great river, still fed by its tributaries with alpine snow, and listen to Beethoven's

'Pastoral Symphony' conducted by his name-sake Otto Klemperer – and all at the same time. And if he took his eyes off his float he could see on one side the ferris wheel in the Prater, and on the other the towers of UNO city: the one promising innocent pleasure, the other world peace. A Hungarian cruise boat, bedecked with flags, low because of the bridges, carrying Mozart fans in Mozart year down the Danube to Budapest, slipped away from the port.

The pipe drew well, Beethoven awakened pleasant feelings on entering the Vienna woods which were only a few miles or so away, and the float bobbed. A pike-perch?

Cranmer shot him behind the ear, gave the body a push so it toppled four feet down a steep slope of dressed boulders and into the water with a solid sort of splash. Then, with a high round arm throw, he lobbed the Makarov fifty metres further out beyond it.

He walked briskly back to the ramp. Two small boys skateboarded down towards and past him. Just as he arrived on the U-bahn platform a train pulled in. He boarded it.

11

He made it on to the 1400 hours train from Wien Westbanhof with five minutes to spare, he already had his ticket, and got off at Salzburg at 1725 although he had booked through to Kitzbuhel. In the open bus station opposite the Salzburg Bahnhof he caught a bus up into the mountains to Berchtesgaden. Almost immediately there was a *grenzcontrole* at the German border: this time the guard merely swung down the aisle checking that all the passengers were carrying documentation. The Biedermann passport was not even opened. He looked around. Some of his fellow passengers were prosperous peasant women returning from Salzburg market, but most were single or paired backpackers travelling on the cheap with complicated ticket arrangements which claimed reduced tariffs on some buses and trains and not others. The inspector was a lot more thorough over checking these than the border guard had been with passports.

It was a smooth ride on a smooth road in a smooth bus. The elegant, unblemished engineering conferred a well-groomed domesticity on the grandeur of the mountains, the denseness of the forests, the splendour of the alpine meadows. One felt that at the top of every mountain torrent a discreetly-placed uniformed inspector tested the water for acidity or radiation on the hour, every hour, before letting the immaculate whiteness plummet on down the well-polished granite of its particular chasm. None of the big alpine cows, beige and white, had shit on their backsides, and their bells, easily heard over the whisper of the Mercedes-Benz engine, chimed in well-tuned cadences. Cranmer began to feel he had made a mistake. He had expected something a touch more basic, Wagnerian.

Nevertheless he checked in to a luxury hotel on Stang Gass, for two nights, swam thirty lengths in the twenty-five metre pool, had a sauna, and dined off grilled trout and what purported to be wild boar. He slept well, in coddled luxury which he more than half despised, but which the deprived side of his nature could not help relishing – but first the little boy who had had toys instead of love played with the toys in his room, the colour TV with multiple channels including an in-house porn video, the large bathroom with its huge towels and finger-touch water controls.

The next day, Sunday, he took the post bus up to Obersalzburg. He ignored the lift but took the steep walk, through forest for the most part but always tamely signposted, up to the Eagle's Nest. He felt deeply irritated by the bland and noncommittal way the place was laid out, the exhibits displayed: nevertheless a deep and uncomfortable emotion began to swell behind his breast bone, in his diaphragm, around his balls. It

72

was uncompromised by value judgement either way: it was the response of his whole psyche to the bigness, the enormity of one man's project to build a kingdom that would last a thousand years and whose boundaries would one day extend into space. Finally a deep satisfaction overrode the irritation and he made the walk back down in a mood of deep elation.

On Monday he caught the 0946 train down from Berchtesgaden to Traunstein, the suburb of Salzburg that lies in Germany, where it joined the semi-fast Wien to München train. At Traunstein he had time to buy the morning edition of the *Bayerische Zeitung*. The train was not crowded and he had no difficulty finding a corner seat. He waited until the Alpine scenery had receded before opening out the paper. There was a picture of Dr Otto Schumacher on the front page – in full academic fig this time – and the headline – 'SCHUMACHER SLAIN'. The story began 'The ex-Ukrainian Jew who hunted down Ukrainian war-criminals was finally himself the victim.' There was a second headline 'WARRIORS OF CHRIST CLAIM KILLING'.

At one o'clock he turned off the Arnulfstrasse, Munich, into the Augustinerkeller, looked round the big room, with its huge quartzy granite pillars, white walls, plastic ivy, real deer antlers. There were long tables in the centre, smaller booths in alcoves to the sides. Already it seemed full: mainly with Münchener businessmen eating Münchener *weisswürst* with cabbage and potato purée, and huge glasses of beer. Waitresses with trolleys took orders and served. It was very noisy with piped Bavarian band music under-cutting the general din with braying brass over a mind-drilling rum-tum-tum. He eventually found Willi Weise in a small alcove near the other door on Augustiner-strasse. The fat man was dressed exactly as he had been on Montmartre – the Tina Turner T-shirt, the leather jacket, the jeans. He had just started a huge and elaborate ice-cream featuring gobbets of real cream and piped *vermicelle* – sweet-chestnut purée. Cranmer looked down at him.

'You want to talk to me here?'

Weise shrugged.

'Why not?' He pushed a big spoonful of ice-cream into his mouth, talked through it. 'Not much chance of us being overheard.'

'Not much chance of me hearing you at all.'

'Not unless you sit down.' Weise heaved his big bottom along the short bench, Cranmer squeezed in beside him. A waitress handed him a big laminated menu.

'Take the set-meal, it's cheaper. You're in Munich – you drink beer.' Weise looked up at the waitress. 'One menu of the day and a beer.'

Cranmer tried to reassert his right to choose for himself.

'A *small* beer.'

Weise settled back into his ice-cream.

'The doctor told me I should eat only one dish at lunchtime, so I have what I like best. You did well in Vienna. My bosses are pleased.'

'The Warriors of Christ? You want me to believe Herz is broking on their behalf?'

'I don't give a shit what you believe. What is important is that everybody else believes that the Warriors of Christ killed Schumacher. And the next guy we've got lined up for you, too.'

'The Warriors of Christ are rubbish. They tried to bomb a British financier a year ago, he came from the Ukraine, was born there, and the bomb went off while they were trying to fix it. Killed two of them.'

The waitress put a half-litre of beer on the table, a wrapped knife and fork, a pot of mustard.

'I asked for a small beer.'

'In Munich that is a small beer. A large coffee with cream and schnapps, please. Yeah, that was the last the real Warriors of Christ did. And that's why you're going to use a similar bomb this time.'

'You want me to blow myself up?'

'Certainly not. We want you alive for the third which will be the really big one. I take it you can handle a bomb?'

'Certainly. But not the way the Warriors of Christ did.'

Weise laughed. The waitress put a plate in front of Cranmer – large white sausage, cabbage, potato purée. He unwrapped his knife and fork, stuck the fork into the sausage, watched liquid ooze clear of the prongs. He cut it, dabbed mustard, ate it. Not as bad as it looked. Drank some beer. That was good, too. He wiped his mouth on the paper serviette, went on.

'I'm making a serious point. If the police are to believe a bunch of Ukrainian nationalist nutters are behind these killings they've got to look like the work of really stupid amateurs who got lucky. Well. It's a challenge. Do a pro-job and make it look lucky.'

He ate some more. Then: 'So. Tell me about the third. The big one. Another Ukrainian? I suppose so. I can't help wondering what it is you have against Ukrainians.'

By now Weise was clearing out the bottom of his ice-cream dish. The spoon clanged against the glass, and he froze. Then he stabbed the air in front of Cranmer's face with the spoon.

'Don't ever ask a question of that sort again. Not ever.'

Cranmer ate on in silence, annoyed with himself. He had, and he knew it, committed a solecism, broken a rule – of etiquette merely, but it lifted a corner on him, revealed his unproved status as an apprentice still learning his trade.

12

Three days later Cranmer alighted from the Munich–Berlin express at Leipzig at ten minutes past two in the afternoon, having had his ear bent by a nun travelling from Nuremburg to

Berlin (East) to see relatives she visited for a week each year – nephews and nieces. Her main gist throughout was how the journey now took an hour and a half less because there were no more border controls between the Volksdeutsch. Her second subject was a jeremiad against the fallen DDR government. They had left a heritage of squalor, atheism, and pollution (which included the right of her sister to murder her unborn children) that had been left for Chancellor Köhl to clear up. During the last half hour she wove the two together and added a third – a ray of hope. At least one thing was sure: the Turks would have to go home now, whether they liked it or not. With all the labour pouring in from the east there was no longer any need or room for them.

Leipzig Hauptbahnhof is the largest railway station in Europe, but Weise's instructions had been precise, and Cranmer soon found the lunch counter on the left-hand side. It was little more than a large alcove with elbow high shelves at the sides and circular ones round the pillars that supported the roof, no tables or chairs, no stools even. He put the new, smart, black suitcase he was carrying beneath one of them, together with the document case Weise had given him on the Sacré Coeur belvedere. He bought another white sausage on a paper plate and a beer, and waited.

From the nearby entrance to the men's lavatories Weise watched him for a moment and approved. Cranmer was now wearing a conventional dark grey suit with a pinstripe, and had had his hair cut. His black shoes shone. Weise checked his own zip – he was still wearing his usual clothes – emerged on to the concourse and walked across to the lunch counter. He was carrying a document case identical to Cranmer's and he placed it carefully on the floor beside it. He also bought a sausage and beer.

Presently Cranmer drank a little beer, but clearly his heart wasn't in it.

He murmured, very quietly.

'Be my guest.'

76

He picked up the document case Weise had put down, and his own suitcase too, walked smartly away heading for the exit marked Platz der Republik.

Weise shrugged, and started on his own sausage. Presently a cleaner in a white overall came to clear the shelf. He was dark and unshaven, and looked Turkish: a sign that in spite of everything the nun had said the west's immigrant workers were moving east just as the east's workers hungry for marks were moving west. Weise told him to piss off, and ate and drank Cranmer's sausage and beer when he had finished his own.

Cranmer checked into the Astoria Hotel on the other side of the big square, where a single room, with bath, was waiting for him on the fifth floor. He unpacked the suitcase – just ordinary clothes, but many of them new and still in shop-wrappings. When he had finished he turned to a table under the window and opened the document case. The bottom half was lined with Swiss francs again, exactly as before, but there were twice as many: second instalment on the first job, first instalment on the second. Above them was a large manilla envelope. He shook it over the writing table set in the window embrasure, and a large glossily laminated card wallet dropped out. Its two compartments were filled with assorted documents, but all in the same style as the outer wallet: glossy white backgrounds, smart printing in a strong blue ink. He pulled a high-backed chair from its place in front of the dressing table, and set about going through them, slowly, carefully, methodically.

The repeated heading on the material, in English, French, Spanish – Interpol's official languages – with German added, announced again and again: *Leipzig 1991: International Conference Contra-Terrorism.* Clearly it was the pack that delegates received on arrival. But there were also photographs of two men taken without their knowledge and enlarged. One was of a Russian, a Kruschev look-alike, with two heavy minders almost blocking off the view of his face. The other was of a British plain clothes policeman leaving Scotland Yard and doing up his jacket as he

77

came down the steps round the familiar circling triangular aluminium sign. Finally there was a plastic strip with punch-holes labelled 'Hotel Merkur: third floor passkey', and an ID pin-on tag. The name: Superintendant Ken Wright, London Metropolitan Police Force. The photo space was blank.

In the lid were two one kilo bags of Semtex, a small Japanese alarm clock, batteries, and a miniature explosion initiator, also Japanese.

Cranmer turned them over in his hands, sighed.

'What sort of shit is this?'

He answered himself.

'The sort of shit the Warriors of Christ use.'

At eight o'clock the next morning he crossed the open spaces in front of the Hotel Merkur, passed through the main doors. At that moment Commander Ken Wright, a youthful fifty-five with three small children from his second marriage, was sitting up in the bath, with his back to the open bathroom door, shaving himself. He was enoying a luxury that was rare – a hot bath undisturbed by small persons coming in for a crap or a wee or to clean their teeth. Very aware of where he was, and he had not been this far east before, he sang: *Lili Marlene* in the English version. Underneath the lamplight, Somewhere over . . .

Suddenly he stopped, froze. In the small shaving mirror he had placed on the edge of the bath, he had caught a movement behind him. He reacted quickly, striving to stand and turn at the same time to face his assailant. He deflected the first blow, a karate chop aimed at his neck, but it knocked him off balance and he could do little to protect himself from the vicious kick that now caught him in the pit of his stomach. A double-fisted blow swung up at his chin sent him crashing back into the bath. The back of his head hit the taps, and his eyes glazed.

Cranmer looked down at him from the other end of the bath, thought about it. Then he stooped, got a firm grip on Wright's ankles, pulled. Wright's head slipped under the surface of the bath-water.

Cranmer went into the bedroom. On a side-table there was a litter of papers including the same pack relating to the international conference of anti-terrorist police officers. Amongst them he found Wright's ID badge with a photo. Cranmer held it in one hand and from a pocket took the one he had received in the Astoria Hotel. This now had a photo of himself on it. He compared them closely for a moment.

'Near enough, it'll do. Well done, Willi.'

He pinned the second badge to his lapel, looked round the room, back into the bathroom. No change apart from a yellow cloud of urine above the man's hairy stomach. He closed the bathroom door, used the screw-driver attachment on a Swiss Army knife to slip the bolt, locking the door on the inside but from the outside. He picked up a 'DO NOT DISTURB' sign, hung it on the outside knob of the outer door. He then let himself out into the corridor, closed the door, checked it, too, was properly locked. He withdrew the passkey, put it in his pocket. Finally he stripped off the surgical gloves he had been wearing and pocketed them. He used his elbow to touch the button in the lift.

A hundred or so policemen of several nationalities slowly gathered in the reception area of the Social Sciences Faculty of Leipzig University. Slowly because in an outer foyer each was checked: the name and description on the identity tag against a list, the face on the photo against the face that wore it. Apart from those dressed in ethnic costume they were all very much of a type – large, suited, with ties and polished shoes and all carried black document cases. A notice board on an easel in the middle of the area displayed a programme.

'TERRORISM: THE WAR WE WILL WIN' 9 AM: Plenary Session: Official opening of the Conference – the Mayor of Leipzig, Lecture Theatre I. 9.30 AM – 10.30 AM: Group A, The Russian Experience Part I: Colonel Kalnitzky of the Ukrainian anti-Terrorist Squad, Lecture Theatre II . . .'

Cranmer, carrying the document case and wearing the Ken

79

Wright photo-badge with his own photo not Wright's, moved through the crowd. He stood for a moment in front of the notice-board. No change – the information matched that in the brochure. From it he already knew that Lecture Hall II was down the second corridor to the right. He moved off in that direction.

Meanwhile the entrance area continued to fill. Almost the last to arrive before the Mayor of Leipzig were the Russian delegation led by Colonel Kalnitzky – no doubt he was well aware that he was a Kruschev look-alike and deliberately chose to wear a soft leather trilby to point up the likeness. He paused in front of the notice-board, turned, clasped his fists above his head in a handshake for all. Then he turned to his minders.

'OK. You're off duty for . . .' He looked at his watch, 'Four hours. Meet me here in the foyer at one.'

He beamed at all the policemen around him and spread his arms.

'Here at least I know I am among friends . . .'

Three-quarters of an hour later he was on the podium in Lecture Hall II. His notes were in front of him, occasionally he glanced down at them through heavy bi-focals. His delivery was slow, giving the simultaneous interpreters in their booths at the back of the hall a reasonable chance.

'. . . with perestroika, and the slow but steady institutionalis-ation of Ukrainian nationalism, the situation has radically altered, groups like the Warriors of Christ no longer have the same sort of foundation to build on. One result of this has been that their choice of targets has ceased to be predictable or even rational – I am thinking of poor Otto Schumacher – and this has made our task more difficult. On the other hand, no one can believe that the silly bastards will be around for much longer.'

He glanced at the clock facing him on the far wall of the theatre. 9.45. In Lecture Hall III, next door, the podium exploded – killing a cleaner.

*

The newspaper headlines played variations on the same theme: 'WARRIORS OF CHRIST CLAIM BLUNDER – KALNITZKY ESCAPES.'

13

A small boy, perhaps eight years old, who had lost his parents and did not seem to mind, stood in front of the gorilla cage and pulled slow faces in imitation of its occupant. Presently he moved on to the yellow baboons, *Papio cynocephalus*, which also brought into view a corner of the café terrace where two men sat at a table and talked. The small boy found the monkeyness of the men as amusing as the humanness of the monkeys, particularly that of the fat man with the ice-cream. The small boy wanted an ice-cream, and for the first time it occurred to him to wonder where his mama was. The other man was boring – just a grey suit really, nothing more. A third man approached the table, short, compact, neat, tough. The fat man stood up to welcome him.

'Herr Herz, Herr Biedermann.'

Cranmer did not stand and Herz did not shake hands. He sat opposite Cranmer, peeled off thin yellow leather gloves and unbuttoned a light top coat. Although it was sunny and July a cold breeze blew off the Zürichsee.

The waiter appeared at his elbow. Would the new arrival have ice-cream? No, the silly man ordered coffee, which, the small boy knew, was yukky. The new arrival looked round.

'This is a fool place to meet. It could rain. You can never tell in Zürich. If a second meeting becomes necessary we can have it in the AlterLog Office, right?'

'No.' Biedermann was firm.

Weise attempted to be conciliatory.

81

'Herr Herz is anxious to create an atmosphere, even a bond of mutual trust. Isn't that so Heinrich?'

'Of course.'

His reply had no warmth and an uneasy silence fell over the table. The small boy came closer. When at last they spoke again he imitated their expressions, just as he had the gorilla's and the baboons'.

'This is the big one,' Weise said and spooned up ice-cream. It did not look particularly big to the small boy – he'd had bigger ones. On his birthday. 'You'll like this one. The money's . . . serious. Real money.'

'Yes?' Cranmer concealed any excitement he might have felt, waited.

The waiter brought Herz's coffee. He stirred in sweeteners dropped from a small plastic dispenser he took from his pocket, drank, put down the cup, caught and held Cranmer's cold grey eyes.

'Three hundred thousand Swiss francs,' he murmured. 'Of course for that sort of money you will realise that we are asking for something . . . rather special.'

Weise leaned in over his empty dish.

'Five people,' he said. 'Five designated people. They will all be at the same place at the same time. But it must look as if the attack is aimed at only one of them. That only one of them is the intended target.'

'There will be security?'

'Oh yes,' Herz answered. 'I think so.'

'Thanks to your previous efforts, I think we can safely say there will be security,' Weise sounded unctuous, flattering. 'There are other parameters too.'

But Cranmer was no longer listening. He was staring at the small boy and his eyes looked like year-old ice. The small boy slowly broke up, turned and ran . . . into the arms of his distraught mama.

*

82

For their second meeting Cranmer chose the pleasure steamer on the Zürichsee. They sat on the upper open deck beneath an awning on polished teak slatted seats, by the brass-mounted rail. It was all very clean and bright – shipshape. The Swiss flag flapped behind them, and stirred in Cranmer's British mind old jokes about the Swiss navy. There were water-skiers and rainbow sail boards in the foreground, wooded hills and a saw blade of snow in the distance. Idyllic.

'And it has to look as if it's a Warriors of Christ job?'

'That is vital,' Herz was adamant. 'We can't shift on that.'

'You realise how difficult that makes things.'

Weise wheedled again in his fluty voice: 'The main target fits the Warriors of Christ pattern.'

Cranmer did not think this very helpful.

'The point is the Warriors of Christ are bunglers. They use unsophisticated equipment,' he grimaced with distaste. 'A Makarov pistol, a time-bomb fired by an electric charge connected to an alarm clock. What you're asking for now needs something better than all that. A lot better. Five targets in one go can't be left to a timing device. It has to be remote control.'

Herz gave way a little.

'If you know exactly what you need, we can get it. Never mind right now if it breaks the pattern.'

Weise offered assurance. 'We'll think of a way round that.'

'All right. Now. A remote control device requires the person who initiates the explosion to be in visual or at any rate aural contact. That creates a security problem. Furthermore the charge will almost certainly have to be brought through a cordon and placed where it will kill all five people at once. You really are asking a lot. I shall need helpers. Two . . .'

He was aware of their consternation. They were not happy. He went on.

'I can recruit them. I know the right stuff.'

Herz sneezed, turned his coat collar up against the breeze coming in off the lake.

'I can't authorise that without checking back to my . . . to the people who are paying.'

The very lack of expression on Cranmer's face exposed his intense curiosity as to who those 'people' might be.

The boat had turned, was heading for a landing stage. Herz sneezed again.

'We'll have to have another meeting,' he declared. 'But next time we meet indoors, right?'

Cranmer did not realise the place was gay. At five o'clock on a bright afternoon when he checked it out the Edelweiss Café-Bar had been almost empty. Two smartly-dressed and heavily made-up ladies sharing an English tea in silence had been the only customers – only later did it occur to him that they might have been transvestites. He had not stopped long, just long enough to check out that the public pay-phone was in a small dark booth outside the men's downstairs toilet. After that he had some shopping to do – and since Zürich is the sort of place where being in the know can help you to make or save very large sums of money, there had been no problem about finding what he wanted.

At nine o'clock at night the Edelweiss showed itself in its true colours – mainly pink. The waiters and barman wore make-up and while there were three or four people in women's clothes now they were very clearly in drag. It was busy too: most of the clientele drinking outlandish cocktails which involved the barman in routines of acrobatic juggling with bottles and shakers, deployment of cute paper parasols and silver swizzle sticks.

Cranmer checked the tiny apparatus he had bought was in place and functioning, then went into the toilet. Two men, one old, one young, were at the urinals, both tried to look at his prick as he unbuttoned, seemed disgruntled when he shielded it from view. He was more put out though when he returned to the bar. Herz and Weise were both already there, six minutes ahead of the appointment – they were watching the street door

84

and so there was no hope of concealing from them the fact that though they were early he had been even earlier.

Nevertheless he got close enough to hear what they were saying before they saw him.

'Why the fuck did he choose a place like this? He's not queer is he?'

Weise wriggled his huge behind in the soft leatherette of the low chair he was sitting in.

'Not as far as I now.' His voice squeaked with petulance.

A waiter, with a single gold cross twinkling below one ear, hovered with a menu. Weise reached for it eagerly – perhaps thinking it was the sort that all but the most pretentious restaurants carry separate from their own to advertise proprietory ice-creams. This one, however, listed and illustrated the complicated cocktails with joky copy telling you what they'd do to you.

'Can't I have a beer?' More plaintive now than petulant.

Cranmer stepped in using the waiter's intervention as a diversion which he hoped would distract them from realising he had been watching them, was there first.

'These are my guests. Three beers.'

The waiter began a roll-call of all the beers they had – most of them clearly the sort that come in bottles with more silver foil on them than you get on a cheap champagne. Cranmer cut him off.

'Three from the tap please. That's all.'

When it was all settled Herz leaned over the centre of the low round glass table they were sitting at.

'Right. In a nutshell. We have two areas of difficulty. One. We take your point that for this to work you need highly sophisticated equipment. And you shall get it. So long as the items on the shopping list you have given us . . .' He took a slip of paper from his breast pocket and spread it on the table beneath his nose, 'are as available as you say they are. But, I have to reiterate. At the end of the day it must still look like the work of the Warriors of Christ.'

85

He drank beer, wiped his mouth. When he began to speak again it was in far more measured tones, and quiet enough to force Cranmer to lean forward to hear him.

'Two. The helpers you say you need. Clearly two extra men imply a quantum leap in risk. I don't think I can go forward with this without solid assurance that it will be quite impossible for either of these two men to present any sort of threat at all to us . . . after the event.'

He sat back, fixed Cranmer with a look whose lack of expression was meant to speak volumes. But it was Weise who spelled it out.

'They have to be snuffed.'

Cranmer appeared to give this some thought. He sipped his drink, looked up and around. The waiter, back at the bar to collect drinks for other customers, thought he was being eyed, made a *moue* with his lips and grinned. Then he shuddered, turned to his companion.

'Someone walked on my grave.'

Cranmer leaned forward, twisted the slip of paper, and with a Parker ball-point stabbed one item on the list.

'Get me two of these. Not just one. That will take care of it. It will take care of both of your worries. One and two.'

They thought about it, about the possible reasons for wanting two of the infra-red signalling devices that could arm the mercury trembler detonator.

'Yes. I think I see what you're getting at. All right.' Herz folded up the paper, slipped it back in his breast pocket. 'We can move on from here. Meet Willi in Barcelona, on the . . .'

But Cranmer was shaking his head. He tapped the glass table with his Parker, leaned back, looked at both of them.

'No. You are asking me to . . . to waste two valuable assets. That costs.'

Weise knew it was his line.

'Three hundred k Swiss, and you want more? Come on!'

He glanced at Herz, seeking approval, but Herz overrode him.

'How much?'

'Double.'

Silence fell over the table. They realised he meant it. Herz sneezed.

'Double. I have to . . . I have to make a phone call.' He stood slowly, buttoning his jacket, looked around, caught the waiter.

'Is there a pay-phone?'

'Downstairs, duckie. Outside the toilet.'

Herz threaded his way through the tables. Weise and Cranmer looked at each other and Weise looked away, pulled out a nailfile and began to poke his nails.

An hour later Cranmer was back in the privacy of his hotel room. He sat on the bed, and pulled out what looked like the smallest and neatest of the Sony Micro-Cassette recorders. A thin black wire led from the microphone input to a thin oblong plate, a half centimetre by a quarter, metallic on one side, the other padded plastic. There was a blob of blu-tak on it. He disconnected this, pressed rewind, let the squeaky gabble run until it stopped, adjusted the volume, pressed play.

There was the distorted noise of telephone numbers clicking, and a connection being made. A female voice spoke.

'Herr Winckelmann's residence. Who's calling?'

Then Herz: 'Heinrich Herz. Could you put me through to Herr Winckelmann please?'

Pause, then new electronic gates opened. Cranmer thought: Mr Big he may be – certainly he's serious. He has a manned private switchboard well after working hours in his own home. The voice that came was heavy, deep, a brandy and cigar voice with serrated steel in it.

'Yes, Heinrich. What is it?'

'He wants double.'

'But he'll do it?'

'For double, yes.'

'And he'll do it properly?'

'Yes.'

'Tell him OK. Haggle a bit. Make him think it hurts.'

The click of the replaced receiver was final. Cranmer sat for a moment, grimaced with irritation. He had not liked the tone of the exchange – there was a hint of conspiracy in it, of shared knowledge, decisions already taken, no need to discuss them again. But nothing certain, a matter of nuances merely. Still, the main point had been achieved. He rewound to the beginning, listened to the clicks again.

He murmured to himself: '73 31 35, six digits only, local number.'

The following morning, at eleven o'clock, he rang the same number.

'Herr Winckelmann's residence. I am afraid Herr Winckelmann is no longer in.'

'Ah. Could you tell me where I might be able to reach him?'

'You should try the Prolebentek head office in Zollikerstrasse. The number is . . .'

But Cranmer did not wish to know: for the time being the name of the office was enough.

PART II

14

Carlos Negrín, manager of the Barcelona branch of Prolebentek, stood in the centre of the inner concourse of the Estació de Sants and watched while workmen in blue monos strung a large banner along the space above the ticket offices, banks and so forth that faced the passengers coming up the escalators from the platforms below. The first thing they would see. It was a good banner, he thought – with the pride of an impresario who has commissioned a work of art to fit his own requirements and believes the artist to have contributed nothing but fairly ordinary manual skills.

He turned to Willi Weise.

'What do you think?'

'Very pretty.'

They made a contrasting pair. Willi short, fat, in his leather jacket, denims and Tina Turner T-shirt; Negrín tall, crinkly black hair, pocked pasty face, wearing a conventional business suit, but all a bit flash – a hint of gold at his cuffs, an onyx amongst the hairs on his pinky.

The last knot was tied, the last workman began to descend the ladder. The banner read, in Catalan, Castilian, German and English:

'International Conference of Greens, 2 – 6 September, 1991. Barcelona welcomes the delegates.' Smaller lettering in one corner read 'Sponsored by Prolebentek' with the Prolebentek logo: PLT in sans serif, crunched up so the space between the L and the T made a rectangle. The rectangle was filled with a simple, stylised sunflower. The whole banner was bordered with a Miróesque design in un-Miróesque greens and yellows. Few graphic designers in Barcelona fail to produce work that derives from either Picasso, Dali or Miró. It was a fashon Negrín saw no reason to buck.

Weise ground a cigarette stub into the marble paving, looked at his watch.

'Madame will be here in a moment or so. I don't want her to see me with you. Ciao.'

He trotted away towards the Metro entrance, hands thrust in his leather pockets, head forward, his feet twinkling behind as if trying to keep up with a centre of gravity that had somehow got in front of them.

Negrín turned towards the escalators, looked at his watch too. Presently he saw the white straight hair of a woman coming up from below. She was elderly but fit, with a figure a touch dumpy but honed-down and vital. She had pale visionary eyes, a beak-nose between rosy cheeks of such immaculate softness it was impossible to believe that any impurity such as alcohol or meat had ever sullied her blood. She was wearing jeans and a sweater, had a second woolly slung over one arm, and a large carpet bag on the other.

Although he had never met her she was unmistakable – at least to anyone who had any reason at all for being aware of Green politics in Europe. He stepped forward to see her off the escalator and take her hand.

'Dr Arendt? This is a great honour for Prolebentek, and for me personally.'

She gave him the ironic smile she reserved for anyone foolhardy enough to offer her what she called 'guff', but accepted his hand.

'It's good of you to meet me.' Her voice was brisk. She allowed Negrín to take the carpet bag. It was a lot heavier than he expected.

'Sorry. Books and papers, mainly. Glad to hand it over. Only yourself to blame, young man – you shouldn't have offered.'

She stepped back, looked around: a characteristic gesture –

she was endlessly curious about every new place she visited, indeed about everything under the sun. She read the banner.

'Goodness that's early isn't it? We've still got more than a week.'

Negrín smiled unctuously.

'In Spain we still have a *mañana* complex. We expect other nations to find us unpunctual, so now we do everything too soon.' He steered her towards the outer concourse. 'We have time to check you in at your hotel. Our first meeting with the Guàrdia Urbana is at twelve o'clock . . .'

Ten minutes later, and a kilometre away, in the Plaça de la Universitat Weise watched the man he still knew as Biedermann climb down from a big French bus. He was back in his denims and the suitcase he took from the hold was old, battered, and large. Weise made sure Cranmer had seen him and recognised him from a distance, before crossing the road to welcome him. He was doing his best to alleviate any feeling he might be creating in Cranmer's mind that he was watching him. He crossed the six-lane Gran Via, raised a podgy palm at ten metres distance, and received a similar signal from Cranmer in return. It was an oddly wary gesture, contiguous with the theory that handshaking arose out of the need to demonstrate that one was not carrying a weapon. In fact they did not shake hands, nor did Weise offer to take Cranmer's suitcase. He indicated a small red Panda parked on the other side. The key he used when they got there was on an Avis ring.

Dr Julia Arendt, Member of the European Parliament, had little time for policemen. In sixty years of political activity – she was not quite six when she attended her first demonstration against the pro-Nazi party in her native Brabant – she had been bludgeoned several times, arrested on four occasions, and beaten while under arrest twice. Nevertheless Captain Martín of Barcelona's Guàrdia Urbana looked like becoming the second policeman in her life to prove to be the exception to the rule.

93

Being of an irremediably optimistic turn of mind she always trusted first impressions until they were proved wrong. Being a realist too she was often persuaded to change her mind about appearances – never about fundamentals. Her first impressions of the Guàrdia Urbana Head Quarters at Rambles 43 were almost entirely good. Occupying what had been built as the School of Philosophy in 1593, refurbished in 1786, and allowed to decay through the nineteenth century it was restored and converted to become the headquarters of the recently formed Guàrdia Urbana. It has a narrow frontage on the Rambla faced with hard stone, grey but touched with pink. This modern façade is brutal and hard-edged but leads immediately into a square arcaded courtyard of human, Renaissance proportions. Wide stone staircases lead up to the main offices on the first floor where everything is clean, bright, tolerably comfortable, and pleasant. The guàrdias who were visible looked clean and smart too, and not at all menacing in open necked blue shirts with rolled up sleeves. One of them showed her and Negrín into Martín's office.

This had modern metal furniture, but new and pleasantly coloured. Cheerful posters (not entirely free of the Picasso-Dali-Miró syndrome) were mostly propaganda for the Guàrdia Urbana, included one advertising their policing role in the coming Olympic Games, and another for *The Greens in Barcelona – A Conference on Industrial Waste* with the Prolebentek logo.

Xavier Martín was about forty, good-looking, tough, uniformed like the others but with barred shoulder flashes. His welcome was cordial, but without Negrín's flummery. Arendt quite took to him. She was the sort of woman who, even on the point of becoming elderly, sees no reason for denying herself pleasure at the sight of a strong, well set-up, young man (young to her) or enjoyment of the manliness of his handshake.

'I never expected to feel welcome in a Guardia Cuartel,' she said, accepting the upholstered tubular chair he offered.

He frowned for a moment, then smiled.

'I hope, Dr Arendt, that you are not confusing us with the Guardia Civil.'

'Oh dear. I think I may be. Of course the uniform has changed, but then so many appearances have changed in Spain.'

He was at pains to explain to her that the Guardia Civil no longer exist in Catalunya, that the Guàrdia Urbana were a newly formed Catalan force taking the place of the old municipal police. Their duties, he said, were to control traffic, look after tourists, attend accidents. Their main anti-criminal function was preventative – particularly they patrolled the 'heavy' areas of Barcelona trying to limit drug dealing, and forestalling violence. They also organised and laid on security at the public, street level where it was necessary – which was why she was there.

'As I understand it,' he concluded, 'Prolebentek in conjuction with the Town Hall has arranged a comprehensive list of events for your delegates to attend. What I propose now is that we should take a tour round the town, visit the sites involved, and I'll describe to you the sort of security we think might be necessary.'

She was old enough, experienced enough in the ways of men in authority, even nice ones, to know that this was not the moment to start arguing. Let's see, she said to herself, the extent of the problem before wading in.

A Renault 21 with Guàrdia Urbana markings, driven by another pleasant young man in shirt sleeves, took the three of them first to the Olympic City on the south-west slopes of Montjuic. Apart from the main stadium which dated back to the 1929 World's Fair, most of it, at the beginning of the last week in August 1991, looked like a vast and hopeless if busy building site. Arendt noted that most of the workers were Arab or Afro, but did not comment. Fighting for the rights of immigrant 'guest' workers was one of the many causes she espoused and she made a note to herself that she would check out their terms of employment before she left Barcelona. It was by no means only as a Green that she had a seat in Strasbourg:

she may have won it as a Green, but she was basically a fully paid-up leftie of the old school, unreconstituted by Stalin, or, for that matter, by Gorbachev either.

The Estadi Olímpic itself was impressive. As they walked out into the middle Negrín explained how there would be a finger buffet right there in the centre of the huge green oval and this would be Prolebentek's very own contribution to the conference.

'Hopefully there will be someone from Head Office in Zürich, perhaps Herr Winckelmann himself, to welcome your chairperson or president – '

At last her impatience began to show.

'We don't have a chairman or a president. Look. I cannot go back to the organising committee and recommend these arrangements. We're coming to Barcelona on serious business, not on a junket. We're here for five days and what have we got? Two receptions, a tour of the city, a ride in a cable car, a finger buffet in this stadium. Not to mention an expensive meal in a fish restaurant . . .'

'But Prolebentek picks up the tab, you know that.'

'That's not the point I'm trying to make. We're planning eight intensive sessions. We aim to get out an agreed communiqué. And we do not want to be presented to the world as sixty weirdos on a massive freebie . . .'

But she stopped there. This still wasn't the time or place.

High up on the terraces above them, so far away that they were entirely insignificant, Cranmer looked at Weise. He shook his head. Weise shrugged, but agreed.

The Renault 21 dropped them at the foot of the funicular which took them to the top of Montjuic. There they walked the short distance through the woods and parks (which Arendt enjoyed) to the cable car station. It was a clear hot summer day, and to most people the views would have been magnificent: mountains in the distance, the sweep of the coast, and one of the great cities of the world spread out below in such a way that all the different quarters could be clearly picked out and identified. But as well as all this Arendt saw the fog of car emissions, white dust above the many construction sites, and a yet more pernicious yellowish haze over the industrial areas up the coast on both sides with plumes of vapour above cooling towers.

On the way down in the cable car Martín pointed out the main features with obvious pride and pleasure. First to their right and almost below them a huge building site where the old nineteenth-century warehouses had been pulled down. It spread right back into Montjuic itself whose cliffs showed the scarring of fresh blasting: this was to be the Olympic Village and the Olympic Port. Once a medieval harbour, a nineteenth- and twentieth-century port and dock, it was about to become a huge residential and pleasure complex for the twenty-first century. The two thousand housing units that would be left when the fifteen thousand athletes had gone were already selling for £200,000 each ... All this was said with great pride. Arendt drily remarked that she had already seen posters and graffiti – both done with style – demanding that the old port should be returned to the people.

They passed through the cable car station at the top of a mini-Eiffel tower on the central mole of the old port, a wide finger jutting out into the old harbour, and Martín switched tack, sensing that she did not altogether approve of what was going on beneath them. This time he pointed left to the Columbus monument, the replica of the Santa María, and the tall brick chimneys which had been left to mark where the great textile factories once were, the factories that made Barcelona, in the first two decades of the twentieth century, Europe's second richest and largest city. And in the distance to the north the fairy-tale pinnacles of Gaudì's Sagrada Familia. He even recounted a story against his police force: how on Innocents' Day (Spain's April Fool's Day) a newspaper had reported that terrorists had blown up the Columbus Monument during the night.

'Everyone who had a car drove there to see it. The whole

town became one huge awful traffic jam. We were powerless . . .
stood no chance at all.'

But her attention was now on the coast beyond and in front
of them: they could see forty kilometres of it, stretching up
towards France. It was dominated by two features: first an
enormous building site, the second half of the Olympic development, an amazing complex of towers and ziggurats, walkways,
malls and shopping centres, stretching for five kilometres east
and north with new marinas sheltered by artificial coves built
on D-Day lines and on as big a scale – that was what it would
be, in less than a year.

Dr Arendt privately doubted. In spite of the presence of four
or five impressive towers glittering in the sun, and hundreds of
giant cranes, it still looked a mess. She wondered again about
the extent to which the labour that had made it, apart from the
upper echelons of architects, planners and designers, would
benefit from it in the long run. In the short run, yes – work
when work was short elsewhere, and tolerably large pay-packets
too, the EC saw to that. But, like the Irish Navvies of Britain in
the 1830s, also immigrant labour, there would be no lasting joy
from it for the Andalusians, Moroccans, and Africans from the
far side of the Sahara who actually built it.

Beyond this enormous building site that was to become the
Parc de Mar, the coast faded into purple distances filled with
refineries and chemical works with sad little beach resorts sand-
wiched between. These were what had re-created Barcelona's
wealth once textiles ceased to be very, very big money.

As they approached the second tower, Negrín grasped her
elbow – she hated him for doing so – and directed her attention
to the nearest beaches, sand on the other side of the mole.

'Barceloneta,' he exclaimed. 'And some of the most famous
fish restaurants in the world. That's where we take you for
lunch on Monday.'

'Oh no. I don't think so. I know I speak for all of us. We
would prefer something much simpler.'

'Ah, but then you would miss a very big opportunity. The

98

water down there is poisonous. No one can swim off what should be one of the most glamorous beaches in Europe. We'll get the cameras on you, not on me, let you say your bit about it.'

The Renault 21 was waiting for them at the foot of the tower beneath the cable car station in Barceloneta. As they approached, the driver, outside and leaning against it and chatting to a patrol – a male officer and a female – chucked his cigarette, saluted.

'Captain, the Policia Nacional have been on the RT for you.'

'What do they want?'

'Deputy Chief Estrada wants you to call in on the way back. He said it's connected with the Green Convention.'

'I can't see what business it is of his.' Martín opened the passenger door for Arendt. 'But all right. You'd better take us to Via Laietana.'

Less than half a kilometre away Weise and Cranmer followed a waiter to a corner table on the terrace in front of the Casa Pez. Terrace is perhaps too grand a word: it was an area covered with boards, fenced off from its neighbours and filled with plastic tables. Each had a blue and white San Miguel parasol. In front of them sand sloped down to the Mediterranean. The sand was filled with sunbathers, mostly in their thirties and many even older. They wore very little, the women almost all topless, some down to the skimpiest of bottoms known as dental floss, the men in brief briefs, that were often shiny, satiny. Most were tanned to a deep brown, and all took it in turns to smooth handfuls of oil or cream over each others' well-developed musculature. Some stood or knelt, flexing muscles that were robust. None swam, a point Cranmer made as they sat.

'Why not?'

'Because the water is poisonous. You get rashes, ulcers, sores if you swim in it.' Weise took the menu, handed it to Bieder-mann. 'I'll just have an ice-cream. But you should try the zarzuela, fried bits of fish in a spicy sauce.'

99

15

The Policia Nacional Head Quarters at the top of the Via Laietana was much more what Arendt expected from a police station. For a start Laietana has none of the prettiness or glamour of the Rambla – it's a busy city street with tall buildings, either modern or built at the turn of the century. And in spite of the changes, liberalisation, quite extensive Catalan autonomy and so on, the Policia Nacional still maintains some of the ethos of an occupying garrison set in hostile territory. Their predecessors were the Policia Armada, Los Grises, the grey ones, as feared in the cities as the Guardia Civil had been in the countryside. While the Guàrdia Urbana answers to the Mayor, the Policia Nacional are commanded by a general in Madrid and answer to the Minister of Justice. Though the uniform has been changed, and their powers limited, many of the personnel remain – in the senior ranks men who worked for Franco. Not many at that level are Catalan.

Outside, the building has a stone-faced, nineteenth-century baroque grandeur, though there is a permanent queue outside of the poor, the frightened, the angry: mostly women trying to see husbands, boy-friends, sons arrested the night before, and African or Moroccan 'guest' workers who have suddenly been told that papers they paid large sums for are no longer in order.

As they passed this chain of sullen unhappiness and climbed wide but shabby stairs to the second floor Martín explained how the role of the Policia Nacional differs from that of the Guàrdia Urbana.

'Here their first pre-occupation is major organised crime. We deal with the petty stuff, with what happens on the streets, they are meant to go for the Mr Bigs. They never get them.'

'It's the same everywhere.'

'Maybe. But there are overlaps, grey areas where we often have problems. Drugs mainly. Especially when they use under-cover agents without telling us. It's the same with security. We put the men on the streets, the human shield, but they have the marksmen on the roof tops. And it's them of course who are actually meant to identify and arrest terrorists. Here we are.'

They were outside a door with glazed frosted glass. Stencilled letters in a script fashionable half a century ago spelled out: Brigada Justicial – Teniente-Jefe Juan Estrada.

Both Estrada and his office reinforced Arendt's preconcep-tions. It was a cluttered, dirty, untidy room and it smelled of cheap brandy and stale tobacco. Set in the embrasure of a tall but unwashed bay window there was a large but scuffed and undistinguished desk with a PC, telephone, intercom, and a litter of papers. A second frosted glass door flanked with grey-green filing cabinets appeared to lead to a toilet and wash-basin. The few personal touches were connected with the Lidia: a calendar with a charging bull picture, a framed and signed black and white photograph of Paco Camino performing a stylish *derechazo*, a pen holder made from a bull's foot.

Estrada was tough, fat, corrupt. He joined the Policia Armada under Franco in 1960 and since then he had eaten too much, drunk too much, seen too many evil things, done too many evil things. He turned from the window as they came in, sketched a peremptory acknowledgement of Martín's introductions, prod-ded printouts on the desk in front of him with a fat but hard nicotine-stained index finger. A Ducados was clamped between it and its neighbour, and his voice was a Ducados voice, rattling out of a deep but emphysemic chest.

'Martín, you've got a problem. Mikhail Sasonov. Coming to your conference. He's Ukrainian. The KGB have wired us via Interpol that he's a likely hit for the Warriors of Christ. He'll have two KGB minders protecting his arse, but so did Kalnitzky.'

Arendt, whose Spanish was good, it was the reason why she

had been chosen as the conference committee member to liaise with the Barcelona authorities, jumped in.

'Before we go any further – may I make one thing clear? Greens do not appear in the media, on TV or anywhere else, surrounded by minders – '

'Listen lady. With the Olympics only months away, no newsworthy visitor to this city gets mugged even, let alone blown-up. If this guy is under threat, then he gets full protection twenty-four hours a day, and he goes nowhere where Martín can't provide it.'

Martín, for all the antagonism he felt for Estrada, acknowledged he was right.

'All right, all right. First. We can cut the more obviously risky venues – the cable car ride across the old harbour, maybe the funicular to Montjuic. At any rate for this Sasonov.'

'Well, thank goodness for that.' Arendt batted Estrada's cigarette smoke away from her face. 'I've been trying to find an opportunity all morning to say this. Cut them for all of us. There was far too much rubbish in the programme anyway.'

Martín continued.

'Second, in the indoor meeting places, both where your conference is convening and at the municipal receptions, we can keep the cordon more or less invisible, something that has to be crossed between the outside world, and the inner rooms where the meetings or whatever take place. Neither cameras outside or inside the cordon need see it. It's the routine we use when the Royals come. And I think we should not lose sight of the fact that Kalnitzky was nearly killed because he dismissed his minders prematurely. Presumably that won't happen with Sasonov.'

'I'm told they even piss together.'

Arendt felt the deliberate vulgarity was aimed at her, rose above it.

'And what about the Gaudí church, the fish restaurant at Barceloneta, the stadium?' she said. 'I don't see how you can cordon off places like those invisibly. Don't get me wrong. They don't frighten me – I just don't want TV pictures taken of us over the heads of an army of armed men.'

'We'll look at each place individually, carefully, analytically. We are, you know, quite experienced in these problems.'

'All right.' Estrada seemed grateful that he wasn't faced with as much opposition as he had expected. He had not relished dealing with a combination of the Guàrdia Urbana whom he took to be fit to help grannies cross roads and little else, and a bunch of loonie lefties. 'But who pays? This sort of policing doesn't come cheap.'

'Prolebentek,' Negrín provided the answer. 'But our support does depend on our getting reasonable publicity, and that does mean public appearances, exposure on the media, and so on. I think we have to leave in the stadium and the Casa Pez.'

Estrada ground out his cigarette.

'OK. It's your problem, not mine. I just wanted to be sure you know what the score is. Fuck up and they'll cancel the Olympics.' He laughed throatily, cleared phlegm. 'We should be so lucky.'

16

Weise and Cranmer came away from the Casa Pez an hour or so later and turned up a back street. The buildings were twenty or thirty years old, built as cheap state-assisted housing for dockers and fisherman. The fish were dead and the port had closed – moved to a new container port on the far side of the old harbour. If the sea had been cleaned up it would have been a prime site for luxury re-development, but the money remained down the coast where the water was cleaner. They were now rented by a nucleus of the original occupiers, retired or unemployed, and 'guest' workers who felt their papers were legal

103

enough to allow them to live in a place exposed to visits from the immigration branch of the Policia Nacional. There were always some empty.

Weise led Cranmer up a shabby flight of stairs to a landing, where he unlocked a door from which a Sacred Heart had been prised leaving an unvarnished patch.

'Here we are then.'

Cranmer pushed past him, swiftly explored the whole apartment. It had one reception room, one bedroom, a kitchen and a bathroom. The few pieces of furniture – a kitchen table, six rush-bottomed upright chairs, an iron bed with a thin mattress – were cheap and tawdry. There was a girlie calendar, 1988, in the reception room, and centre-folds from a magazine on the bathroom wall. The women on them had been photographed in postures that made the bunnies of *Playboy* seem like something out of Beatrix Potter. These and the missing Sacred Heart, and the general air of wretchedness suggested a squat occupied by immigrant Moroccan males, followed by repossession.

Cranmer ended up at the one large window in the reception room, parted the slats of a blind with two fingers, looked out. At the end of the drab modern street he could just see a glimpse of the Barceloneta beach and the sea. He turned back into the kitchen where Weise leant against the sink.

'All right?'

'Yes, Willi. It's OK. Bit close if we do fix on the Casa Pez, but . . .' he shrugged.

'Convenient though.'

Weise now stepped to one side, opened the cupboard door beneath the sink, heaved out a large cardboard box, clearly it was very heavy, and panting slightly, dumped it on the kitchen table.

'Everything you asked for.'

Smaller boxes wrapped in oiled brown paper, sealed with printed paper slips filled the top. Cranmer took them out one by one, examined them carefully, read the Cyrillic script. He was not familiar with the language but he had seen these labels

104

before. He unwrapped the paper and lifted the heavy duty cardboard lid and gently shook out the object inside. The main part was a small brown box made of a hard plastic similar to Bakelite. Two thin wires protruded, and met in a metal tube about four centimetres long with a diameter of one.

He returned to the big box, found a smaller pack which he carefully unwrapped. It contained four cylinders each of which would fit exactly into the tube. He took the Bakelite box and tube into the reception room, and carefully slotted one of the cylinders into the tube, then he returned to the kitchen.

There were two more wrapped packages but this time the wrapping was tissue paper. He tore it off and revealed a simple infra-red signaller – exactly the sort of thing you use as a remote control for your television. He opened it, checked that it was loaded with a simple MN1500 battery. Then he paused.

'I take it the tremblers have got batteries?'

'It looks as if we're about to find out.' Weise had taken himself as far from the living-room as he could get – into a small pantry at the back of the kitchen. Already he had his hands close to his ears. 'There's no chance a bang could set off the rest?'

'None. If it's the grade of Semtex I asked for. You know how all this works?'

'I guess so.'

But Cranmer was enoying himself, went on.

'The explosion initiators have inside them batteries, two MN 1604s wired in relay to give a charge of eighteen volts. Enough for a spark, enough to set off the detonator. The circuit is closed when a drop of mercury slips between two terminals inside. It has about one inch to travel, but at the moment is held in place by a thin piece of plastic.'

He lifted the infra-red remote control.

'If I dab the 'on' button . . .' He did so, and smiled. 'Nothing apparently happens. But inside the small piece of plastic has shifted, and now the sightest movement will cause the mercury to trickle into place and close the circuit.'

105

He stooped, balled up a piece of oily brown paper into a tight ball, threw it hard and accurately.

Flash, a bang, about as loud as a pistol shot or the more vicious sort of firework, smoke.

'Perfect. What sort of range do you reckon this has?' He lifted the signaller.

Weise came out of the pantry.

'Fifty metres for sure. Can work, if there's nothing between, at up to a hundred.'

Cranmer nodded, bent over the cardboard box again, counted the eight one kilo plastic packs of grey Semtex.

'There's this, too.'

Something in Weise's voice said danger. Cranmer turned just as he heard a hard, solid metal click. Weise was slotting together a short-barrel pump-action shot-gun. On the larder shelf there was a box of cartridges. He fed them into the gun.

'Willi, I hope you know what you're doing with that.'

'I know what I'm doing.' He sighted at Cranmer, uttered his high-pitched laugh like a cock crowing. 'It's not that long since I used one of these for Herr Herz. But now he prefers to use me as a cut-out man. The fact that I've done what you're doing is the reason why I'm such a good back-up man for you.'

He unloaded the gun, began to dismantle it again.

'You ran scared for a second, didn't you? Serves you right. Fooling with that detonator you had me shitting myself. OK, Herr Biedermann? Anything else?'

'No. And listen Willi, don't fool with me again.'

'All right, Herr Biedermann. But don't you mess me about either.' He packed the dismantled gun away into its case. 'Biedermann. That's a shit of a name. Isn't there anything else I can call you?'

'Niemand.'

'Niemand.' Weise laughed. 'That's worse still.'

He shifted into English.

'No Man. Not Tom, Dick or Harry?'

Cranmer's voice matched his icy eyes.

'No Willi. Just Biedermann. Or Niemand.'

He repacked the big box, but kept the infra-red remote control he had used. That he put in his pocket. They exchanged knowing grins when he did so.

Next morning, at a quarter past ten, Cranmer went into the Casa Pez by the rear entrance, on the Passeig Maritim. He took a small camera with him, a Ricoh YF-20. The restaurant part, both outside on the beach and on an inner verandah, was closed, but the bar, an indoor area between the kitchen and the verandah, was open. He had a coffee and a sandwich, sitting on a stool, watched the slow preparations for the long lunchtime which would not start until two o'clock. Without bothering to explain himself he took six photographs, covering as much of the area as he could, including one shot into the kitchen. He came out at ten to eleven. Fifty metres away, leaning on the parapet that separates the Passeig Maritim from the sand, he could see Weise waiting for him. He was eating an ice-cream. Cranmer came up to him.

'You're early. How long have you been here?'

'Does it matter? Not long.' Weise shrugged. 'What do you think? Will it do?'

'It matters if I get to think you're spying on me. Yes, it'll do.'

They began to walk along the promenade. The sands were crowded with the same posing sunbathers as the day before. They would be there every day until the sun lost its warmth. Amongst them a very black African moved, attempting to sell personal cassette players, statues of African women with sharp-pointed breasts, woven cotton bed-spreads like the one Inger had on her bed.

'There may be a complication.' Weise binned the ice-cream wrapper, was aware of Cranmer's reaction. He went on: 'The police here have rumbled that Sasonov is a likely Warriors of Christ target. The security will be tighter. They've cancelled the cable car and funicular ride.'

'So that makes it sure that this is the best bet. And so long as the security is routine, I can handle it.' Cranmer stopped, put his hands on the parapet, looked down the coast into the chemical haze that hung above it. 'So. A week to go.'

'Eight days. Take a trip, in the country. Wherever you like. Here, you might as well have this. I don't need it.'

He handed Cranmer the Avis tagged car-key.

'Why? I thought I'd stay. It's a good town. Has possibilities.'

The women on the beach were eyeing him. Or he supposed they were.

'No. It's too hot.' Weise wheedled, but there was steel in it. Cranmer had learned that when Willi wheedled, he meant it. 'You can't swim, the water's poisonous. And already people are noticing you, especially the girls. Have a good time, but have it somewhere else.'

Cranmer gave it a moment's thought.

'OK. But I'll rent my own car.'

He handed back the key.

'Why?'

'You've got a naughty streak, Willi. Don't think I haven't realised that. I don't want to drive off in a car you might have bugged.'

He turned and walked firmly away. Weise grimaced, shrugged. You can't win them all.

Late that afternoon he was back in Zürich, took a taxi from Klöten airport to the Prolebentek building in Zollikerstrasse. A receptionist with long, long legs beneath a fanny-pelmet – she looked like a Barbie doll and about as real – showed him into Herr Winckelmann's office. It was a large room with a deep white carpet, grey walls simulating marble, and plants lit by concealed lighting so the greens and reds of the variegated foliage glowed with a poisonous virulence.

Winckelmann sat behind a desk covered in soft black leather mounted on chrome tubes. He was a large man, built like a tank, his close-shaven head the turret, swivelling above heavy shoulders in response to Willi's arrival. In spite of his size there was something weasely about his face – the way it all seemed to slope down past high cheek bones towards the tip of his nose. Herz was with him, sitting in a soft black leather chair.

Winckelmann barked.

'Well?'

Willi Weise ran his tongue over his top lip, took a breath.

'Nothing,' he fluted. 'Nothing at all. He fended off any questions, evaded surveillance with complete professionalism, even refused my offer of the car. I tell you though – he is professional. He's been very well trained in undercover work, knows his stuff with explosives. It's not easy to acquire the sort of skills he has. I'm pretty sure that somewhere along the line he was legit. Police, special services, something of that sort.'

'All the more reason for finding out who he is.' The gun turret shifted. 'Herz, you realise you might have employed a fucking policeman?'

'Maverick if he is. Whatever else, he killed Schumacher.'

'Nevertheless, I want to know who he is, what his background is, how far we can trust him.'

'We don't have to trust him.' Herz's voice rose, became almost plaintive. 'Willi will take him out as soon as the job's done.'

'Willi will try to. But if he's as skilful as you say, Willi might fail.'

Weise's tongue again made its flickering appearance, and he fought off a revealing shudder of angst. Winckelmann growled on.

'Heinrich, you have to make Finchley-Camden tell you who he is. If he's kosher then we can let Willi off the hook. But we have to know.'

'He won't say. He won't even answer the phone to me.'

'Heinrich. Just go to London and find out. OK?'

17

Cranmer messed about on the Metro for half an hour until he was sure he had no tail, emerged at the Estacio de Sants. There he changed some Swiss francs, bought a ticket for Madrid and a place on the 1227 Electrotren, took the escalators down to the platforms and boarded the semi-fast, air-conditioned express. At twenty to five he got off at Zaragoza, just as the train was about to leave the station. Nearby he hired a VW Polo, the fastest car available, checked there would be no problem about driving it into France. He drove north across the Ebro plain, through Huesca and into the mountains south of the Pyrenees. He spent the night at Sabiñánigo in the Hotel La Pardina. He left early next morning, drove over the Portalet Pass, leaving the spectacular twin peaks of the Pic du Midi d'Ossau on his left. It looked a good mountain – he thought he might have a go.

A little later he got peeved because all the cars in front of him had slowed down for no apparent reason. Some even pulled in off the road, their drivers and passengers got out, walked into the mountain grass, filled with the dried stalks of asphodels, climbed up onto outcrops of rock. They gazed into the sky, shaded their eyes, pointed.

Then he saw why. A huge bird, perhaps the biggest he had ever seen, was cruising effortlessly a mere hundred feet or so above the road. Like the others he parked, got out onto the grass and waited. It passed directly over him: a gold body, black wings with a spread of nine feet and a long, black, wedge-shaped tail, and he turned with it. For a moment its size blotted out the sun. Some eagle, he thought, and then *some* eagle. He was in no hurry, he stayed and watched. Presently, without apparently shifting a feather the bird began a long low sweep towards the huge rock faces of the mountain, and began to soar.

The sight of its effortless power, its domination of its environment filled him with a warm glow: it was an animal he could identify with, he saw himself like that. Only when it was a black dot against the deep blue of the sky, confused with the spots on his retinae, did he at last turn back to the car and drive on.

The bird was a Lammergeier or Bearded Vulture. He would not have been pleased to discover it was a vulture rather than a fully paid up bird of prey. And it is not all that efficient at survival either: there are probably no more than fifty pairs left in southern Europe.

He arrived at Inger's farmhouse shortly after one, parked the Polo in front of the house and studio/barn, got out, looked around. The high doors of the barn were open, and framed her sculpture of him, of his re-birth from fire to a new life. It was about eight feet high and set on a solid table that raised it a further two feet. Made out of leaf, flame, blade-shaped pieces of metal the main armature angled it forward so wings of fire seemed to stream behind it. Some of the metal was polished, some painted in deep blues with flashes of orange, yellow, and bright green. He guessed it was pretty good, that she was pleased with it. He was.

Then he looked round a bit more, became quickly aware that things were not quite as they should be. The Volkswagen camper had gone, and there was no other vehicle to replace it. But the barn doors were open. He looked under the stones in the patio where she normally left the key. There was no key there. He went back to the front door, pushed, and it gave. He glanced round, checked he was not leaving a possible enemy in his rear, then silently pushed the door open, entered, lifting the heavy velvet curtain that acted as a draught excluder as he did so.

The kitchen was a mess. There were unwashed glasses and plates in the sink, the rubbish bucket was full, a half empty

111

bottle of Madiran stood in a pool of red wine on the big pine table beside a half eaten baguette, and a tin of half-consumed sardines. A fork rested on the edge of the tin. One fork, one glass by the bottle, one person. If that was all, no problem.

Moving noiselessly, he turned and slowly checked out the rest of the room. By the door to the patio, which he saw was unbolted, Inger kept a small notice-board where she pinned notes to herself – shopping lists, dates to be remembered. It was clear but for one piece of folded note-paper. On it, in her art school italic script, the two words: Herr Niemand. No Man.

He remembered he was no longer Biedermann, Mr Worthy – he became No Man again.

He unpinned the paper, folded it out, read, heard her voice in his head.

> My mother has had a fall and is probably dying. It
> may be some weeks before I can get back. Please
> stay, please wait for me. Inger.

That was all.

Then the stair creaked. He froze for a second, like a fox caught in a headlight, pushed the note into his pocket. He remembered the living-room on the other side of the tiny hall. Whoever it was had been hiding there, was now attempting to get up the stairs without being heard, and had failed. A second creak, this time from above. He looked up at the wooden ceiling, moved back into the vestibule, began to climb. He avoided the stair that creaked. At the top he had a choice – one way led to Inger's bedroom, Laura's bedroom which he had used, and the bathroom. The other was the door into the part of the house Inger had never got round to converting or even clearing up: three dark, shuttered rooms, inter-connected and filled with large ancient furniture, some of it sheeted. The door was ajar, and had a key in it.

He paused, opened the door into Inger's bedroom, noticed that the bed had been used, and left untidy. He glanced into the bathroom and Laura's room, but already he felt pretty sure that the intruder had gone into the unused part – Inger never left the door to it open. He went through it, easing the key out as he went, silently locked the door behind him, pocketed the key. Then he stood, let his senses take over.

It was dark, but by no means completely so. There were shuttered windows on both sides but the one at the back of the house faced the sun and tiny shafts of light littered the floor immediately in front of it. His eyes soon adjusted to the gloom. He could make out a big tallboy with a mirror, chairs and maybe a bed covered with sheets. He smelled dust, mice, and fear – not far away.

He coughed, quite loudly, and banged his fist on the door. Then he walked briskly into the second room – lit and furnished in much the same way as the first, and on into the third. He looked around it apparently perfunctorily, and caught a glimpse of her bare foot in a sunbeam by the south-facing back window. He turned, walked back to the outer, locked door, banged it again, and then silently slipped into the middle room.

Presently Laura flitted through. She was wearing a short white night shirt, nothing else as far as he could see. He listened as she reached the locked door, listened and grinned. She gasped, turned back, panic-stricken, knowing she was trapped, but thinking that she had merely been locked in almost accidentally, that he would now be looking for her elsewhere.

Turned, and found him facing her in the doorway to the middle room. Almost she fainted, had to heave in breath two or three times. When she spoke it was in a whisper.

'No Man . . .?'

'What are you doing here?' He made it loud, peremptory.

'Waiting for you. I've been here . . . days. I knew you'd come.'

Slowly she began to undo the buttons of the shirt, but the fear rushed back into her eyes as he stepped towards her.

'You stole my money.'

His right hand rose above his left shoulder, the outer edge of

113

the palm angled like a blade. But as it smashed out and down, in a back-hand slice, he altered the plane that might have killed her. It was the back rather than the edge that smashed across her face. She staggered against the wall, and then sank to the floor, to her knees. Blood spilled from the cut on her cheek bone. She looked up at his face, then buried hers in the pit of his stomach. Presently she pulled back and pulled down the zip of his jeans.

18

For an hour in the afternoon he lay on Inger's bed, smoking and listening to the Miles Davis *Tutu* album on her stereo-cassette player. He liked its abrasive, ultra modern quality, the fact that only the trumpet and some of the percussion were unsynthesised. Downstairs Laura worked – cleaning up the mess she had made. But he felt restless. Enjoy yourself, Willi had said. With a dolly like Laura and a document case half full of Swiss francs in fifties, the rustic charms of the farmhouse were too tame a setting.

Presently he heard her on the stairs again. She came in, stood at the end of the bed. She still had nothing on but the night-shirt, cut short like a man's. She looked thinner than when he had seen her before, more haggard. The bruise beneath the cut on her cheek was swelling well, the colour spreading up into her eye, but she looked flushed too, excited. He realised she had liked what had happened, wanted more.

'I've finished.'

'Come here.'

His hand struck like a snake, caught the hair above the nape of her neck, wrenched her head down on to his stomach. He pulled on the cigarette, made it glow, touched her thigh with it, let her go. She didn't move, waited.

'Have you got any good clothes here. I mean . . . good, smart.'

'No.'

'Then we'll have to get you some.' He lifted the shirt, smacked her bottom. 'Come on. Make yourself half-way respectable anyway.'

He drove as fast as the Polo would let him, down the A 64 autoroute to Biarritz, booked them into the Hotel Palais, sent her out with two thousand Swiss francs and instructions to get herself proper clothes. She came back with a Courrèges small black backless, black pantyhose, satin evening slippers, a smart white rain-coat and very little change.

'Where do we eat?'

She'd already given that some thought.

'Le Jour se Lève. It's a Japanese-style fish restaurant in St Jean de Luz. Probably you ought to book first.'

The A 63 down the coast, twenty kilometres in ten minutes. They parked on the edge of the car-free zone just as the evening light was beginning to fade on the high cone of la Grande Rhune, turning the water in the fishing harbour to mother-of-pearl. The boutiques were lit up, each an Aladdin's cave. He sat at a café table, gave her another five hundred.

'Get yourself a gold chain. Or whatever.'

Then they walked through the little alleys and out on to the promenade, just as the sun sank into the Bay of Biscay beyond the distant moles. The lights on them flickered and died, flickered and died, and the fishing boats chugged out between them. On the horizon a square-rigged three-master stood up like a ghost.

The restaurant was at the end, overlooked the fishing port on one side, the bigger harbour on the other. Inside the décor suggested the far orient without being too extreme about it, and

115

while the menu offered raw fish and cetacean meat, most of the dishes were Thai or Vietnamese. The pictures on the walls though were Japanese reproductions of nineteenth-century coloured prints, and if one looked at them properly, grossly erotic beneath the folds of silk kimonos and fans. The waiters were from the east too – but no further than Cambodia or Vietnam.

One of them showed them to a table in the corner of the big curved window that filled one side. Laura refused the chair he offered, sat so her cheek was exposed to the rest of the room. She had decided to wear her bruise and black eye like a trophy. They ordered appetisers of spicy fried sea-food, and then followed the waiter back to the big fish tanks on the other side of the room. Lobsters, deep blue and coral, meandered meaninglessly about the bottom of one, large black fish with barbels swirled more gracefully in another.

They stood in front of the fish tank, holding hands as if they were in love. She hesitated, reluctant for a moment to sign a death warrant. Slowly he increased pressure until she had to respond to the pain. She flinched, gasped, swallowed, pointed with her free hand.

'That one. Down in the corner on this side.'

Cranmer released her, laughed, turned to the waiter.

'The largest,' he said.

Back at the table, the appetisers had arrived with spicy dips of varying hotness. But Cranmer waited until Laura was sitting again, then turned to the waiter.

'You have a pay-phone?'

'Of course. In the foyer by the cloakroom.'

Laura looked up, alarmed, caught his sleeve.

'Will you be long?'

He shrugged. 'Ten, twenty minutes. Depends. You stay here, eat those. Don't come out after me.'

'Can I have a drink? Please?'

'Gin? With tonic?'

Surprised, she shrugged. 'All right.'

'Two. And we'll have champagne with the fish.'

116

The waiter attempted to make a scene of it.

'May I recommend the Dom . . .'

But Cranmer was having none of that.

'Champagne. Brut. Cold. All right?'

He was no more than ten minutes. When he came back he was in a good mood. Both calls had gone well – the help he would need at the Casa Pez in seven days' time was on the way. He lifted his untouched glass, touched hers although it was nearly empty.

'Cheers.' He drank. 'I've got six days. Do you think Inger will come back in that time?'

'Less than a week? What are we doing here if we've got less than a week?'

'How soon before Inger comes back?'

'I don't know. Does it matter? We can go somewhere else if she turns up. Oh, I'll phone her when we get back to the farm, check it all out for you. But please don't go on about her.'

The waiter was back, first with the champagne then the fish on chafing dishes. He served them and they ate in silence. When she had eaten as much as she could, she put aside her fork, looked up at him with filling eyes. Her bottom lip trembled.

'Where do you have to go when the week has gone? Will you take me?' She tried not to sound pleading, failed.

Cranmer looked up at her across the bones of the fish that now lay in front of him. He thought about it. Perhaps it might not be such a bad idea – to have help, an ally in Barcelona that no one knew about but him. He flipped the fish over, started on the other side.

'You've got to take me.'

She almost whined.

'Maybe. We'll see.'

They bought surfboards, towels, drove north, looking for surf, real surf. The N-10 arrowed through Les Landes, Europe's second largest forest, mile upon mile of flat sandy land covered

117

with tall pines. It smelled of the turpentine that leaked into cups attached to the trees. Occasional clearings held chicken farms, advertised *miel* and *gelée royale*. At a small village called Castets he filtered off the by-pass, and then in the village itself took a left. He was following her directions: she claimed she knew where the best surf was. They drove through an even smaller village, St Girons, where they bought cold dry white wine from a refrigerator in the one small shop, and two small round melons. They bought Coca-Cola from a dispenser – she drank hers, he chucked his. He'd bought it just for the cup. Eventually they came to St Girons-Plage: a small settlement of self-catering apartments, a couple of shops, a camp-site, all set behind the huge dune that runs almost from Arcachon to Biarritz interrupted only by four or five small rivers. It's thirty, forty feet high, sometimes more, and varies in width from fifty yards to two hundred. In places giant nets are staked to keep it from drifting, but for the most part it's covered in a hard, shiny grass that squeaks when you walk on it.

They parked, in the big car park behind it. It was quite full. Laura scanned it for the psychedelically painted 2CV her boyfriend used – thought she could see it, but wasn't sure. They went through the gap, walked along a short promenade in front of the apartments. Already they could see the dune stretching almost white into the deepest distance the thirty miles or more back to Biarritz, losing itself in the permanent haze of fine sand and sea spray which lies like a heaving, constantly shifting snake above it and the beach. In front of it fine white sand, then hard dark wet sand, then the sea, the ocean.

There had been some wind and the waves were high, up to eight feet and the water was filled with surfers. They walked on, Laura said they should, and he was pleased to get away from the August crowd. Eventually notices warned: beyond this point there were no life-savers, there was an undertow, bathing and surfing were dangerous. Beyond that point there were far fewer swimmers or surfers. Most of them were young, and many wore no clothes at all. They left the hard wet sand they had been on for ease of walking, tramped through the dry soft stuff, crossed the belt of plastic bottles and other litter, much of it smeared with tar, climbed into the dune. Cranmer found a shallow hollow.

'This will do.'

He chucked down his board and towel, pulled his shirt over his head, stripped off his trousers and pants. He squatted, hunkered down over the plastic bag that held the bottles and melons, opened one of the bottles with the cork-screw on his knife, poured into the polystyrene cups.

'Don't want it to get warm.' He drank. 'Aren't you going to take your clothes off?'

While she did, it took her even less time than it had him, he picked up one of the melons, pushed the fingers of both hands through the rind at one end and pulled it in two, offered her half. They drank, ate melon, spat out the seeds around them. Then, with juice and wine dribbling between her breasts, and the wind buffeting about them, and the deep roar of the surf always in their ears, he pushed her on to her back and fucked her, quickly and roughly, but urging her to a swift orgasm.

Then he stood, looked down at her out of the sun.

'I'm going to surf. Coming?'

She sensed that he did not want her to, shook her head.

'Maybe later.'

He turned and left her, bounced down the loose sand. She wondered what the marks on his back were – a sort of liverish-brown now with fiery pink edges.

The first time he left the surfboard just out of reach of the sea, waded in without it, felt the smack of the run-on from a couple of breakers bursting on his thighs, his stomach; then suddenly he grinned with real pleasure as a vicious undertow almost swept his feet from under him, sucking the sand away from under his feet. It was dangerous, and that was what he wanted. He duck-dived into the next one, came up and swam with a fast strong crawl beyond the line of breakers, to where the water was blue. Out there he let the great rollers heave him up, and slip him down the other side, heave and drop, heave and drop. Then he turned, swam back to the sand, waded the last bit, picked up the board.

She watched him from the crest of the dune, forced herself to make objective judgements, rated him good if not stylish, strong enough to take it but out of practice. But it was no use, or not for long. Her head filled with the wretched brew of loneliness, angst and boredom which was her normal state of mind if nothing totally distracting was happening. She finished the bottle, and the wine with the sun and the wind gave her a headache. She knew what she needed and felt a biting, gnawing yet somehow listless despair at the thought that she might not get it.

But then she heard voices. Familiar voices. Raising herself on her elbows she saw them, scouting along the land-side of the crest – Siegfried and Kurt. Not, thank God, Peter. She saw them spread themselves, their towels, boards and so on, fifty metres away, ducked her head back down, waited, thought about it. Had they seen her? It was not entirely necessary that they should have done, this was the area they usually came to, but was it not a coincidence they had placed themselves so close? Did it matter, either way? No.

She hoisted herself on to her elbows, looked down on to the beach. He was coming in again, much better now, not bucking the curver he was on, but letting it take him – it all looked more effortless. He is good, she thought, just out of practice, but it's coming back. She glanced sideways, caught Kurt looking at her. He raised a hand, opened and closed the palm. So. They knew she was there, had known all along. She reached for Cranmer's trousers, found the wallet, found five hundred francs. Not enough, really, not enough for enough, but it was all she dared. A quick look down. He was on his way out again, brown buttocks twinkling against the swirling foam.

Still keeping an eye on him she pulled on pants and then scampered along the dune, across the fifty metres, looked down at them. Kurt was blond, tanned; Siegfried fatter, darker, with spots, both about her age. Kurt looked up at her, hand across his eyes against the glare.

'Hi, Laura. It's been a long time.'

'Hi. Hi, Siggy.'

'Hi.'

She took a breath.

'It's not been so long. Four days.'

'Five. You left Saturday.' Siggy had taken charge. He usually did. 'You said you'd be back that evening. With some money.'

'OK. My mother's gone. She's away. I stayed on up there. That's all. Where's Peter? Is he here?'

'No.' Kurt this time. 'Went back to Düsseldorf day before yesterday. The guy you're with now. He surfs well. But he's a dude. Loaded. Bourgeois shit.'

'Knocks you about too. You like that sort of thing don't you? Have you got any money? We're broke.'

'Don't be silly. I got hit with a board. That's all.'

'Have you got any money?'

'Yes.'

She let them see the five hundred franc note. Siegfried made a grab for it, but she pulled her hand away in time. She looked out over the dune again. Cranmer was far out, waiting for the big one.

'Have you got any dope? I mean with you?'

Kurt shrugged: 'Speed. Not much.'

She struggled not to show desperation.

'Is it good? Real?'

'Durophet. Twelve point fives.'

'Five for five hundred.'

Kurt glanced up at Siegfried, who nodded, pulled a foil card from the bum-bag tied round his waist. He tore off a strip holding five black and white capsules. But Cranmer was up and coming in fast, the sort of ride one doesn't expect to repeat.

'Oh come on, come on, please, please hurry.'

121

'OK, OK.' Kurt handed them over, took the money. 'At last we eat.'

She ran quickly back across the dunes, stumbling as she went, just as Cranmer left the water. She pushed the foil strip into the slipper she'd been wearing, looked around, checked that everything was more or less as it had been, lay on her front. He climbed the last steep slope, made it over the top, picked up a towel. She turned again and sat, knees drawn up and held in her arms.

'Was that good? Did you enjoy that?'

'It was all right. I'm fit.' He scrubbed at his genitals, in the groove between his buttocks, spread the towel, sat facing her. 'Tell me about Barcelona.'

'Only if you promise to take me.'

'Tell me. It's got an old part. A medieval slum.'

'The Barri Gòtic. I lived there. It's wild. Wicked. I know how to get a room there too. You just ask in the Caracas bar in Argenteria.' She shifted into a provocative pose, leant back on her elbows, spread her legs, rubbed her toes against his shin. 'Take me with you. I'll show you. There are things you can do in Barcelona you can't do anywhere else.'

'Really? But you can score junk anywhere.' He looked up and around. 'Those two men. You spoke to them.'

She tried to pull her foot in but his hand struck again, caught her ankle, and, coming forward into a crouch over her as he did so, he twisted her on to her front with the foot he was holding pressed down towards the small of her back.

'Scream, and I'll break your leg. Tell me. Who are they?'

'Friends. The guys I hung out with here.' There was excitement as well as hysteria and fear. 'Until I got bored with them.'

'What did you take them?'

He turned up the pressure. She moaned and not only because of the pain which was real enough.

'Money.'

'How much?'

'Five hundred. From your wallet. It's what I came to the farm for. Four days ago. They're hungry.'

'Like shit, they're hungry.'

He released her foot. He knelt up above her for a moment, then spread her legs, lifted and pulled her buttocks towards him. She squawked as he penetrated her back passage, but he reached forward and slapped her ear from behind. After that she just moaned. When he came, he dropped her, and she rolled on to her back, her arm up against the sun, and to hide the tears.

'Please, take me with you to Barcelona. Say you'll take me.'

But now he was almost sure he would not. In little more than two days he had learned too much about her – she would be a liability, not an ally. He looked at the anvil cloud that had formed to the south and the east, above the distant mountains, and realised too that he could not leave her behind either, like an untaken city in the rear of an advancing army.

19

She stood in front of her mother's full-length mirror and looked into an arch filled with light. She had placed herself under the central overhead light. The lamp over the dressing table and the reading light over the bed also shone full on her. The corners of the room, and the mirror itself were in near darkness, but the centre, and its reflection in the mirror, made a cave of light.

On the bed were three boxes: one padded and frilled, boudoir-style, a birthday gift from an aunt when she was fifteen, one was plain wood, nineteenth century with a small brass key-hole, the third was serious – gun-metal steel lined with velvet, with a proper lock. Together they held a lot of jewellery, a lot of treasure. There were simple gold chains and strings of pearls, one of which was the real thing. There was a white feather and diamanté tiara she had worn when she did the Dying Swan at ballet school. There were necklaces, bangles, and rings made from or studded with Inger's favourite shades – topaz and amethyst. And there was a whole mass of lesser stuff – paste costume jewellery collected over two decades by both women. Thunder crackled in the mountains, rain drummed on the roof and the gutters filled and spilled, filled and spilled, but it all made the room, heated by the two bars of an electric fire, that more cosy, secret, rich, a fit harem for the Sultan's concubine to prepare herself for her master's bidding.

A night, a day, and now another night of rain had apparently pushed him near to overt recognisable madness, had brought the concealed, innate, permanent madness that she knew possessed him into the open. He had drunk more than he usually did, and made her do things which . . . well, she'd only read of them in the Olympia Press books her mother kept because they were, she said, curios from an earlier age. And at last, as dusk came, he said he was going out, out into the rain.

'Where? Why? Can't I come too?'

'No.'

'Why not.'

'Because I want to be alone.'

'What shall I do?'

'Go upstairs. Make yourself pretty.'

'How long will you be?'

'As long as it takes. Go on. Go now.'

He had gone out through the front door. She waited to hear the noise of the car, but it didn't come. She went up to her own room, looked out from its darkness into rain and deeper darkness, saw briefly the beam of a torch swing round the entrance of the barn, conferring on her mother's statue of him brief, dramatic life. Then nothing. Make yourself pretty. For half an hour she played with make-up and Inger's clothes, but they were wrong for her, always had been. All right for a forty-year-old to swan about in up-market versions of early seventies styles but . . .

One floppy silk blouse with huge carnations printed on it briefly made something of her with a chunky piece of gilt costume jewellery – and that gave her the idea. She'd do without clothes, do it with jewellery and paint. But first she went to the kitchen, mixed a jug of white rum and Coke, one to two, and took it upstairs. She had three durophets left and she took one. Then she set too.

She used up every cake of eye make-up and every lipstick, gave herself huge elf eyes with black outlines, made her nipples the centres of exotic flowers, caused a snake to leak out of her navel and wander down her tummy. And then she started in on the jewellery.

Two hours after he'd gone, she felt she had it as right as she was likely to get it: the danger now was a let-down, to come off the high, to see herself as a tawdry gew-gaw, to face the lonely panic which was too often the mental landscape she lived in. Two-thirds of the jug had gone, she had only two capsules left.

What to do now? Her eye fell on her mother's stereo-cassette player. And suddenly it came to her. Through the five days she had been with Cranmer the one thing she had longed to do was somehow to let her mother know what had been going on. But how? A letter could be torn up part-read, and anyway Laura hated writing, knew she lacked the ability to capture on paper the extent of her conquest of her mother's boy-friend. Face-to-face would never do either. And a telephone could be cut off. But record a message? Yes. And the player had a microphone built-in. She knew that because the player was six years old and had been used to record her first, and finally aborted attempts to play the piano.

Excited again she rummaged through the little bedside drawer beneath the machine, found cassettes once blank on which her mother had made recordings from the radio or her friend's tapes. Leonard Cohen, 'I'm Your Man'. Yes. She'd play that sooner or later. And there was a splendid irony tying

125

what she would hear to what she expected to hear. I'm Your Man. Oh no he's not.

'Mumsie, I'm on your bed, and I'm dressed in your jewellery. Why? Because he's done it to me three times already today, and I want him to do it again. Your hunky No Man.'

She broke out a Durophet, only one left, poured what was left in the jug. Now she was enjoying herself. Really.

'Mumsie, I bet I know a lot more about him than you do. I think he's a crook. A fabulous real crook, like something out of . . . oh I don't know. But really wicked, wicked beyond wicked, way out in a sphere beyond wickedness, like a sort of angel. A Fallen Angel? But there's nothing fallen about him is there? That sculpture you've made says it a bit, even if it is just junk and scrap . . . And now listen to this. He came back with lots of money. Really lots, but not enough for ever. But now he's going to take me to Barcelona. And we're going to shack up in the Barri Gòtic, like I did before, and when he's done what he's going there to do we'll have all the money we'll need for ever . . .'

Footsteps on the stairs. Quickly she switched off the recorder. But she was twisted, half on her front, half on one side when Cranmer came in – her attitude expressed guilt and concealment. His clothes, thin sweater and jeans, were streaked with mud and rain, his hair and face too. He looked at her for a long moment, taking in her appearance, the jewellery, the paint.

'Why are you like that? Why have you got those things on?'

'You told me to. Be pretty, you said. Aren't I pretty?'

He moved to the bed, looked down at her, fingered one of the chains, sat beside her.

'Leave them on. What's this?'

He picked up the foil card of capsules, broke the last one out, looked at the tiny lettering on it. She shifted on the bed – beads, metal, stones shifted too.

'Where have you been?' She pouted, made it teasing, petulant. 'You're all wet.'

'Durophet. Speed? Where from?'

'The beach. Those men. The money I . . .'

'Took from my wallet. There's no way I can take you with me. To Barcelona.'

She pulled away from him, her knees under her, moved into partial shade.

'Why not? What have I done?'

'And I can't leave you, either.' He sniffed her glass, looked at the jug. 'You drink too much. Drop pills. Inger told me in Barcelona you got yourself a heroin habit.'

Noise of rain and distant grumbles of thunder. She asked the question but had already guessed the answer.

'What are you going to do with me?'

'Kill you.'

She moved very swiftly, the door was on her side, the bed impeded him. Nevertheless he got his hand on ropes of beads and pearls. The strings burst in his face, pearls and beads, hundreds of them, scattered and bounced down the wooden stairs behind him. Some got under his feet and he tumbled noisily to the bottom, flailing legs and arms. Silence as he sat, huddled up at the bottom, then a door banged and the velvet curtain moved in a sudden draught.

He picked himself up, staggered, overcame the pain. He moved into the kitchen. It was brightly lit and empty. His eyes scanned everything, a meticulous and virtually instant check. There was a space in the wall-rack of kitchen knives. The cleaver he used when he killed the rats had gone.

There were two doors, two ways out – beyond the curtain that moved there was the small vestibule to the front door. The other door led straight into the patio. He pulled down the curtain and wrapped it round his left arm. He picked up the heavy and powerful torch he had been using outside, but did not turn it on. He turned out the kitchen light and counted to ten – something he had been taught, give his eyes time to adjust – then he opened the front door and hurled himself through in a crouched position, holding his left, protected arm above his head.

127

Nothing. He shone the torch, which had a long and penetrating beam, over the yard, the entrance to the barn where it picked up Inger's sculpture, down the road, and over the meadow. Only the silver rain, the trees and the more distant sculptures shone back. He turned out the torch, moved back into the patio, felt under the stones where the key was hidden, returned to the front door, locked it and pocketed the key.

By then Laura, who had been in the patio, was back in the kitchen, where she heard the key turn, realised what he had done. She banged the door between patio and kitchen, slipped into the patio and pressed herself against the wall in which the opening to the yard was set.

Cranmer moved across the patio to the kitchen door without seeing her, snapped on the light, saw no sign of her, no wet footprints on the kitchen floor, span to see her disappear into the yard. He followed her, paused in the opening to the yard, turned on the torch. Its beam briefly caught then lost her as she ran into the barn.

He moved to the wide high entrance to the barn, dominated by the sculpture. He turned on the torch, let it sweep round, let it find her crouched in a corner near the entrance.

Any magic there might have been had gone. She looked vulnerable, dirty, wet. She was blinded by the torch, threw an arm over her eyes. All she could see was the eye of light staring at her. She moved towards him, but she still held the cleaver.

'No Man? It's just a game, yes? A game?'

'Yes. A game. It's over now.'

She threw herself at him, sweeping the cleaver which he took on his shielded arm. He struck her with the torch, again and again and again, and the light wheeled about the barn, bounced off the skylight, whirled over her mother's tools and equipment, off the statue.

When it was over he buried her in the grave he had already dug, near the rats.

20

Finchley-Camden opened the fine oak door that separated his inner sanctum from what was in effect a waiting-room. Herz looked up from the copy of *Country Life* he had been leafing through with increasing bewilderment.

'My dear chap, I'm so sorry to have kept you waiting. What can I do for you?'

He stood back, let the compact sturdy-looking Swiss pass through, pushed a chair closer to the desk for him, got back behind his desk, behind, as it were his fortified lines. Torres Vedras.

'Would you like a coffee? I'll get Gwendolyn to send us in coffee.' He flipped a switch. 'Gwendolyn, coffee please, there's a dear. For two. Now, Heinrich, what can I do for you? I'm so sorry we weren't able to accommodate your last request, though what I read in the papers inclines me to believe you got what you wanted elsewhere, eh?' He ha-ha-ed like a bugle, you couldn't call it a laugh. 'Tell me, did you miss Kalnitzky on purpose or were you out to get him?'

Herz felt dizzy: this was all very confusing, even more weird than *Country Life*.

He waited while Gwendolyn poured coffee from silver into Limoges. She was a sensible girl in a sensible dress, a near clone of the plain but jolly girls who tramped grouse moors in Scotland and got photographed while they did it. Neither she nor the expensive tableware could make the coffee drinkable.

'Jolly lucky you found us in, actually. Only re-opened yesterday after the summer break. Swanning around the Med until Saturday, been away three weeks.'

Herz took a breath, set aside the cup.

'I have been trying to get in contact.' He was determined not to allow his confusion to show, determined to get what he had come for. 'You see . . . Your man has as you say done very well for us, but before he takes on the really important commission my client is insisting that we know who he is.'

Finchley-Camden's turn to be confused.

'I'm not quite sure I'm catching your drift, old chap.'

Herz attempted to explain: how a man who wanted to be known as Biedermann had phoned the AlterLog office, had claimed to be the contract killer Wolf-hound had found for AlterLog. How Biedermann said all monies should be paid direct to him, how Wolf-hound would bill him not AlterLog for their commission. How . . .

'And you took all this on board without checking back?' Finchley-Camden was scandalised by such unprofessionalism.

'We could not do so for two reasons. One. Biedermann said that if we contacted you the deal would be off. At first we accepted this as part of your security procedures. Then later you were always out when I tried to phone . . .'

'The hols, old chap. I told you. Put up the shutters first of August, always do that.'

'And for the fortnight before that you were not available. The girl always said you were out. Meanwhile, Biedermann had performed very well for us, was very competent, very professional. But now, as I said, my client feels we ought to know a little bit more about him, before he carries out the main task. We cannot leave ourselves exposed. And that is why I am here. If you can give me assurances that he is reliable, not a risk, will keep his word not to . . .'

'But my dear chap. I can't tell you anything at all. I have not the slightest idea of whom you are talking about.'

The big clock ticked. Herz looked sightlessly at a large painting on the wall. Men in tall peaked caps bayoneted men in bearskins on a mountainside. Black writing on the gilt frame

130

said: 'A company of the Riversdale Rifles takes out a French Piquet in the Pyrenees, August 1813.'

'Biedermann, whoever he is, knew that I had approached you. How?'

'My dear chap. That precisely is the question I am asking myself.'

'I think you had better find out the answer.'

'I think so. At the moment it looks like a bloody great hole in our security. Below the water-line at that. You must know something else about him? I mean, have you met him? What does he look like?'

Herz described Cranmer. Then: 'There's just one other thing. He claims to be dead. Officially dead. We rather liked that. The idea that if he was identified by appearance, finger-prints, or even recognised it would lead to . . . a dead-end. This was the reason he gave for insisting we provide him with new documents – Swiss passport, Euro-driving permit.'

Finchley-Camden struggled with himself to keep Herz from knowing that the penny was dropping, light dawning. But Herz was not fooled. He left feeling pretty sure Finchley-Camden had guessed who Biedermann was, but was certainly not going to admit it until he had checked it out for himself.

As soon as he had gone, after exchanging mutual assurances that they would be in touch, that it was in the interests of everyone concerned to sort this thing out, Finchley-Camden thought it through again and then called Gwendolyn on the intercom.

'Gwendolyn? Get hold of Sam Dorf. Tell him if he's free I'm buying him lunch at whatever chop-house he's using these days. Right?'

Boiled onions, game chips, two fatty chops. With surgical skill Finchley-Camden separated the strip of fat from the lean, then the lean from the bone.

'Sam,' he said, '*Nil nisi sed bonum* and all that crap, but just

131

how deep was the shit Tom was in when his number came up on that aircrash.'

Sam Dorf, nearly sixty, pale grey suit, sharp dark eyes that could be jolly, plump pink cheeks, had the reputation of a killer shark. Which, Finchley-Camden thought, is fair enough. Dorf and Co, Commodity Brokers, was one of the very few small firms to survive Big Bang and two recessions. He had a deep voice, and vowels which occasionally betrayed their origin a mile or so away in Whitechapel.

'Deep, Roderick. Very deep. Stride at the Wood Street nick was reaching for his collar. No doubt about that.' He took a good pull at the house red, a Rioja reserva.

'And Judith. How was he making out there?'

'Not good at all.' Dorf dabbed his lips with a napkin. The corners could lift in an angel-smile, but now they compressed into a thin line, as he thought for a moment about his daughter's marriage to Finchley-Camden's nephew. 'They spent . . . he spent more than he earned, which is why he had his finger in the till on the Metal Exchange. That worried her. But there were more private things too. Well. What other people get up to in the sack is nobody's business but theirs. But Judith let on to her mother that your Tom had some pretty funny ideas she couldn't always go along with. And she's no nun, herself. I mean, you know, she does like it. So long as it's reasonably straight. Still. All water under the bridge, now.'

'She's getting over it? Not grieving too much?'

Dorf laughed, sawed into one of his onions. 'Not really. Tell you the truth she's shacked up already with the second violinist in a string quartet. Much more her sort of thing really. I reckon it was under way before that crash widowed her.'

'Did Tom know?'

Dorf shrugged. 'Maybe.'

Finchley-Camden thought: the lovers are lucky to be alive if he did. He said: 'So all in all Tom was going through a bad patch when he snuffed.'

'Yes. I'd go along with that. Come on, Roddy, play square with me. Why the free lunch and questions about Tom?'

'He was working for me when it happened. There's a bit of a mystery about one or two aspects of it. I can't rule out the possibility of suicide.'

'You mean he topped himself and took out twenty innocent people with him? All in all Tom was a bad lot, Roddy. It won't surprise you to hear me say that. But he wasn't psycho.' He put down his knife and fork, looked across the table. 'Or was he?'

21

Sunday, the day before the official opening of the conference of sixty-three Greens from all over Europe, west and east, and at three in the afternoon, the concourse of the Estació de Sants looked like a small eco-demo with banners and placards. Raul Singer, charismatic leader of the Rainbow Fraction of Frankfurt was about to arrive. Dr Julia Arendt, Carlos Negrín of Proleben-tek, and the deputy mayor of Barcelona made up the official welcoming party but most of the Greens who had already arrived were there, and a couple of hundred of Barcelona's wilder lefties, green and otherwise too. A mobile freelance television crew consisting of a woman reporter, cameraman with the camera on his padded shoulder, a soundman with boom, mike and recorder, and lightman with mobile lamps who doubled as producer, jostled press reporters and photographers and were jostled back in turn.

Cranmer prowled like a wolf in denims, dark blue jersey and trainers, on the edges of the crowd, and near the wide exit on to the outer concourse, Willi Weise, leather-jacketed and Tina Turner-ed, peeled the wrapper from a Pop-Eye (in Spain pronounced Eh-Yeh) and watched.

But the charismatic Singer, who was nothing if not a self-publicist, stayed on the platform below until his fellow passengers had cleared up the escalator: he had no intention of allowing his welcome to take place amongst a litter of kids and baggage as Barcelona returned from summer holiday. Amongst them two men in their early thirties attempted to pick their way through the litter of surfboards, sail boards, golf clubs and even a hang-glider. The shorter was redheaded, wore an anorak over jeans, had a small gold ring in his left ear. He had small blue eyes and hands that were red but compact and hard like rock, the knuckles tattoed – Love and Hate. The other was dark enough to be identified as Afro, but only just. He wore a brightly coloured 'shell', the top half of which was padded. He was tall, had long wrists and hands which he tended to swing or allow to flop. Both carried simple hold-alls and small duffel-bags.

Cranmer watched them and his smile twisted one side of his mouth for a moment as they checked, spoke to each other, looked about them – Brits abroad, expecting to be met, where the fuck's the courier got to? Except it wasn't a courier they were looking for. He stepped round an extended family, all in huge Mexican-style straw hats, which he had been using as a stalking horse, spoke quietly.

'Corporal MacTaggart, Lance Corporal Smith.'

The Afro spun towards him, stamped his feet to attention, snapped up a very British Army salute.

'Lance Corporal Winston Smith, reporting for duty, SAH!' Then his hand came down and was thrust out palm-up. 'Mr Cranmer, you bastard, we thought you was dead, man? Lay on five.'

Cranmer submitted to the ceremony with a bad grace.

'OK, Winston, that'll do. Hullo there, Kevin. You're looking fit.'

Brusquely he patted the shorter man's shoulder. He answered in a broad, working-class Glaswegian accent.

'All the better for finding you alive and well, sorr.'

'All right, lads. I'd rather you didn't go on about that,' and he shepherded them towards the Metro entrance.

Weise chucked his Pop-Eye lolly, twinkled away to the street. He looked pleased.

Shortly Raul Singer, who was much of an age with Cranmer and his associates, emerged from below. He had long coarse blond hair tied back in a pony-tail, wide-spaced pale blue eyes lit with fanaticism, thick lips. He wore combat-style fatigues badged not militarily but with rainbows. There were cheers and fast rhythmic hand-clapping from the wilder fringes which he acknowledged with both hands clasped over his head, then he fell into Julia Arendt's deep embrace. Behind him a small, very blonde, very pretty girl, like a porcelain doll except that she too was dressed in fatigues, hovered shyly. Cameras flashed, the TV crew moved in. He pulled back from Arendt, but left his hands on her shoulders.

'Julia. We've cracked it. We can prove a Mafia link.'

'But of course!' She smiled back at him, her face full of warmth, affection. 'The story would not be complete if the Mafia were not in it.'

'I'm serious, you know?'

She was generous, apologetic.

'Of course you are.'

He took her arm, surged with her through the crowd which parted in front of them like the Red Sea in front of Moses.

'Essentially, what we are talking about is garbage. Organising garbage collection was where the Mafia started. In Sicily. Then the Camorra in Naples. And Cosa Nostra in New York. Garbage. They're experts. The experts.'

'It's an interesting idea.'

'Julia. I'm not talking about an idea. I'm talking about facts. Is Sasonov here yet? We've come across a Ukrainian link too, a strong one.'

'No, he was held up. He'll be here tomorrow, midday. Lucky man will miss the Mayor's reception, but he should make it to lunch at a fish restaurant. You know there's still far too much of that sort of thing on the programme, but it's what you get when you lie down with local politics and local capitalism. Anyway we're shot of most of it by seven tomorrow evening when we'll be able to get down to serious work . . .'

As they rounded the corner into the outer concourse, the TV reporter, a tall brunette in a red suit with padded shoulders and pencil skirt slit at the back over long black stockings, pounced. The pretty little German girl whom Singer had picked out of the other Greens travelling on the train to be his conference friend felt suddenly a touch left out, wondered if she shouldn't just melt away.

'Mr Singer, Dr Arendt, a few words, please. Is there a central theme to your conference?'

'There will be a full press conference at the end of the week when we have completed a communiqué.' Arendt wanted to push on, hear more of what Singer had discovered. Singer, however, never refused an interview, and certainly not from Mediterranean goddesses.

'I can tell you right now that garbage is our theme. Industrial garbage on a huge scale and how the big corporations are developing ways to circumvent the new EC regulations . . .'

Cranmer unlocked the door of the Barceloneta apartment, led the way in.

'It's not much, in fact it's a pretty crappy dump. But it's in the right place, the gear's here, and if all goes well we shouldn't have to spend more than one night here.'

MacTaggart and Smith followed and like a pair of dogs went through the place sniffing and wagging their tails. Not much had changed – some food and a crate of 25cl Mahou beers had been brought in, and two suits of waiters' clothes.

Cranmer hauled the box out from under the sink, put it on the table.

136

'Here, Smith, you'd better check this out. Make sure I've got it right. You're the expert.'

He spilled photographs out of a commercial fast processing firm's envelope.

'This is the site. It's practically at the end of the road. Have a good look at it all, have a beer or two, get familiar with it, then we'll move on to a proper first stage briefing.'

Presently Winston Smith knocked the top off his second bottle of Mahou.

'Why is Spanish beer like copulating in a canoe? Because it's fucking close to water. Here's to Sergeant James Wilkins.'

'Aye,' said MacTaggart, and reached for a bottle for himself. 'I'll drink to Jimmie.'

They sat for a moment and remembered the fourth member of their Special Services team, shot in the head by an IRA gunman. They remembered too how they had taken their revenge by luring the gunman into the toilets of the Duke of Wellington pub, Belfast, where they had let him know who they were and why before Cranmer broke his neck. They'd paid for the crime with their army careers – no more.

Winston shook himself, perked up.

'This gear's OK, you know that? Especially the mercury tremblers and the infra-red signallers, lovely jobs. Did you test them?'

'Of course.' There was a black mark on the wall to prove he had. Cranmer prodded one of the pictures. 'I'm afraid this was the best I could do for the kitchen. But I've made a plan of how I think it goes.'

He unrolled a sheet of thin drawing paper. Winston put down the opened pack of detonating charges, came over to the table, looked over Cranmer's shoulder.

'You took these photos.'

'Yes.'

'Somebody saw you do that. They could fit you up with a photofit.'

Kevin MacTaggart turned on him.

137

'No way.'

'Why not?'

'You black git,' he tapped Winston's head. 'Nothing in that coconut but coconut milk.'

A moment of anger – Winston threw a punch at Kevin who blocked it stylishly.

'OK, darling, so I'm an ignorant black bastard, that's what you always used to say, right? But now tell me.'

'Who can they identify him as?' Kevin stood back and grinned. 'Captain Thomas Cranmer, Military Cross, late of the Royal Buff Caps and Special Services? But Captain Cranmer's dead. D, E, A, D. Snuffed. See? Identification . . . false. Error.'

Winston thought about it.

'Jesus. That's fucking brilliant, that is. For the rest of his life he can do what he fucking likes.' He turned to Cranmer. 'Whatever you fucking like.'

Cranmer thought about that too. For nearly two months he had ranged over Europe like a Lammergeier or a wolf, he had been Mr Worthy, Mr No Man. That had given him . . . not courage, he'd never been short of that, but confidence.

'May be. But already I'm a touch less dead than I was.'

The Glaswegian asked the question.

'How's that then?'

'There's two chaps now know I'm alive and well and in Barcelona. One of them's a blabbermouth, and the other's a nasty wicked little schemer.'

A moment of doubt, fear even, then Cranmer laughed and they did too, confident that he was joking.

'OK, let's get on with it.'

22

Mayor's reception, noon until one. Coach-trip to Barcelona's most famous landmark – Gaudí's Sagrada Familia, church of the Holy Family. 2 PM: Lunch at the Casa Pez. 7 PM: First plenary session at the University.

A big new bus had been laid on, was waiting in the Plaça Sant Miquel outside the Town Hall. Although the Mayor's reception had been the first and only official event so far, by the time the delegates were trickling into the bus, what might have become the two main themes were emerging. And since Raul Singer and the Rainbow Fraction were at the centre of both, controversy was simmering with the possibility of a major split.

Walking across the square, an elderly Norwegian in a heavy cotton checked shirt with rolled-up sleeves and corduroys attempted to take Singer to task. He considered it no anomaly at all that after a lifetime protesting the British outfall of acid rain on his country's forests he remained an unrepentant and continuous pipe-smoker.

'You can't prove a thing without admitting you obtained the information illegally.'

'It doesn't matter. OK, one or two of us end up in jail. It's no big deal.'

'Not for you.' The Norwegian used his pipe stem to stab the air in front of Singer's face. Singer flinched away from it as if it were a turd. 'You can all rot in jail for as long as you like for all I care. But it could be a big and bad deal for the movement. The whole thing could be turned against us. You can imagine what the right-wing press would say, right-wing politicians. Your Rainbow Fraction did us incalculable harm last year when you blew up railway track in front of a train carrying nuclear waste. This could be as bad.'

'Oh come on. That was quite different. On that occasion the bastards tried to make out we'd endangered lives, even though we'd tipped them off. There's no way they can make that sort of claim over hacking the accounts and fax lines of ten crooked companies. Listen you're not going to smoke that thing on the bus, are you?'

The Norwegian tapped it out on the heel of his solid walking boot, followed Singer and the pretty girl into the bus, took the seat in front of them but remained standing, leaned across the back of his seat.

'That's how you see it. It's not how they'll see it. And how they see it is how the public will see it. The public we are still trying to get on to our side. No, believe me, letting it out that you've been hacking on behalf of the Green Movement is pissing in the wind.'

The bus began to move and the Norwegian had to sit down. Singer put his hand on the pretty girl's knee, whispered in her ear.

'Believe me, boring old farts like him do our image far more harm than the Rainbow Fraction.'

She whispered back: 'What does he mean "pissing in the wind"?'

A local Barcelona Green sitting on the other side of the gangway knew.

'Pissing in the wind? Not necessarily an environmentally unsound practice, but silly all the same. Who's been pissing in the wind?'

'We all will be if we tell the world we use illegal methods to get our information.' The Norwegian would not give up.

The pretty girl was getting the picture. 'There's a gender difference here, anatomically unavoidable. Girls tend to say spitting in the wind.'

'Spitting, I guess, is less environmentally sound . . .'

*

At the Gaudí church there were several units of the Guàrdia Urbana waiting for them, making a cordon they had to pass through, separating them from the rest of the tourists as they filtered through the turnstiles, climbed the shallow ramp to the west entrance beneath the stark image of the Crucified Christ.

'The other end is much prettier,' the Barcelona Green remarked. 'It has the Nativity, and the Mysteries of Joy.'

'Why are there so many police about?' asked the pretty girl. 'There's not been a bomb scare or something has there?'

'It's because of Sasonov. They reckon the Ukrainian Warriors of Christ are after him.'

'But he's not here yet.'

'Where is he?'

'He's arriving at the airport about now. Julia Arendt has gone to meet him.'

'Well then, that's where all the fuzz should be.'

They moved into the central area. The fantastic walls and pinnacles rose up on every side but the middle was a building site, a hole in the ground, filled with huge and noisy plant. The walks open to tourists were on boards and fenced off.

The pretty girl took Singer's arm. 'What did your hacker find out?'

'Information that links ten companies whose business is disposing of very widely differing forms of noxious waste with the Genoa bank the Mafia uses. Also that payments from accounts in that bank have been used to buy long leases on virgin forest land in the Ukraine. And on still unpolluted lakes in Lithuania. Sasonov gave us the first lead when he found out where the Swiss francs came from that had found their way into the pocket of a Ukrainian land agent.'

The police presence at the international terminal at the airport was much more serious. Patrols armed with Beretta machine pistols filtered through the arrivals area, sniffer dogs with their leads got in the way of luggage trolleys. In front of the doors to the customs and passport control it all thickened into a knot of which Julia Arendt and Captain Xavier Martín were the centre. On the periphery the television crew and its gear added its own brand of muddle.

The reporter perked up the lapels of her red suit.

'Do we have time to do a lead-in?'

The lightman looked at his watch.

'The plane should have landed – and he'll come straight through, but we can try.'

The four of them bustled about for a moment or so, getting even more in the way of police and frustrated travellers.

'Right?'

'Rolling.'

She coughed, cleared her throat, took a hand-mike from the sound man.

'The star of the Green show opening here today in Barcelona has to be Mikhail Sasonov and he's due right now off the Frankfurt plane. Sasonov was a senior forestry official in the Ukraine when democracy and the free market came to Kiev two years ago. After spending his working life locked in hopeless struggle with the old bureaucracies, a struggle on his part to save the forests of the western steppes and the Volga valley from the effects of acid rain and clear-felling, he entered politics, was elected a member of the People's Assembly. Almost immediately he made a name for himself as new enemies to his beloved forests emerged, for in less than a year it became apparent to him that free market forces menaced his beloved trees as dangerously as ever did . . . Shit, I've lost it.'

But in any case the police were pushing back in front of the doors, and the cameraman was jostled.

'We'll patch it in later. Get ready to grab him as he comes through.'

Flanked by two KGB plain clothes minders, surrounded by Guàrdias, a round podgy man of about fifty came through the swing doors, and offered a big but shy grin to everyone. He was wearing an ill-fitting suit with a virulently green tie, a small

Lenin and Red Flag enamel badge on one lapel, the Greenpeace dove on the other. Arendt folded him in her arms.

'Mikhail!'

'Julia!'

'It's so good to see you again. It really is. And so brave of you to come.' She broke out of the embrace. 'Look, I'm so sorry we've got all these police here, and I'm afraid they're going to be a nuisance – '

'But, Julia, it's all my fault. And I too have these bears with me all the time.' He took her elbow and as they walked on, leant into her with jokey confidentiality. 'They even go to the bathroom with me, and when there isn't room for us all together, like on the plane, they check it out first – it can be embarrassing, you know? At my age sometimes one is in a hurry . . . And who is this charming young lady in red? Ah, the media, I am still not used to all this sort of thing, you know?'

'Mr Sasonov, please. I'm here for Catalan TV, we'll probably make the national news too, could you spare me a moment?'

'Of course, my dear, why not? We're in no hurry, are we?'

Martín intervened.

'Two minutes. You must understand that security depends on keeping to schedules, especially when you're on the move.' He turned to the crew. 'No more, right?'

He got his men to herd the group away from the main thoroughfare and into an alcove. They formed a cordon isolating them from the ordinary travellers. The crew quickly set up their gear again, the cameraman signalled satisfaction and readiness.

'Mr Sasonov, is it true that you have brought with you evidence that western European industries are buying one hundred year leases in tracts of Ukrainian land with a view to using them for dumping industrial waste?'

'We have evidence there is an undercover operation going on, whereby shell companies, companies whose real ownership is carefully concealed, are buying land, and lakes, for such purposes. And we've linked them with other companies who are taking noxious waste from certain chemical conglomerates

143

which have recently been hard-hit by new EC legislation. And at school they taught me two and two make four.'

'Mr Sasonov, your concern demonstrates what might be interpreted as Ukrainian patriotism. Is it not odd then that the authorities believe that you might be in danger from a nationalist Ukrainian group of terrorists?'

'No, no. Not in the slightest odd. The Warriors of Christ are Catholic neo-fascist nationalists. They will do anything to gain power in the Ukraine. Certainly they will be prepared to sell themselves to international capitalist corporations, sell themselves and our country – '

But Martín was already making frantic winding-up gestures.

'Try for a goodbye,' the cameraman pleaded.

'Thank you Mikhail Sasonov, patriotic Green. Just how far the final communiqué will reflect Mr Sasonov's views . . .'

But the caravan moved on, leaving them suddenly stranded and meaningless.

'Shit. Where now?'

The soundman was already winding in coils of black line.

'Barceloneta. The Casa Pez,' he said.

In the apartment in Barceloneta Cranmer and MacTaggart, both wearing light raincoats over waiters' uniforms waited. The previous night, after the shops had closed, it had occurred to them that it was just possible the Casa Pez did not use soup tureens as large as the one they would need. Winston, who had some Spanish, had been sent out to get one. He'd been gone over an hour. For the fifth time MacTaggart assembled the shot-gun. Cranmer timed him on a stop-watch.

'Five point six seconds. That's good enough. Just. Don't fuck up on it, though.'

'I won't.' More slowly the Scot dismantled it.

The door buzzer sounded, a normal, ordinary buzz. The two men looked at each other with anxiety and MacTaggart got the gun together again in four point three, though no one was

144

timing him. Then the buzz came again, this time in the rhythm of the opening bars of 'Colonel Bogey'.

'Stupid black bastard.'

He went to the door, pulled back bolts and released the chain as the buzzer repeated the rhythm. Winston Smith came in. On his head he carried the big soup tureen they were waiting for. Picking up the rhythm of 'Colonel Bogey' he mocked drum majorette marching, flapped his long free right hand, and sang.

'Hitler has only got one ball. Goering has two but very small. Himmler is very sim'lar, and poor old Goballs has no balls at all . . .'

MacTaggart made him give up the tureen.

'It's big. But no way will we get all the plastic in it.'

'You're right. Winston, stash two kilos in that rucksack, with the spare detonator.' Cranmer looked at his watch. 'We'd better get a move on.'

He carefully placed the remaining six kilos of Semtex into the tureen, and in the middle of it the other of the two mercury tumbler detonators. Then he picked up the infra-red signaller. MacTaggart reached for it.

'Do you mind? Strict procedures. I carry the bomb, I carry the arming device, right?'

Cranmer grinned.

'Just testing.'

23

The big bus cruised down the Passeig Maritim parked behind a VW Polo close to the rear entrance of the Casa Pez. A Guàrdia who had come on board when they left the Sagrada Familia stood up and asked them to remain seated. The area had not yet been completely checked – it was obviously important that the last sweep should be made as close to their arrival as possible.

Those on the beach side of the bus looked down, many of the others stood in the gangway, leaned over them. They could see the sand sloping down to the sea littered with sun-worshippers – fewer now that Europe was back at work, mostly women. To the left the beach curved into the sea beneath gas containers and then more distant chimneys all shrouded in a haze such as Monet liked to paint in Paris and London when the rot first set in – presumably he was not then aware of its chemical composition. To the right the fish restaurants – the first being the Casa Pez. The tables on the open-air boarded area above the sand had been rearranged into a large square horse-shoe, the parasols left in place, and laid with fresh white linen, and small vases filled with red carnations trimmed with green hibiscus leaves. The pasteboard arch which made a beach side entrance now had a banner strung across it – a smaller version of the one at the station, with the Prolebentek logo. The general air of genial smartness was completed by two uniformed Guàrdias with two well-groomed dogs who sniffed and wagged their tails over the whole area. Eventually one of the Guàrdias spoke into an RT, lifted a thumb towards the bus.

'All clear,' remarked the Barcelona Green. 'No plastic under the boards.'

'No smelly plastic, anyway,' muttered the Norwegian, feeling for his pipe.

They began to de-bus, but as they did a line of Guàrdias began to move down across the sand towards the sea, and a message crackled through a loud-hailer in Spanish as well as Catalan. Most of the sun-bathers began to pull their gear together, slipped on tops, prepared to move. But some held their ground, began to argue.

Singer reacted.

'Christ, they can't do that. Julia would be furious if she could see this.'

Pushing through the Greens in front of him, he trotted down

146

to what was clearly the most confrontational group. The Barcelona Green was close behind and the pretty girl too.

The sun-worshippers – three middle-aged to elderly ladies, anorexically thin, topless, virtually bottomless, and walnut brown apart from dayglo carmine lipstick and nail polish, greeted his arrival enthusiastically.

'Look, we're very sorry, it's not our fault, we didn't want this to happen. Tell them please, translate.'

A Guàrdia pushed him in the chest, Singer pushed him back.

'Come on. These people have more right to be here than we do. It's their beach.'

The oldest of the three gripped his arm with a thin claw whose mottled wrist supported a diamanté bracelet.

'You are quite right, Herr Singer. We do indeed have more right to be here than you.' Her German was immaculate. In fact it began to dawn on him that she was German. 'But you mustn't worry, we'll move. Fifty metres did you say? That's no great sacrifice.'

One of her mates leant in, gripped Singer's upper arm.

'Tell you the truth, we just wanted to see you. See if you're as good looking in the flesh as you are on TV.'

The third chimed in.

'Not that we agree with you, not at all.'

Three bottoms, sadly wrinkled beneath the tan, framed with pink dental floss, bobbed away.

Their retreat was marked by wailing sirens and flashing blue lights: two Guàrdia Urbana cars and four outriders stormed down the Passeig, parked behind the bus. A KGB minder got out of the second, on the offside, ran round to the passenger door, doing up his jacket as he went. First the white head of Dr Arendt, then the bald one of Sasonov appeared momentarily before more minders and police moved in. The Greens who were on the beach or already in the restaurant moved back towards them. There was a sporadic salvo of clapping.

'It's Julia. And Sasonov, that is Mikhail.' Singer was always

147

quick to claim intimacy with the more charismatic leaders of the movement. 'Come on.'

But the TV crew had followed as briskly as they could on his heels. The lady in red took his elbow with one hand, with the other thrust a hand-microphone beneath his nose, urged him to the water's edge.

'You can't swim in the sea. You get spots, ulcers, sores if you do,' she said. 'Would you care to comment on that Herr Singer?'

He looked into the lens of the camera that retreated unsteadily before him. The cameraman looked likely to get his feet wet, perhaps ulcerated. But, yes, certainly Singer would like to comment.

Behind him the pretty girl took the Barcelona Green's hand.

'But we're going to eat the fish. Won't they poison us too?'

'Oh no. The sea here is dead. The fish comes from at least thirty kilometres away. And they will be well-cooked in our famous zarzuela – spiced fish stew.'

Pipe smoke billowed round them.

'The prawns are probably Norwegian,' said the Norwegian with glum satisfaction.

Behind them the tables were filling. Three waiters moved amongst them popping Cava bottles, handing out chafing dishes of scarlet prawns, orange mussels in ebony shells, sliced jamón Serrano – the mountain-cured ham which is desperately tough but much better flavoured than its Bayonne or Parma equivalents – manchego sheep's cheese and four different varieties of olives.

'What do you with the shells?' One Green asked another.

'This is Spain – you drop them on the floor. They'll be swept up sooner or later.'

Singer and his mini-entourage at last approached the bannered archway. He looked up at the Prolebentek logo.

'You know, these people may not be quite as squeaky clean as you might imagine.'

Only the Barcelona Green and the pretty girl were now close to him.

'Really?' The pretty girl injected chirpiness into the word.

'The companies we've been investigating pay them really substantial sums of money. Of course it's made to look like investment in a cleaner Europe, grants for research and so on. But we've got a feeling Prolebentek is doing more for them in return than just helping them to refurbish their image.'

'Please, please,' the Barcelona Green pleaded. 'No more of that now. If they overhear you they'll take away our lunch. And that *really* would be pissing in the wind.'

As they went through the arch the noise of excited chatter welled around them. It froze for a moment on a muffled percussion. Suddenly they were reminded of fear.

'What was that?'

'Did you hear that?'

'It was some way off. I think.'

'A car back-firing?'

But since it was apparent no one had been hurt, the chatter rose up again, louder than before.

Arendt called through it and across the space between the entrance and the middle of the centre table.

'Raul! Come here and meet Mikhail Sasonov. I've kept a place here for you.'

Singer turned to the pretty girl and the Barcelona Green.

'I'm sorry,' he said, 'but I think really I should.'

She was chirpy again, perhaps relieved.

'Of course you must, I'll see you later.'

Singer took his place between Arendt and Sasonov, the other two took the last empty chairs on the periphery. A waiter – there was now only one in evidence – filled the pretty girl's glass, emptying the Cava bottle he was holding. He shrugged, grinned at the Barcelona Green and said, in bad English: 'I go – I come back.'

And he set off across the boards, into the covered area and

the bar, through the double doors with round windows that led into the kitchen . . .

As he came through, backwards, waiter-style, a masked man, black balaclava with eye-slits, grabbed him, locked his neck and arm, twisted him so he could see a second masked man with a short-barrelled shot-gun, four kitchen staff and three waiters against and facing the far wall with their hands up, and the body of the Chef with most of his head missing. Some of it was blasted against the wall. Being a good waiter he did not drop the empty Cava bottle, but placed it carefully on a central table, before joining his colleagues.

A third intruder, unmasked, red-headed, dressed as a waiter, moved round the big pots on the stoves lifting lids, and looking in. Like the other two he was wearing surgical gloves.

The first man, the one who had grabbed the real waiter, was back at the door and peering through the round window.

'At last they're all there. In place. Shit, Kevin, get a move on. We can't hold on to this much longer.'

'Mr Cranmer, Sorr, this will do.'

It was the unmasked man who had spoken. He ladled soup into a big tureen, put a napkin over his arm, moved towards the door, which the first man held open.

'Right, Kevin. In the middle of the middle table – as planned.'

Without taking his eyes off the men he was covering with the shot-gun, and with his back to the others the third man spoke.

'You've got the signaller, haven't you?'

The man with the tureen paused, answered.

'Of course I have. In my pocket.'

'Don't hang about then.'

'Darling, I shall be right back.' The redhead mouthed a kiss over his shoulder, went through the door.

'Fucking arse-hole.'

But Winston Smith's eyes never left the backs in front of him. With Mr Cranmer in charge you did like what you was told.

*

Singer popped a prawn he had carefully peeled into his mouth, and then sucked brains and juice out of the head.

'Basically,' he said, 'we want a communiqué that spells out the fact that Western Europe is adopting a neo-colonial approach to the East – one aspect of which is the abuse of your land-space as a dumping ground for our muck.'

'Ah, but our problem in Russia is that we want to be colonised by the West.' Sasonov put a friendly plump hand on Singer's delaying the arrival of Cava at its intended destination. 'Pepsi-Cola culture still has enormous glamour for us. We got it wrong for seventy years. None of us wants to believe you got it wrong too. I don't remember seeing a waiter with red hair before.'

At some distance the pretty girl turned to the Barcelona Green.

'Is that the zarzuela?'

'I don't think so. It's usually served from a big pan, like paella.'

The red-headed man put the tureen in front of Singer and with a flourish took off the lid. Six kilos of Semtex exploded.

PART III

24

Inger Mahler watched her mother die in Schleswig. The process took a long time, most of August. She went to the hospital every day and sat at the old lady's bedside: it was a hideous business.

Before her accident Mrs Mahler lived on her own in a small chalet-style house set in a field behind low stone walls. She made her husband buy it when he retired after a life spent earning not very much as portrait painter to the burghers of Schleswig and drawing-tutor to their children, eked out with part-time work in the town *oberschule*. Deprived by retirement of anything interesting to do he quite swiftly drank himself to death. Mrs Mahler lived on for twenty years – a nuisance to her neighbours, to the Lutheran minister, and, as far as she was able, to Inger as well.

Mrs Mahler's kitchen had a floor of quarry-tiles which she washed everyday. In her seventy-ninth year, her cat walked in while the floor was still wet. Mrs Mahler went to chase the cat off the tiles, slipped, and broke her hip. There were complications. The hip had to be reset after three weeks. Told she would only ever be able to walk again with a Zimmer frame, and that in a home for people no longer able to care for themselves, she decided to die. Dying is not easy after seventy-eight years of determined living. But she managed – mainly by refusing to eat and drink. In her last hours she found the strength to push over the stand that supported the saline drip.

During these last weeks of her mother's life Inger lived in the little house. She slept in the one spare room, spent an hour every day travelling to and from the hospital in a bus, and an

155

hour in the hospital where she found that she had no more to say to her mother now than in the previous twenty or even forty years. It had never been a good relationship: for the first twenty years of her life Inger and her weak-willed but easy-going father had conspired together against the mother's tyranny and got on well enough. When her father and ally died the only escape that seemed possible was marriage – and since Inger's husband, Laura's father, turned out to be a very poor substitute for her father, that too was a disaster.

In the evenings Inger went through her father's sketch-books. Most of the work was competent and banal. There were drawings though of a thin ethereal woman, severely and spiritually beautiful, that were touching in the yearning they expressed. She guessed they represented no reality at all but the fantasies her father had woven about her mother during their courtship. There were also drawings of herself as a child, in some of which she caught a disturbing similarity between herself and her own daughter at that age.

Against this background of loneliness, boredom and anguish Inger's mind focused itself on her brief affair with Cranmer. She relived many times each day and night every moment of the few days she had known him. Sexually aroused to levels she had never previously experienced she longed for the ecstacy he had provoked, for the possession he had taken of her, for the hard, robust, but fine beauty of his body. She was not in love, not that is in any way recognised by the writers of romantic fiction or ballads. Indeed she feared and hated many aspects of the man who had so suddenly and completely come into her life: he was callous, capable of cruelty, he had shown consideration only when it was clear, after the event, that he hoped to gain something by doing so. Yet out of all this, as well as out of her experience of his body, his physique, the way he moved, the way he made love, she created for herself an image of something pure, strong, elemental, free, uncompromised by a social system she found hypocritical and shitty. She had tried to express this image in the sculpture she had completed before the phone call from her mother's doctor dragged her away; it was an image she longed to return to.

Time was heavy on her hands. She became obsessed with the idea of penetrating the mystery that surrounded him. The idea of doing so bloomed like an evil flower in her mind, waiting to be plucked, promising poison as well as revelation. She knew that if or when they came together again knowledge of the past he had broken from would give a terrible new dimension to the relationship. She had always said that she did not want to know his past, that Cranmer's glory was his newness, but she relished the thought of knowing, of not telling him she knew. It would enable her to stand back, to reserve something, to observe and be detached even at the most overwhelming moments of love-making. It would give her something of the sort of power over him, that he had over her.

It was easier than she had expected. A newspaper friend in Hamburg knew the local stringer for *The Times* of London. The stringer had a modem link to Wapping – through it she was able to read everything that had been published in the news-paper concerning the Hanover air-crash – far more than appeared in the German papers after the first day or so.

She knew he had been on the plane as a minder, a body-guard. Among the dead was listed Captain Thomas Cranmer MC, employed by the Emir as a personal bodyguard during his short business trip to Europe. Two days after the crash *The Times* published a short obituary. The Hamburg stringer, a crazed anglophile, interpreted it for her. Cranmer had been educated at a small public school, noted for the roughness with which it treated its pupils. He had gone on to Sandhurst, and then, for two years, to Cambridge University where he did a crash course in German paid for by the Ministry of Defence. He served for three years in Berlin, almost certainly doing under-cover work through The Wall (here the stringer was reading between the lines) and probably attached to one of the Special Services. Certainly during the Falklands he was seconded from his regiment, the Royal Buff Caps, to the SAS. He was decorated for killing a picket of six Argentinian soldiers sheltering from a snowstorm in a shepherd's hut. Later in the fighting he received a shrapnel wound from 'friendly' fire. In the late Eighties he served in North Ireland for two years before being given an Honourable Discharge. The stringer guessed that this probably meant he had been implementing the shoot to kill policy over-enthusiastically and the army had dumped him before a scandal broke. Married, no children. Born in 1957 he was thirty-four when he died.

Inger was not overly surprised by any of this, nor even particularly upset. If anything surprised her it was her own failure to be upset. She wondered at the strangeness of it all. She believed herself to be a compassionate person, and in her early twenties she had been a protester: against war and abuse of the environment, for civil rights, rights of 'guest workers', and so on. But she had always distanced herself from the people who organised these activities: she believed herself to be whole-heartedly committed, but she was never a joiner, she could never become a member, a part of an organisation. And now that part of her that stood aside and watched was amused that the first great physical passion of her life should be for a man from the other side – a career soldier, a man who had killed for a living.

Inger attended her mother's funeral, the only mourner apart from the paid functionaries, and caught a plane to Paris and then on to Tarbes the same day. She arrived back at her farmhouse at eleven o'clock at night after fantasising for hours that he would be there, waiting for her.

Instead she found that some of her jewellery had disappeared, and that other items were misplaced. The next day she found pearls from a missing necklace in the vestibule in front of the front door, and two more in the barn. But before that, at ten o'clock in the morning, she found Laura's message on the Leonard Cohen tape 'I'm Your Man'.

The message created a storm of contradictory emotions. At first the overriding one was anger. She had never conceived that she could feel anger like this, that anyone could. But it was undercut by guilt: she knew she had been a bad mother to Laura, that everything that was wrong about Laura could be traced back to emotional neglect from birth. Inger had not wanted Laura, had never learned to like her. She loved her in a way – they were the same flesh, there was a biological bond. Only very dimly did she realise that she had recreated with Laura the relationship that had existed between her and her own mother, though in the previous weeks this had become clearer. The point was that as a mother she had failed, and she knew it, and it had become a point of honour with her to do her best at least to pick up the pieces when Laura went badly wrong.

Which was why, sixteen months earlier, she had given up work in Schleswig and then much of her precious Pyreneean summer rescuing Laura from a heroin habit in Barcelona and concomitant prostitution. After a second sleepless night, she knew for sure that the right thing was to go to Barcelona and rescue her again. During the night she had put together a scenario based on Laura's tape: No Man (she still called him that in her head, even though she now knew his name) needed money. He had persuaded Laura to go to Barcelona and use her knowledge of the drug scene to get into it, perhaps investing the mysterious large sum he had brought back to the farm.

She did not attempt to conceal from herself that she also wanted to go there because No Man was there. That there could well be a battle between Laura and herself over him. That she would win. And at the back of it all there was a presentiment. At times she felt sure that her daughter was dead. It was a feeling she decided was irrational in one sense, easily explained in another: irrational because there was no evidence to support it, explicable because the dark side of her nature wanted Laura to be dead.

Driven by anger, guilt, jealousy, and desire, Inger went to Barcelona, arriving in the Plaça de Catalunya shortly before the bomb went off two kilometres away in Barceloneta. There were

159

two courses of action open to her. Laura's tape indicated that she and Cranmer might have shacked up in the Barri Gótic, where Laura had been the year before. She could follow that line. Or she could just go to the police and report her daughter as missing, presumed in the company of a criminal. Exhausted by the events of the previous day and sleepless nights she settled on the simpler course.

Her first view of it, as she came up from the Metro, was a disappointment. The marvellous Plaça itself with its fountains and spaces, as big as a small park, was boarded off for some sort of gigantic refurbishment – an underground car-park for the Games perhaps. But the Rambla itself on the other side of the big and busy intersection looked unchanged. She paused outside the Café Zürich, thought about taking a coffee in the warm September sun, but decided not to succumb to tourist pleasures. She was not a tourist.

She crossed, and set off quite briskly down the central reservation of the Rambla, beneath the tall plane trees. In spite of everything she was momentarily distracted by the gorgeous flower stalls with their gladioli, roses, late lilies, the first dahlias, gypsophilia and then the cages of jewelled birds. It was imposs-ible to be in the Rambla, in sunlight, without feeling something of its very particular *alegría*.

But it was a long walk all the way down to number 43, the flower and bird stalls gave way to kiosks selling porn, the shops began to lose some of the glitz and glamour of those nearer the top end. And just as the red, white and yellow flag bearing the arms of Barcelona showed through the plane tree leaves there was a sudden cacophony of noise. A high alarm bell, with an ear-shattering beat started it, but it was almost instantly followed by wailing and yelping sirens, the explosive roar of powerful motorbikes. Motorbikes, cars, vans spewed out of the squared stone entrance, blue and yellow lights whirled and flashed. And above it all a helicopter thrashed low over the trees. Horrified, she turned away, and after all found a seat in the nearest café, ordered tea with lemon.

160

When the waiter returned she asked if he knew what it was all about. He shrugged, spoke in a Spanish that was too quick for her, something about a bomb on the beach at Barceloneta. The TV programme had been interrupted by a newsflash. She decided that this was probably not the moment to persuade the Guàrdia Urbana to take much note of her story of a missing daughter on the run with a criminal: they clearly had more serious matters on their hands. In a way she was relieved, quite glad to postpone the moment: she had serious misgivings about going to the police. She would not have considered them for a moment if she could have afforded a private investigator.

25

When the bomb went off Cranmer and Smith followed the routine they'd planned for all three of them as though nothing at all had gone wrong. Smith dismantled the shot-gun and stuffed it in a hold-all. They ripped off the masks and ran out of the back exit from the Casa Pez. The car Cranmer hired in Zaragoza was parked on the kerb. He drove it fast down the Carrer Sant Carles into the Passeig Nacional and the old port, took a right, drove it into the filling station opposite the Barceloneta Metro, parked it on the forecourt. Cranmer took three bags from the boot, Smith picked up one, they crossed the road. Within three minutes of the bang they were safe in the underground. They travelled only one stop, to Jaume I, walked down Argenteria past the Caracas Café-Bar and into the Plaça Santa Maria. Within twelve minutes of the bang they were pounding up a flight of old wooden stairs to the top of a six story house in the north-east corner of the square.

On the top landing there were two doors: one large and heavy though old and pitted with woodworm, the other a simple affair of planks with an enamel black on white label – 'Toilet'. A short flight of wooden steps, little more than a ladder, climbed up to a third door, also planks, which gave access to the roof. Cranmer unlocked the Yale-type, self-locking latch on the big door, looked at his watch.

'Not bad. A minute less than I reckoned.'

Winston slung his two bags, one with the gun in it, on to a big double bed, looked around. He saw a high-ceilinged room that once might have been grand, but now there were damp marks on the ceiling, the wallpaper below the picture rail had begun to drop and someone had peeled down shards of it and left them in crumpled heaps on the uncarpeted black wood floor. The bed had an iron bedstead, a dirty russet-coloured quilt and a bolster. There were also two tables, four chairs and a large old wardrobe. In a curtained alcove a basin, a kitchen dresser and a double gas burner.

There were three windows. The middle one was larger than the others, with two wood shutters. Cranmer opened the two glass doors, folded back the shutters, pulled up the faded green blind on to a very narrow balcony with a wrought-iron rail. Warm sunshine flooded in.

At first sight the little square looked attractive. The area in front of the church was laid out with fine tile-like bricks; the church itself, Santa Maria del Mar, the church of the dockers, sailors and fishermen, had a sombre grandeur. There were three or four small and heavily pollarded trees, some of the narrow small iron balconies had trailing potted plants and others had scarlet geraniums. Many of the faded green blinds were down but draped over the balconies to create draughts as well as shade. But much of the ironwork was rusty and unpainted, stucco flaked off to reveal ancient brickwork, and the sculptured decorations of the church's façade were crumbling with sea air and pollution. Opposite there was a café-bar, the Nemesis.

Cranmer heard the chunky metal click again as Winston reassembled the shot-gun. He turned to find it was pointing at him. He was not surprised.

'I reckon you fucking shafted him.'

'No.'

'Blown into bite-size bits like a Chinese stir-fry. Fucking idiot half the time, but he understood plastic.'

'He was unlucky.'

'He knew what he was doing. The equipment was kosher. So you shafted him. Buggered if I can see how. He had the infra-red signaller all right.'

'In his pocket. Maybe he bumped into something on his way out. He did. He went through the door backwards, pushed it with his backside. He must have pressed the on button then.'

'No. He was moving all the time. It would have gone off straight away and we would all have been blown.'

Cranmer allowed his irritation to show.

'OK. It happened when he got to the table. He bumped something, someone bumped him. Now put that damned thing down and forget it. These things happen.' This was Captain Cranmer MC talking – to a Lance-Corporal. 'There are some beers under the bed. Be a good chap: knock the top off one for me and have one yourself. There are sandwiches too. Then we'll have a kip. We've got six hours . . .'

Smith did as he was told. Generally you did when Mr Cranmer was talking. Still . . . it wasn't right, it wasn't straight up some-how, but fucked if he could see the why and the how of it.

Four o'clock in the afternoon came and went before Scene of the Crime Officer Ramón Gómez of the Policia Nacional allowed them to bring in the black zip-up bags for the legs and lower bodies of Singer, Arendt and the man who had carried the bomb. Doctors and ambulance men had coped with the living and those whose death was still to come, then two concentric cordons of plastic ribbon were set up and the inner one put out of bounds to all but a team of forensic technicians and photogra-phers, masked and in sterile overalls. Their progress from the outer perimeter to the blood-splashed shattered epi-centre of the explosion was slow, meticulous and thorough, measured out by

163

the steady accumulation of hundreds of filmy plastic bindles labelled and carefully filled with samples of tissue and bone, of shards of wood, crockery, and glass, of documents ripped by the blast and doused in the blood of their owners.

Only when they had reached the centre and the last dreadful remains had been cleared did Gómez feel he could present anything like a coherent report to Teniente-Jefe Juan Estrada of the Brigada Justicial who was already in overall charge of the case. He walked over to where the large, grey man was waiting, shook a Ducados free in its pack, let Estrada's podgy short finger and thumb lift it clear, lit it for him, lit one for himself.

Estrada coughed, spat, his voice rasped.

'Right then. What's the score?'

'Eight dead, twenty-two in hospital. At least three of them are not expected to survive. Plus the Chef, found in the kitchen with his head blown off by a shot-gun blast.'

'Are they all identified? The dead I mean.'

'All but one. The man who brought out the soup tureen which blew up. It seems clear he was one of the bombers. All kitchen staff are accounted for and the delegates.'

'It could have been worse.'

They looked back over the ruined area, the shattered glass and façade of the Casa Pez. Gómez was big, dark, and, like his boss, in a suit not a uniform. However, he remained unmistakeably a policeman. He added:

'Really, it should have been worse.'

'Yes. Names?'

Gómez looked at his note-book.

'Raul Singer, German, of the Rainbow Fraction of Frankfurt, who was immediately in front of the bomb; Dr Julia Arendt, Member of the European Parliament for Brabant . . .' He stopped. Yet again they heard the sirens of approaching vehicles. This time they heralded the arrival of a big black limo with the Barcelona arms centred above the windscreen. Estrada straightened, tried to peer over the heads of ambulance men, the Guàrdia Urbana, ghoulish sightseers and reporters on the periphery.

'Don't tell me, let me guess,' he rasped. 'It's the fucking mayor?'

Gómez nodded. Silently they waited, watched as the Guàrdia Urbana saluted, and then grinned sourly at each other as the man they both hated and despised ran into trouble with their own men.

The mayor of Barcelona was a robust fifty-five, wore black-framed glasses, had thinning dark hair. He was a socialist and had a past that included beatings and imprisonment under Franco. Estrada himself had interrogated him once, back in 1972. There was no love lost between them. He got through, stormed across the littered sand, nearly tripped on a shattered bin in two shades of grey plastic with a red lining. It was a design he had chosen himself.

'Estrada, one of your men held me up.'

'He was doing his job.' Estrada chucked his Ducados, shook out another for himself and Gómez, lit them, did not offer one to the mayor. 'Strictly speaking he shouldn't have let you in at all since you're not involved in forensic procedures. What do you want?'

'I want to know how the hell you were able to let this thing happen to our guests.'

'Ask Martín. He was in charge of their safety. I'm here to find out who did it.'

'We know who did it. It was the Warriors of Christ. They've already said so. Aiming to get poor Mikhail Sasonov. How is he?'

Estrada shrugged. Gómez answered.

'In intensive care. He was wearing a vest. Not enough to save him though. He won't live.'

'That's terrible, terrible news. I take it there are road-blocks in place, the port and airport watched and so on? One of our main concerns must be the restoration of the credibility of our security procedures well before the Games open.'

165

'That's not my job. Catching crooks is.'

'These madmen. The Warriors of Christ.'

'I'm not trying to lock up a name.' Estrada was beginning to let his anger show. 'I aim to lock up people. Flesh and blood. And I'd like to be left to get on with it. What is it, Gómez?'

During all this a forensic technician had joined the group, holding a small object in a labelled bindle. He wanted to show it to Gómez, but felt he should not interrupt the mayor. Eventually he handed it to Gómez, whispered an explanation. Gómez now repeated it.

'We've got this. A finger.'

'Only one? No hands? Toes? Feet?'

'This finger is wearing a surgical glove. They think it belongs to the bomber.'

Estrada took the bindle, thrust it under the mayor's nose.

'Ah. We've made a start then. People. That's what I'm after. Flesh and blood. Take it away, Gómez, lock it up . . .'

At about the time MacTaggart's finger was taken into custody Inger summoned up courage to enter the Guàrdia Head Quarters. She had walked away from her unfinished tea with lemon, first into the pretty Plaça Reial with its palm trees and lamp-posts designed by Gaudí when he was young, then further into the Barri Gòtic before rejoining the Rambla at Plaça Boqueria – not really a square but simply a spot where four roads intersect with the Rambla but marked by a pavement mosaic designed by Miró. All this was displacement activity: she was bothered by the sight of intolerable carnage that was already appearing on the café television sets, as well as by doubts about whether or not she was doing the right thing by going to the police at all. Many forms of criminal activity did not bother her. Since first world conglomerates built empires on the backs of third world labour paid at starvation rates, and did so with the connivance of banks and governments, it seemed to her hypocritical to condemn the street thief or cat burglar. She detested the criminalisation of any sexual behaviour between consenting adults no matter how bizarre, and she had no time for a legal system that allows the sale of alcohol and nicotine to habitual abusers, with immense social damage, but jails people who trade in pot. Above all she hated the police, the corrupt guardians of a corrupt society.

However, she had seen at first hand the effects of heroin abuse, and that too here in Barcelona, and she retained the scenario she had created for herself that it was to help him trade in heroin that the man she still preferred to call No Man had brought her daughter back here.

When she finally passed through the brutal rectangle that forms the entrance to number 43 she felt instant if partial reassurance. A second glass door took her into a glazed corridor whose glass wall was set inside a perfectly proportioned and restored colonnade in Palladian style, almost entirely unornamented, but gentle and human in scale. It formed one side of a small, elegant courtyard. On the corner to her right, the corridor became a wider square space with a staircase coming down into it and a duty desk. It was all modern, clean, simple, with polished oak benches for people to wait on, and a handful of well-designed public service posters. There was no one about apart from the rather elderly police sergeant behind the counter. A plastic name plate said that he was Sergeant Arranz.

He looked up at her over half-moon spectacles as she approached, shuffled straight the paperwork he had been looking at, leaned over the counter towards her. He lacked, she decided, the weight that might be called paternal. He was like a favourite uncle. A critical voice in her ear suggested that the effect was almost certainly designed – nevertheless she was seduced, ready to talk, confide, it not actually trust.

'How can I help you?'

'Do you speak French?'

'Reasonably. We can speak French.' His voice was deep but not loud.

She explained that she wished to report a missing person, her daughter, and he agreed that she had come to the right place.

167

She took a year-old snap of Laura from her peasant weave bag. It showed her at the table in the patio at the farmhouse beneath the vine with plates and a bottle, the end of a summer dinner in front of her.

Arranz pulled out a pad of self-copying forms, took her name, Laura's name, queried the disparity in family names Mahler and Christoffersen.

'I divorced her father twelve years ago and reverted to my maiden name . . . I think she might be with this man.' And to the photograph of Laura she added a glossy black and white of Cranmer in the bull ring, holding the *cocarde* above his head. She had bought it from the office of '64', the Pau free newspaper. Her confidence that she was doing the right thing had strengthened during all this and she pushed on more quickly.

'She left a message for me. She said he's a crook, that they're coming here to Barcelona, to make enough money to last them . . . for ever.'

'Can I copy these?' He meant the pictures.

'Of course.'

He fed them into a copier, checked the copies for quality. The one of Laura came out coloured.

'Man's name?'

Her heart missed a beat.

'He calls himself Niemand. That's all I know.'

Arranz thought for a moment, and then tapped even dentures with his ball point.

'As far as we're concerned the situation's complicated by the fact the girl is over eighteen. Adults are free to go missing.'

'I doubt if my daughter will ever be fully adult.'

He shrugged, asked her to sign the top form, separated it from the copies. Then he guillotined the surplus paper from the picture copies, stapled them to the top copy. His movements were quick and precise. The questions came.

'Has your daughter ever taken drugs?'

'Yes.'

'Heroin or hashish?'

168

'Both. Others too. Amphetamines.'

'Barça is an H and H town.' He leaned across the counter again. 'You really want us to find your daughter?'

'Of course.'

But she felt a tremor of doubt. He went on, rather earnest now, voice filled with sympathy.

'If I file this under missing persons it will be dead on the file. If I put it under drugs, it will go on the computer, and officers will pay some attention. You've told me enough to make it reasonable for me to do that.'

'All right. Do that.'

Had she committed an act of betrayal?

'Where can we contact you?'

'I don't know. I've only just arrived.'

'Drop by and tell us when you have an address. Have a good stay.'

Suddenly his smile was inhuman, totally artificial, false. He handed her the yellow version of her statement which, she was horrified to see was headed 'Denuncio'. She thanked him, with an insincerity as deep as his, and walked back into the evening light of the Rambla. She felt like Judas on Saturday.

26

She still had a daughter to find, and it now seemed a matter of even greater urgency to find her before the police did. The spiteful message was stored in her head verbatim, she could retrieve it at will.

'And we're going to shack up in the Barri Gòtic, like I did before, and when he's done what he's going there to do we'll have all the money . . .'

The Barri Gòtic, the Gothic Quarter, a warren of ancient

streets and alleys between the old port and the cathedral, is sliced in two by the Via Laietana. To the west, between the Rambla and Laietana and south of the cathedral much of it has a tawdry smartness, the kitsch appeal of a barrio chino, a red-light district, with good restaurants, and awful tourist traps. To the east of Laietana it is poor and squalid, many of the tall houses empty, the alleys dark and very narrow. It was in a room east of Laietana in the Carrer Argenteria, opposite the Café-bar Caracas, that Inger had found Laura sixteen months earlier. She had been sharing a needle as well as the pad with a Romanian girl who had exchanged the horrors of life under the Ceauşescus for a scene that was different but not a whole lot better. They supported the habit by selling themselves cheap to backpackers and that way didn't get into hassles with the pros.

Inger crossed Laietana, and headed down the Carrer Argenteria, turned into the Café-bar Caracas. It was very small, very simple – a narrow room with a counter no more than three metres long. On one side three tiny tables with chairs no one used, on the other a coffee machine, cups, saucers, bottles, and a grill for making toasted sandwiches. There were three fixed stools in front of the counter. Inger sat on one of them.

A young lad, no more than thirteen, perhaps less, sat on a wooden stool in front of the coffee machine, picked his teeth.

'*¿Qué quiere?*'

The fact he spoke Castilian showed he had identified her as a foreigner. Foreigners don't bother to learn Catalan.

'*Café con leche.*'

The boy shifted into espresso coffee-making mode, steam-heated the milk.

'Is Don Pedro still here?'

'Papa? Sure. He's in the kitchen. Do you want to speak to him?'

'Please.'

He put the coffee down in front of her, went back up the narrow space, through a floppy swing door. Presently a fat grey

170

man with the lined face of a controlled alcoholic came out. The boy followed him. She asked:

'Do you remember me?'

He shrugged.

'A year ago my daughter lived in a room in the house opposite. I believe you arranged the let. She . . . had problems.'

She pushed the snap of Laura on to the counter.

Don Pedro lifted his head, scratched the stubble in the turkey folds of his throat.

'Yeah. I remember.'

'Has she been back? Have you seen her recently?'

Somewhat clumsily she pushed a folded thousand peseta note under the saucer of her cup.

'No.'

She added the photograph of Cranmer.

'If he's the guy I think he is he came in yesterday, had a coffee and a sandwich. He was looking for a room too. But I don't do that any more, so I told him no and he went.'

She felt the panic again, coupled with despair, fought them off. What had Cranmer done when Pedro turned him down? Almost certainly he had gone to another bar, asked the same question. It was the thing to do if you wanted a room in the Barri. There were no concierges, the landlords were absentee but barmen often held the keys of empty rooms or knew where they could be found. She'd just have to make up her mind to do the same.

She worked her way round the quarter in precisely the wrong way, setting off from the Caracas towards the Picasso Museum, then south into the warren of tiny, narrow alleys to the east of the Plaça Santa Maria and west of the Plaça Comercial. Frequently she felt like giving up, but she felt it would be absurd to, having started. Questioning bartenders and showing them the photographs became a steadily more unreal activity, dream-like, the sort of repeating dream you can have under an anaesthetic. But she told herself this was irrational: if she had

171

employed a private investigator this was precisely what she would have expected him to have done.

It was almost dark when she got to the Nemesis bar. It had a high curved counter with a canopy, high black square stools, five or six low tables with laminate tops and matching chairs, a quite deep and poorly lit interior. When Inger went in she found a very fat lady of about forty behind the bar, who had, in spite or because of her size, taken some trouble with the rest of her appearance: she wore an expensive-looking black silk dress, had black hair piled high and fixed with two silver-mounted combs, her hands were well manicured, the nails newly painted. Her eyes were hard and her mouth mean – it was a tough area to run a bar in. Her husband had been knifed to death five years earlier for refusing drink to a drunk.

Again Inger brought out the photographs and a thousand peseta note. She failed with the snap of Laura but at last and for the second time drew recognition of Cranmer.

'He was here yesterday, asked if I knew of rooms nearby he could rent.'

'Yes?'

'He was very precise about what he wanted. Had to be on the top floor, and no other tenant up there.'

'And?'

The fat lady put fat fingers with rings on her arm, pointed with the other hand across the square.

'The house in the corner, behind the trees.'

Five floors climbed from a large, open entry, each with three windows, the windows getting smaller towards the top.

'He rented the room on the top floor. I look after it for the landlord. He paid a month in advance. But he didn't stay. He didn't stay there last night.'

She picked up the thousand peseta note, turned, opened the till, folded it in. She turned back and her hard eyes met Inger's. Inger felt a moment of panic, simply she did not know what to do next. Then she realised, put another note on the counter.

'Is he there now?'

172

'Yes. He came in about two o'clock. Just after. He wasn't alone.'

'But not with the girl?'

'No. Another man. Looked African. But not black. Not Moroccan either . . . like an American afro.'

'Did they have anything with them?'

'Couple of bags each. Nothing much.'

There was nothing else to say, nothing else to ask. Inger ordered a coffee which she didn't want, took it to one of the tables near the back but from which she could see the entry. The panic returned. She did not know what to do. 'I think he's a crook. A fabulous real crook, like something out of . . . oh I don't know. But really wicked, wicked beyond wicked, way out in a sphere beyond wickedness, like a sort of angel.' Well, yes. May be. And the Afro too. And still no sign at all of Laura. What could she do? She was tired now, not ready for a scene, for confrontation. She'd wait. At least she'd found him.

27

Winston was still not happy when they left. On the way down the stairs he started again.

'You'd have shafted me by now. Only you need someone to cover your arse in this pick-up.'

But Cranmer was now carrying the reassembled gun in an airline bag that was long enough. He looked at the back of Winston's brightly panelled padded shell – they'd changed during their wait.

'No. I'll be covering your arse. That way you get your hands on the loot and you'll know I can't run off with it until we've shared it. Right? You can have Kevin's share too. All of it. I guess that's how he would have wanted it.'

Winston was at the bottom of the dimly-lit stairs. He turned. After a moment's thought, he assented with a grin. White teeth in the gloom.

'All right then. Shame about Kev though. He was a fucking good mate, even though he was an ignorant bastard. I expect he did bump that button.'

They passed through the door and into the square. One dull street lamp, and a red glow from the Nemesis. Cranmer could see the fat lady on the corner of her bar, up by the door. She was always there he now realised, where she could see the whole space, keep an eye on things. A weak spot, but what the hell. He didn't expect to be back.

But he had made a second mistake too without knowing it. Weise had designated the Estació Cercanias as the place where he would be paid off. Three times they had met at stations, quick meetings in busy places where people were on the move, anxious, preoccupied, not inclined to be watchful or remember who they had seen with whom. Places too where Willi could buy himself an ice-cream. So it had not occurred to Cranmer to check out this particular station. It was a surprise to find when they got there that it was in the process of being demolished. The fact was that the old station, next door to the much bigger Estació de França, was built to serve two functions: it provided the freight yards for the old port, and the terminus for the suburban lines that ran up the coast. The port had moved west, the suburban lines were closed. The whole area, including much of the Estació de França, a huge nineteenth-century glass and iron barn of a place, was being torn down and rebuilt to make way for the western approaches to the Parc de Mar.

There was high chain link fencing across the forecourt, but one or two cars were parked inside it. They followed the fence towards the Estació de França and found a gap guarded by a striped pole-barrier which was up. There was no one around to control it and they walked in. There was a modern concrete canopy in front of the two-storey nineteenth-century façade which still had faded elegance although there was no glass in the windows.

'Mr Cranmer, are you sure you got this right?'

'More than ever sure, Winston. He said platform one. That's where he'll be.'

No problem about finding platform one, the original art nouveau sign still swung awry above it though the old concertina barrier hung awkwardly from one corner like a curtain with its rail detached at one end. They walked along it, glass crunched beneath their feet. On one side there was a long curtain wall, the north side of the station. At the far end the sky, framed in a semicircle, still held a glow of daylight and they could see the last martins and swifts swirling like the midges they hunted across it. Presently they walked through the arch into the open air, but still on the low continental platform.

A huge derelict space opened out in front of them. Over to the left the hangar of the Estació de França was lit, glowed dully, but in front of them there was what looked in the fading light like a wilderness of churned-up yellow clay. Further off there were high black stacks of what could have been rail ties, and also reinforced concrete footings of new buildings, some with what would be columns ending in black fingers of steel twisted against the sky. And beyond them buildings finished or nearly finished, some of them already columns of light, others with cranes still in place: the advance posts of the fabulous development which would eventually march into Barceloneta from the east, sweep aside the Casa Pez as well as the railway station to link with the Olympic Village.

In the foreground there were small fires in front of abandoned rail and truck containers, and as their eyes got more accustomed to the darkness they realised they were looking at a small settlement of shanty-dwellers living in the steel rectangles, for the time being tolerated as the huge building projects sucked in all the cheap labour they could find.

Willi Weise came from behind one of these, and began to pick his way across the rubble towards them. He was not easy to see in his black leather jacket and black Tina Turner Foreign Affair Tour T-shirt, but one of the small fires threw him briefly into silhouette and they could see he was carrying a document case. Suddenly he stopped, still at fifty metres distance, and his voice squeaked across the space like a faultily played oboe.

'Biedermann. You've got someone with you. I expected you to be alone.'

'Well, Willi, there you are. I know you can be a touch naughty at times, so I thought I'd play safe.'

'We agreed that both of us would come alone.'

'Willi, that's tough.' Cranmer lowered his voice to a murmur. 'Right, Smith, off you go. He'll give you the case, you take it, and then move off to the side, to the right and come back. I'll be covering for you, and he knows I will.'

He let Smith get ten yards ahead, pulled the shot-gun from its bag, and followed at that distance. The Afro's dayglo bright shell jacket was easy to see. As Smith got near Weise, Weise lifted the document case, held it across his chest.

'Mr Cranmer says you're to give me the case, and then piss off fast. Right?'

Weise shifted the case so it was end on to Smith, took a step to his left to bring Cranmer into view.

'Willi, give him the case.'

He heard a mechanism click, the wrong sound, but he knew precisely what it was. He threw himself sideways and into a crouch as Weise activated the machine pistol concealed in the case. It was no more than a burp gun and the slugs sprayed wildly across both targets. Cranmer felt one rip the side of his left arm, and another screamed like a red hot needle into his right inner thigh, but in spite of the pain he fired, pumped, fired, pumped, fired and both men in front of him were down, but then the more distant one was up and moving, hobbling, clutching the pit of his stomach with both hands – he'd dropped the case.

Cranmer was after him, found the case, dropped the shot-gun. The effective accurate range of a Heckler and Koch may not be much but it's more than that of a short-barrel twelve bore. He tracked Weise to a gap between two containers where the fat man's legs finally turned to cottonwool.

Cranmer stood over him for a moment, looked down at the deathly-pale face, lit by the flickering of a nearby fire, at the narrowly-spaced piggy eyes now wide with fear and pain, at the bloody mess beneath the pink and blue lettering on black – Foreign Affair.

'Nice try, Willi.'

He knew about Heckler and Koch machine pistols in document cases. They were developed for West German police undercover agents and he had been asked to test one for the British Special Services when they came out. He knew how to alter the setting to single round without opening the case. He put the hole in the end of the case, the muzzle, against Weise's ear and pressed the catch that made it fire.

Walking was now searing pain and he could feel the warm stickiness of the blood spreading down his inside leg. He got back to where Winston had fallen, looked around, there was no sign of him, no sign at all.

'Winston? Where are you? Come on you stupid black bastard, don't fuck me about.'

No answer, but from the shadows and from the gaps between the containers expressionless black faces looked out at him – wary, menacing, waiting. After a pause he sensed the hostility, turned and limped away.

An African, really black, came out and picked up the shotgun, grinned. He was pleased, his day made for him.

It took Cranmer nearly an hour to get back to the Plaça Santa Maria – a walk of less than ten minutes. When he had to he pretended to be a drunk who had pissed himself: hence the black stain down his jeans. The climb up five flights of stairs was, almost literally, the killer.

She heard him coming – the dragging footsteps, heavy breathing, groans of pain.

177

He was still carrying a document case which she later found to be heavy and locked. His left arm hung limp, and the right side of his jeans was soaked in blood. He put the case down, struggled with his right hand to extract a key from his pocket on his left side.

'Oh shit. Bloody, bloody shit.'

He leant against the wall, and began to slip to the floor. She came out from the toilet, snapped the light on as she did so. He looked up at her, a cutout against the light.

'Laura? Oh Christ. I must be dying.'

29

For a moment this stunned her. She felt sure he thought he had seen a ghost, that therefore her presentiment was right, that Laura was dead. Then came the temptation, to walk down the stairs, leave him to die. But she couldn't, not now, not after finding him after a pursuit of twenty-four hours and hundreds of kilometres. She found the key in his pocket, got the door open, cajoled him into one last effort, back on his feet, into the room and on to the bed. There was a sharp knife in the kitchenette, no scissors, and she cut his clothes away over the wound with that. Then she washed him. The leg wound seemed the worst. Although there was some clotting it still seemed to be bleeding quite badly, especially from the exit wound just below his right buttock. It was a mess, the shredded muscle pushed out like the feathery petals of some exotic, fleshy scarlet flower with inner depths of darker reds. It frightened her, though she told herself the artery had escaped, he'd be dead by now if it hadn't, that the effort of getting there from wherever he had come had probably retarded the body's normal reactions to such trauma.

Sterile dressings? She must find something, think of something. No point in stopping the bleeding if he ended up with gangrene. The sheet on the bed beneath a large but old quilt and the cotton cover on the one bolster both looked lethal. She had the answer in her hand-bag – Tampax, she had four, all 'super'. For a moment she considered trying to get one actually into the wound on his leg, but in the end merely shredded them, made pads out of them and bound them in place with strips torn from a more or less clean shirt she found in one of the three holdalls. She found tea, sugar, condensed milk in a tube, in the kitchenette and managed to make him drink some. But none of this was enough and she knew it.

'I'm going to have to find a chemist, buy proper dressings, antiseptics, an antibiotic. Will iron pills be any use? You must have lost so much blood, a litre, two?'

She covered him with the quilt, found the key again, money.

She wasn't gone long. On Laietana she looked up and down the busy and well-lit street, it was still not ten o'clock and Barcelona goes to bed late, spotted the flashing green neon cross of a *farmacia* still open. It was a big shop, a marvellous mixture of porcelain jars and glass beakers with Latin names on, and huge modern cabinets that rolled out like the shelves in a book repository. It was manned, or rather womanned, by an extremely competent lady, short, perfectly groomed in a starchy white overall, who maintained total professionalism throughout.

Inger described the wounds, described the bleeding; the pharmacist pushed back her shelves on wheels, found dressings in sterile packets, a bottle of mercurichrome, rolls of adhesive tape. While she looked for them the thought crossed Inger's mind: lucky we're not in England, where chemists have been little more than shop-keepers for a century, and never touch anything serious without a prescription. In Spain where doctors were expensive, you could rely on pharmacists for expert advice and Hippocratic discretion too.

'He should have an antibiotic. Is he allergic to penicillin?'

'Not as far as I know.'

179

'And he should start the course with a major dose. Can you give injections?'

'Yes.'

'It should be injected – he might not hold it down if it's taken orally, and from what you've told me it is very important indeed he has an antibiotic as soon as possible. Right I'm setting you up a pack: needles, capsules with penicillin in powder form, distilled water, a three day course. You inject the water into the capsule, shake it . . .'

'I know.'

But the pharmacist insisted on explaining the whole procedure. When she had finished she looked Inger very hard, very straight in the eye.

'There must be considerable pain.'

'I think so. Yes.'

'Then you must also give this.' This time she had to unlock a cabinet built like a safe. From it she took a wrapped, prepared needle and syringe. 'One dose of morphine. Tomorrow you must rely on ordinary painkillers. The needle is for single, one time use, and should be properly disposed of. You understand?

'Yes, of course.'

She understood. She understood because of Laura, sixteen months before.

The pharmacist ended up with packets containing powders which, reconstituted, would make strong sugar and salt solutions.

'Apart from these wounds, is he in good health?'

Inger thought of his lean, muscular body, its hardness and perfect proportions, his muted overall tan and the unblemished condition of his skin – apart from the burn marks, still visible as liver-coloured patches on his back and hands.

'Very good health.'

'These only tonight. In the morning these . . .,' and she reached down jars of beef extracts, 'and a little white bread. If everything is going well by lunchtime you can try a good soup, with an egg in it, not a packet one, fish in the evening or

180

chicken. Day after tomorrow whatever he likes. No alcohol until tomorrow evening and then only a little.'

'Should I give him iron pills?'

'No. Certainly not. He'll replace the blood himself very quickly. The main short term problem is fluid loss. Long term, there could be, well almost certainly will be damage to nerves and the circulatory system, especially in the leg. Change the dressings twice a day, and call a doctor, no matter what the circumstances, if infection sets in in spite of everything. You'll lose him if you don't.'

She packed it all away in a plastic bag, accepted Visa. Inger paused at the door.

'What do you think caused these wounds?'

At last the pharmacist lost a little composure.

'You mean you don't know?'

'No.'

Perfectly plucked and pencilled eyebrows rose into semicircles.

'What you described to me are bullet wounds. Presumably small calibre or the damage would have been greater. At the moment your friend's greatest danger is shock. Shock can kill as readily as blood loss or tissue damage.'

Inger ran back.

She gave him the penicillin and morphine injections, she cleaned the wounds again and applied the dressings she had bought. It was midnight before she was through and utter weariness and despair filled her head with a black fog of unreality. Gazing down at him his honey-coloured body seemed to sway as if in a boat or on a magic carpet. She longed to lie beside him but she couldn't bring herself to accept an intimacy beyond that of a nurse – the thought of Laura with him stood between them like the ghost he had believed her to be. She pulled the quilt over him and turned away.

The four chairs in the room were all wooden and upright. She tried to sleep in one, with her head on her arms on the table that stood in front of the centre window but it was impossibly uncomfortable. At last she curled up on the floor, using her bag as a pillow. She slept for a short time a deep dreamless sleep of exhaustion, but woke weary and cold.

Inside her bag the casing of a small old-fashioned cassette player which she used to record ideas that came to her at night, or when her sketch books were not available, pressed into the side of her face. She sat up, pulled it free, let it rest on her knees for a moment.

The first pre-dawn grey light filtered through dirty glass. Outside sparrows chattered. She pressed 'play'.

The voice murmured: 'Mumsie, I'm on your bed, and I'm dressed in your jewellery. Why? Because he's done it to me three times already today, and I want him to do it again. Your hunky No Man.'

Inger turned up the volume.

'Mumsie, I bet I know a lot more about him than you do. I think he's a crook. A fabulous real crook, like something out of . . . oh I don't know. But really wicked, wicked beyond wicked, way out in a sphere beyond wickedness, like a sort of angel – '

Cranmer stirred, moaned. She pressed 'pause', listened.

'Laura?' His voice was a hoarse whisper.

She dragged herself to her feet, moved into the deeper darkness near his head.

'Yes?'

'Is that Laura?'

'Yes.'

'Then . . . this is it. I'm dead.'

She turned back to the window in anguish and pain – certain that he had killed her daughter, or been the cause of her death.

30

The TV crew, together with the small crowd that always collects when a TV camera is about to be used in the streets, were waiting for them when they arrived at the Policia Nacional Head Quarters at the top of Laietana. Gómez got out of the front passenger seat, held open the rear door of the large new Citröen in Policia Nacional livery. Estrada heaved himself on to the kerb, straightened his jacket, grunted. His pock-marked, lined face, never healthy, was the colour of old putty, and the small effort of getting out of the car had left him short of breath.

The cameraman pushed his elbow in the stomach of a woman with a shopping-bag, the soundman dangled the padded cylinder of a microphone over the steps. Estrada was ready to ignore them entirely but when he saw the tall brunette in her red suit and black stockings he paused beneath the stone canopy.

'Chief Estrada, can you give us some indication of how the investigation is going?'

'Jesus. I haven't even had my breakfast.'

'Do you think the bombers are still in Barcelona?'

'We have good descriptions of them, we know they abandoned a car and took to the Metro, so yes, we're working on the assumption they're holed up somewhere in town.'

That was enough – while he relished her sexiness he was wary of it too: he'd look a fool on the telly standing on a step gossiping with a TV tart.

'How soon before you make an arrest.'

The silliness of the question got him off the hook.

'Gómez, tell them something, then have someone get me a sandwich.'

*

He walked on past his own office on the first floor without going in. Was it only eight, nine days since he'd warned them in there? The Arendt woman, the man from Prolebentek, and that wet fart Martín from the Guàrdia Urbana – telling them that what had happened would happen.

He was heading for the Casa Pez Incident Room which had been set up three doors along in a large airy room on the corner of the building. It had a big semi-circular bay window with three frames and two more windows on each side of it. A quite grand white stone balustrade ran round the building in front of them. Nevertheless it was shabby, had not been decorated for half a century. The only picture was a large coloured photograph of the King in the uniform of General-Commandante of the Policia Nacional. It hung at the furthest end of the room above a large table covered with a green baize cloth.

The rest of the room was filled with tubular-legged tables, matching chairs, each carrying video computer terminals, modems, telephones. A team of about twenty senior detectives had been assembled, several from the Brigada Informacíon as well as the Brigada Judicial, and most of them were already there. Already the room was filled with smoke, a litter of polystyrene coffee cups and computer printout.

An explosives expert from the forensic sub-section was updating them on the work his team had done through the night. A tall, cadaverous man with sunken cheeks and long wrists that his suit cuffs could not cover, he had a flop-over board and a pointing stick, was in full flow. However everything stopped while Estrada padded through to the table, took the only chair with arms in the room, waited for a moment while the youngest detective there put a small French loaf with a French omelette for filling at his elbow and a polystyrene cup of coffee.

'At the moment I am assuming the bomb was armed by an infra-red signaller, similar to the one found in the pocket of the man who carried the tureen.' The expert's delivery was dry, precise, quick. 'Inside the tureen there would have been a mercury trembler detonator. Batteries provide an electric charge which initiates the explosion when the circuit is completed. Once the bomb is in place an infra-red signal frees a drop of mercury to move into the gap completing the circuit. This happens instantaneously, as soon as the bomb is subjected to even the tiniest movement. But until it receives the signal the bomb is unarmed and relatively harmless. This is sophisticated equipment, not easily improvised, and it requires expert handling.'

'But it killed one of them.' Estrada forced the words through his sandwich. The last word took some sandwich with it. 'Experts?'

'The only explanation is that one of the two in the kitchen used a second arming device . . . prematurely.'

'Accidentally?'

'Possibly.'

'But not likely – assuming they were experts, knew what they were doing . . . Yes?'

He was looking now at a severely attractive woman of about thirty. She had dark hair fastened in the back of her neck with a black banana clip, lieutenant's silver bars on the black shoulder strap of her white shirt, black pencil skirt. The only make-up she wore was brick-coloured lipstick precisely painted on shapely lips. Her long fingers held fax printout.

'I think you should see this straightaway.'

'You're from Información, aren't you?'

'Yes. Concepción Claret from Foreign Liaison. I speak French, Eng . . .'

'Have you read it?'

'Of course.'

'Tell.'

'Information ex UK National Identification Bureau, London, via Interpol, Lyons. The finger belonged to Kevin MacTaggart –'

The name got to him.

'Is that an Irish name? The IRA use bombs like this one.'

'I think not. Though he could be of Irish extraction.' She

185

looked back down at the printout. 'Age thirty-two, born Paisley, near Glasgow . . .'

'Not then a Ukrainian madman. Go on.'

'Criminal record: one prosecution, London, burglary using explosives, 1987, sentenced to five years, released on parole after three, parole still has a month to run and he failed to report in last week. A good record in the regular army leading to an honourable discharge after service in North Ireland . . .'

'That's an Irish connection.'

'Yes, but then he was on the side of the security forces.' She let her impatience with his interruptions show. 'His good army record was the reason for granting parole.'

'Is that all?'

'So far.'

'We want everything the Met has on him. Profiles, work career, associates, the lot. Go direct to Scotland Yard under the anti-terrorist procedures. Tell them what you like but make them move.' He slurped coffee, leant back in the chair, looked round at Gómez, the expert, the nearest detectives. 'Comments?'

Gómez offered: 'London connection with an earlier Warriors of Christ attempt. That was a car-bomb that also went off too soon.'

'I don't like it,' the expert was sceptical. 'The London car-bomb initiator was an amateur device that could easily go wrong and did. It was similar to the one used in Leipzig. But this one was a professional device that went off prematurely because the man on the button pressed it too soon.'

'They must have wanted to blow MacTaggart to bits.'

'I think so.'

'But smaller bits than they did.' He rasped a laugh, thinking of the finger that had set things moving. Then he frowned. 'We're speculating too much. Not enough hard facts. We're meant to be narrowing the frame, at least defining it. Give me something real.'

One of the detectives flipped a page in his note-book.

'One of the Casa Pez waiters knows a little English. The

bombers spoke very little to each other, but according to this waiter they spoke English.'

'Jesus. What did they say to each other?'

'He doesn't know. It just sounded like English to him.'

'And you let it go at that? Dickhead.' Estrada slapped his own forehead in a Spanish gesture of frustration. 'Get someone who really knows English. Do we have anyone who knows English really well?'

'Lieutenant Claret,' said Gómez.

Estrada stood, looked down the room. The woman lieutenant was at her desk in one of the windows, keying in his requests to London.

'Conchee!' he bellowed, using the standard abbreviation of María de la Concepción Immaculada. She ignored him. 'Shit. Lieutenant Claret. Oh, what the hell.' He turned back to the detective. 'Go get the waiter back up here. And when he's here interview him with Claret, and get her to transcribe whatever he heard the bombers say – if he can't identify the words then a transcription of the sounds . . . are you following me?'

The detective nodded assent.

'And then ask her to put the meanings on.' He stuffed the last mouthful of sandwich into his mouth, washed it down with the end of the coffee, looked around. 'Well, none of that's a bad start at all. Right. What's next?'

Winckelmann, fat and evil, lane-swam in his swimming-pool, a gentle breast-stroke. Presently his personal servant, male and sharp, helped him out, wrapped him in a bathrobe as white as the fresh snow on the peaks on the far side of the Grieffenzee, as white as the clouds above them. Winckelmann pulled off his rubber cap, which was all he had been wearing, sank into a seat at a pool-side table laid for breakfast. The personal servant made a minor adjustment to the sun-shade, checked the table, poured coffee and cream from silver.

'Herr Herz?' he murmured.

'I'll see him now.' Winckelmann broke a roll, savoured the

187

fresh bakery smell, spread butter – the best. He savoured too one of the more expensive views in the world: the steep wooded shore, with just a thin scattering of villas all as secluded, as well-protected and as luxurious as his own, the sapphire blue of the lake, the mountains beyond. It's not easy to amass the sort of fortune which allows one to live in such places without occasionally paying people to break the law on one's behalf. Herz and his firm AlterLog – Alternative Logic – were the means Winckelmann most often resorted to when it became necessary.

The personal servant returned with Herz in tow, held out a chair for him, saw him seated, withdrew.

'You have had breakfast? The details then.'

Herz cleared his throat, tapped the short strong thumb and fingers of his left hand with the index finger of the right.

'Sasonov. Arendt. Singer. The three Greens who had specific knowledge or suspicions about the Ukrainian connection. And the other two you weren't fond of.'

'The newspaper says three more Greens, all important ones. And two likely to die.'

'A bonus. No extra charge.'

'No extra charge!' Winckelmann's laugh was throaty and prolonged. 'That's good, that's very good. And last night Willi tidied up Biedermann?'

There was no mistaking the subtle shift in Herz's posture and expression. Winckelmann's change of mood was abrupt.

'No? So what went wrong?'

'Only one of Biedermann's associates was killed in the bomb blast. That's what the newspapers say. So the black man escaped with Biedermann. Willi didn't know that. He thought he was dealing with just Biedermann on his own.'

'And . . .?'

'Willi's not been seen since. Apparently he was with Negrín at the Barcelona office of Prolebentek when the news of the explosion came in. He sent Negrín out for food, McDonalds, that sort of thing. Then went to sleep on the office sofa. Negrín

188

woke him at half past seven. He had a shower, checked out the
document case, left at eight. Negrín locked up the office and
went home. Willi was meant to phone me at nine, confirm that
it had all gone off all right. He didn't.'

'And that's it? Nothing more?'

'Nothing.'

Winckelmann leant back, pushed a crumpled napkin on the
table. Sunlight reflected from the pool played over his pink
jowls. Briefly he poked the nail of his little finger between two
teeth, dislodged a flake of crust.

'All right. So what happened?'

'Willi got himself killed.'

'So what are you going to do now?'

'Nothing. Wait.'

Herz looked out over the lake. A speedboat with a water skier
cut a cicatrice out of the blue, but it healed instantly, as if it had
never been there. Willi Weise, gofer to the gofers of the rich,
had cultivated anonymity, moved under three aliases, had no
fixed address, was like that vanishing white scar. The space he
had occupied would close in as if he had never existed.

'That's crazy.'

'Biedermann will surface. He wants his money, and he'll
want a guarantee we leave him alone. We'll deal with him when
he does.'

'You've got to be more clever than that. If we wait, he'll
surface with something clever. No. He must be found. Listen.
You contacted Wolf-hound? I told you to.'

'Yes.'

'And?'

'You're not going to believe this. And you're not going to like
it either.' No comment, and he didn't expect one – yet. Herz
continued. 'Finchley-Camden, the Britisher who runs it, claims
he knows nothing about it at all. He says he didn't like the
proposal we had made, but he stalled, didn't want to offend us
with an outright refusal. Told his secretary that he was out if

189

ever I called through until he went on his summer holidays. And he was.'

'But Biedermann contacted you. Said he was doing so because Wolf-hound had asked him to.'

'Yes.'

Winckelmann thought it through. Though he was angry and disturbed his mind was keen and quick.

'Either Finchley-Camden is lying, or his security is rubbish – Biedermann knew we had gone to Wolf-hound and what for. Or your security is rubbish. Which?'

'My security is foolproof. I've been working for you long enough for you to know that, you've checked it out yourself. And Biedermann is English, Willi and I were sure of that. Though he spoke good German he had an English accent, and manner. You know what they're like – the British junker-class. Arrogant bastards. Finally when I spoke to Finchley-Camden, who is very much one of the same breed, there was a point when he began to understand what had happened, how Biedermann might have breached his security.'

'But he said nothing.'

'Of course not.'

Winckelmann took longer this time. He did not rush into decisions unless he had to. He slumped back in his chair and slowly let his big broad hand caress his forehead, descend over closed eyes, close over his cheekbones, and end holding his weasely nose between thumb and forefinger. He did this two or three times.

Herz waited, his gaze back on the lake, on the speedboat and water skier. All very well to think that the official Weise would disappear, the documented Willi, without anyone wondering or worrying about what had happened to him – but the corporeal Willi might still turn up. Almost certainly would. Something to deal with when it happened. Certainly not something to bother his client with right now. Winckelmann grunted, Herz turned back. Winckelmann was sitting up again, his eyes sharp and hard.

190

'You are wrong, you know. To recommend we wait for Biedermann to come out, show himself. He won't until he knows he has the advantage. We must find him, get to him before he is ready for us. And the only line we have on that is this Finchley-Camden. He must know who Biedermann really is, what his name is, where he can be found, where his probable hideout is.'

'I doubt he'll co-operate.'

'Make him. We know enough about his operation to embarrass him.'

'Herr Winckelmann, I really don't want to do this. It exposes us further, we shall be giving hostages to fortune. I think it will be a mistake – '

But once Winckelmann had made a decision he was immovable. Moreover Herz's report had distressed him far more than he had let on. He was worried and angry that so much had gone awry: Weise's disappearance, Biedermann's and his black associate's, and this confusion with Wolf-hound.

He let it show now. He tipped the coffee pot so it spilled into Herz's lap. Herz didn't move.

'That was a mistake. Let's not make any more. Do it.'

31

'It's less numb and I can move my thumb.'

Morning now, broad daylight. Half a mile away Estrada was starting his second cup of coffee and six hundred miles away Claret's requests for details about MacTaggart were hitting a fax machine in the intelligence room at New Scotland Yard. By the Grieffenzee Herz reached for a napkin. Cranmer was propped up on the bolster in the centre of the bed, naked apart from the dressings. His left arm was strapped to his side to the elbow, and the forearm bent across his chest. Inger had just finished dressing it for the second time with the proper dressings.

'So the nerve is all right after all?'

'I think so.'

Inger came out from behind the screened alcove, drying her hands. She looked down at him – her tired face empty of all expression.

'Good. You were lucky. Torn muscle, chipped bone possibly cracked but not a proper break – I might not have to send you to hospital after all.' She sat on the middle of the bed. 'That is if the leg is all right. Let's have a look at it. You'll have to spread your legs a bit, and if you can, shift on to your right side.'

She began to undo the dressing on his thigh, exposed the entry wound. Already it all looked a lot less horrifying. The bullet had really no more than clipped the inside back of his leg, the fleshiest part, passing through skin and muscle about an inch and a half thick. She began to clean it with swabs and mercurichrome. He winced frequently, grunted once or twice and she could see how his good arm clenched the bolster by his head, clenched and relaxed, clenched again. But she felt nothing for him, for his pain. Emotionally drained and exhausted now, she could not withstand the hammering question that beat obsessively in her inner ear. She gave in to it.

'Where's Laura?'

'I don't know.'

Believing it helped to tell whether or not a person is lying if you can see his eyes, she glanced up at his. They were shut.

'When you came back last night, when you saw me, you thought I was Laura. Did she come here with you?'

'No. I left her . . . at your farm.'

She worked on for a moment, then stood, went back to the alcove for adhesive tape and the knife, cursed herself for about the tenth time for not buying scissors at the pharmacist. She cut strips the lengths she thought she would need, stuck them on the iron bedstead rail, tore a dressing out of its packet.

'When you came back you had money. Stolen?'

'Not exactly.' His voice was alert now.

She taped the dressing over the entry wound.

'Turn over and let's look at the other side. Oh dear. That looks like an infection in spite of the penicillin.'

More swabs and mercurichrome. This time the grunt of pain was nearly a shout, and she felt the muscle clamp and give, clamp and give in some sort of mini-spasm.

'But the money did come from . . . something against the law, criminal.'

He shifted his shoulder, but kept his eyes closed, screwed up, perhaps because of the pain.

'How do you know all this? How did you know where to find me?'

'Wait. I'll tell you when I've finished.' She worked on. 'This is going to leave a nasty mess when it heals. Like the one on your front, under your ribs.'

'That was shrapnel. What you're looking at is an exit wound.'

She taped a new dressing over it, cleared away the stuff she'd been using into the kitchenette alcove, came back, swung one of the rush-bottomed chairs into his bedside (the rushes collapsing out of the bottom but they held for her) shook a BN out of a pack, lit it, gave it to him, took it back, made it her own as well as his. BN's were the nearest she'd been able to find in Spain to the Gauloises Lights she preferred.

'How did I know all this? I'll tell you. She left me this. It was in the player beside my bed.'

She took a cassette from her bag, tossed it on to the quilt.

He picked it up, looked at it. The label, hand-written, still said – Leonard Cohen: 'I'm Your Man'.

'Can you play it, now?'

'Yes.'

She pulled out the player, slotted in the cassette, pressed a button.

'Mumsie. This is just to tell you that you won't see your No Man again. He's mine now. When he came back he had lots of

193

money, and he's taking me to Barcelona to do another big job and then we'll be rich for ever. I'll be his guide there, show him where I lived . . .'

Inger pressed stop, killed her daughter's voice.

'No need to hear the rest. She says you're wicked. That you're about to make a lot of money here. And there's spiteful stuff about me too.'

Cranmer heaved himself on to his back, opened his eyes. For a long moment they stared into each other. The twisted smile came and went.

'She tells lies.'

'I know. She always did. But go on.'

'I came back from Paris, with money. I have information that people believe died with me. They'll pay for it. Or they'll kill me because of it. In Paris they paid. Here they tried to kill.'

She picked up the cigarette, drew on it.

'None of that is my business. But I do want to know what you've done with my daughter. I think you killed her. I know she's dead.'

'You know.'

And at that moment she knew too. He had not questioned her assertion – how could he? At that moment he believed she had found Laura's grave. But she was not yet ready, not by a long way, to believe what she knew. She needed to give him a way out, opportunities for explanation, denial, excuses even. She was too tired to cope with her daughter's death, a death she must, however obliquely, have had a hand in; unable too to allow that this wounded god in front of her had done it.

'Are you still in pain?'

'Nothing I can't handle.'

'So no more pain-killers.'

'No.'

'Right. So now you can tell me why you killed my daughter.'

He closed his eyes again, turned onto his side, away from her, grunting with pain as he did so.

'I did not kill your daughter.'

194

'I know she's dead. I don't want to believe it, but I know.' She got up, moved about the room, touched things, looked at the mess. The thought was irresistible: it needed cleaning. She would have to clean it. 'So tell me what happened.'

'We met. At your farm. It was . . . OK – for a time. But she drank too much, took speed, we quarrelled. I left her with some money. Quite a lot. That's all. As far as I know she went back to Biarritz with it.'

In the howling rain he looked down at Laura, naked but for her paint and the gold chains and the beads that had not snapped, and he pushed wet earth on to her breasts, her stomach and her sex. From a great distance he heard her mother's voice.

'Oh shit. All that sounds likely enough. And if it's true then she'll turn up when she's spent it.'

He knew that for the time being it was all right. She had not found the grave. The voice went on.

'Make me believe it. Make me believe you're telling the truth.'

It sounded more like a command than a plea. And he was satisfied with that. He slept.

32

That Tuesday afternoon, at about half past one Spanish time and European time, half past twelve British Summer Time, printout began to appear in the Incident Room – ex-New Scotland Yard, London. Claret collected it as it came, tore off the sheets, ran through it all with a pen and a dictionary. By a quarter past two she was about ready to report, took it all to Gómez at the green baize table. The room was now almost empty – only three detectives were in, playing cards with a

Spanish pack. The rest were out, combing the area around the Casa Pez for the second day running, following up reported sightings of two men, one Afro, generally making a nuisance of themselves and resenting the fact that they were. Almost everyone now believed that the bombers were away: back to North Ireland, the Basque country, wherever. Perhaps even the Ukraine.

'Where's the Chief? He ought to see this.'

Gómez looked up from the sports pages of *El Periodico*.

'Over at the Town Hall. The mayor wanted a progress report. He could be back by now. What is it?'

'More stuff on MacTaggart. It looks good.'

The telephone on the table buzzed. Gómez answered it, looked up at Claret, covered the mouthpiece.

'He's back. If there's anything important he wants it now.'

'Tell him I'm coming.'

She paused at her desk for a quick glance in her pocket mirror, was entirely satisfied with what she saw, clicked on low heels down to the door, out into the corridor, tapped briskly on the frosted glass – making a point of rapping her index knuckle on the 'J' of 'Juan'.

She heard him bellow: 'Come!' and she went in.

Estrada's uniform shirt, jacket, tie were untidily hung from a coat hanger suspended from the filing cabinet. The inner toilet flushed, a tap ran. She wondered whether or not she should sit down on the chair in front of the shabby, cluttered desk, had decided that she might as well when he called out.

'Who is it?'

'Lieutenant Claret.'

'Conchi.'

Estrada appeared in the wash-room doorway. He was naked to the waist, rubbing his armpits with a towel. Fat, hairy, pasty – not a pretty sight.

'Bastard mayor. Press conference. Wanted me in uniform. Fucking waste of time.'

He threw down the towel, pulled on a stained T-shirt

196

decorated with 'Cobi' – the Barcelona Games mascot, a sort of dog-like creature *sui generis*. He sat in his chair, shook a Ducados out of a pack, lit it, put it carefully on an ash-tray. Bending to a drawer on his side of the desk he found a glass, a bottle of Osborne Brandy, poured half a tumbler, drank.

'Wash the taste of shit out of my mouth.'

The exchanges that followed were fast – two antagonistic people scoring off each other.

'We've got a lot more on Kevin MacTaggart.'

'You've read it?'

'Of course.'

'Tell.'

'Ex the British Police National Computer, Hendon. Direct.' She pushed one sheet of printout out of the way, crossed her legs, put the sheaf on her knee. 'MacTaggart joined army cadets at sixteen, full-time army at eighteen, served in the Royal Buff Caps.'

'I remember them,' Estrada drank a little more, leant back in his old wooden backed swivel chair, pulled on his Ducados. 'They were in Gibraltar.'

'He was seconded to the Special Air Service in 1981 and served behind the lines in the Falklands Conflict . . .'

'The what?' Scoring a point.

'Las Malvinas.' Mentally she kicked herself, she'd just read the words off the printout, had forgotten to translate them. She pulled in a breath tried to steady herself, but the smell of the cheap tobacco and the brandy were getting to her.

'Then North Ireland. Honourable discharge, two years early, three years ago.'

She looked up.

'I'd like to find out more about that,' she said. 'Early discharge, even honourable, needs to be explained.'

She went back to the printout.

'Then the safe-blowing charge. He used plastic that may have been stolen from an IRA cache, discovered by the British army. And that's it for actual bio. But there is a psychologist's report . . .'

'Garbage. Sure to be. And as for the rest it doesn't add up to a monkey's fart of an advance on what we've already got.'

Did he mean it? Or was he trying to needle her? Or both – using the one as an excuse to do the other. Nevertheless she stayed cool.

'I think you ought to hear the psychologist's report. My digest of it anyway.'

'I've nothing to do all day but drink brandy and smoke.'

That's what he did. She sighed, let her expression show as much dumb disrespect as she dared, rattled her printout.

'At school MacTaggart was always in trouble until he found a role model in an older boy. Then he did well. Ditto in the army – wouldn't settle until he found an older man he could respect, could obey without damaging his own self-image.'

'Like I said.' Estrada's laugh crackled round the phlegm in his throat. 'Garbage. Never read a psychologist's report without finding a dirty mind had written it.'

Taking the printout in one hand only, she recrossed her legs, smoothed her skirt.

'I beg your pardon. Dirty mind?'

'Older boy, older man. The message is clear. He thinks MacTaggart's a rent-boy.'

'That's not what he's getting at.'

'No? Please yourself. Is that it then?'

She hesitated. Strictly speaking it was not her job to interpret the significance of what she had told him. She prepared to go.

'Well yes.'

But something in her manner was a warning, and Estrada remembered that he'd given her another job too.

'What about the waiter who knows English?' He came forward on the swivel chair, put his elbows on the desk. 'But he doesn't know any English, at all really, does he?' He tried three words himself, with satirical intent. '"That'll do nicely" to AmEx cards.'

She'd had enough, came back to the desk, put her hands on it only inches from his elbows, leaned into him. A face as severely pure as Athene's looked into a morass – Silenus on a bad day.

'Listen, Señor. I don't have to put up with this. I think I have something here. Either you let me spell it out, or I file it so it's on the record, and I remember it when I'm proved right. OK?'

There was a long pause, then he thrust himself and the chair back with a sudden violent movement. His bloodshot eyes were hard, very angry.

'If a lieutenant with balls spoke like that to me, I'd smash his head in. Then I'd listen to him. Go on.'

'Right.' She got her breathing under control, hoped that the flush that she felt sweep up her neck was not too visible, sat down again and smoothed out the printout. But she didn't look at it.

'MacTaggart functioned well under orders from someone he had learnt to respect. At one point in the Casa Pez kitchen, he came to attention, like a soldier, and said, to the taller man, in English, 'Meester Kramer, Sir!'

'And what the fuck is that supposed to mean?'

Claret spelled it out slowly as if to a child.

'I think it means that in the past the older man, the man who had MacTaggart's respect, for whom he functioned well, had been his commanding officer in the army.'

33

At about a quarter to three in the afternoon direct sunlight edged under the lintels of the tall windows and a bar of sunlight fell across the floor beneath them. Almost immediately the old room felt a touch warmer, brighter. Already it was cleaner since Inger had swept out the torn wallpaper, cleared away the fallen plaster and other rubbish. She opened the central window, pushed a chair into the sunlight so two of its legs were on the tiny narrow balcony, two still in the room. She sat on it, looked out, over and down into the little square. At this time of day it looked less squalid, almost picturesque. A small cascade of purple flowers dripped from a nearby balcony and the sun drew from them an almondy, frangipane scent. From where she was she could just see the façade of the church. On the lintel above the west door there was a jolly statuette of the Virgin, Romanesque, almost primitive, and it cheered her whenever she saw it.

She tilted the chair back so her head rested against the wooden window frame, closed her eyes, turned her face to the sun, and her eyelids filled her brain with bright warm smooth vermilion. She let her thighs fall wide, left her hands relaxed on them, palms turned up, accepting the warmth. Bird-song, a liquid trickle of silver sound, cajoled her ear – she did not know it came from a caged goldfinch, would have enjoyed it not at all if she had. The almondy fragrance filled her nostrils, and presently she slept.

He woke her sharply with a shout, it sounded like a warning: 'Look out' very abrupt, a command as well as a warning. The front legs of the chair thudded beneath her, and she sat up, head turned, still in the sunlight.

'What is it?'

His head twisted on the bolster for a moment and she could see he was flushed, hot. Her own neck hurt, was stiff, and she rubbed it with her long fingers. Then he opened his eyes – for a moment they were blank, then wary, finally the twisted grin came.

'I need a piss.'

'Can you manage? I could . . . arrange for you . . . not to get up. If you can't.'

'I'll manage. Give me a hand though.'

She left her chair, stood over him as he swung his strong legs over the edge of the bed. He paused for a moment, then gritted his teeth and pushed down. She caught his elbow as he came up, was ready to take his weight, but he needed her only to keep his balance.

He had an erection, the glans moist and pink pushing through the foreskin. The sight of it momentarily took her by storm, made her melt.

'Here. Put the quilt round you. You're hot, you mustn't get cold.'

She draped it over his shoulders. It was big, faded red, but not very thick, and it fell about him like a mantle. She recalled for a slow second a German painting, Renaissance, the *Mockery of Christ*; then he let a little weight fall on to her arm, and began to make it step by step to the door.

'It's not so bad. Not as bad as I thought.'

She reached for the latch, but his hand was there first, turned the knob. He frowned.

'Put the catch on. Always. It's not difficult to get these things open from the outside if the catch isn't on. There's a bolt too.'

She was irritated by this assumption of authority.

She waited on the landing, heard him urinate. When he came out of the tiny toilet, she had cleaned that too, the erection had gone.

'Back to bed. I think you've got a fever. It must be the infection.'

'No.'

'Please.'

'No. I just got hot under this thing. The window. I'd like to sit in the window. At the table. I'm sick of the bed.'

'All right.'

She shrugged, went ahead of him, pulled out a second chair so he could sit at the solid deal table, facing the chair she had been on. She didn't sit down again, but stayed standing, her hands clenched on the back of her chair. She had been disturbed, quite badly disturbed by the sight of his erection, by the nakedness of his legs. Desire was a fuse – for a sudden, hot helpless anger that almost overwhelmed her.

'I want to know all about it. About you and Laura.'

201

He was surprised, his dark eyebrows met for a moment, quizzing her.

'Why? What's the point?'

'You don't understand how hurt I am. I hated you when you left. So suddenly, without warning. But I knew you'd come back. I knew it had been good for you too. And then I came back . . . Hoping you'd be there. And then, I found you had been there, and that . . . slut, that worthless bitch had . . . Oh shit. What happened? Was she there when you arrived?'

'Yes.' He was coiled now, fists clenched, ready to strike if she attacked him.

'And how long did it take before . . . before you were fucking?' She was deliberately lacerating herself, forcing herself to imagine the worst so she could not be further damaged when she discovered the truth. 'Ten minutes? Five? Where? On my bed? Our bed?'

Outside, across the square, a small metal wheel squealed between the metal jaws that held it. Head up, she looked across. An old woman, white hair scraped to a bun, face walnut brown, walnut wrinkled, short and dumpy in black, wound in washing, felt it, wound it out again. The anger burnt itself out. Shaking she turned away, fumbled for a cigarette, lit it, swiftly smoked nearly half.

'You read my letter? The one I left for you at the farm?'

'Yes.'

'So you know why I went away.'

'Your mother . . . was ill?'

'My mother died.' She pushed the smoke into the sunbeams, it settled in banks of blue about her head. 'Because of a fall.'

'I'm sorry. I am sorry.'

'Well. You have to say that. One is meant to. But there's no need. She was old and unhappy. Why? Because there was nothing real left in her life at all. She had lost relevance. Unlike the old woman opposite she had no one to wash for. She would have died years ago if she could.'

'Anyone can die.'

202

'Not if they're afraid to.'

Because he sensed she wanted the conversation to go on, he cast about for something else to say.

'Still. You must miss her.'

'In a way. There's a gap, like a tooth that's gone. But the tooth hurt.'

She turned, rested her back against the window jamb, faced him across the room with her arms folded across her chest, the cigarette still between the fingers of her right hand above the watery glow of the pale amethyst ring. She was wearing a brown and black blouse printed with muted orange flowers with big floppy sleeves, a dark skirt of fine wool to below her knees, thonged sandals. Her long dark hair was looped loosely up above her ears and pinned.

'Do you know what parents do to you?'

The expression on his lean face hardened, she could see the sinews in his cheeks and neck go tense.

'Yes. You know.' She breathed in smoke and her voice went higher as she let it out, the words came quicker. 'One way or another they fuck you up. With me it was guilt, from the moment I was born. Guilty for waking her up in the night, guilty for soiling the clean nappy just after she'd changed it, guilty for having teeth, guilty for wanting things she said they couldn't afford, for having needs and desires she couldn't cope with. Then guilty, later, for marrying, guilty for divorcing, guilty for neglecting her. Everything I should feel grateful to my mother for is blighted by that guilt. And, too, every reason I might have for mourning her now she is dead. And of course I feel guilty because I can't. And finally – the worst of all. I know I reproduced the same pattern with Laura.'

She dabbed the cigarette end on the blackened brick work, considered letting it drop five stories to the cracked paving below, thought better of it, lobbed it to the bin where she had put the syringes.

'I didn't come here to find you. I came here to find Laura. Last time she was here she got hooked on junk and sold herself cheap to backpackers, American and Australian, to pay for it. She said, on that tape, she was coming here to make a lot of money, that you're a criminal. So. I suppose you were going to use her to find your way round the drug trade here – '

'But she didn't come here. I've not seen her since I . . . kicked her out of your house.'

'So you say.' The weariness felt like an old and dirty Afghan coat. 'Well. If that's the case, I ought to go back to the farmhouse and find her. I've done all I can for you. All I want to do for you. It's time I paid off some of what I owe her.'

He looked up now, suddenly believing her, believing she was planning to go.

'You go on about her all the time. Why? Forget her. She doesn't need you.'

She cried back at him:

'Because she's dead? Because you killed her?'

'No.' He was angry now, but there was something theatrical in the way he showed it, over the top. 'Because she's a cunt, a bitch. Not worth the time you spend on her, spend worrying about her.'

She caught the tone, threw it back at him.

'Oh yes? How long did you spend with her? Two, three days? You got to know her well, didn't you? In all of three days.'

'Yes, yes I did. Well enough.'

She looked down at him, he held her eyes, both struggled with feelings that were confused and conflicting. Then she turned away.

'Anyway. She needs me. I'm going. I'll go out and get you some food first. Then I'm going.'

But a question hung in the air, a hint that she might respond to an appeal to stay. His lip twisted.

'You could give me a cigarette before you go.'

'I am sorry.' She managed a small laugh. 'That was thoughtless of me.'

She lit one, handed it to him. He seized her wrist, but gently, held on, made her keep her face close to his.

204

'Can we have a decent meal before you leave? Fish and some wine. Like we had at your farmhouse, after the bullring thing?'

Her breath went again and again inside she melted. Tears startled her through the weariness.

'No Man, you really are a bastard. But grade A. A solid gold bastard.'

He let her go, and she moved about, found money, her big peasant-weave bag, pushed a comb through her hair and pinned back a lock that had fallen. He watched.

'I'm off. Shall I take the key?'

'No. Leave it. Just pull the door to. I'll let you in when you come back.'

Cranmer stood by the window and watched the square until she had crossed it. Five minutes later, long enough to be sure she was not coming back for anything she might have forgotten (plastic, money, whatever), he made it to the door, engaged the latch, threw the bolt. Then he pulled the Heckler and Koch in its document case from the wardrobe, and began to check it out. There were two spare magazines and he slotted one on to the machine-pistol in place of the one Weise had almost used up. When he had finished, had satisfied himself again that he had remembered all he needed to know about how it worked, he put it all away, and readjusted the combinations on the locks. These acted as safety catches – the pistol would not fire until they'd been turned to the right numbers.

He smiled grimly as he did all this, recalling the history that lay behind the weapon. They had been made for undercover agents of the West German Polizei but withdrawn following a report in *Der Spiegel* and protests from liberals and lefties. Market forces demanded they be sold to someone, and it was inevitable that if the police were not to have them, then the other side would.

34

Inger made the fifteen minute walk through the *barri* across Laietana, into the Plaça Reial and so out on to the Rambla. She walked up to the Mercat La Boqueria, close to the Plaça with the pavement mosaic by Miró. The market was one of her most favourite places in Barcelona – a huge hangar of black steel and glass put together with an elegance that looked towards Modernism rather than back to the nineteenth century out of which it had come. It was filled with hundreds of stalls and shops selling, one would think from the profusion of items on sale, every foodstuff in the world – certainly everything Catalan, and most things Spanish. And all arranged with an eye for colour, contrast and design that wooed the eye as seductively as the brightest Picassos. Of course many of the stalls had not reopened after the midday break, but there was still no shortage of choice. She was only limited by the thought that she was shopping for two only and for an evening meal and a breakfast, and that she had a good fifteen minutes walk to complete once she had loaded herself up.

She did well. She bought thin sliced mountain-cured ham, tough, dark and rich, thinking he needed the richness; a cooked lobster; a bottle of Cordoniu Cava; and a good brandy, bread, and everything one puts in a classic Spanish salad – lettuce, onion, cucumber, tomato, oil, lemon, olives scooped from barrels, fat, plump and garlicky, black and green.

Back out on the Rambla she took a right, thinking to head to the next intersection, the Carrer de Ferran, and her easiest route back to the other side of the Barri Gòtic.

'Frau Mahler.'

A voice almost in her ear, speciously avuncular. Her heart

missed a beat, she looked up into the face of Sergeant Arranz. It was a moment before she remembered who he was. He was wearing a dark padded jacket over jeans, both garments over-filled and sitting slightly incongruously on a man of over fifty. Probably she would not have recognised him at all if he had not been chatting to a patrol, one man, one woman, of Guàrdia Urbana. They were wearing the uniforms he had been in when she went to 43 Rambles, a hundred metres or so further down the avenue.

'You never came back to us with your address. Suppose we had found your daughter?'

'I really should have told you . . .' She felt first confused, then angry. Anger was almost always her reaction when a policeman spoke to her.

'Told us what, Mrs Mahler?'

'My address and . . .'

'Did you find the man your daughter was supposed to be with?'

It was a way out of what had become an embarrassing and possibly dangerous conundrum.

'Yes. I found him. And he told me that Laura never came to Barcelona after all.'

'So why are we looking for her?'

She shrugged weakly and walked on down the Rambla. Arranz watched her for a moment and then followed her. When she turned left into Carrer de Ferran he considered for a moment whether or not he should too. He did not – because there was only the smell of something wrong about her, nothing definite, and because he had only just come off duty after a hard shift. He made the compromise, went back down the Rambla to 43.

Martín was at his desk, lit by a single desk light, a pen in one hand, a bottle of Fanta at his elbow, catching up on the paperwork the Casa Pez bomb had created.

'Andreu. Hi. What can I do for you? I thought you'd gone home.'

'Have you got a moment?'

'When I'm up to my ears in this shit, yes.'

'Can I use the computer?'

'Be my guest.'

Arranz went behind the desk, leant over Martín's shoulder, dabbed in entry codes. An entry scrolled down.

'I logged this yesterday. German woman reporting her missing daughter. Very disturbed. Said the daughter, ex-heroin habit, was involved with a man who was a criminal, they were here to make a lot of money. I asked her if I could put it on the drugs file – it would get attention there. On Missing Persons it would be dead. You get the picture?'

'I'm not an idiot.'

'Anyone who works here is an idiot. This evening she walked by. Shopping. I asked her if she'd found her daughter. She was confused, didn't know what to say. She did say though that she had found the man involved and he had told her that her daughter was not coming to Barcelona after all. She wasn't just confused. She was frightened. Of me. Of the conversation we were having. She wanted out.'

Martín leant back, drank Fanta Naranja from the bottle.

'So what do you reckon?'

'Well,' Arranz moved back round to the front of the desk, swung a chair in, sat on it. 'She could be here on a drug deal with the man. And she didn't want her daughter involved. Oh shit . . . how should I know?' He laughed. 'I just didn't like the smell of it. And all along she's refused to tell us where she's staying. That's it really. I just feel it ought to stay on file, on the drug file, even though the missing daughter's no longer missing. The main thing is, on both occasions she was unwilling to tell me where she's staying. It might be worth finding out. She had a load of shopping from the market, so she's not in a hotel. But she told me the first time that she was looking for one.'

'You could have followed her.'

'Come on, Xavier. She'd have spotted me. And anyway, I'm off duty.'

'OK.' Martín grinned back at him. 'I'll put out a reminder to patrols, with the photos. Anything else?'

'No. That's all. I'm off now. Enjoy your paperwork.'

'Piss off Andreu.'

When he had finished with the document case and its lethal contents Cranmer put it all back in the wardrobe, and hoisted out the hold-all he had put there after the Casa Pez bombing, took from it the Micro-Cassette player he had bought in Zürich as part of a telephone bugging device. With the input from the actual bug removed it functioned like a normal player. He lit one of Inger's cigarettes, pressed play.

First the clicks of a number dialling. Then the female voice: Herr Winckelmann's residence. His own answered: I'd like to speak to Herr Winckelmann please. Right now Herr Winckelmann is at the Prolebentek Head Office. May I take a message?

Cranmer pressed stop, then play and record. In a quiet murmur, with his mouth close to the corner of the slim small box where the microphone was sited, he began to speak.

'Herr Herz. From what you have just heard you will realise that I know precisely who paid me for the first killings I did for you, and who it is who still owes me six hundred thousand Swiss francs for the Casa Pez bombing. You will appreciate, and I am sure Herr Winckelmann will too, that this knowledge gives me a very important advantage in the game we are playing . . .'

He continued for sometime, often rewinding, playing back, re-recording, getting it right, right through until he heard her steps on the stairs, her knock on the door.

'It's me. Inger.'

He turned off the recorder, opened the door. She came in with her shopping, a plastic bag as well as her peasant-weave.

'Did I hear you talking? Is there someone here?'

'Only this.' He showed her the recorder. 'It's a message for the people who shot me up last night. Tomorrow I'd like you to take it to an office here in Barcelona. Will you do that? Do you

209

mind? There's no danger – it's just a case of leaving it with a receptionist.'

He paused, watched her back as she unpacked her shopping on to the deal table. There seemed a lot – surely a good sign.

'That is . . . if you're going to stay here until tomorrow.'

'I might. I'll see.'

She filled the small sink with cold water, tipped lettuce, cucumber, tomatoes into it.

'You were quite right,' he said, his voice level and reasonable, 'I can see you should go back to your farmhouse. Or Biarritz anyway. I'm sure Laura went back to Biarritz. But please. Stay here until tomorrow afternoon. She'll survive without you a day, a couple of days more. By tomorrow afternoon I should be able to look after myself.'

She turned. Her face was pale again, big shadows round her large dark eyes.

'So. After all, you are persuading me, helping me to believe Laura is alive.'

'Yes.'

'But you said things, things that made me sure that she was dead. And probably that you had killed her.'

'I was in shock. And in a bad way. You know that. And then you gave me morphine. I had fantasies, hallucinations.' He hoisted himself up in the bed, leaned forward over his knees. 'Look. You've bought nice things to eat, to drink. Can't we forget her? Just for a few hours. Let's enjoy ourselves, eh?'

She pulled the lettuce from the sink, shook it, pulled off the outer leaves, the stalk, began to shred it with her hands. Never cut a lettuce – the steel makes it bitter. She asked the question without looking back at him.

'Are you trying to tell me you need me?'

'Perhaps. It's not something I say easily.'

She worked on, without speaking for five minutes or so, chopping tomato, onion, cucumber on the wooden draining board which she had scrubbed earlier in the day, laying it all out on a large cracked dish she had found with other crockery

210

and utensils on curtained shelves beneath the sink. Finally she added the olives and a sprinkling of salt. She looked at the lobster and the tiredness returned and hunger too. Later, she thought, and remembered the ham. She cut small rounds of bread, laid the ham out with it, and the last of the olives, brought it to the small locker that stood by the bed.

'A snack. Starters. I'd like a drink. There's Cava, that's Catalan champagne and just as good as French, or brandy.'

'Brandy. Save the Cava for the lobster. But put a lot of water in it for me.'

She mixed brandy and water for both of them, sat on the bed, but in the middle, not too close. She reached for the ham and bread, folded a slice on to the bread, passed it to him, made one for herself. Then she drank some brandy and water, and felt stronger again, but excited too, recalling she still had an advantage that he did not know about. It gave her power, but frightened her too – she feared his anger if he found out what she knew. But at the same time it was a temptation, like playing Truth and Dare when you're twelve, thirteen years old, and you know someone might ask you to do something really awful, and you rather hope they will.

'You kill people.'

'Tell me why you say that.'

Right away the anger was there, but playing with fire as she was, she had her answer ready.

'People who are shot at, people who get wounds from bombs or whatever,' she was thinking of the scar below his ribs which he said was shrapnel, and which she knew he had received in the Falklands, where he had killed six young men, boys really, hiding in a shepherd's hut, 'are generally people who shoot back, or first, people who throw bombs.'

He straightened his back, pulled away from her so his face was in shadow. His eyes were ice-cold, and his voice matched.

'You know more about me than you say. You must have thought about it, made guesses.'

Had she gone too far, already?

211

'It's not something I want to talk about.'

'But you brought it up.' He pulled his knees up again, cradled the glass above them. 'You could have found out who I was. While you were away you could have read detailed accounts of that air-crash, found out who was on board. You knew I was a bodyguard, that would have been enough. You could know my name. The name I had then.'

Yes. Too far, too soon. She drank, almost finished her drink, then head on one side, said the lie quietly.

'But I didn't. I didn't do that.'

'Why not? I would have done. Most people would.'

'You know how it was with me. You came to me without a past.' Her voice was warm now, she spoke slowly, carefully. 'It was perfect. No wife, no children, no regrets, no hang-ups. I couldn't spoil that.'

She reached towards him let her fingers slip down his shin, his calf, towards his foot, and skillfully turned the course of their talk.

'I wish I hadn't told you so much about myself,' she said. 'Knowing things leads you to expect things.'

'I don't expect anything from you.'

'But you do. You expect help. And you trust me. Why?' She stood, reached for his glass. He emptied it, and she went back to the table to refill them. 'Why?'

'I have to. There's no one else.' Her hand froze on the bottle it was about to lift. He hurried on. 'That's how it was when I came into your camper. But the way you reacted then said a lot about you. About the sort of person you are.'

'I didn't scream, nor call the police. I didn't make you go to hospital when you didn't want to. Is that the sort of thing you mean?'

'Yes. Not many people would have done what you did. There aren't many people like you.'

At last there was a smile on her face when she turned to bring him back his brandy and water. She handed it to him, looked down at him.

'Not many. But we always recognise each other when we meet. It's a family, a secret society, a Masonry of loners.' She turned back to the table. With neat competent movements she began to dismember the lobster, cutting the back in half with a sharp heavy knife, using the handle to crack the shell-casing on the claws. 'We never let each other down. We hate all social conventions and hypocrisy in general, and the law, legal systems and so on, in particular.'

'It sounds like the Mafia.'

'No. The Mafia stands outside society and the law but it exploits them, exploits the systems. We ignore it all, pretend it isn't there, as much as we can, and help each other when we get tangled in them. We mind our own business. But we help when help is needed. You needed help.'

'Still do.'

She turned again, stabbed the air in front of her to make the point.

'I thought you were like that. One of us, one of the family. But you're not.'

'No?'

'No. But that doesn't mean to say we can't eat together. It doesn't mean to say I won't help you. The food is ready. Can you open the Cava?'

She handed him the bottle.

'And when we've eaten, and drunk a little, I'm coming to bed with you. And when I've slept a bit, because, No Man, I am very tired, when I've slept a little, then we'll make love. Does that surprise you? After everything? The bad things, you going away, you and Laura, and me thinking you've harmed or even killed her? But it shouldn't. It was good before. It can be good here too.'

35

'I told you, didn't I? That she had a big mole on her cheek?'

'You did.'

'And that she was fat. Very fat?'

'That too.'

Late evening. Already out in Laietana the street lamps were on, and Barcelona was warming up – the bars filling, shops here and there putting up their shutters, while the coloured lights outside the discos and clubs began to flicker and spin. Reaching for the climax of his story Estrada let the front legs of his chair thump into the floor of the Incident Room. From her desk Claret looked up from the screen in front of her, grimaced, and then with eyebrows knitted ducked back down, doing her best to shut out whatever new enormity her temporary boss was about to perpetrate.

'But what I didn't tell you was this. I spent the next ten minutes massaging another mole on her stomach, thinking it was her tit!' He bellowed with laughter. Gómez and the two other detectives sitting with him beneath the portrait of the King joined in obsequiously. 'OK. Back to the bullshit. Offence-profiling, offender-profiling. Fancy names for horse-sense. Come on Conchi – tell us what the perverts at Interpol have sent you.'

She lifted a plastic suspension file from the box that stood on casters by her chair, put it on the desk, stood, smoothed her black pencil-line skirt, picked up the file and walked as unself-consciously as she could towards the big green baize-covered table. Not easy in a skirt that hugged her flat tummy and long shapely thighs above black-stockinged knees and calves. It was clear from the slightly glazed expression she provoked in the eyes of many of the men she worked with that the uniform had been designed either by a male chauvinist pig or the madame of a brothel. She took an empty chair at the furthest point she could get from Estrada. She coughed – the need to was not psychological, but the result of passive smoking.

'It's not clear from what we are getting just to what extent Interpol believes the Casa Pez bombing is part of a series or not. Or at any rate to which previous killings claimed by the Warriors of Christ it should be related. The name was first used in the mid-seventies by a group who assassinated Ukrainian performers travelling in Europe on exchanges and schemes paid for by the central Soviet culture ministry. Their worst atrocity was the machine-gunning of the Kiev String Quartet on the steps of the Royal Festival Hall, London. As far as we know all members of that group are either dead or in British maximum security prisons, and it seems pretty certain that they have nothing to do with later users of the name.'

She paused to refuse a cigarette from the youngest detective. He blushed, and looked at his nails for the next five minutes.

'Three years ago a second sequence began of attempts on the lives of Ukrainian officials travelling abroad, or on Russians who had held senior administrative or industrial posts in the Ukraine. There were four episodes before the murder of Schumacher. The most recent was six months before Schumacher, took place in London, and ended in the death of the bomber as he tried to place his bomb under the target's car.'

'OK.' Estrada cleared his throat. From where he was sitting Claret wore the white shirt and black epaulettes, each with the single silver bar of a lieutenant. It was just about possible to forget her knees and crossed ankles. 'Apart from the claims, which probably came from some nutter, perhaps a left-over from earlier Warriors, and may have nothing at all to do with these events, what other factors suggest Casa Pez is part of a series?'

'Interpol suggests two. The victims, and the general configuration, including method, success rate and so on. "Victims" is clear. Arnold Kagan, who survived the London bomb seven

215

months ago, is in the process of setting up a branch of his British based home-computer empire in Kiev, with central Russian support. He is a known moderate, a federalist, and these are the people the extremists most fear. Kalnitzky was the anti-terrorist police chief in Kiev – the motives for his attempted murder are obvious. The case of Schumacher is rather different. He was directly responsible for the successful prosecution of fifteen Ukrainian nationalist socialist war criminals, five of whom were arrested in Russia and hanged. But in 1980 he declared he had done enough and since then he has been no threat to anyone. So the likeliest motive for killing him now that I can see is revenge. On the face of it Sasonov is part of the pattern. Like Kagan he was a moderate federalist. There is also some evidence, little more than rumour at the moment, that he was about to uncover or reveal that the nationalist movement was planning to lease Ukrainian land to Western industrialists for dumping toxic waste. I can go along with all that. I accept the victims fit a pattern, suggest a series.'

'But you're not happy about configuration.'

'Not really. No. The killings were all very different. The common factor Interpol finds is the element of bungling. This characterised the second series up to the Kagan car bomb which killed the bomber not Kagan. But the Interpol analyst sees the same pattern continuing. Kalnitzky survived because the bomb was in the wrong room. And here, at the Casa Pez, one of the bombers was blown up.'

'But nothing like that with Schumacher.'

'No. Though Interpol suggest that it was done with a sort of wild bravado – the killer could very well have been seen in the very act of doing it in such a public place. Then it would have been bungled.'

'Come on Conchi. Come clean. You're not happy with the Interpol assessment. But you must have good reason. If I found you questioning my ability I'd have you back blowing a whistle at the jay-walkers in the Plaça de Catalunya by eight o'clock tomorrow morning.' He thought: I'd rather see you doing a

216

strip-tease in one of the Barri Xines clubs. 'Are you saying Interpol is wrong, and this isn't a series?'

'No, I'm not saying that – although I think there is quite strong evidence that it may not be. Let me just run through that. First. I exclude the Kagan affair from the series. It was six months ago and your forensic explosives expert didn't think there was a connection. What else suggests it is not a series? We have a pistol shooting in broad daylight. We have an unarmed killing of exceptional skill and brutality on a man normally able to look after himself, followed by a bomb apparently similar to the one used in the Kagan affair except that it went off properly, expertly, but in the wrong place. Then we have the Casa Pez – a very different sort of bomb using sophisticated equipment, not easily obtainable, used in a very professional way.'

'But blowing up one of the bombers.' Gómez at last felt on sure enough ground to intervene.

'But the Chief himself, this morning, hypothesised that that could have been done on purpose. Anyway we have four incidents, three if we conflate as everyone agrees we should, the murder of Ken Wright and the attempt on Kalnitzky, all carried out in very different ways, using very different equipment. On the face of it the only reasons for supposing a series are the Ukrainian connection that links all the victims but Wright, and the fact that someone is telexing the media and claiming they are the Warriors of Christ, and they did it.'

'And they could be nutters.'

'Well yes.'

'So no series. We should just be looking for the gang who did the Casa Pez and forget the rest.'

'No. That's not what I'm trying to say.'

'Shit, Conchi, just what the fuck are you trying to say.' This was not said in anger, but tired boredom. He yawned grossly to underline the point. Claret remained red but mute. Estrada sighed. 'Lieutenant María de la Concepción Immaculada Claret y Gasset, please do enlighten us. If you would?'

'Señor, I am sorry if I am keeping you from a very well

deserved rest,' she contrived to suggest she was talking about early retirement rather than early bed, 'but I would like you to hear me out.'

'Feel free.' He crushed an empty Ducados packet in his big square fist. 'Gómez, have you got a cigarette?'

'The common factor that might link the incidents is not the bungling but the professionalism of the leader. Maybe the bungling is fed in to disguise it, but he is a pro. He can kill in a variety of ways. He always gets away, and his victims, apart from Kalnitzky, always die. But just think, he shoots, he uses brutal and effective methods of unarmed killing, he can handle different sorts of bomb. If you'll forgive me, Señor, I am now moving into offender-profiling.'

'Shit.'

'What I believe we are looking for is someone who has been professionally trained in killing skills to a very high level. That means he was either trained legitimately, in an army or a police force, or he was trained by someone who was. It also means he has almost certainly killed before. We should ask for information on all recent unsolved crimes, across Europe, that match these for brutality and skill. We have the technology, capacity, and authority to do that, you know?'

Estrada thought back across a long and difficult day. His breath rattled in his trachea, he dragged tired hands across a tired face.

'MacTaggart was a trained killer, trained by the British army,' he said at last. 'And earlier you suggested the leader of the gang might once have been his commanding officer in that army. Aren't you just framing a new hypothesis to substantiate the first one?'

She was surprised, she was shocked. First, that he should accuse her of what amounted to an immature not to say unprofessional manipulation of facts and arguments; second, that he was intelligent enough to see the possibility; third, that it was just possible . . . he might be right.

Maybe he sensed her discomfort.

'Anyway, Conchi, if you're right, one thing is for sure. If he's that professional, he'll have pissed off out of Barça long ago. I guess by tomorrow night we'll be able to close up shop here and go home. Put up the shutters, tell the world the bombers have flown the coop, back to Belfast, Bilbao, or wherever bombers come from these days. Gómez of course won't go home, he'll go back to the little Japanese girl he pokes when his lousy job gives him the chance, eh? Am I right? Susie Nissan, we call her. Tell me, Gómez, is it true what they used to say when we were kids – oriental ladies are fitted up horizontally? Not vertically?'

They ate most of the lobster and salad, drank all the Cava, and a fair bit more brandy. By the time they were finished Inger was almost asleep in her chair and outside it was dark. She helped Cranmer to the toilet again and on to the bed. Then she turned out the dim unshaded light that hung from a high plaster rose in the middle of the ceiling, slipped out of her clothes and got under the quilt beside him. Briefly she let her fingers run over his rib-cage, across his stomach, and into the pubic hair. For a moment she played with his sex and his balls, then her hand went back to his stomach and with her head on his shoulder she slept. Presently he moved her head on to the bolster without waking her, and moved her knee from where it lay across his uninjured thigh, and he too slept, but far more lightly than her.

Towards dawn a moon just past full filled the room with silver light, magicking the shabbiness and the dust into a memory of medieval grandeur. Inger woke slowly with it, presently saw that he too was awake, lying on his back, but head propped high. She pulled herself up and closer, rested her cheek on her hand, and he half turned to her, mouth twisted a little in acknowledgement that she was there and awake. For a time her right hand cradled his cheek, her finger traced in the moonlight the line of his hard, emotionally deprived mouth, of his strong neck.

219

'One day I will know who you really are. Who you are, not who you were.'

He allowed himself one of his rare laughs, little more than a chuckle at the back of his mouth.

'You know more than you say. I'm sure of it. Anyway, as much as you, or anyone else needs to know.'

'But it's not enough. You always hold something back. Emotionally, physically. You never reveal what's inside. Why?'

He said nothing for a moment, then spoke very quietly, as if to himself.

'Since the crash, since I became dead, I cannot be seen or hurt. It's as if, when people look at me, all they can see are reflections of themselves. That's good. I don't want that to change.'

'Like Perseus. He had a helmet that made him invisible, winged sandals that could take him anywhere, a polished shield that was a mirror.'

She turned his head so she could look into his eyes, fancied the moon was bright enough for her to see her own face in his large pupils.

'Because I cannot see you I invent you. And what I invent is what I want.' She gave a little laugh, lay on her back, but felt for and caught his hand. 'Andromeda invented a demi-god to kill the sea-monster. I too needed a demi-god.'

'I saw no monster.'

'There were several.'

'Yes?'

'Oh yes. Middle-age: fear my sexuality could no longer delight anyone but me, could exist only as a lonely secret; fear my talent was a myth, fear that I was the last person on earth to know it was a myth. Bastard though he was the No Man I invented enjoyed me in bed, and helped me make the best sculpture I ever made.'

The silence spread through the room unblemished by the murmurs of a waking city.

'No Man, what would happen if you lost the gifts Athene

220

gave Perseus, if she took them back – your invisibility, your polished shield that shows only reflections . . .?'

Out of his inner darkness he replied.

'I'd fall. I'd fall out of the sky, like Icarus when his wings caught fire.'

She sensed he was troubled, and she was troubled too by the guilt of the lie she maintained – she knew she could perhaps hurt him by revealing that she knew his name, and at that moment she did not want to hurt him at all. She lifted herself above him, and sat, knees on either side of his legs, but carefully well below the wound. She carried the quilt with her so it hung like a tent from her shoulders over both of them. Then she lowered her head and her long rich dark hair spilled forward past her cheeks. Lightly she kissed the bandages, first on his arm then on his leg. The dryness of medicated cellulose made her want to sneeze but she headed it off.

'When these happened you could be seen and hurt.'

'There was someone there who knew my name. And I don't know what happened to him.'

'My darling. My poor darling. But you're still a god to me.'

Her kisses moved on over his chest, his stomach, and gently she took his sex into her mouth.

It hardly stirred, and did not thicken. Presently she gave up, pulled herself away, still sitting, still with the quilt around her, but no longer shared with him. All the pleasure had leaked away, distress flooded back.

'She's here. She's still here in bed with us. What did she do with you that I can't?' Her voice rose in anger. 'What nasty little tricks did she get up to?'

He closed his eyes, as if, she thought, he was remembering, then he hoisted himself higher on his elbows with his head against the bars of the ancient bedstead. His eyes looked dark, like polished pebbles in the moonlight. But as dawn approached its silver had shifted to the whiteness of lead. She turned her head away, but couldn't let go, couldn't leave it alone.

'I can guess. She liked to be hurt, yes? And that turns you on.

221

You hurt me before. Not much, but enough. Do you want to hurt me now? Will that do it? Will that get it up? She said you did it three times in one day – '

'Oh come on.' At last he responded, his head twisting in irritation, dismissal perhaps. 'She tells lies, we both know that. Thirty hours ago I was shot. Twice. If I'm not the same god for you that I was, blame that, not Laura.'

'No. It's Laura.'

She slipped off the bed, taking the quilt, went to the table – still littered with the remains of their meal, squalid in the pre-dawn light – sat on her chair, fumbled with cigarettes, gave up and hurled them away. She stormed on.

'May be its because you killed her. May be you cannot make love to the mother of the girl you killed. May be it was an accident. These things happen – when people play stupid sex games.'

'No. It wasn't like that.'

Her stomach lurched with panic. She repeated the words, spacing them out.

'It was not like that.'

She scrunched the quilt closer about her, stifled a sob, stifled the desire to call it out, his name, his real name, and demand from him the truth. The whole truth. She made a decision which she knew was wrong but which she could not deny herself. She spoke quietly but firmly.

'Don't tell me. Not yet. Please. I don't want to know because I know if you tell me that will be the end. The end of everything.'

She turned back to the window, watched the old moon, shredded by television aerials, dip between crumbling chimney stacks.

'It's cold,' he murmured. 'Can I have the quilt back?'

'Can I come too.'

'Of course.'

She lay beside him and with a gesture as close to tenderness as anything he had ever shown he slipped his arm beneath her back and turned her so her head rested on his shoulder.

222

'I need help tomorrow. A lot of help.'

'I won't hurt anyone, or help you to hurt people.'

'No. That's not the sort of thing I mean . . .'

Dawn and the sea-borne sun cast long purple shadows from the glitzy new skyscrapers of the Parc del Mar across the churned and impacted sand of the wasteland that still remained. Between them the light momentarily bounced off the windscreen of a Guàrdia Urbana patrol car as it turned off the finished road and onto a track which marked where a railway line had been. It lurched awkwardly over the indentations left by sleepers and three Africans, all black as midnight, impassively noted its slow progress towards them.

One of them rolled balls of dough between his big hands, slapped them flat. His companion slipped them on to the top of a half oil barrel. Inside it they had a small fire of wood debris going. The dough blistered, he turned it brown-side up. When it was done he scooped it onto a cracked plastic plate and handed it to the third, shaking his long black fingers from the heat. The third poured coffee from an aluminium jug and took the bread and the cup up into the container behind them.

Winston Smith lay inside, on a rear seat taken from an old Seat, half covered by a blanket woven in coloured stripes. There was a pile of them in a corner. When the Africans couldn't pick up casual work on the building sites they peddled them along the beaches. Winston shifted, winced, careful not to allow his back which was pitted with suppurating scabs of shot wounds to come in contact with anything rougher than air.

'Cheers, mate. You don't understand a word I say, but you're a good bloke.'

Outside the patrol car came to a halt fifty metres away beside what looked like a low fat heap of dirty clothes. The Guàrdias got out, looked at Weise's body. One of them came over to the container. He was a big man with a red face, gun and baton on his belt, his blue shirt morning fresh. He looked down at the three impassive black faces.

223

'So who saw it happen?'

When they did not answer he kicked the oil drum over, scattering ashes, burning wood, bread.

'Filth. Scum.'

He walked back to the body. The second Guàrdia looked up from it.

'One side of his head's gone. But first he got shot in the groin with a shot-gun. Since then the rats have been at him.'

'It has to be homicide. I'll give the lads at Via Laietana a buzz.'

'They'll love you for that. I suppose we'd better stay until they come.'

He shook out a cigarette, leant against the car while his companion reached in for the RT handset.

36

The Information Room in the Policia Nacional building in Via Laietana takes no account of day or night, since it is in one of the basements. It's a big, drab room, with faulty air-conditioning and poor sound-proofing – a disadvantage not only because Linea IV passes under it, but also because a corridor of pens backs on to the longer wall. The arrest of ninety per cent of drunks, petty thieves, drug-traders at street and club level, illegal immigrants, unlicensed prostitutes may be entirely justified, but none admit it, and the only way to protest once you have been locked up is to shout. Or scream.

Nevertheless the Information Room functions, and the people who work there have the benefit of the latest in data processing, storing, and retrieval equipment, and chores which might have taken three or four bored detectives a week in the past, such as processing or searching the list, say, of legal guest workers with their addresses and jobs, can be done by one person with a net-worked IBM in a matter of moments. But not only is the IBM net-worked with similar computers throughout Spain, a handful of keys put it on line with police databases across Europe. Needless to say this has all been laid on not because Madrid Head Quarters and the Barcelona City Fathers want to give Barcelona the leading edge in urban policing, but because if something went badly wrong during the Olympics, another Black September, or something of that sort, there would be every possible aid to crisis management available. And no kickback that they were under-resourced.

An hour after the discovery of Weise's body a detective from homicide came into the smoke-filled room. He moved between the six consoles each with its own VDT, keyboard, fax, modem and telephone, looking for the girl he usually liked to deal with, chat up, when duty brought him down there. But she was very busy. Data slowly scrolled down her screen, and the bubble jet printer spewed listing paper. He paused long enough to see it was a report from French police of a killing near the German border, six weeks earlier – an Englishman had been found dead of a broken neck in a motorway service station toilet.

He moved on, picked out an older woman busy knitting a chunky jumper with Cobi on it. He leant over her shoulder and from a plastic bindle spilled a Euro ID card on to her table-top.

'Be a sweetheart and run a couple of checks on this for me?'

She set aside her knitting, picked up the ID. A photo of Willi Weise, and his name. Issued in München.

'Check with Munich that it's real, then check the register of foreign hotel users, back day by day for a fortnight. OK? Results to room 303.'

'You might as well wait.' Already she was keying in the information on the ID. 'These things don't take long.'

As data began to scroll across her screen she leant across to her neighbour.

225

'Willi Weise, Euro ID No. 683079992, DBR. Check back foreign visitors registry fourteen days.'

She leant back in her chair. The detective from homicide offered her a cigarette, which she refused.

'I'd like a Coke. Diet Coke.'

He went to a vending-machine sited by the door he had come in through, fed in two one-hundred peseta coins, pressed buttons. Plastic cups dropped, were held lovingly but loosely in metal claws, a Diet Coke then Fanta Limón streamed from spigots. He returned with the drinks.

'Looks interesting,' she said, but was already reaching for her knitting. He thought: surely she can afford a knitting machine, but read the script on the screen.

Words and numbers in German, but the meaning was clear enough.

'Euro ID No. 683079992, name Willi Weise, INVALID. Details follow.'

The male operator next door caught his attention.

'Willi Weise checked into the Hotel Bristol, in the Travessera de Gracia, Friday 30 August using that ID which appears to be false . . . Hang on. I'm getting a blip. The reservation was made in the name Prolebentek and that's flagged to the Casa Pez Incident Room.'

Siren blasting, the big Policia Nacional Citroën cruised up the Passeig de Gracia past Guardi's fairy-tale Casa Milà with its sweeping balconies and cavernous recesses. Madrid-born Estrada no longer bothered to notice such things: simply they symbolised for him the general looniness of all things Catalan. A light flashed on the dash board and Gòmez, in the front passenger seat leant forward for the RT receiver.

'For Christ's sake turn that damn thing off,' Estrada snarled at the driver. 'He won't be able to hear a damn thing.'

But he himself went on talking – to no one in particular, though Claret was sitting next to him.

226

'Bastard – this link between Prolebentek and this stiff they've found. What's his name again?'

'Weise. Willi Weise.'

Estrada shook out a Ducados, Claret's eyes and mouth crinkled in disgust.

'If nothing had turned up by nightfall today I was ready to wind the thing down, hand it over to Madrid and go home. Right. What have we got?'

Gómez replaced the handset of the RT.

'Forensic, preliminary,' he said. 'They reckon the shot-gun wound in his groin could match the one that killed the Casa Pez chef. Anyway there's nothing to suggest it wasn't the same one.'

'And the guy who fired it and the gun itself are still out there somewhere.' Estrada shifted himself about in the back seat. The cigarette had got to his bowels. 'Why the fuck have we stopped?'

'Usual snarl-up at Plaça Joan-Carles.' The driver was laconic.

'Then use the goddamn hooter. But just for long enough to get us across.'

With the siren blasting again they crossed the busy intersection of Gracia and the Diagonal. When it was quiet again, Estrada turned to Claret.

'Did you get anything from the Brits about the officers MacTaggart worked with?'

She looked up, her dark brown eyes making contact with his watery blue.

'They won't reveal names of officers who served with the Special Forces. But I pleaded. Anti-terrorism and all that. So they did say one was a junior minister in the Major government, another a Buddhist monk, and the third is dead.'

'Didn't I tell you?' Estrada beamed. 'Psychologists' reports are always shit. Just like all that offender-profiling you bent our ears with last night. Is this it? Looks a pretty crummy dump.'

The car pulled into the pavement outside a medium-sized, medium-priced hotel – the Hotel Bristol. All except the driver piled out on to the pavement, followed Estrada into the foyer.

'Room number,' he barked.

'707. Seventh floor.'

'Lift?'

'Over to your right.'

In the lift Claret spoke up again.

'Well I didn't leave it at that. I went back to them.'

'Whatever for?' Estrada trod on his Ducados, shook out another, but his bowels which were imperatively on the move said no and he put it back.

'For details of the dead officer. I argued that if he's dead there's no need to protect his identity.'

'Did you get a result?'

'Not yet.'

The lift stopped, they moved out into a corridor, set off down it then Estrada stopped.

'They must think you're crazy.' A penny dropped. 'Whose authority was on these requests?'

'Yours.' The corners of her mouth lifted. 'Of course.'

'Jesus. Now they think I'm crazy.'

They pushed on into room 707. It was a normal anonymous middle-rank hotel room. The young detective was already there, watching an in-house soft porn video. He turned off the sound, stood. He was very tall. Upright he made the room seem small. When they were all in it became like a cell.

'Well. What have you got?'

'Nothing.'

'What do you mean, nothing? This is Weise's room isn't it? This is the hotel Prolebentek booked him into.'

'Yes.'

'So?'

'So the guy went out the morning of the bomb. At the moment this room is taken by a Catholic priest, Irish, and he's not pleased I'm sitting here waiting for you.'

'Eh?' Estrada's attention was momentarily held by the pretty redhead on the video. She wore suspenders and black stockings, nothing else, and she was silently grinding her groin against that of a large naked black man. Large and getting larger. 'Turn

228

that damn thing off. So where's Weise's luggage? His plastic? His money?'

The detective hesitated over the off-switch but finally pressed it.

'I don't know.'

'What the fuck am I doing here?'

'When we got the address and number from Information you sent me straight over, told me to wait here for you.'

Estrada struggled with several problems at once, both psychological and animal.

'OK. OK. So what did happen to all Weise's stuff? And what about the bill?'

'A guy called in yesterday took his baggage, paid the bill on a Prolebentek AmEx card. The signature says C. Negrín. He's the manager of the Barcelona branch of Prolebentek.'

'Great, marvellous.' Estrada reached out and pinched the young man's cheek. 'You see, you did get something after all. I need a crap.'

He pushed past him, squeezed into the tiny bathroom – just a shower-stall and a toilet. They stood around, waited, pretended they couldn't hear. Explosive wind heralded a downward-forced basketful of effluvia. At last the toilet flushed. Estrada came out, drying his hands, grinned.

'That's better. Now will someone get me back to Via Laietana before I commit a second felony?'

Back in the car Gómez put his elbow on the back of his seat, looked over his shoulder.

'Drop me off at Passeig de Gracia. I'll get over to Prolebentek, check them out. See what they know about Weise.'

Estrada closed his eyes and smoked. A deep smile spread slowly across the caverns and pock-marks of his prematurely aged face. Whatever else was wrong for him, one thing was clear: Gómez was not ready for his desk. His voice rattled.

'No. We can be more clever than that. We'll set up an observation post, see who comes, who goes. You can do that now. Use the RT. Let's know as much about them as we can

229

before we alert them. Is that rain on the windscreen? Summer's over.'

Back in the office he pulled out glasses and Osborne. Gómez left his untouched. When Estrada went over the top he did not want to go with him – indeed he wanted to walk away in the old man's shoes. But Estrada put the first away, poured another.

'I'd bug them if I didn't need a magistrate's warrant. Fucking new laws. In the old days you bugged people you knew were villains and if they didn't confess you beat the shit out of them until they did. Yes?'

Claret came in.

'What is it?'

'I've had a response from London. The dead officer, the man MacTaggart served under in North Ireland, was a Captain Thomas Cranmer. He was killed six weeks ago in the Hanover air-crash.' She hurried on before he could interrupt. 'In the Casa Pez, MacTaggart saluted the leader and, according to the waiter, called him "Mr Kramer".'

Estrada thought about it.

'Neat. But the bugger's dead. It has to be a coincidence. Leave it Conchi. Listen. Prolebentek. Get anything Interpol or the Zürich police can come up with. And forget about this Cranmer. Right?'

37

The showroom and office of the Catalan branch of Prolebentek (Zürich) were three blocks north of the Gran Via intersection on the Rambla de Catalunya, in the heart of the *ensanche* built by Cerda, the great late nineteenth-century architect and town-planner who enclosed the medieval town in a grid of fine

avenues, parks and city streets. It remains unsurpassed anywhere and the inspiration for a hundred or more similar
developments all over the world. It is the commercial centre of
the city: filled with smart shops, grand hotels, hospitals, col-
leges, opulent restaurants and street cafés, parks, and above all
offices and show-rooms.

The PLT logo with its smart sunflower made a distinctive
square sign in hard shiny materials above a big plate glass
window filled with glossy displays that glamorously repeated
again and again the same message: Prolebentek made a lot of
money out of recycling industrial waste wherever possible and
disposing of it with total safety where recycling was not possible.
Inside were more displays including one for the International
Conference of Greens which an expensively sexy receptionist
was in the process of dismantling. She was standing on a small
set of steps and reaching up to take down a streamer which
echoed in smaller scale the one that had been put up in the
Estacío de Sants. Negrín sat on her glass-topped desk and
watched her.

Herz prowled around the big room behind him. It had a very
high ceiling, almost as high as the ceiling of the floor above. The
back wall was curved and hung with purple velveteen wall
covering, lit by discreet spots. A chrome staircase made a half
sweep up to a railed landing which had two doors upholstered
in padded black leather. Below, and facing the bottom of the
stairs was the low desk with a smoked glass top with telephones,
blotter, diary. The chair behind it was made of black leather
slung between chrome tubes. Three similar armchairs were
dotted about with smoked glass ashtrays also mounted on
chrome tubes. Big coloured photographs, flow charts and cut-
cake charts, brochures in dispensers, all grouped into separate
modules, filled most of the rest of the floor with all the
razzamatazz of glitzy PR. The message was clear – Prolebentek
cleaned up the planet, coverted industrial squalor and waste
into landscapes of natural but friendly beauty. Herz came back
to the big window, looked out on to the street.

231

'Will you please stop staring at my legs? You know: it was only last Friday I put this lot up.'

As her arms dropped her skirt fell back an inch or so and Negrín looked up at her painted face instead.

'It's been cancelled,' he said.

'I know. But why?'

'Because of the bomb.'

'But it didn't kill all of them, did it? I'd have thought . . .'

Herz, still in the window, spoke over his shoulder: 'Taxi pulling in. It's him. He's here.'

Negrín moved to the door, held it open as Finchley-Camden came through. The Englishman was wearing a light-weight cavalry length Burberry over light-weight tweeds, and carried the brown derby he wore to the races. He ignored Negrín, shook hands with Herz.

'Wasn't too sure of the parking situation, so I left my wheels at the hotel, took a taxi. Not late am I?'

'If you'd like to come to my office . . .' Negrín offered from behind.

'I'll see the Colonel on my own.' Herz was brusque.

Negrín, mortified, watched them climb the stairs. The receptionist revelled inwardly, smiled sweetly.

'You can help me with this,' she said.

Herz moved straight to the managerial desk, leant over it, made the meeting a confrontation.

'Right. Who is Biedermann? I think since we met in London you have found time to discover his real identity. Yes?'

'My dear chap.' Finchley-Camden looked round, took in the dark walls, black furniture, concealed lighting, and a Swiss Cheese plant. He walked over to the window, got the light behind him, sound defensive position. For a moment or two he contrived to find that his perfectly manicured nails were more interesting than Herz.

'Come on.' The tone now was more than confrontational. 'Who is Hans Biedermann? We have every right to know.'

232

Satisfied that his nails were as perfect as he expected them to be Finchley-Camden looked round, smoothed the silvery corrugations of his hair.

'My guess is that he is Tom Cranmer, my nephew. Back in July, when you made your second call, he was in my office. You remember: I dialled you back on your private line.'

'That was careless.' Herz was smug now, pleased Finchley-Camden had cracked at last, pleased the mess had started with Wolf-hound not AlterLog. 'It's easy to train yourself to pick up a number from the sound of the clicks. I can do it myself.'

'Well, of course I'll do well to remember that, if I ever have occasion to make a phone call in your company. But he was my nephew. I trusted his discretion. And of course I am using the past tense because he is dead. He was killed in the Hanover aircrash. He was declared officially dead.'

'Ah so. Yes. I'm beginning to understand.' Herz sat down in Negrín's managerial chair, leant forward on his elbows, tapped his teeth with clasped thumbs. 'In Paris Biedermann told Willi he was officially dead. Could this Cranmer speak German?'

'Very well. He read German at Cambridge on a Ministry of Defence scholarship. There is another factor. On the plane there were officially twenty-one passengers and crew. Twenty-one bodies were found but some were too damaged to be identified with complete certainty. But I happen to know that there were twenty-two people on the plane. Including Tom.'

'So. We know who he is. How do we find him?'

'It won't be easy. You tried to kill him. That was a damn silly thing to do. Tom can take care of himself.'

'Willi was no amateur.'

'But not good enough for Tom. Anyway. He'll be around, before long. He'll want his money, and either he'll kill you before you can kill him, or he'll screw a guarantee of immunity out of you. We'll think of something when he shows.'

'But you do agree he must be dealt with.'

'Oh certainly. He's put my whole operation at risk. Can't have that. Severest penalties in order. *Pour encourager les autres.* I

233

say, old chap, do you mind if we don't meet here again? There's a car parked on the other side of the road, on a double yellow line, and the traffic chappie just walked past without asking the two men inside to move on . . .'

Towards midday on the same morning, under a sky that had clouded over since dawn and was grey, through streets that with the change in the weather suddenly smelt of the sea, Inger made her way the short distance to the main Post Office at the bottom of Laietana. Inside the big neo-gothic building with its big decorated turrets she wondered which out of the many counters was the one she needed. But a recess on one side showed the way: it was filled with rows and rows of tiny pigeon-holes, lockable on the outside, open to the clerks on the inside. There were over a thousand of them. The clerk at the counter told her she could hire one for five hundred and fifty pesetas. He entered her name in a book, took her money, gave her two keys and a number – 649. She opened the small oblong door, put inside it a small envelope containing a Micro-Cassette, locked it, put the keys in her bag.

Next she caught the Metro to Urquinaona, and made the short walk to the Plaça de Catalunya branch of her bank, the German Deutsche Bank. She approached the nearest free counter clerk, plump, with black-framed spectacles and wearing a dark suit that would not have looked cheap on a cabinet minister, and identified herself as the holder of an account in the Schleswig branch. She asked to see the branch director.

The counter-clerk checked on an internal telephone and told her that she would have to wait for twenty minutes. He offered her a comfortable chair and an in-house glossy magazine. She leafed through it almost sightlessly: apparently it outlined all the extra banking services that were being laid on to help visitors and athletes during the coming Olympics.

Presently she was ushered through a heavily secured door, passed an electronic metal check, then through another door and so into the director's office.

Señor Prat was Catalan but of course spoke excellent German. He was about fifty, suited like a prime minister, wore German spectacles with a very slight violet tint. When the light from the window caught them they became reflective, she could see only bright rectangles instead of eyes.

'Frau Mahler, how can I help?'

She explained. She was expecting a large sum of money to be paid into her Schleswig account. Six hundred thousand Swiss Francs. Possibly late this afternoon, certainly during the next morning's business. She wanted the bank, that is Señor Prat's branch of the bank, to buy Euro bearer bonds – it didn't matter which so long as they weren't rubbish – to the value of five hundred and ninety thousand Swiss francs, and have them ready for collection shortly before the bank closed at two o'clock the next day when she would hand over a cheque on the Schleswig account for the right amount.

'Can all this be done, in the way I've outlined?' she concluded.

Señor Prat made a church of his finger tips.

'It can be done. But this is a very unusual request. And one I can't really recommend.'

'Why not?'

'My dear Frau Mahler, Euro bearer bonds are liquid financial instruments, like cash. If someone snatches your bag as you leave the bank . . .'

She was annoyed. She disliked banks almost as much as she disliked policemen. They patronised, they made excessive charges, they generally just got in the way of things.

'If it is possible, do it.'

He pulled out forms.

'As well as the cheque you intend to present tomorrow I shall require a written instruction to our Schleswig branch. I'll fax it to them, and datapost the original so they get it tomorrow morning. If they agree to clear your cheque then we shall be able to provide the bonds.'

In the end it all turned out to be simpler than she had

expected, with no further hassles. When it was done she walked on up the Rambla de Catalunya to the Prolebentek office.

Gómez was having trouble negotiating an observation post in the block opposite Prolebentek. It had to be the top floor because of the trees in the central section. The small lady, dark and full of energy, who ran the literary agency that occupied the whole floor wanted assurances he could not give that the surveillance equipment he wanted to put in was legal, and that he had the right to take over the small office used by her redheaded colleague. She threatened to phone her lawyer, she said she wanted to speak directly with Jefe Estrada. He fought that one off – he knew his boss would be impossibly rude, alienate her even further.

Consequently when Inger arrived observation was still limited to the two detectives in an unmarked police car on the other side of the road. One was down the street buying a beefburger, the other, the young tall one, was in the driver's seat, flipping through a small format hard porn magazine featuring quartets in unlikely positions.

Presently his colleague got in beside him, holding a polystyrene box. He opened it, bit into the bun.

'Who's the visitor then?'

'What visitor?'

'There's a woman in there. Went in, just now.'

'Oh shit.' The young tall one pushed the porn magazine to one side. 'What does she look like? We don't have any instructions about women except young Miss Sexy Tits who's on the desk.'

'See for yourself. She's coming out now.'

The older man recovered a blob of ketchup that was running down his chin, licked his finger. They watched as Inger set off back down the sidewalk towards the Plaça de Catalunya.

'What do you think?'

'She's a casual. Leave her.'

Only a few moments later though the receptionist came out,

236

now wearing a light coat and carrying a bag. She altered the 'open' notice to 'closed' and locked up.

The detective in the passenger seat looked at his watch.

'No where near her lunch time yet. It just as well we hung on. There she goes and here I go after her. See you.'

He put his half-finished beefburger back in its box, let himself out, leaned in through the window.

'Don't chuck that, I may need it when I come back.'

But the driver was already back into his magazine.

Inger walked on across the Plaça, into the top end of the Rambla, also looking for fast-food or takeaway, but preferably one selling something a bit more inspiring than beefburgers. She paused for a moment at the bookstalls, her eye caught by a big book devoted to modern sculpture. She wondered if she or her work were featured at all, but the book was sealed in cellophane, and she moved on past the flower-shops and bird-stalls. There was quite a breeze now, blowing up the street from the Columbus Monument and the sea, and she quickened her walk, wished she had a coat or a jumper. And at that moment she was identified by a Guàrdia Urbana patrol, one male, one female. They began to follow her and the male half murmured into his RT.

On the corner by the Hotel Monte Carlo she took a left into the narrow but smart Carrer Portaferrissa, found a classy baker's shop, bought *empanadillas* stuffed with tuna in a *picante* sauce. The patrol lingered outside, and made a reason for staying put of ticking off two small boys who had been playing football with a Coca-Cola tin. Inger came out of the bakers' and the patrol fell in behind her with elaborate casualness.

One of the small boys shouted after them.

'Why are you following that lady?'

But he spoke Catalan and she did not understand.

She cut down the narrow alley on the west side of the cathedral, paused to listen to buskers playing Mozart on a flute and guitar, gave them money. She moved on into the cloister to

237

the south of the cathedral. In its centre there is an enclosed and rather mysterious tropical garden with palms and white geese. They seem talismanic, like the geese on the Capitol in Rome or the ravens in the Tower of London. A fat man was trying to feed them with bread. A second patrol of Guàrdias, again one man and one woman, was waiting for her, approached her, again with studied casualness.

'Excuse me, señora.' It was the man who saluted, spoke, first. 'Do you have your passport with you, or any other means of identification?'

'Yes, of course, Let me see.' She made a business of it, making him hold the pasties, delving into her bag, trying to conceal the sudden wave of agitation that was almost overwhelming. She brought out her passport. 'And my Euro ID too, if you want it.'

'Please.'

'Is anything wrong?'

'Nothing, dear. Nothing at all.' The female one smiled sweetly. 'Just a routine check. Have you been in Barcelona long?'

'Not . . . not very long. Three or four days.'

The male officer handed the female the documents. She noted the numbers and other details. 'And you're a tourist. Yes?'

'Well, yes.'

The female looked up from her notebook. The smile remained fixed.

'And where are you staying, Mrs Mahler?'

She took a deep breath, bit her lip.

'The Monte Carlo. The Hotel Monte Carlo.'

'That's fine then.' He saluted again, pasted in a smile of his own. 'Have a lovely stay in Barcelona, Mrs Mahler. Enjoy yourself.'

They saluted yet again and walked back in the direction from which Inger had come. She waited until they had left the cloister and then walked off in the opposite direction. The fat man gave up trying to persuade the already well-fed geese to eat, followed her.

238

He entered the Plaça de Santa Maria ten metres or so behind her in time to see her disappearing into the entry opposite the bar. He went into the bar, sat on a stool at the counter in front of the barlady. As immaculately well-groomed as ever in her widow's weeds she was polishing the coffee-machine with a yellow duster.

'Coffee with milk and a Maritoñi cake.'

She slotted the coffee holder into the machine, pulled the lever which would force steam through it, placed a cup to catch the drip.

'Some time since we saw you here, Sergeant.' She put the wrapped cake on a plate in front of him.

'You may have a chance to get used to me again.'

He began to peel off the wrapper, exposing the small sponge filled with pumpkin jam – Angel's Hair. She steam-heated the milk, added it to the coffee, waited for the question she knew was coming.

'Foreign lady, German. About forty, but still a looker. Just used the entry opposite. Does she live there?' He slipped a thousand peseta note on to the counter.'

'She arrived on Monday.'

'Alone?'

'No. She's got a man there. But he doesn't come out. They're in the top floor room.'

'Tell me about them.' He began to eat his cake, drink his coffee. 'Everything. Anything.'

38

It was half past one before before the tiny spools began to turn. Cranmer's voice spilled slowly out into a large room furnished in upholstered reproduction furniture; the big windows had velvet drapes, a paler shade of dusty pink than the deep carpet. Near the centre of the room there was a large, low, round marble top coffee-table, with coffee jug, sugar, cup and saucer, all monogrammed HR, Barcelona. Incongruously the player had been placed in the middle of them, brand new and black, standing up on its end like a tiny version of the monolith in *2001: A Space Odyssey*. Procuring it had been the main reason for the delay. The Prolebentek receptionist had been sent from the Ritz in a taxi to El Corte Inglés to get it. Herz then phoned Negrín, told him to close down the office. He and the receptionist were to take a holiday, a fortnight, preferably abroad and at once.

Herz played the tape through, it took less than five minutes, then he made two phone calls. The first was to Zürich, the second was local – to the Hotel Diplomatic just three blocks away.

'Finchley-Camden? Your nephew has made contact, left a recorded message at the Prolebentek office. I've got it here now. I think you'd better come over and hear it.'

Ten minutes later there was a knock on his door and Finchley-Camden came in.

'Weather's taken a turn for the worse,' he remarked, taking off his Burberry. He nodded at the Sony player. 'Is that it?'

'That's it.'

Finchley-Camden sat on the edge of a chair, head on one side, long fingers loosely twined between his knees.

'Neat. Does it work?'

'Of course.'

Herz reached forward, picked the player up, pressed a button. There was a tiny burst of fast-forward scream, then Cranmer's voice.

'. . . appreciate, and I am sure Herr Winckelmann will too, that this knowledge gives me a very important advantage in the game we are playing . . .'

'Hang about.' Finchley-Camden raised a finger and Herz stopped the motor. 'I want to hear the whole tape. The beginning too.'

'Three sentences. Demonstrating why he feels certain that we will pay. They have no relevance to the rest.'

'Let me be the judge of that.'

'Certainly not. I and my associates are already over-exposed in this affair. Shall I go on?'

He did not wait for an answer, but reactivated the tape. The voice came again.

'Right now, as you listen to this cassette, another with full details of how I was employed to bomb the Casa Pez is sitting in a locked post office box in Barcelona. Tomorrow, Thursday, an envelope containing the key will be posted to the Casa Pez Incident Room, which it will reach on Friday morning. You will want to obtain the second key before Friday morning, so you can open the box before the police do. To do this you must authorise the immediate transfer of the six hundred thousand Swiss francs . . .'

Finchley-Camden reacted with wry admiration.

'. . . you owe me to account number 04932021 in the Schleswig branch of the Deutsche Bank. I shall then arrange for that money to be transferred to another account in another bank. If all these arrangements have been satisfactorily completed by the time the banks close tomorrow, that is at two o'clock, Thursday, then I shall phone you at the Prolebentek office in the Rambla de Catalunya, at precisely that time, and tell you how you will be able to obtain the number of the box and its second key. That's the deal. The timer's already running and the only way you can stop it is to do as I say.'

Herz pressed stop.

'That's it. There's nothing else on the tape. I've run it through.'

'Ingenious. Clever bastard, my nephew. Is there any possibility of finding a way of getting it out of the Post Office?'

'By burglary? Bribery of a counter clerk? Very probably, but that sort of operation requires time and careful planning. It's not even clear which Post Office it's in. And as he says – there's very little time.'

241

'He knows what he's doing. In the next twenty-four hours you'll be so busy doing what he wants you to do, you won't be able to put together a counter plan.'

'"You?" What do you mean "You"?'

'Well, us. Anyway, if you do intend to make that transfer to the Schleswig Bank, you'd better get a move on.'

'It's already in hand. But is that all you can offer?'

'At the moment, yes.'

'It was delivered by hand. A tall woman, dark, good-looking, about forty. She spoke poor Spanish with a German accent. Does that suggest anything?'

'No. Not at all. Nice to think he's got a bint in tow though. He never had much trouble getting nookie, even if he did tend to knock them about once he was in.'

The irritation which the Englishman always produced in Herz smouldered towards anger.

'Nice? There's nothing nice about any of this at all. Do you have nothing to suggest?'

'My dear chap, I do entirely agree with you. It's a bugger, and Tom is way out of order. I have no sympathy for him at all, and quite accept that the extremest measures are called for. But for the moment there's no practical course we can take except ride with it. Tomorrow, when he shows his presence again, we might be able to do something. But until then he has us by the short and curlies.'

Herz had no idea what a short and curly was, and felt it would be an irrelevance to ask.

A quarter to five, the Incident Room in Laietana. Lieutenant Claret looked out of the big window at the busy street below as it filled up again after the midday break. A fine drizzle was falling, there were bright umbrellas, coloured raincoats. She chewed her lip, sighed, drummed her carefully groomed but short nails on the desk. She was deeply fed-up, almost distressed. No chagrin quite equals that felt by someone who knows they are absolutely right but whose seniors refuse to listen — especially when those seniors are male chauvinist pigs and/or lecherous drunks. She had at her elbow three pages of printout and two of fax relating to Captain Thomas Cranmer late of the Royal Buff Caps. In Berlin he had done undercover work across the Wall using the excellent German he had been taught on an army sponsored crash course at Cambridge. Then the SAS, the Falklands and North Ireland. Honourable discharge, followed by a brief career on the London Metal Exchange. How that ended was chronicled in a further eight pages from the City of London Fraud Squad summarising charges they had been about to bring against him when he died.

She looked round the room with deep distaste. Accidie had descended like a mantle, the spiritual equivalent of the tobacco smoke, cigarette ash and crushed polystyrene cups that were already there. Up at the big table Gómez read the sports pages; the young tall detective, relieved now from watching Proleben-tek, had his magazine; three others played cards with a Spanish pack. All were listless. The machines were quiet.

She turned back to the pile of printouts on the other side of her desk, and began to sift through that: details of unsolved murders with factors that could tie them in with the series that ended with the Casa Pez bomb or perhaps with the murder of Willi Weise. Twenty-five from all over Europe. The latest to arrive via Paris described a young woman battered to death with a blunt instrument, probably a heavy duty flash-light, and buried in a shallow grave outside a farmhouse in the Pyrénées Atlantiques. Police wanted to contact Inger Mahler, German national, owner of the farmhouse, believed to be the mother of the victim . . .

Estrada came in, moist raincoat billowing about him, eating an omelette sandwich. The young detective tried to hide his magazine, but Estrada spotted it as he passed, grabbed it, looked at a set of pictures.

'That's not possible. I've tried. One of them would need a rubber cock to make that work. Get me a coffee.' He swept on up to the table binned the end of the sandwich, sat in his chair, shook out a Ducados which Gómez lit. 'So what's new?'

'The mayor wants your report on why security broke down at the Casa Pez.'

'I said: what's new?'

The young detective brought him his coffee.

'Pedro? That magazine? You're back at school and I'm teacher. It's confiscated, see? Bring it to me, there's a good boy, and I won't tell your mummy I found you with it.'

Sheepishly the young detective did as he had been told. As he handed it over Estrada leant round him, looked down the room.

'Conchi? What's with you? Got any ideas? Shit, she doesn't like being called Conchi.' He put on a mewling voice. 'Lieutenant Claret?'

She gritted her teeth, picked up the Cranmer file, eased herself out from the desk, went up to the table.

'Tell.'

It occurred to her that it was possible that he couldn't read, rather than just plain lazy. She pushed the thought aside.

'Thomas Cranmer. In 1982 he killed six Argentinians who were holed up in a shepherd's hut. Although he was given a medal a Labour member of Parliament questioned the necessity of the massacre. Later he served with the Special Services in Ireland where he was responsible for blowing up a car of IRA gunmen on their way to a rendezvous. At that time he worked with Kevin MacTaggart and another man called Winston Smith who was part West Indian. In 1988 he was discharged from the army because he killed, by a blow that dislocated his vertebrae, an Irishman known to belong to the IRA. The problem was this time he acted entirely on his own initiative. MacTaggart was an accessory. In July this year a warrant for his arrest had just been issued when . . . You're not listening to me.'

'No, Conchi, I'm not.'

'Why not?'

'You know very well why not.' He turned a page, leaned sideways so he could nudge Gómez. 'Now this is possible. There

244

was a girl in Bilbao, when I was stationed there, she'd circus-trained as a contortionist . . . Lieutenant Claret, tapping your foot and going tut-tut is damned close to inappropriate behaviour to a senior officer. Have you read the report of the Hanover air-crash?'

'Yes.'

'Well, so have I. Ah. That surprised you. There were twenty-one people on board and twenty-one bodies were found. Or to be precise the human tissue recovered was sufficient if reconstituted to make twenty-one. And there is absolutely no doubt at all that Cranmer was on the plane.'

'Not all the bodies were identifiable – the bomb was a phosphorous fire . . .'

'And the experts said that it was not possible for anyone on the plane to have survived it.'

'Scarcely possible is what the report I read said.'

'Oh, piss off, Conchi. The man is DEAD.'

She went back to her desk.

Accidie, scarcely ruffled, fell back into place. After a decent pause while they waited to see if anything more serious was going to be required of them, the card players shuffled, cut, dealt. Gómez went back to his paper. Estrada sat slumped, facing the room, legs stretched out in front of him, fat hands face down on the arms of his chair, head sunk in and back like a defensive turtle's. Presently he began to speak, as if to himself but clearly expecting to be attended to.

'What have we not got. One. Absolutely no indication to suggest that the bombers are still in Barça. No indication to suggest that they are not Warriors of Christ apart from the fact that they are no more than a name on electronic messages faxed to the newspapers and probably don't exist anyway. But Sasonov was a Ukrainian and on record as believing the Ukraine should remain part of a federal USSR. It's simple, too simple, but it adds up. All of this points in one direction. We should put up the shutters and go home. We've collected the forensic evidence which may be useful later, from it we know

245

the name of one dead bomber – it's not been wasted effort. And before Conchi chips in again let me say New Scotland Yard may yet come up with news MacTaggart was flashing roubles or whatever about the place, or had a Ukrainian exile girl-friend. There's a big community of them in London. In which case her incomprehensible desire to tie MacTaggart to a dead man will be seen to be as wilfully stupid as it is.'

He shifted his big bottom in the big chair, held up a hand. Gómez gave him another Ducados, lit it. The big man drew on the rough smoke, cleared his throat. Down the room Claret looked out of the window, clenched her fists into tight balls, bit her lip. I will not cry she said to herself, I will not let the bastard see me cry.

'So why don't we do that? Shut up shop, I mean. Because a patrol of Guàrdia Urbana wankers were pointed at a corpse by a family of illegal Afros living in a container who had decided said corpse was a health hazard and beginning to smell. And then homicide tied him in with a false ID and with Prolebentek, a firm we had tagged because they booked the Casa Pez and picked up the tab for the lunch. They look fruity all right, especially as homicide says the manager, Negrín, paid the stiff's bill and took his baggage after he had been killed. Incidentally his actual death was caused by a 9mm parabellum fired into his ear at point blank range. Probably fired by a Heckler and Koch MP5. They've found three more slugs and some blood that is not Weise's but which might be related to the incident. Now all this is very interesting – but at the moment it adds up to sod all. Prolebentek has gone dead. Negrín is on holiday in Corfu, the receptionist leaves tomorrow for Tunis. Have we had a response yet to our requests for information on Prolebentek? Lieutenant Claret, I'm asking you.'

'Not yet.'

'That leaves us with Heinrich Herz at the Ritz, and Roderick Finchley-Camden at the Diplomatic . . . Yes, Conchi?'

'Who is Finchley-Camden?'

Estrada sighed wheezily, sarcastically, but answered.

246

'At about a quarter to one this afternoon the receptionist of Prolebentek called on Herz at the Ritz. She then went to El Corte Inglés, where apparently she bought a Sony pocket recorder which she took back to the Ritz. She then went home to her flat in Gracia. At about a quarter to two Herz was visited by an Englishman staying at the Diplomatic. His name is Finchley-Camden. All right?'

For Claret brass bands began to play, flowers bloomed in the garden of her mind. But she checked before she spoke. On her desk, amongst all the other stuff relating to Cranmer was a faxed photocopy of *The Times* obituary. Some clerk at New Scotland Yard had chosen to do it that way, rather than type out a copy of Cranmer's military record. It began: Cranmer, Thomas Roderick, son of George Allen Cranmer (d. 1976), and Anne Mary, *née* Finchley-Camden . . .

39

Towards evening the weather cleared a little and a watery sun sank towards Montjuic. On the other side of the old port the forensic effectives who had been combing the area where Weise died packed away their bags, stripped off overalls, took down the fluttering cordon of plastic ribbon and went back to Via Laietana. Winston Smith watched them go. Then he struggled back into his blood-soaked shell top, crying and cursing as the scabs and suppurating pits came in contact with the shredded cellulose and nylon that had initially saved his life. The three Africans who had continued the process sat or stood, watched him, faces impassive. Incidents like this were not uncommon in lives lived in a limbo between legality and criminality. Close up they were faced by the immigration police on one side and on the other by petty crooks who ran extortion rackets or sold the right to labour on the huge building sites. Behind them more shadowy and threatening forces loomed: organised crime and the drug syndicates recruited pedlars and mules and the drug squads, both Policia Nacional and Guàrdia Urbana, regularly beat up the innocent with the guilty in futile attempts to discover which was which.

A sudden shoot-out in the urban wastelands was not a regular feature of their lives – but it occurred more often than a traffic incident does in the lives of regular citizens.

Nor was it the first time they had helped an anonymous wounded man whose skin and desperation claimed fraternal rights, even though they had no language in common. Nevertheless they were glad to see him go. Such visitors could bring problems, could even, after all, turn out to be dangerous in their own right.

Smith climbed down the short drop from the container on to the churned, impacted sand, was glad to find that his legs, though a touch rubbery, worked well. He lifted a hand in salute.

'You're good lads. See you around, all right? Take care.'

One of them briefly flapped a pale palm in answer. Winston turned, headed for the disused platform and the shattered station a hundred metres away. In front of him dereliction, behind the shining pillars of light that would march over it in the next months, turn the wasteland into glass and concrete, sweeping walkways, galleried shopping centres, leafy malls with fairy-tale fountains: Europe's most glitzy development – ever.

In the rubble of the station he picked up a short flat metal bar which he hoped would serve as a jemmy. He emerged from the wasteland not a hundred metres from the filling-station where Cranmer had left the car. The last rays of the sun briefly illuminated the figure of Columbus ten blocks down the palm-edged sea front, his right arm flung out towards the west he had just conquered. It was here, in Barcelona, in the Plaça Reial, that he told the tale of it all to the Catholic Monarchs four hundred and ninety-nine years earlier. Winston got his bearings

248

too, headed towards the small apartment Weise had rented for Cranmer in Barceloneta.

The single flight of stairs were a problem: by now he was dizzy, the infections in his back were producing fever, terrible sweats, nausea and breathlessness. He had just enough strength left to burst the lock mounted in cheap pine and push his way in. He found a light switch, leaned on the table. Suddenly he was seized with a fit of coughing that brought up phlegm. He spat in the sink. There was some staining that he feared might be blood – but it was brownish, not bright red.

He looked around. There was food – a half finished French-style loaf, a hard sausage they had been slicing when they felt like it. There were also mouse droppings. The crate of 25cl Mahou beer bottles was still under the table with six left unopened. And there was the broom cupboard by the sink.

He opened it. The small webbing rucksack was still on the floor. He lifted it and a mouse scuttled into the gap between the broomhead and wall.

'Hi there, Mickey. I won't hurt you, darling. Mates? Know what I mean?'

Christ, I'm going barmy. Talking to a fucking rodent.

He hoisted the rucksack on to the table, winced again as torn muscle in his back took the slight strain. He unpacked the two kilos of plastic explosive he had put there when they found they had too much for the tureen – and the spare mercury trembler detonator. Satisfied with what he'd found, he knocked the top off a bottle of Mahou.

'Cheers, Kev,' he said. 'Don't worry about a thing.'

She found Cranmer standing by the window in his briefs, doing the Canadian Air Force exercises – as far as his injuries let him. She was suddenly angry, rounded on him, told him off for being a fool. It was all a symptom of the strain she was under. She had hated almost everything about the morning: she hated forms and officialdom at the best of times, she hated underhand dealing and clearly, though she knew next to nothing about

249

what was going on, that was what he had involved her in. She had enjoyed getting her way with the Director of the Deutsche Bank but that was about all. They ate the *empanadillas* and the end of the night before's salad while she recounted what had happened. When she got to her visit to Prolebentek he interrupted.

'The girl actually said Herz is here, in Barcelona?'

'Yes, yes I think so.' She tried to remember the actual words. 'She said she couldn't give me his address, but that she would see he got the cassette right away. That must mean he's here, mustn't it?'

'Yes. I think so.' Cranmer looked pleased with himself. 'I was pretty sure he'd be here. Looking for Willi.'

'Who?'

'Never mind. Actually – the guy who shot me.'

She felt again the weight of confusion and despair.

'You're not going to tell me any more than that, are you?'

'No. So, it all seems to have worked out then. No problems.'

'Not until almost the very end.'

'What happened then?'

'It was in the Cathedral cloister. I was stopped by a police patrol. One male, one female.'

'Why?' He set down the cheap tin fork he had been using – it went with the room. 'What did they want?'

'I don't know. They said it was routine. They checked my ID. Asked how long I'd been here.'

He stood up, picked up a hand towel.

'What did you say?'

'Four or five days. And they wanted to know where I was staying.'

He moved behind her, twisting the wet towel between his hands.

'Yes. They would. What did you say?'

'I told them the Hotel Monte Carlo, in the Rambla. I . . . I'd just passed it.' She shifted in her chair, looked back and up at him. 'The name stuck in my mind.'

'SHIT!'

Suddenly he was out of control, a spring whose anchor had snapped. He swiped her across the face with the towel. She jumped up and back, knocking both chair and table over. Her eyes blazed, she was very angry.

'Don't ever do anything like that to me again. I'll kill you if you do.'

'I'll kill you if you try.'

And he hit again, one, two, forehand, backhand, and she backed away, covering her face with her arms. He threw down the towel, leapt at her, grabbed her wrists, forced them apart, forced her against the wall. She threw back her head, defiant, her cheeks crimson with the blows.

'Oh yes. You could too.' She made the sarcasm sing like a too taut violin string. 'You're good at killing, aren't you?'

'What the devil do you mean?'

'You're a killer.' But something in his eyes held her, deflected her. 'At any rate . . . you like hurting. And Laura liked being hurt. Just tell me one thing – did you kill Laura?'

'She liked being hurt.'

'You didn't have to kill her.'

He shouted now, but spaced the words too.

'I did not kill her.'

The violin string snapped. She had no gift for anger, not personal anger.

'Oh, No Man. Make me believe that.'

He pushed himself against her, his stomach against hers, and she felt the pressure, the warmth, the power. She let her head fall on to his shoulder, and he felt the heat of her tears against his cheek, and the power grew.

'Oh yes, yes, yes,' she shuddered, 'take me, please take me.'

The sun that lit Columbus shone on Inger and the man who had become again not the Thomas Cranmer who killed, but the No Man she had taken to her farm. Its warmth prolonged the languorous satisfaction she felt, a pleasure less sharp than the

251

ecstacies that had stormed her, but deeper. She sat up on the big bed with her back to the bedstead and her feet tucked to the side, like Copenhagen's mermaid. He was spread out in front of her – the back of his head on her thighs, in her lap, the lower half of his body twisted to the side with the knees up. Blood stained the dressing on the back of his leg, shortly she would have to change it. For all her romanticism and spontaneity, and in spite of the relaxed, melting state she was in, a state her tired mind and body had hungered for for days, the intelligent, cultivated, ironical side of her brain whispered: Venus and Adonis? Who do you think you are.

'From the start I valued the mystery you are.' She fondled his cheek, ran her finger on his lips. 'Always the mystery. To meet a man who does not bring a past with him.' She knew it was a lie, but preferred to stay with it. She shifted a buttock where pins and needles threatened and snaked out a long white arm for her glass filled with water and the last of the brandy.

Later though, after the sun had gone and the post-coital glow with it, the anxieties nagged back.

'A million Deutsches marks, not far off a million, is a lot of money. More really than you need. Than anyone needs.'

'But they owe it to me, as part of an agreement. I kept my side of it.'

'Normally I would say: all right – if you feel strongly, OK. But when it's as much money as that, and just for you, no one else, then it's greedy, and talking of debts, and honour and owing when there's greed there too is Mafia talk. It's getting cold. Now the sun's gone.'

He recognised a dead-end or at any rate a point it would be foolish to push beyond.

'I don't think we should see each other for a time . . . after it's all over.'

'No. Possibly not again at all.' She allowed herself a small sad laugh. 'But I shall always have the best sculpture I ever made to remind me of you.'

'Not for sale?'

'Not until I'm hungry. Or unless you want to spend some of your million on it.'

'I might.'

The room was now almost dark. The last light glowed on her hand as it stroked his cheek.

'Kiss me, No Man.'

But he never had, never did.

The sun returned to the other side of the square, shone between the stumpy spires of Sante Maria del Mar, touched with gold the low parapet and mossy tiles and forest of TV aerials on the other side. Down below the fat barlady sluiced arcs of silver water from a hose over cobbles it would not touch for several hours. Already she had serviced her first customers, the pre-dawn crowd coming back from the wholesale markets, a post-man and a couple of bus-drivers and Metro workers on their way out, serving them with coffees, omelette sandwiches, shots of brandy and anis. Normally now there would be a long lull in trade until as late as eleven when the first tourists, backpackers and couples for the most part, leaked in with their guide books, keen to see Europe's last genuinely medieval ungentrified slum and the gothic church which had been on the waterfront when it was built.

She did not at all like the look of Winston Smith when he showed up. She distrusted Afros, even pale ones, and while at first sight his shell tracksuit looked trendy and not cheap, when she caught a glimpse of the back she felt her worst fears were justified: she knew the effects of a shot-gun blast when she saw them. Nevertheless she followed him in, went behind her counter, prepared herself to serve him. The reason why was the presence of her only other customer – sitting in the table nearest to the window a thin man whom she knew to be an undercover member of a Guàrdia Urbana drug squad. It seemed likely that there was a connection between them.

Winston ordered coffee and a toasted cheese sandwich in guide-book Spanish and took them to the rear of her bar, as far

253

away from the policeman as possible. He paid English style, as soon as he had been served, with change from the money Cranmer had given him for the tureen.

At nine o'clock the fat policeman arrived and the thin policeman left.

At ten Cranmer and Inger appeared in the entry. Cranmer was carrying a document case. Without looking towards the café they disappeared up Carrer Argenteria. The fat policeman was up and away as soon as he saw them.

'I'll pay you later.'

The barlady shrugged, cleared away his coffee cup and a half eaten cake with Angel Hair jam. Then she sensed and heard a movement behind her. Turning she saw the Afro was also on his feet and her heart sank as she realised all police protection had evaporated. But his gaze was fixed on the entry opposite, and his face was lit with knowledge and determination. He hoisted up his webbing bag and made for the door.

40

At ten o'clock the Incident Room was packed with as many detectives and uniformed men as could be got in, about fifty in all. Any early morning freshness the room might have had was obliterated by the smells of after-shave, cologne, body sweat and gas, and cigarette smoke. The blinds were down at the end near the table and a black-and-white photograph was projected on a screen.

The projection's origin was a news agency's glossy: it had suffered remarkably little deterioration during electronic transfer from London. It showed Cranmer in formal morning dress, standing outside Buckingham Palace, displaying his Military Cross in its case. Gómez stood beside the screen and completed his briefing. Estrada sat beside him in his big old armchair with his feet on the table.

'Sometime he's going to come out from wherever he's holed up. He's going to buy food. Or an air ticket. Use the Metro. Your job is to see him do it and recognise him when he does. Then you follow prescribed procedure for known terrorists. You radio for assistance and you make no attempt at an arrest unless you are certain you are going to lose him if you don't. And if you do attempt an arrest, you shoot him before he shoots you. He's armed – with a Heckler and Koch burp gun probably concealed in some sort of bag, and or a pump-action, short barrel shot-gun, ditto. It's possible he still has access to Semtex and detonators. That's it for now.'

He killed the projected picture and the meeting broke up with general noise of moved chairs and chatter. Claret came through the crowd with printout in her hand.

'Tell,' Estrada barked.

'Ex Interpol, Lyons.'

'Jesus they took their time.'

'Apparently the initiating police forces, German and Swiss, especially the Swiss, were reluctant to authorise release. Anyway. Following information laid by the Rainbow Fraction, a radical Green group who have declared themselves prepared to break – '

'Terrorists in white armour. Commie bastards.'

'. . . the law, and pressed by the European Commission, Bonn is trying to mount an international investigation into the affairs of Prolebentek. They believe Prolebentek is involved in co-ordinating a billion dollar scheme whereby the laws regarding disposal of toxic industrial waste are either broken or circumvented – '

'Trying? What do they mean trying?'

'Prolebentek is registered in Switzerland, it has Swiss directors and offices in Zürich. The Swiss police won't assist without a prima facie case against them and the Prolebentek lawyers are arguing the Rainbow Fraction evidence has no validity.'

255

'So why are you telling me all this garbage?'

'Because in the Barceloneta Bombing two of the dead were leaders of the Rainbow Fraction.' Claret let her impatience show. Had the fat bastard forgotten why she had been instructed to look into the Prolebentek parent company? She spelled it out slowly. 'And I reckon that gives us, you, enough to go to a judge for a wire-tapping and surveillance warrant on the Prolebentek offices here.'

'He'll say the bomb was aimed at Sasonov by Ukrainian loonies.'

'Well, may be. But there are two men in town we've tied in with Prolebentek, apart from the local staff. Heinrich Herz, who runs a shady outfit of fixers called AlterLog, also out of Zürich, and the Englishman Finchley-Camden who runs Wolf-hound, employed Cranmer, is Cranmer's uncle. And we're all now pretty sure Cranmer was the leader of the bombers. That's enough, surely?'

Estrada swung his feet to the floor, let the front legs of his chair drop.

'Yes. It could be. Gómez, the judge who hates Brits? The one with a cousin who's an Argentinian general. What's his name?'

'Judge Jaime Ibañez.'

'That's the one. Tell him we're coming over for a bugging warrant. Come on, Conchi, you come too. You can tell him how solid the British link is with Prolebentek.'

Cranmer and Inger went straight to the Telefonica office at the Plaça de Catalunya and joined the queue for booths. The Telefonica had a small marble hall with eight numbered telephone booths. Opposite them was a counter where two clerks allocated booths, monitored the meters, and charged the users when they left the booths. It's a more sensible way to make an international call than standing in a pavement box, blasted with traffic noise and fiddling for large change. When Inger and Cranmer arrived there was only a Moroccan woman in front of them. She had sallow skin and heavy eyebrows that met above

256

her nose beneath a white head-scarf, and she tapped a five hundred peseta piece against her teeth. Behind them a fat man lit a cheroot with a particularly foul aroma.

A booth door folded inwards on its central hinge and the first user to finish his call came out.

'Number three,' one of the clerks called, and the Moroccan lady moved.

Cranmer fidgeted.

'Don't be so impatient. It's only just gone ten. We've got plenty of time.'

'I know. I'm sorry. It's just that there's someone here smoking something vile and there's a no-smoking sign.'

A second door opened.

'Number one.'

Inger and Cranmer moved to booth one. A moment of clumsiness followed as they discovered that because of the way the door folded in they could not both get in at once. Inger left Cranmer on the outside with his back to the glass door which she left as wide open as she could so he could hear what she said. Because she was in booth one the fat man now at the head of the queue was close to Cranmer. Cranmer leant across, tapped the fat man's shoulder. For a moment the fat man looked terrified and his right hand moved towards his left arm pit, then he realised Cranmer was pointing to the No Smoking sign. He shrugged, dropped the cigar and ground it under his foot. Cranmer watched with cold expressionless eyes as the fat man wiped his suddenly perspiring face on a handkerchief. He could hear Inger in the booth speaking German and he wondered if it was a language the fat man could understand.

'But that's what I'm trying to explain to you. I sold my farm in France, with the sculptures . . . yes, to a Swiss called Heinrich Herz. Yes. He actually likes my sculptures very much. Yes. For six hundred thousand Swiss francs. Oh? Really? Just a moment.' She pushed open the door. 'He says the money came in Deutsches marks. Six hundred and sixty thousand and . . . some hundreds. Does it matter?'

It sounded about right.

'No. That's all right.'

If the fat man was a crook employed by Herz probably he could speak German. And it was possible Herz had got clever and realised they would be making international phone calls.

'Booth seven,' the clerk called.

For a second the fat man went rigid, then the tiniest of eye movements expressed thought followed by resignation. He moved to booth seven, unhitched the handset and without taking his eyes off Inger and Cranmer tapped out random numbers. Presently Inger came out, took Cranmer's arm.

'That's fine. He got the dataposted letter. He'll instruct the Bank here to honour my cheque. Bastard made a fuss though, even though I've been a customer for twenty years.'

She went to the counter. The clerk asked for nine hundred and sixty pesetas, she put the change in a charity box.

'Is that OK?'

'That's fine.' But he was still worried about the fat man.

The fat man was worried about him. He waited until they were on the street then he burst out of his booth and tried to follow them. But the clerk yelled:

'Hey! You haven't paid.' She reached for an alarm button.

'But I never spoke to anyone.'

'You dialled a number. In Seoul, Korea. And someone answered.'

'Shit.'

He put his Guàrdia Urbana ID on the counter, charged on out, checked that his back-up was in place and went back to settle up. In the event he recovered from the stomach wounds he received later, so all in all it was a blessing for him. If Cranmer had seen him on his tail again during the next hour or so he would have found a way of killing him.

By this time Winston Smith had arrived at Cranmer's door at the top of the stairs in the Plaça Santa Maria. He tried his

258

jemmy on it but this one, though attacked by woodworm, was seasoned oak – seasoned through five hundred years. Each succeeding generation had refurbished the place but none of them threw away what they could still use. The jemmy snapped. Smith looked around, climbed the plank stairs to the planked door at the top – not really a door, more a sort of square hatch. It was bolted too, but on the inside.

He opened it, climbed through, looked out onto tiled roofs, not steeply sloped, chimneys, parapets, the skyline of Barcelona and the sea and the mountains beyond.

Estrada got the warrant he wanted. With Claret and Gómez he was driven back to the literary agency opposite the still deserted Prolebentek office. From another direction a surveillance team with elaborate equipment were also on their way to the same address. But he was not happy.

'It's gone sour. I believe you now, Conchi. But Cranmer's gone. Why should he stay? Nothing has moved at Prolebentek for twenty-four hours. When Finchley-Camden and Herz leave town we'll pass the file to Madrid and put the shutters up. In the meantime, let's do our best to have a nice day.'

He considered putting his hand on her knee, but thought better of it.

'Shit. Conchi? What's with you? Got any ideas? Lieutenant Claret?'

'I've told you. I think Cranmer's still around. That he was involved in the killing of Weise, that there was some dispute over money, something like that. May be the other blood is his, and he's holed up somewhere wounded. Finchley-Camden wouldn't be here if he wasn't. I think we ought to involve the Guàrdia Urbana. Another couple of hundred men and women looking out for him is bound to . . .'

'Come on, Conchi. They're wankers. You know that. If they saw him they'd either go up to him and say, hallo sir, are you Captain Thomas Cranmer, the well-known mass-murderer, and get their heads blown off, or they'd stop the traffic to help him cross the road. That's what they're best at, what they're trained for.'

He watched the avenues go by, relished the thought of waving his bit of paper at the women (naturally he had decided they were lesbians) in the literary agency. But he could not shake off a feeling of failure that had become a habit.

'You gave us the name. Cranmer. But a name is a name is a name. And you can't arrest a name. It's useful, yes. I shall feel proud of you when I go up to him and say: Meester Thomas Cranmer, I arrest you for many murders and I shall take great pleasure in shooting you if you twitch. But where's the flesh and blood? Where the fuck is he? Is this it? Have we arrived?'

Nothing much happened for nearly four hours. Cranmer declared that he wanted to remain in the open, preferably amongst trees. They hung about in the splendid Parc de la Ciutadella – or at least Cranmer did. After a fairly bright start the sky began to fill with cloud again and the temperature dropped. Inger took the opportunity to visit the Museu d'Art Modern, which had less modern art than she had expected. It was mainly devoted to what is now called 'modernist' art, and there were only two galleries of contemporary Catalan painting and sculpture.

Meanwhile, Estrada and the Policia Nacional occupied the offices of the literary agency and a bug was put on the Prolebentek phones. Towards one o'clock the fat man moved back in as back-up to the tail the Guàrdia Urbana had maintained on Cranmer. At twenty past one Cranmer and Inger moved from the Ciutadella back to the Plaça de Catalunya, where at just after half past they took an inside table in the Café Zürich. By now Cranmer's leg was playing up and he was limping. He was glad to sit at the table.

The Café Zürich is on a corner with the then still boarded up park and fountains of Barcelona's central Plaça on one side and the Rambla opposite. The outside terrace is smart, has the air of one of those cosmopolitan places every great city has that says this is where film stars meet directors; rock stars are seen with their latest girl-friends.

The inside was rather plain with white walls and dark wood tables, and benches in alcoves. A large round clock with Roman numerals was hung above the bar. Inger and Cranmer sat in an alcove, ordered coffee for him and a bottle of mineral water for her. When the long hand of the clock moved to the eight, Cranmer nodded. Inger reached out a hand and squeezed his, got up and left. When she had gone he caught the waiter's attention and made the universal scribbling gesture which means 'the bill, please'.

Inger waited on the pavement of the four-lane and very busy Carrer de Pelai until the Guàrdia on point duty blew his whistle, held the traffic up, and waving like a windmill signalled the waiting pedestrians to cross. The fat man hiding behind the green newspaper kiosk on the corner realised he needed reinforcements and he used his RT to call them up. He was still murmuring when he saw her turn into the Deutsche Bank, a few doors down the Rambla. Inside the ministerially-suited clerk recognised her. He already had a slip of paper ready saying that after paying bank charges and commission the Eurobonds could cost her six hundred and fifty-seven thousand, five hundred and thirty-two deutsches marks. He took her cheque for this sum on the Schleswig branch of the bank, her Euro ID card and her bank card into the rear, presumably to Señor Prat. A five minute wait followed. This time she did not sit down.

He came back with a thick, strong envelope from which he took a bundle of engraved certificates. He explained what they were: bonds issued by the Bayerische Bundesrepublik to finance the building of a hydroelectric dam in the Bavarian Alps, with a face value of six hundred and fifty thousand deutsches marks, how their value on the open market shifted according to interest rates, and a lot more of the same sort, which, even at the best of

261

times she would have found incomprehensible and boring, and which now filled her with panic.

He concluded: 'Please put them in a very safe place as soon as you can.'

She did her best to smile, dropped the envelope into the bottom of her peasant-weave bag, and left.

From the Guàrdia Urbana Renault 19 they had driven up from 43, Captain Martín and Sergeant Arranz saw her come out on to the Rambla. A sudden gust of wind tossed the tops of the plane trees and threw a handful of rain across the pavements. The bookstall owners started to spread plastic sheets over their wares, securing them with clothes pegs.

The big digital clock on the corner advertising Seven-Up twitched on to one forty-nine and the temperature display dropped from twenty-three to twenty-two. Cranmer came out of the Café Zürich carrying his document case. The thin Guàrdia detective who had been reading a newspaper under the awning, folded it up and followed him. Cranmer did not go far – just one block up the side of the Plaça to the telephone kiosks outside the entrance to the Catalunya Metro. He went into the first kiosk to fall free and waited. It was now one fifty three. Martín and Arranz left their car, crossed the Rambla, and went into the bank.

Five blocks away, up the Rambla de Catalunya, Finchley-Camden crossed the avenue, his Burberry flapping about him, his right hand holding down the crown of the brown derby. On the other side he met Herz who had a key and was unlocking the Prolebentek showroom door.

'We're early,' Herz said.

'We'll need to be,' Finchley-Camden replied, as he followed the Swiss in. 'He'll be punctual.'

Up in the observation post opposite, relief spread, blossomed into euphoria amongst the watchers. The surveillance equipment was working, they could hear everything that was said, and the video was turning. But best of all after nearly four hours during which Estrada had smoked a whole packet of Ducados and Claret had read one of the manuscripts on the literary agent's desk, something had happened – at last.

Back in the bank things were going less well for Martín. Last minute users had filled the waiting area as closing time approached. They respected his uniform and let him through, but the overworked clerks were less forthcoming.

Martín leaned across the counter, tried to get the attention of the clerk in the black-framed spectacles and ministerial suit.

'The manager please and quickly. This is very urgent.'

The clerk did not look up from the number keyboard he was working at until he had finished his calculation, then he swung his swivel chair to face his neighbour, a young woman in a pale blue blouse and slate-coloured suit with a pencil skirt.

'Lola, see if Señor Prat is free.'

'No. Don't see if he is free. Take me to him now.'

'Could you show me your warrant card, please.'

Martín fumbled in the breast pocket of his shirt. His colour rose. He turned to the young woman.

'Get the manager, while this arsehole checks out my ID.'

The clerk still took his time. Without rising he reached up for the warrant card, took a long look at it, at the photograph in it, handed it to Lola.

'Take this to Señor Prat and ask him if he's free to see Captain Martín.' He looked up at the policeman, allowed him a conciliatory smile. 'It's not unheard of for bank robbers to carry out raids disguised as policemen or security guards.'

Martín gave him a corrosive look, turned back to Arranz who was still at his shoulder and was using his RT to keep in touch with the street.

'What's happening?'

'She's crossed Carrer de Pelai again, seems to be going on past Café Zürich.'

'Where's the man?'

263

'Still in the phone box up by the Catalunya Metro, as far as I know. No one's reported anything different.'

A large man with tinted spectacles reflecting the overhead strip lights and a bonhomous smile pasted over obvious anxiety, emerged from his office with Lola behind him.

'Captain Martín? Good day. I am Prat, manager of this bank. How can I help you?'

He offered cigarettes across the counter. Martín refused and was annoyed when Arranz accepted. The clerk snapped a small gold lighter. Martín talked through it all.

'You have a client called Inger Mahler. German. We suspect her of drug-dealing. Under the anti-drug trafficking laws we are empowered to ask you to reveal any transactions which could possibly indicate involvement with drug trafficking.'

'What exactly do you want to know about her?'

'Oh for Christ's sake man,' Martín's fuse was almost burned up. 'Is there anything at all suspicious about her account?'

'Not as far as I know.'

Lola coughed.

'Excuse me, señor.'

'Yes?' Prat was annoyed this time. Confidential instructions from Head Office asked employees to check very carefully the appropriateness of revealing details of clients' accounts to the police, even when drug-dealing was the pretext.

'Just now Inger Mahler bought Euro bearer bonds across the counter with a face value of six hundred and fifty thousand deutsches marks – '

'And what's that in pesetas?'

The ministerial clerk swung back to his desk top calculator. He tapped away, tore off the slip of paper it spewed.

'Eighty-one million, five hundred and four thousand, eight hundred and thirty-six pesetas.'

'Shit.' Martín turned to Arranz. 'Tell them to pull them. Now.'

41

Herz stood behind the absent receptionist's desk with his hand poised over her telephone. Finchley-Camden, stooping slightly, began to read through the copy of a display showing how a truly enormous amount of concentrated acid sludge had been successfully treated after six firms with separate areas of expertise had been co-ordinated by Prolebentek. He wondered to himself if Prolebentek was quoted on the Zürich bourse, it might be an idea to buy a slice. The electric clock on the wall moved silently on to two o'clock and the telephone rang. Herz's hand pounced.

'Herr Herz?'

'Herr Biedermann?'

Up in the office of the redheaded half of the literary agency Estrada said: 'Not Cranmer. Shit.'

Claret said: 'Shush!'

The telephone conversation continued.

'I shall only go through this once, no questions after. All right?'

'I'm listening.'

'Do you know the Sagrada Familia, the church designed by Gaudí?'

'I know of it. I've never been there.'

'Then you will have to listen very carefully. After you pass through the turnstiles you go up ramps into the area where there are postcards for sale, posters, right? Go through that into the main body of the church. On the far side there is a wall of towers and windows which are in fact basically two towers with screens of stone galleries and so on between them. Both towers have spiral staircases. There is also a lift. Take the spiral staircase on your right, climb past two unglazed windows to a gallery. Turn right off the stairs into this gallery. On the stone ledge of the first window you will find the key you are looking for.'

'Herr Biedermann? Will you be there?'

There was a click, followed by a second, different, double click.

'Herr Biedermann? Herr Biedermann? He's hung up on me.'

Down in the Prolebentek office Herz had gone pale.

'Did you hear that?'

'I'm afraid I did old chap. I think we'd better go.'

Finchley-Camden put out a hand to take Herz's elbow, urge speed, silence and caution, but Herz was already moving fast. As Finchley-Camden came out on the street behind him, he turned, locked the door, mouthed the one word: 'Bugged.'

High up above them Estrada swore.

'*Coño. Hostia.* They rumbled us.' He turned on the technicians. 'What sort of shit is this equipment you are using?'

'They're crossing the road.' Claret was still at the window. 'The Englishman has a car at the Diplomatic.'

'Right.' Estrada got himself under control. 'Where did he phone from?'

'Public phone box,' one of the technicians answered. 'Downtown, not far from here.'

'Not from the Sagrada Familia then?'

'Can't be sure without analysing the tape, but I'd guess not.'

'Right then. Let's move. I'm assuming the caller was Cranmer whatever he chooses to call himself. Get a mobile there straight away ahead of them. We'll get there too as quick as we can – we know where they're going so we don't have to follow them. But leave an unmarked set of wheels on their arse just in case. It can pick them up at the exit to the Diplomatic underground car park. Listen. Gómez, make sure everyone involved understands this. He spoke of a key. I want it. But I want Herz to pick it up, I want to take it from him, I want him to take it to whatever door it unlocks. Right?' He turned to

266

Claret. 'You're the only one with real brains here. Will Cranmer be there?'

'Probably. Yes.'

He turned back to Gómez.

'If he is I want him alive. I want them all alive. So softly, softly till we have them, right? We let them get into the church before we seal it or even let our presence be felt. But if it looks as if he's going to kill again, then kill him. Is that clear? Kill him.'

On the west side of the Plaça de Catalunya, Cranmer replaced the handset, came out of the booth into the gusty rain. Inger moved to meet him, drawing the envelope of Euro bearer bonds from her bag as she did so. Suddenly, nostalgic angst hit her in the diaphragm like a blow and she felt she might faint with it. This was it. The last moment. He would take the envelope, tell her what had happened to Laura and go. That was the deal. In a moment he would be out of her life for ever, leaving her to pick up the pieces of whatever mess he had left behind. He would not even kiss her goodbye, he would just take the envelope and go.

As he reached for the envelope the fat man came at them from his right, her left. Two uniformed Guàrdias flanked him. The fat man held up his opened warrant card.

'Inger Mahler, I am asking you and your companion to accompany me . . .'

Cranmer raised the document case and fired a short burst. The case leapt in his hand as it had in Weise's – it was not like holding a machine pistol in the way it was designed to be held. The fat man went down with his hands over his stomach, howled like a dog as he rolled into the legs of scattering pedestrians. One of the Guàrdias in uniform whirled away as if a giant had buffeted his shoulder. The other got out his revolver, but the street was too crowded and he didn't dare risk a shot as Cranmer charged down into the Metro. Catalunya is a busy

267

junction, two o'clock the time Barcelona goes home for lunch. In the crowds and maze of tunnels the Guàrdia lost him.

Above, a siren and screeching tyres heralded Martín's arrival. Inger, her face a white mask, shook off the thin detective's hand but remained motionless by the telephone booth.

'No Man, you should not have done that,' she screamed. 'You didn't need to do that.'

A handful of engraved certificates drifted about her feet, lifted with the wind, drifted into the road, twisted and turned in the slipstreams of the traffic.

After that she refused to say a word – it was the only thing any of them could persuade her to say for nearly an hour.

Martín listened to the report of the Guàrdia who had attempted to follow Cranmer into the Metro. Arranz networked a description and an instruction. A man with a limp, carrying a document case, the same man they already were looking for connected with Inger Mahler, they had all seen his photograph taken in a bull-ring, was in the Metro. He was dangerous, the case concealed a gun. All effectives should move to the nearest Metro exit and observe . . .

For forays on to the mainland, Finchley-Camden kept a 1970 Aston Martin garaged privately in Calais. When asked why he chose this method of transport he was wont to reply: 'Once you're across the water, door to door, under six hundred miles, it's the quickest.' And if he had been asked by someone he could trust he would add: 'And it's easier to take a shooter with you in a car, and in my line of business you never know when you might need one.'

They came up the ramp from the Diplomatic by the rear exit onto Carrer D'Arago, and Herz told him to take a left.

'Keep straight on now for ten or eleven blocks. Who do you reckon was bugging the place? Your nephew?'

'Could be. But why not your man Winckelmann? He seems a pretty shifty sort of bastard if you ask me.'

'Not the police, then?'

'Well let's hope not, old chap. If we don't get that key we're going to have enough on our hands with Mr Plod as it is.'

He drove through the wide avenues of Cerda's Eixample with considerable skill but he had to rely on Herz's map-reading, and with the rain the lunch time snarl-ups were even worse than usual. The sudden arrival of police-cars and ambulances five blocks away also had a knock-on effect. He changed lanes to get round a bus, found himself hemmed by traffic waiting to turn right, sounded his horn, stuck out an arm, and switched back.

'That's the handy thing about having a right-hand drive when you do that. They can't help seeing your signal and they know you mean it.'

But Herz had his mind on what was coming.

'The reason for making me go to this place to pick up the key must be that he intends to kill me there.'

'Yes. You tried to kill him. He not only wants his money, he wants to make sure you won't do it again. Clever bastard, my nephew.'

'It's not a comfortable situation to be in.'

'I imagine you can look after yourself.'

'Up to a point. But your nephew has a remarkable track record in this sort of thing.'

'He's good. But you'll have me right there behind you.' Finchley-Camden laughed. 'Or, better still, behind him. And he's not expecting that at all. It'll be the devil of a shock to him when he sees me.'

'I can rely on you?'

'Certainly. As I said: he's put my whole operation at risk, considerable risk. I have to make absolutely sure he can't do anything like that again. Chaps who mess me about can't be allowed a second bite at the cherry.'

'The fact that he's your nephew doesn't bother you?'

'Yes and no. Damn bus up my arse again. Didn't like it when I squeezed past and then cut him out again. What was I saying? Yes. Poor Tom. Since the job has to be done, I owe it to him to do it properly. Some years back I had a dog, Irish Wolf-hound

269

actually. Lovely brute. Got a brain tumour though, and frankly became something of a menace. Got loose, went for a sheep and a couple of kiddies, that sort of thing. Well, you don't call the vet in for that sort of job. You owe it to him, you owe it to yourself to do it yourself. It'll be the same with Tom. Now listen. He said there was a lift . . .'

Although the Sagrada Familia lies outside Cerda's original *ensanche* it is still within the grid system and the whole complex occupies three blocks. Moving (roughly) west to east these comprise the Plaça de la Sagrada Familia, the church itself, the the Plaça de Gaudí. On the north side of the middle block, across the street, is the exit/entrance of the Metro. On the west side of the church, facing the Plaça de Sagrada Familia, are the ticket office and turnstiles. Once through the turnstiles ramps lead to the façade and the entrance to the church itself. At the time these events took place the church was undergoing very extensive building operations.

In 1926 Gaudí, already an old man when it happened, was run over by a tram before the building was completed. For decades it was left as it was or only tinkered with – a shell, a rough square or circle of pierced walls and eight perforated pinnacles that soared to over a hundred metres enclosed an unroofed nave. Everything but particularly the east and west ends were encrusted with decoration and sculpture. Gaudí left plans but also instructions that the work should continue, as in medieval times, over many generations, each adding what they liked according to the spirit of succeeding ages.

But by 1991 it seemed there might not be any succeeding ages, and Barcelona decided to finish it either before the Olympics or the Apocolypse, whichever should arrive first. The result was that in September 1991 it was a building site surrounded by a fence of spectacular masonry.

At two seventeen Cranmer emerged from the Metro, and was spotted by a Guàrdia who reported the sighting back to Martín, and then followed Cranmer, but discreetly, and at a distance, through the turnstiles, up the ramps and into the church.

The next arrivals were two unmarked Policia Nacional cars which arrived and parked on the south side. Then came the Aston Martin. Finchley-Camden had more difficulty parking since he felt constrained to make it legal. He eventually found an underground parking lot a block away. He and Herz walked to the turnstiles, bought tickets and went in. They climbed the low black ramps and passed beneath the Alpha and Omega keystone of the west entrance. Above them St Veronica and her veil, and at the top the Crucifixion done in starkly modernist designs appeared as if hewn from stacked caves. They moved into an enclosed hall with Gaudí's framed plans on the walls and at the end a foyer selling posters and postcards.

Meanwhile Estrada, Gómez and two uniformed police got out of their cars and followed them at a distance. As soon as their quarry were out of sight of the turnstiles Policia Nacional appeared from police buses parked down a side street. Moving swiftly, efficiently, and above all silently, no sirens or flashing blue lights, they closed the turnstiles and began to filter out the sightseers but always from behind Estrada and Gómez who kept Finchley-Camden and Herz in view in front. Rain on a blustery wind smoked across the squares.

The last arrivals were Martín and Arranz. The Policia Nacional officer on the gate let them through almost without thinking, they were after all uniformed Guàrdias, but when moments later four more car loads arrived he radioed through to Estrada. Estrada using the sort of language everyone was accustomed to hearing from him told him to keep the blundering wankers out, and what the hell had they turned up for anyway.

Finchley-Camden and Herz moved out of the foyer and into the 'interior' of the church. Already it was more enclosed than it ever had been, the beginnings of soaring fan vaulting beginning to spread across the sky, but the southern wall was still far from finished, indeed would be left to the end so there would always be access for the plant and materials needed to finish the

271

rest. These were enormous. Huge webs of red scaffolding screened the inner walls, the floor alternated between deep holes dug to put in the footings for the huge columns that would support four more pinnacles and a big central tower, and massive hoppers of cement and sand, mixers, stacks of dressed stone and so on. A JCB was being positioned close to one of the holes. Walkways were left for sightseers skirting all this, fenced with low rails, and the two men followed these round the plant to the inside of the east end.

Here they found things precisely as Cranmer had described them. The middle section was pierced with windows some containing the only glazing as yet in place, predominately blue, Mary's colour, whose part of the building this is. This was flanked by two stacked columns that contained the two spiral staircases and climbed to succeeding stages of galleries and unglazed windows. Sightseers can climb these elegant, simple but narrow and steep stairs – but most prefer to take the lift whose shaft and entrance is on the left-hand side. Finchley-Camden assumed that his nephew was somewhere on the right-hand side, waiting for Herz. He touched the brim of his brown hat in farewell, and using plant and hoppers as cover got to the lift entrance with, he hoped, a fair chance that he had not been seen by his errant nephew. Herz gave him four minutes and then moved to the south staircase and began to climb.

Already there were noticeably fewer visitors. None had come in behind them – many had left since their arrival. He met two backpackers cursing the narrowness of the stairs as they bumped their packs on the walls and that was all. Above him the white stone stairs, fixed to the outer wall of the tube, inner edges curved and without rails or central column and stacked one above the other, perspective up in a perfect spiral almost to a vanishing point. The problem for Herz was that he could not see who was above him beyond the turn he was on. It occurred to him that this could be a reason for Cranmer's choice of venue.

Presently a narrow gallery branched off. There was a low parapet between slender columns that formed the stone frames of unglazed apertures that looked out over the 'interior'. On the central parapet he could see the key and on the floor below it Willi Weise's document case. He knew what was in it. Questions whirled through his mind. Finally he stooped for the case first but sensed as he did so rather than heard Cranmer's presence behind him. However, he heard Finchley-Camden's voice all right, amplified by the stairs.

'Tom? I'd rather you didn't do that.'

Herz turned, saw Cranmer lower the angled edge of his right hand which he had been about to smash into his neck. His expression was terrifying – that of a Medusa rather than of one who has looked into her eyes. Herz took the step that allowed him to see Finchley-Camden duck through the low entry and level the Smith and Wesson .38 army issue revolver he was holding.

'Tom, you've been a very silly boy, up to all sorts of silly games, and dangerous too. Still, all is not lost. If you come quietly with us now, I'm sure we'll be able to work something out . . .'

Herz could see the shift in Cranmer's expression, his uncle could not. Cranmer swung himself down and simultaneously scooped the smaller man in front of him. Finchley-Camden fired, hit Herz in the side. With a superhuman effort Cranmer heaved the wounded man across the small space, scooped up the document case. Finchley-Camden loosed off one more shot from the floor but the bullet screamed off stone. By the time he was free of Herz's flailing arms and legs, Cranmer had gone, the one turn of the stairs taking him clear. The tall Englishman scooped the key from the parapet and climbed the stairs, back the way he had come.

On the walkways below Estrada and Gómez were still unaware of the presence of Martín and Arranz – a three-metre high cement hopper remained between them. All four had heard the shots, even above the roar and clatter of the plant around them. When Cranmer appeared in the entrance to the stairs Arranz drew his Browning, went into crouch position, steadied his right

273

wrist with his left hand. Martín moved in to make the arrest. But at the same moment from the other side of the hopper Gómez made his move and came between Cranmer and Arranz. Cranmer fired a second burst from the Heckler and Koch, the few remaining tourists scattered as did the site-workers, impeding the police. Cranmer swung himself over the barriers into the site area before they could shoot or stop him. He fired the remaining rounds of his second magazine into the driving cab of the JCB, leapt in, tipped the dying driver out into the churned-up debris below. Revving the engine so clouds of diesel fumes filled the air he wrenched it round, raised the shovel and the scoop and smashed into the boarding that separated the site from the street. He drove the JCB round the west end of the church where it finally smashed into the side of a coach filled with Japanese tourists – but now he was in sight of the Metro entrance. A quick dash through the swirling, scattering and umbrellaed crowds was all that was needed and he made it.

Back on the floor of the Holy Family Estrada and Martín confronted each other, Martín kneeling over Arranz who was bleeding heavily from a wound in his face.

'What the hell do you think you're playing at? Cowboys and Indians?'

'Estrada, you're a bastard. If he dies . . . then you killed him, you know that?'

'Listen. That man will live. He'll live to help old ladies cross the road which is all he's good for.' He turned to Gómez, who came running back from the staircase. 'Did you get them? Were they still there?'

'Only Herz. He's hurt, shot, but still alive. It's going to be a hell of a job getting him down those stairs. No sign of a key.'

'Shit. And thanks to these wankers, we've still got an armed killer on the loose.' Suddenly the muscles in his face dropped and his face went tired. 'So what do we do now?'

Martín straightened, came closer.

'You mean you don't know where he lives? And who he's been living with there?'

274

'And you do?' Estrada looked into Martín's face, saw the hard half-smile. 'Shit. You do.'

At just about that moment Finchley-Camden emerged from the lift. There was no need for him to go back into the interior. Passing under the arches of the east end encrusted with jolly sculptures of the Nativity and the Mysteries of Joy, he was able to use an exit-only turnstile on to the Plaça de Gaudí. Ever the unruffled British gent, he strode away, unheeded.

42

It was a relief after so long, after so much pain, to hear Cranmer's footsteps on the stair, the key turn in the lock. Winston made the last effort he knew was necessary and directed the second infra-red signaller he had found amongst Cranmer's things in the wardrobe towards the window and pressed the 'on' button. He got it back under the bolster just as the heavy door which had defeated him swung open.

'Mr Cranmer, SAH!' His attempted shout came out as a hoarse croak.

'Smith! What the hell are you doing here? And how . . .? Ah.'

Still in the doorway he took in the hole in the high ceiling. Joists dangled at the edges. Beneath it the table that had stood beneath the mirror, the table on which Inger had kept the very few toiletries she used. On the floor a broken chair and plaster everywhere. A little daylight seeped down, swirling wind, and some rain. It had formed into a steady drip that occasionally quickened into a trickle. A puddle was forming beneath it.

'Through the roof. And you hurt yourself doing it.'

'Got in all right.' Winston gasped, wriggled his back which

275

was now a fiery hell of pain. 'Hurt myself trying to get out. I reckon my leg's broke.'

'Playing silly buggers.' Cranmer watched him warily. Did he have the shot-gun? Probably, had to be the answer. 'But why?'

'Came here to kill you. Sir.'

'Join the club. Most of Barcelona seems to be having a go.'

Holding the document case at the ready, he was pretty sure its magazine was empty, but Winston wasn't to know that, he limped in closer. The wound in his thigh had opened, was painful and seeping blood. Winston was sprawled diagonally across the bed and yes, definitely his left ankle was broken: the foot was twisted in a way that left no doubt. Poor bugger had weed himself too, which probably meant he'd been there some time. No sign of the gun though – not at any rate in the West Indian's reach. He found a pack of Inger's BN on the floor near her table, and her little gold lighter. He lit one, handed it to Winston, lit one for himself.

'Why, Smith? Why do you want to kill me?'

'You killed Kev. Good bloke Kev. And then you set me up.'

'It wasn't like that.'

'Mr Cranmer, it was. It's clear enough. We knew who you were, we knew you were alive. You needed us, but when you didn't need us any more, you killed Kev, set me up, and blew a hole in me back. And I know how you killed him. With this.' He showed the signaller. 'You had two of them. That was a bastard trick, you know? Planned too. So I came here to kill you. Least I could do really.'

Cranmer's mouth creased into a grimace, then he turned to the alcove, and with the cigarette clamped in his mouth and his eyes screwed up against the smoke he filled a saucepan of water, lit one of the gas-rings. He drew on the cigarette, turned, elbow of right hand on wrist of left hand, looked down at Winston.

'Shame you see it like that. I'm going to have a coffee. Do you want some?'

He put the cigarette in a saucer, pulled out two mugs from

276

the cupboard below the sink, turned to put them on the second table, the one in front of the central window.

Winston winced, shut his eyes and murmured: 'I'd rather have tea if you've got some.'

'I think we have.' Still holding the mugs he turned back to the alcove. 'Tea-bags, anyway.'

'We? Would that be the woman I saw you with?' Winston seemed to need to keep the conversation going.

'Ah. You've been spying. Yes actually.'

'Will she come back here?'

'There's just a chance.' Then, responding to crescendoing police sirens outside. 'On the other hand it's possible she has set me up.'

He went round the solid deal table to the window, looked down and out. Intense headlights swung round the tiny Plaça, turning the leaden rain to silver. Police cars arrived in each of the narrow entrances, sealing it. Blue lights span.

'Shit. It rather does look as if she has set me up.' He moved back into the room, back to the gas-ring. 'Tea-time. I think you're right. Tea better than coffee at a time like this.

Down below Guàrdias, now in light blue nylon anoraks against the rain, erected barriers at the further ends of the streets that led in, police in black oilskins above padded flak jackets moved against the parked cars, drew beads on Cranmer's three windows and the entry below with high velocity rifles. In the street most nearly opposite the entry others began to erect a powerful spotlight, unspooling a black lead to the nearest shop – a tiny place that sold milk, eggs, and withered vegetables scavenged from the market. Two more cars arrived behind them, one Guàrdia Urbana, the other Policia Nacional. Estrada, Gómez and Claret joined Martín and other uniformed Guàrdias. In the centre of the group they had Inger. She held her head up, let the rain stream down her face, refused the coat a female Guàrdia tried to put over her shoulders. Eyes screwed up she peered through the gloom at his high window. The outer blind was up, the slatted shutters closed and there was no light beyond. It must, she thought, be almost dark in there – even though it was still not quite three o'clock.

A policeman saluted Estrada.

'He's in there all right. The woman in the bar saw him arrive.'

'So. How do we get him out? Martín? Is that woman going to help?'

Martín stood beside him.

'No.'

'As long as he's got that burp gun no one's going to get near him without being hurt.' He shook out a Ducados, shielded it against the rain. Gòmez tried to light it for him, failed. 'Oh shit, leave it. I'm open to suggestions.'

Claret came in on his left.

'Surely the woman, Mahler, could talk him down.'

'She's not co-operated at all yet.' Martín was brusquely dismissive. 'She's not said a word since we arrested her.'

'May be she'll listen to me.'

'Women's talk?' Estrada gave a rueful laugh. 'Give it a try.'

'No. Not women's talk. You said her name is Mahler. Is she Ingrid Mahler, a German?'

Cranmer moved about in what was now almost complete darkness. Heavier clouds had rolled in from the south, purple, black. On the bed Winston's cigarette glowed but did not move. Cranmer murmured to himself.

'What have we got here, Smith? Small rucksack? Where have I seen that before? Damn it, yes. In the flat Willi found for us. And what did it have in it? The plastic, Smith. And there was what . . . two kilos unused? Jesus, Smith, you really were the king of the nasty little schemers, weren't you? SHIT.'

Suddenly the room had filled with stark light – from the spotlight, penetrating the slats of the shutters. Winston did not react. His head lolled on the pillow in an attitude as impossible as his twisted foot. The cigarette burned towards his lifeless fingers.

'Time to go.' Cranmer recovered from the sudden glare, but kept back from the window, looked around him, took in again the chair that had been piled on the table beneath the hole and that it had toppled as Winston jumped for the joists above.

'Silly bugger. No wonder you broke your leg. But what have you been up to? You broke your leg on the way *out*. So you had done what you came to do. You had laid your bomb, then you planned to get up into the roof again and activate it from there before doing a runner. But you fell. So somewhere in here there is a little bomb, little, but plenty big enough, and almost certainly armed. Definitely time to go.'

He made careful preparations for his departure. First he took the Heckler and Koch from its case, replaced the spent magazine with the third and last, slung it on his back. Then he looked very carefully all over a chair before touching it. Once he was satisfied that there was no plastic stuck to it he picked it up and was about to put it on the table under the hole, when he stopped, and checked the table. Satisfied at last he put the chair on the table, climbed on to the table, and then on to the chair, reached up. He got his hands into the hole. Got a grip and hoisted himself upwards, but the joists and plaster gave way, dumped him first on the table then on the floor in a shower of debris. He froze, waited for the explosion which did not come.

'Christ. No wonder you broke your leg.'

He moved towards the table in front of the window, was stooping to look under it when a loudspeaker crackled, boomed with feedback.

Inger looked up through the curtaining rain at the spotlit window. She felt dead now, beyond caring, beyond feeling. But these people, these people she hated, and especially she hated the woman who had told her what she had known all along, wanted her to speak to him again, once more. She forced herself to find something to say, to make the sort of noises they wanted to hear.

279

'No Man? Are you still there? Please listen, No Man. You've killed enough now. They'll kill you if you don't give yourself up. But the killing has got to stop.'

She heard her voice, distorted and amplified, not really her own but appropriated by gadgets and the law, boom around the square, bounce from the façade of the church with its naïf madonna on the lintel of the door. 'I've never asked you for anything. No Man, that must mean you . . . owe me. Does that count for anything? Oh I don't know . . . But. No more killing. Please. Not you or anyone.'

She could hear the despair in her voice. It wasn't working, she knew it. She felt pressure from the woman by her side, reminding her of her new knowledge. She looked down into the policewoman's dark eyes and shuddered convulsively.

'They've told me about her. They discovered her body. At the farm . . . Laura . . .' She choked on the word, then drew breath, for her last effort.

Up in the room he snarled, giving up on her. He turned from the window, back towards the table.

'*Tom?*' The name was sung, high and clear like a trumpet. '*Do the people who love you call you Tom?*'

'Bitch.'

He seized the table with one hand at each end. Surely it was too heavy.

The window, shutters and glass, billowed and his burning body hurtled through it, arms and legs spread, trailing shards and petals of flame. Apart from the fact he was now coming out backwards the moment echoed his exit from the plane, Inger's sculpture, and Icarus falling out of the sky.

EPILOGUE

Winckelmann stood behind the huge sheet of tinted glass that formed the window of his office and looked down fourteen stories to Zullikerstrasse below. It was dusk and the busy-ness of the day was leaking away. Amongst the commuters leaving the offices and shops a few residents were out walking their dogs, making last minute purchases at the kiosks or pâtisseries.

He squeezed his enormous fist and felt the plastic corners of the tiny Micro-Cassette press into his palm. He was very angry, but determined if possible not to show it.

Behind him Finchley-Camden, sprawled insolently in deep black leather, cleared his throat, recrossed his legs.

'Of course I've had it copied.'

The rage blossomed like a scarlet flower filmed with a frame shot every five minutes. The Micro-Cassette shattered and Winckelmann let the shards drop into the deep white carpet.

'Of course.'

Winckelmann opened his palm, glanced down at the welling blood. He pulled a big white handkerchief from his pocket with his left hand and folded it into the other.

Finchley-Camden continued: 'One can't be too careful.'

'You mentioned a quite large sum which you said was for this . . . thing. But clearly what you came to sell was not a recording but your discretion.'

'That's right.' The Englishman's voice was as bland as his smile. 'And I have to say that I'm not really prepared to negotiate the price.'

Amongst the dog-walkers was a whore Winckelmann

281

occasionally spent time with – especially on evenings when things had not gone too well. She was tall, Nigerian, glamorous in a very conventional way, dressed today in a light silk coat, a sort of muted scarlet that set off, especially from above, short-cut black hair that shone wetly. She had a large male Rottweiler, muzzled. At private parties she included her dog in her act.

Winckelmann watched her progress up the wide pavement, but dragged his mind back to the problem in hand.

'Would you accept Prolebentek shares?'

'Yes, I think I might. That is if I knew more about you, if I could feel certain that what my poor nephew did for you leaves you where you want to be.'

'We make secret contracts with industries who are having problems with EC waste disposal regulations. We shift their muck for them – to Russia mostly . . . What people still call Russia.'

Down below the dog defecated hugely on the pavement. Winckelmann droned on. 'We have deals, also secret, in seven of the Republics and we are negotiating more. It won't last more than four or five years but thanks to our recent exercise in damage limitation and crisis management, we expect to make very big profits indeed during that time . . .'

It added up, Finchley-Camden had to concede, to what indeed looked like a very attractive investment. He decided it would be foolish to refuse Winckelmann's offer – especially if acceptance would ease any residual bad feeling between them.

'Yes,' he said. 'Yes, that will do nicely. Six hundred thousand Swiss francs worth at today's closing price then, shall we say?'

Winckelmann waited while the beautiful woman with the dog did what Swiss law required her to do with a poop-scoop and a handy Robi-dog – one of the bins the Swiss authorities provide. In waste disposal, Winckelmann reflected, there's always money to be made. He looked at his watch. There was still time to manipulate the Prolebentek share prices a point or two before the bourse closed. He turned.

'It seems it may be some time before poor Heinrich is back at

282

work and AlterLog fully functional again. I wonder if we might explore one or two possibilities this situation might open up for you . . .'

It all quite made Finchley-Camden's day for him . . . shame about poor Tom.

Crikey I'm...

Getting
Married

Other titles in the *Crikey I'm...™* **series**

Crikey I'm A Teenager

Crikey I'm Thirty

Crikey I'm Forty

Crikey I'm Fifty

Crikey I'm Retired

Crikey I'm In Love

Crikey I'm A Mum

Crikey I'm A Dad

Crikey I'm A Grandparent

Crikey I'm...™

Getting Married

Contributors

Julia Cole
Victoria Warner
Eliza Williams

Edited by

Steve Hare

Cover Illustration by

Ian Pollock

PURPLE HOUSE

Published by Purple House Limited 1998
75 Banbury Road
Oxford OX2 6PE

© Purple House Limited 1998

Cover illustration: © Ian Pollock/The Inkshed

Crikey I'm... is a trademark of Purple House
Limited

A catalogue record for this book is available
from the British Library

ISBN 1-84118-020-3

Printed in Great Britain by
Cox and Wyman

Acknowledgements

We are grateful to everyone who helped in
the compilation of this book, particularly to
the following:

Stephen Franks of Franks and Franks (Design)

Inform Group Worldwide (Reproduction)

Dave Kent of the Kobal Collection

Bodleian Library, Oxford

Central Library, Oxford

Condé Nast Magazines, London

British Film Institute

Liz Brown

Mark McClintock

Hannah Wren

Illustrations

Contents

Crikey, I'm Getting Married!

Marriage is the rock on which our whole society is founded. The family unit, stability, continuity – love. There are powerful forces still at work today that predate history. It's why we're here at all.

From time to time the inexorable rise in divorce rates and single parents gives rise to the commonly voiced assertion that the institution of marriage is dead. The closest, perhaps, that this statement ever came to reality was in Margaret Thatcher's chilling belief that there was 'no such thing as society'.

However, 60 per cent of people marrying today will remain happily married for the rest of their lives; they will not be condemned, as couples were once, to years of private animosity and anguish for the sake of convention and outward show. It is more likely that the percentages of 'happy' and 'successful' marriages have probably changed very little over the last hundred years. We are just a little more honest these days.

All the same, in every culture, and every religious and secular service today, couples are advised to treat the matter with due gravity. It is a big step; and tradition dictates that you put yourselves on public view, after long examinations of your feelings and ambitions. It is a milestone – a seminal point in your lives. It is a time for reflection; but it is also a time for the best celebration of your lives.

This book does not set out to preach, or even advise. It provides no checklists, hints or tips on popular hymns or style of dress. It merely celebrates the institution of marriage: an event that unites you with similar people in similar circumstances in every land and culture around the world; that involves you intimately in a limitless past, and defines your own future. It's also the best excuse you'll ever have for enjoying yourselves and delighting in the company of those you know and love.

Marriage Lines

A Short History of Marriage

People have been getting married, and celebrating the fact, for almost as long as there has been any organisation of society. It is one of the main bases upon which society is built. And in many cultures, over many thousands of years, the way marriages were celebrated would not seem so very different to us now.

A Contract to Wed

The events leading up to marriage, however: boy meets girl, they fall in love, they get married – now that is a relatively recent phenomenon. Marriages between families of any social standing were almost invariably arranged; if the couple had ever met, it would only have been by coincidence. The contract had little to do with them, and everything to do with minor alliances, finance and the continuation of the family line. The word itself, 'wed', originally meant a 'pledge'.

According to a MORI opinion poll in 1997, the three most important factors that make a successful marriage are faithfulness (79%), understanding and tolerance (77%), and mutual respect and appreciation (75%). 81% disagree with extra-marital affairs.

In ancient Greece, marriage was a simple business affair, arranged by the parents, and often involving a girl of 15 or so being paired with a man

Spencer Tracy and Elizabeth Taylor as father and daughter in *Father of the Bride*, 1950.

more than twice her age. If he were to die without providing a male heir, she might be obliged to marry his nearest relative, and keep on trying.

Things were much the same in biblical times, though marriages tended to be between teenagers of a similar age. The contract involved a payment to the bride's family for the loss of their daughter – not in sentimental terms, but in terms of the work she would have provided for the household, and the necessity of finding and paying someone to take her place. The whole affair was arranged by the fathers, without any consultation of the couple. Abraham is supposed to have sent a servant over 1,000 miles to collect a bride for his son Isaac; there was intense concern among Israelites to choose wives for their sons from their own kith and kin. The marriage of cousins was very common.

When in Rome

Virtually every general feature of today's Christian marriage service can be traced back to Roman nuptial celebrations. Then, the bride would wear a veil; she would formally be handed into the care of the groom; the two would make solemn declarations; and eventually, the bride would be brought to the groom's house in triumphal procession.

After the Romans introduced their form of marriage into the countries they colonised, Christian values and ceremonies were gradually incorporated over the centuries. Even so, polygamy in Britain was common until the Middle Ages, and even in the seventeenth century, Daniel Defoe could still comment ironically that it was frequent in Essex to meet with men who had 'five to six, to fourteen or fifteen wives, nay and some more'.

Grounds for Divorce in Justinian Rome

A woman might be granted a divorce on grounds of treason, adultery, murder, poisoning, violating sepulchres, forgery, stealing from a temple, robbery, cattle stealing, attempts on her life, introducing immoral women in to the house, and common assault.

A man might gain a divorce on grounds of his wife dining with a man to whom she was not related without permission; going out at night without reasonable cause; frequenting circuses or theatres without permission; procuring an abortion; indulging in mixed bathing; or plotting against him with poison or sword.

From the Prison to the Green

Henry VIII's Reformation, and the split with the Roman Church, had their effects on attitudes to both marriage and divorce. For the common man and woman, however, it was the Civil War and Puritan ethics which introduced the biggest changes; with church weddings banned altogether, along with the wearing of a white dress, itself a recent innovation.

Even the wearing of rings was officially frowned on. Otherwise, from the beginning of the seventeenth century, church weddings were the only recognised ones. The reading of banns was introduced, and the age of majority set at 21; no one below that age could marry without their parents' or guardians' consent. The arranged marriages which had always been the norm among the upper classes now began to encounter resistance: the romantic notion of the love match concerned the young parties involved, more than the economics which occupied their parents' minds. Unlicensed services were often performed, which became known as 'Fleet' marriages, conducted by clergymen imprisoned for debt in London's Fleet Prison but still able to carry on business as usual.

Lord Hardwicke's 1754 Marriage Act put a stop to this loophole for under-age or thwarted lovers, as well as the

Banns

The Archbishop of Canterbury introduced the reading of the banns for Anglican weddings in the four-teenth century to invite the public to come forward if they knew of any reason why the couple should not be wed. They are read aloud in church on the three successive Sundays preceding the marriage.

dubious unions forged there. Now they had to travel to Scotland to take advantage of their more liberal rules – anyone over 16 could marry there. And the first stop over the border – Gretna Green – became the favoured destination for young runaway couples,

she's bound to be a good cook—
and save money *too*...

with a *Kenwood* Chef!

No drudgery for *her*—no dull meals for *him*—there's a KENWOOD 'CHEF' in the kitchen! It does *all* the hard work of food preparation, turns complicated recipes into easy everyday delights, makes exciting new drinks and dishes that used never to be possible at home. Peeling, mixing, slicing, mincing, beating, shredding, juice separating, can opening—it's all done in a moment electrically, and far better than by hand. Look at the list of attachments (many of them have several uses) and you'll realise that the 1957 housewife simply cannot do without a KENWOOD 'CHEF', the world's most versatile Food Mixer. *Appointed electrical dealers and department stores stock the 'CHEF' and attractive easy terms are available.*

Note to him !

You can buy her a Kenwood 'Chef' for an initial payment of only £3.15.0 and eight monthly payments of £3.15.0. Cash price £31.8.0.

Mixing Bowl, taking 6 lbs. of mixture, K Beater, Whisk and Dough Hook are included with every Kenwood 'Chef' as well as Plastic Dust Cover, Rubber Spatula and Recipe & Instruction Book.

The 'Chef' is available in White or Cream with choice of Red, Green, Blue, Yellow or Black plastic parts.

AFTER-SALES
SERVICE

Kenwood Service Engineers call on all CHEF owners twice a year to ensure that their machines are kept in perfect running order. Sign up for Service.

YOUR SERVANT, MADAM !

KENWOOD MANUFACTURING CO. LTD · WOKING · SURREY

The bride's lot has changed rather since this Kenwood advert from 1957!

at the blacksmith's shop. An 1856 law, requiring three weeks' residence in Scotland rather put paid to this means, though such marriages did not actually become illegal until 1940.

Tied Together

In Scotland, until the eighteenth century, a Handfasting Fair used to be held every August; an opportunity for couples to enter into a year's trial marriage. The ceremony simply involved a couple clasping hands and promising to remain faithful to each other for the coming year. They were bound together for only 12 months, and after that they could part company with no obligation or disgrace. Alternatively, they could find the 'Wandering Friar' and renew their vows.

Carefully Arranged

Throughout British history, marriage has been a matter of varying concern to the State, the Church, clans, families and individuals, with one or the other gaining or losing influence over time. After centuries of arranged marriages, the idea today is unthinkable to all but the more traditional families with Asian roots. All the same, today's rich and powerful, while they would not dream of letting their parents arrange a marriage contract for them, will be extremely careful to instruct their lawyers to draw up a watertight prenuptial agreement to protect their interests.

Virgin on the Ridiculous

Double standards are as old as marriage itself. It has been accepted throughout the history of patriarchal societies that men must sow their wild oats, while the women they would eventually marry remained pure and unsullied. A Russian man traditionally displayed his wife's night-clothes the morning after the wedding night, presumably to prove that she had been a virgin before, and no longer was. Some marriage ceremonies included physical checks for chastity, and the whole marriage contract could be annulled on the lack of such evidence. With a combination of virgin brides and wild oats being sown, clearly there was either some strange mathematics at work, some very tired girls who weren't the marrying kind, or a great deal of dishonesty practised.

Bedding the Bride

'Bedding the Bride' was a medieval practice of having the guests accompany the bride and groom to the bedroom – the custom occasionally extended to sewing the couple into the sheets, to ensure, as it were, consummation.

To prevent the latter happening, infant betrothals were often adopted, where a young girl would enter her future husband's household to be watched over

The hot fashion for nineteenth-century weddings, as mod-
elled in the Museum of Costume, Bath.

until such time as she was deemed old enough to marry, thus safeguarding her chastity to the family's satisfaction.

In some societies even this measure was not enough. So important was the concept of bridal purity that considerably worse violation was carried out in the form of infibulation – a crude surgical procedure to make intercourse impossible. There was then the renewed humiliation of its forcible reversal on marriage and, apparently, a repetition of the whole procedure if the husband had to leave home for some time.

It is worth pointing out that the term 'infibulation' comes from the Latin *fibula*, a word with several meanings: a human bone; a brooch with a clasp like a

Droit du Seigneur

Stories still persist of the medieval practice of droit du seigneur; the right of a lord to spend the first night of marriage with any bride under his dominion. Such a right did seem to exist, for a short period in parts of France and Italy, but existing records only mention payments to avoid its enforcement. Certainly lords did have the right to choose wives for their vassals, but this too could be avoided by payment. The practice would seem, therefore, to be more concerned with raising revenue than the expectations of the noble concerned.

safety pin; or 'a stitching needle passed through the prepuce' to prevent intercourse. The mind boggles. The eyes water.

Marriage à la Mode

At the end of the twentieth century, we possess a freedom of choice unthinkable at almost any period in the past: a selection that extends beyond the strictly traditional and includes a wide range of ever more exotic locations (both for the service and for the honeymoon), as well as choice of dress and form of service.

> Just over 50 per cent of people, in response to a MORI opinion poll in 1997, said that the best age for a man and a woman to get married is the mid to late twenties, and just under two-thirds said that marriage should be forever.

The 'traditional' wedding – white dress, bells, choir, reception – is just one option. Hemlines, veils, waistcoats, ties and trousers may change from season to season (to the constant embarrassment of long-married couples reviewing their albums and videos), but marriage itself, whatever the cynics may say, remains very much in fashion.

And long may it prosper.

To love, honour and

plan a family

get this *NEW, FREE book*

What makes a marriage happy? How can you solve the inevitable early difficulties . . . learn how to order your future, plan your family?

Here is a new booklet, **Marriages are Made**, specially written for younger married couples, completely different from anything you may have read before.

Simple, frank information.

In 32 pages of absorbing reading, the booklet tells of problems facing both husbands and wives, of the simple paths to happiness.

The family you want.

Marriages are Made shows how to plan your ideal family, explains all the latest methods, including the 'Pill' and I.U.D. (or Coil).

This is vital reading for both husbands and wives. Send today for your free copy.

An early advertisement for family planning from 1967.

I Do

Wedding Vows and Promises

The vows are the most important part of the wedding, and they tend to follow common themes across religious and secular ceremonies.

In modern Britain, vows can take many strange and unusual forms – it is quite common nowadays for people to write their own, as a way of making the ceremony more personal, and more relevant to the couple themselves. Although they are not always legally binding, their intimate and personal nature can make these vows seem even more important than the legal alternatives.

The Anglican wedding vows require you to 'love and honour your partner, and to remain steadfast until death'. Most wedding vows follow this theme of joining and commitment to one another, although each religion approaches them differently.

I Do... I Don't... I Do...

Elizabeth Taylor and Richard Burton were married in 1964. They divorced in 1974 only to remarry in 1975, and divorce once more less than ten months later.

In orthodox Jewish ceremonies, for example, the bride's silence signals not her reluctance – or a sulky disposition, but her consent. The couple then show their commitment to one another by sipping from a glass, which is later stamped on and broken by the groom, symbolising, amongst other things, the destruction of Jerusalem.

This is another common theme of religious wedding vows – the joining together of the couple, whilst wedding them to their faith. It's an idea found in the Catholic cere-

> **'Just over half the people surveyed agreed that without wedding vows it is too easy for people to walk out of a relationship.'**
>
> From a MORI opinion poll on attitudes to marriage, October 1997

mony where (if both members of the couple are Catholic) the husband and wife are allowed, during a blessing from the vicar, to administer the sacrament to one another, through the act of giving and receiving their marriage vows.

Religious wedding vows also involve sharing and exchange. In many ceremonies this is symbolised by the giving of rings; in Buddhist ceremonies, though, the couple sip from three bowls of increasing size, showing the way their lives will expand together.

The most simple ceremony of all is practised by Quakers. The couple, when they feel ready, rise and say a simple vow to one another, followed by a silence in which other members of the group can offer words of support and inspiration to them.

Sisters take the plunge together in *Seven Sweethearts*, 1942.

Something Old, Something New

The Truth Behind The Traditions

As all the handbooks will tell you, everything about a wedding needs careful planning; nothing must be left to chance. Similarly, the typical church weddings contain no single element that does not have some historical or symbolic significance. Every single aspect of the day is steeped in history and meaning, most of which is given no more than a passing thought by any of the participants. Perhaps the vicar will have a story or two about confetti, but he is more likely to remind guests that it should not be thrown near the church, because it's dreadful stuff to sweep up afterwards.

> **'Marriage is a great institution, but I'm not ready for an institution.'**
>
> Mae West

Much of the significance in customs and clothing, moreover, predates Christianity itself and has no basis in that faith. Their survival, from beyond any written tradition, might just be pure coincidence rather than some awesome folk memory at work, but all together, these myths and legends, custom and folklore add to the powerful sense of occasion and continuity that makes every wedding so special.

Fruitfully Multiplying
Primitive peoples had sex on the brain. Fertility was the key: their very survival depended on the growth

and harvest of crops, the increase of herds and the animals on which they fed. Their gods had normal, and often voracious, sexual desires and had, in legend, often visited earth to satisfy these urges, occasionally taking on odd forms to do so. It was natural, therefore, that early religious rites and ceremonies would incorporate sexual behaviour. 'You may now kiss the bride' might even be the staid remnant of a much more demonstrative act before an approving congregation.

> '**Marriage is the one subject on which all women agree and all men disagree.**'
>
> Oscar Wilde

Christianity, like most contemporary religions, keeps such matters at arm's length. There is no sex in heaven; such thoughts and acts are only ascribed to the Devil and his minions. Nevertheless, one of the prime stated reasons for marrying today is to be fruitful and multiply. In some cultures, married status is only recognised once a child is born, and failure to reproduce can be grounds for divorce.

This Year, Next Year, Sometime...

The month in which you choose to marry is important. These days we think in terms of convenience, arranging the day around holidays and work commitments. June remains the most popular month, for good and venerable reasons. The ancient Romans favoured it, for it was the month of Juno, goddess of

The Wedding Week

The days of the week all have their significance, though with current trends, this nineteenth century rhyme clearly needs a little updating:

> Monday for wealth,
> Tuesday for health,
> Wednesday the best day of all.
> Thursday for crosses,
> Friday for losses,
> Saturday no luck at all.

marriage, who would look favourably on those marrying at this time. April, on the other hand, was devoted to Venus, the goddess of love, and was similarly favoured. To marry in May was deliberately to scorn these two influential ladies, and was inauspicious. May, moreover, was the month of the aged. *Marry in May, you'll regret it for aye*, says a proverb.

Some of the reasons are older still: in primitive agricultural economies there were more practical forces at work. Relying on an increase in herds and the annual harvest, a June marriage would mean a birth the following March: time enough for the mother to recover and work at the harvest! An ancient Scottish proverb sums it up neatly:

> *He's a fool*
> *That marries at Yule.*
> *When the corn's to shear*
> *The bairn's to bear.*

Foot fashion from the ninteenth century.

Tying the Knot

Knots throughout history have been regarded as powerful amulets to guard against evil spirits. Marriage is still referred to as 'tying the knot'. Wedding gifts might include knotted handkerchiefs, and some ceremonies involved tying the bride and groom's hands together with three knots, symbolising the Trinity; or tying parts of their clothing together. The knot was so powerful that accidental knots – twisted articles of clothing – were thought to be possessed by demons.

Unusual Target Practice

As an antidote to various knot-tying spells used to make a new husband impotent, medieval French priests advised the affected husband to urinate through his wedding ring – a practice which survived until last century.

Taboos associated with knots were closely connected with the rites of passage of birth, marriage and death. To help a woman in a difficult childbirth, for instance, all knots in the house might be undone. Even braiding the hair might constrict the baby's passage. Traditions existed of opening all the doors in the house, and opening all drawers and boxes, even uncorking all bottles and letting farm animals loose – all to assist the woman giving birth. In some cultures it was even considered unlucky for the husband to sit cross-legged during his wife's pregnancy. Romans forbade sitting with crossed legs or clasped hands at important meetings, as it signified aggression.

Knots were believed to have the power to kill, or for an enchantress to win a lover and 'attach' him to her. It was believed in Britain right up till the eighteenth century that the consummation of a marriage could be prevented by casting spells on knots at a wedding. To indulge in such sorcery was punishable by death. Thus wedding superstitions concerning the loosening of all knots on the bride and groom evolved. It was once common, in Scotland, for the bride and groom to leave one shoelace undone. Nets, composed entirely of knots, were particularly powerful against the influence of sorcerers: Russians would stand under one to get married.

A Roman bride's garments were fastened with a girdle of sheep's wool and bound with a 'herculean' knot. This had to be ceremoniously untied by the husband. It indicated the binding character of marriage, and symbolised the loss of virginity. Undoing it was a good omen: the couple would be fortunate in raising children. Hercules, never one to do anything by halves, fathered 70.

If You Marry In...

White	You've chosen all right
Blue	Your love is true
Pearl	You'll live in a whirl
Brown	You'll live out of town
Red	You'll wish yourself dead
Yellow	You're ashamed of your fellow
Green	You're ashamed to be seen*
Pink	Your fortunes will sink
Grey	You'll live far away
Black	You'll wish yourself back

* It is considered bad luck to get married in green unless the bride is Irish

Good Luck, Bad Luck

Good or bad luck attended the couple's every move on the day: it was good luck to find a spider in the dress as the bride prepared herself for the wedding, but bad luck not to remove every pin from the dress and veil when she changed out of them later. The bride should look at herself just once in the mirror before leaving, but she must leave one item of clothing off – perhaps a glove. The groom, of course, should never see her outfit before the day. It was good luck to be woken on your wedding day by birdsong, and bad luck to break anything on the day. Seeing a chimney sweep, particularly a filthy one, approaching you was particularly lucky; sweeps are connected with the hearth, the centre of the home, though they are not so common today.

Much of the wedding day seemed to be spent avoiding evil spirits. In some cultures, brides and grooms would go to great lengths to disguise themselves, brides even cutting their hair short and dressing as men. The wearing of a veil served a similar purpose. Otherwise, brides travelled only in the company of bridesmaids, women of similar age, appearance and dress, for the express purpose of confusing malevolent spirits.

Borrowed and Blue

Something old, new, borrowed and blue all have their meanings: old represents the past and family; new – since the sixteenth century at least – is a white dress,

A bride full of pride in *Das Girl von der Revue*, 1928.

part of the necessary purification for this important rite of passage. Borrowed symbolises the shared values of the family and friends; something blue (the colour traditionally worn by the Virgin Mary) suggests purity and is also an ancient Jewish symbol of fidelity. A sixpence on the bride's shoe will ensure wealth.

The average price of a wedding dress in 1997 was £689. The whole wedding outfit costs, on average, £973.

Garters remain a necessary part of the ensemble: men once removed the garter and threw it to their unmarried friends for them to fight over, in much the same way as the bride throws her bouquet. Girls used to place garters under their pillows, if they wished to dream of the man they would marry.

With This Ring

The giving and wearing of rings is as old as the ability to work metal, and no doubt rings and jewellery of bone, wood or clay existed before then. Rings are obviously symbols of permanence and eternity, strength and completeness. Wearing a ring was an outward symbol of fidelity, but perhaps also of ownership. Inevitably, they symbolised wealth and power. In ancient Rome, freemen might wear iron rings; only the nobility could wear rings of gold.

Wearing a ring as a symbol of marriage has been the norm throughout the history of Christianity, and inevitably predates it. Until the seventeenth century, however, the ring finger was the third on the right hand, where nuns still wear rings today, symbolising their marriage to Christ. This finger, the pronubus, was thought to be the only one with a direct connection through the 'vein of love' to the heart.

Confetti

The use of confetti (literally, 'small sweets') is directly connected to the ancient practice of pouring wheat or rice on the bride's head, to ensure her fertility and an abundance of food for the household. Horseshoes, created out of fire and iron, are powerful amulets and bring good luck, either carried by a bride, or nailed (the right way up) over doors.

The Language of Flowers

Flowers have long been ascribed many complex meanings and symbolic powers: orange-blossom signifies fertility and happiness – many nineteenth century brides insisted on having a sprig in their bouquet. Earlier, women may have sprinkled rose water upon their flowers, because it was said to bind a husband to his bride. Bouquets might include knotted ribbons, and brides once carried herbs, again to ward off evil spirits.

The possibilities for different floral combinations are dizzying, and each would have a subtly different meaning according to the flowers used:

Under wraps – a wedding dress from the 1870s.

Carnation	*Fascination*
Daisy	*Innocence*
Gardenia	*Joy*
Heather	*Luck*
Iris	*Passionate love*
Ivy	*Marriage, fidelity*
Ivy Geranium	*The flower of brides*
Myrtle	*Love*
Orchid	*Beauty*
Red Rose	*I love you*
Violet	*Faithfulness*
White Hyacinth	*Loveliness*
White Lily	*Purity*

Party Time

Every society has used a wedding as an excuse for a party, some lasting several days: in biblical times the significant and holy number of seven days was the prescribed time. Their wedding feasts included dancing, asking riddles and singing. The 'Song of Songs' is thought to be a series of lyrics for use at weddings.

The Romans used to employ a fool to tell rude jokes and deflect the attention of spirits from the couple: today's best man's speech might well mirror that tradition.

'Be tolerant of the human race. Your whole family belongs to it – and some of your spouse's family does too.'

Anon

29

Cutting the Cake

The bride and groom sharing a meal is an ancient tradition, and in Rome was a necessary act to formalise the marriage. Cakes symbolise fertility, and traditionally must be shared by all guests, and those unable to attend. Refusing to eat one's slice is both ill-mannered and bad luck, though bridesmaids and unmarried guests could dream of their future husbands and improve their own chances of marrying (and the likelihood of rodent infestation) if they placed the slice under their pillow.

Hasta La Fruit Cake, Baby

At the wedding of Arnold Schwarzenegger and Maria Shriver in 1986 the wedding cake was seven feet high, had eight tiers, and weighed 425 pounds.

Crossing the Threshold

Arriving at the new home meant crossing the threshold. To the Romans and many other cultures, the threshold had particular significance. It was another rite of passage, passing from one stage of life to the next. The Roman bride would smear the door-posts with fat and oil from a wolf or pig, then tie a woollen thread across the door, over which her husband would then carry her. Perhaps this was a vestige of an ancient form of marriage: by capture. Others would sacrifice an animal on the threshold, and the bride would step right foot first, over the flowing blood. To stumble at the threshold was bad luck; it was even worse to sneeze there.

A Taste of Honey

The honeymoon was once associated with a full month, and most commonly with honeyed wine (honey was considered to be an aphrodisiac).

Other sources say, however, that the honeymoon was nothing to do with holidaying. In fact, they say, before the nineteenth century, a wife would be returned to her parents' home straight after the ceremony; she would remain there for a month before her husband eventually got around to collecting her.

Until the middle of the nineteenth century, a wife would always be accompanied by a 'companion' (in addition to her husband) during the holiday. For those with unlimited purse-strings, the honeymoon often included a 'grand tour' of Europe; for the more affluent Victorians with their hugely expansive wallets and large quantities of free time, a honeymoon could last for up to two years.

A Greek Farewell

In ancient Greece, the newly-married couple would set out for the bridal home in a mule cart, accompanied by their friends who pelted them with sandals to drive away evil.

Regardless of where you holiday, however, the bridal bed should always run in the same direction as the room's floorboards, and on a north/south axis. But by now, even the most traditionally inclined couple will have other thoughts on their mind, probably not associated with the ancient customs of being accompanied by various attendants to help the couple undress, or the fact that it was once usual for the bride to wear gloves in bed.

The Wedding Bed-In

John Lennon and Yoko Ono treated their honeymoon in 1969 as a public event in order to bring attention to peace. They staged bed-ins and invited the press to come and speak to them.

The perfect honeymoon? Bride's irresistible offer from 1976.

One Wife or Two, Sir?

An Alternative Approach to Marriage

For primitive man, one wife was rarely sufficient. Polygamous marriages were very common in those days: the more wives a man had, the higher his social status. These relationships were very carefully structured: definite restrictions were placed on the number of wives per individual, and firm rules about the treatment of those wives were imposed. Under primitive Muslim law, for example, men were allowed just four legal wives: for the insatiable, however, relationships with concubines were permitted, and were not considered to be adulterous in any way.

Massively Married

On 28/29 November 1997, 30,000 couples were married in a mass wedding in America organised by the Moonie cult.

Polygamy is, much to the disappointment of some, a dying practice. It is now the preserve of certain religious sects, and a few surviving tribes; although in Kenya, 20 per cent of men and 30 per cent of women are found still to be in polygamous marriages.

Presumably, polygamous marriages usually prevented a husband – and possibly a wife as well – from being either too bored, or over-exposed to the company of one spouse. An alternative method of combating marital boredom is to lend your wife to someone else: once common behaviour amongst the Eskimos (and, legend has it, among suburban couples in the 1970s).

Eskimos were normally monogamous, but the rigours of the Arctic, and the need for a helpmeet, were sometimes too much for any man, and a lone Eskimo would often, in a camp far from home, 'borrow' another's partner.

Which Wife?

For the Thracians who live beyond Creston, it is customary for a man to have a number of wives; and when a husband dies, his wives enter into keen competition to decide which of them was most loved. The one on whom the honour of the verdict falls is first praised by both men and women, and then slaughtered over the grave by her next of kin and buried by her husband's side. For the other wives, not to be chosen is the worst possible disgrace, and they grieve accordingly'.

From Herodotus, *The Histories*
(Trans. Aubrey de Sélincourt, Penguin, 1954)

Returning to the old double standards, polyandry – where a woman has more than one husband – has always been much rarer. It usually occurred where the numbers of men far outweighed those of women. The killing of girl babies left the Todas of Southern India, unsurprisingly, with a disastrous imbalance of the sexes. To combat this, one woman was permitted to marry many men, usually a group of brothers; a practice embraced also by the Pawnee and Nevada Indians. In most primitive societies, brothers shared equal status, and there was thus less opportunity for the inevitable sexual jealousies. Responsibility for raising any children would be shared equally among these men, although the Todas had special rituals which dubbed just one lucky man as the legal father.

Thou Art Strongly Advised Against Adultery

The punishment for adulterous behaviour was, in certain societies, severe; this remains the case in some cultures. Often, unfaithful wives were rewarded with disfigurement or beatings. This was true for the Plains Indians, who would cut off the woman's nose as punishment. A male adulterer might also be beaten or killed, or required to pay damages to the wronged husband: leading, inevitably, to some dishonest individuals pressing claims to compensation at the expense of both husband and wife.

The Marriage Course

In Japan, young women may attend college prior to their marriage, where they will learn skills as a flower arranger, an organiser of the tea ceremony and an administrator of the household.

In Egypt, adultery is against Islamic law as well as civil law. As so often, however, double standards apply: the woman is always punished, whilst the man is punished only if adultery takes place within the marital home – long regarded as the woman's domain. Maximum punishment for either sex can be up to three years' imprisonment.

Popular Wedding Songs

Everything I Do
                    Bryan Adams

Wonderful Tonight
                    Eric Clapton

Unforgettable
                    Nat King Cole

It Had To Be You
                    Harry Connick Jr.

I Will Always Love You
                    Whitney Houston

Can't Help Falling In Love
                    Elvis Presley

Endless Love
                    Diana Ross and Lionel Richie

Unchained Melody
                    Righteous Brothers

When A Man Loves A Woman
                    Percy Sledge

Have I Told You Lately
                    Rod Stewart

Conrad Nagel stares lovingly at Marion Davies in *Lights
of Old Broadway*, 1925.

The Legalities

Who, What and Where

What with British law, and the restrictions of individual religions, getting married in modern Britain can seem a legal minefield – these are just some of the complications to consider:

- As long as you are both free (unmarried, that is), a vicar is legally bound to marry any couple who live in his parish, regardless of their church attending record. He is not legally bound, however, to marry divorcees, and may use his own discretion .

- Special dispensation is required for a Catholic to marry a non-Catholic in the church of their partner's religion.

- Muslim women may only marry Muslim men, although a Muslim man can marry a Muslim, Christian or Jewish woman.

- A Jewish wedding cannot take place on the Sabbath (from sunset on Friday until sunset on Saturday).

- All Muslim, Hindu and Sikh weddings need to be solemnised by a civil wedding to be legal under British law.

- It is possible to marry legally in places other than registry offices or religious buildings as long as they have a licence. However, it is still illegal to marry outdoors in Britain. So no skydiving weddings just yet!

Men cannot marry: their mother, adoptive mother or former adoptive mother, daughter, adoptive daughter or former adoptive daughter, father's mother, mother's mother, son's daughter, daughter's daughter, sister, father's sister, mother's sister, brother's daughter, sister's daughter, wife's mother, wife's daughter, father's wife, son's wife, father's father's wife, mother's father's wife, wife's father's mother, wife's mother's mother, wife's son's daughter, wife's daughter's daughter, son's son's wife, daughter's son's wife.

Women cannot marry: their father, adoptive father or former adoptive father, son, adoptive son or former adoptive son, father's father, mother's father, son's son, daughter's son, brother, father's brother, mother's brother, brother's son, sister's son, husband's father, husband's son, mother's husband, daughter's husband, father's mother's husband, son's son, husband's daughter's son, son's daughter's husband, daughter's daughter's husband.

Las Vegas is the home of unusual and exciting weddings –
you can marry in a drive-thru, in a helicopter, or even with
'Elvis'!

Happy ever after?

Hints For A Happy Marriage

Julia Cole

You can't believe that the big day is going to come and go so quickly. Soon you'll be taking the wedding suits back to the hire shop, showing your friends the wedding photos, and finding a space for the wedding presents – even the strange toast rack from your great-aunt.

The first few dreamy weeks will pass swiftly, and you'll soon be back at work. You may even have a few disagreements. You're about to learn an important lesson – marriage needs commitment and hard work, as well as romance. This is true whether you are marrying for the first or the fifth time. In fact, if you have previously been divorced, you may be hoping that your new marriage will never have disagreements. If you have already lived together you may think that this experience has ironed out all the wrinkles in your relationship before the wedding.

The truth is that the two of you are bound to disagree sometimes – you wouldn't be human if you didn't have different opinions. You will both change, and will need to learn how to manage that change, if you want to stay together. Remaining flexible and open to new ways of doing things, as well as learning to talk openly to one another, are two of the most important ingredients for a successful and loving marriage.

Bearing in mind some of the tips below will help to maintain that loving feeling, and see you still together in 50 years.

Listen as well as talk. When you are discussing something important, listen carefully to your partner rather than jumping in with your own opinion. It's easy to make assumptions, or become defensive, before you know the whole story.

Put aside 'just us' time. It's important to spend time with friends, or to visit your respective parents, but you need to balance this with time spent together alone. Do something relaxing or fun, but aim for at least two evenings a week alone.

Don't avoid the subject of money. You may be tempted to stuff that overdue bill in the drawer, but you do need to talk about finances before the final demands arrive. At the very least, keep a note of outgoing and incoming money. Decide spending and saving priorities together, and stick to your side of the agreement.

Keep your promises. Learning to trust someone takes time, and can only happen if you abide by the decisions you have both made. If you agree to clean the bathroom or put petrol in the car, do it!

Maintain your own interests. At the start of a marriage, it can seem tempting to give up all your own hobbies and dedicate yourself solely to your new husband or wife. But this could cause you to feel isolated and leave you completely dependent on the mood of your partner. If you enjoy rock-climbing, aerobics or folk music, go on doing them. But don't spend every spare hour on them – your partner could wonder what you feel more passionate about – them, or the hobby!

Invest in sex. Your sexual feelings will ebb and flow throughout your relationship – sometimes you will make love every day, at other times, once a month. This variation is normal, and can depend on how tired you are, or whether you are feeling unwell. But sex can become mundane if you always rush through the same old routine at the end of a strenuous day. Put aside evenings or weekend mornings for lazy love, when you will feel unhurried and more responsive to a loving touch.

Cope with conflict. Arguments needn't mean disaster. An argument that clears the air and leads to a problem being sorted out can strengthen a marriage. But rows that go round in circles and leave you simmering with rage are likely to be very destructive. When you fight, don't drag in every disagreement you've ever had. Stick to the topic and keep calm. Don't use insults or sarcasm. Instead, try to understand why you may both be under pressure, and take positive action.

Apologise for hurting each other. It's impossible to live with someone and not occasionally make a hurtful remark. If you know you've upset your spouse, say sorry. Don't wait until several days of

Brand-new 1967 three-programme 19" set. Gets BBC1, ITV, BBC2. Transistorised to give even greater sensitivity, clearer picture, better sound. Extra power on picture tube for brightest picture yet. Smooth, dust-free cabinet lines, diamond-finished controls, silver-trimmed facia. Matching legs available.

What every bride should know about colour TV

Only spendthrifts buy TV sets. Prudent girls rent from Radio Rentals on the Single Payment Discount Rental Plan.

Colour TV starts in just a few months now. Swinging new life for the home screen. But a big disappointment to the unwary couple who've just bought – yes, *bought* – a black-and-white set that's suddenly become completely old hat.

We say buying costs too much

In the first year alone, Government controls can make you pay out £50 or more for a 19" set if you buy on hire purchase. You've possible service bills to face, however you buy. And if you pay cash you can lock up a lot of money on a set that you'll soon want to change to colour TV.

There's only one perfect solution

Rent a brand-new 1967 black-and-white set now from Radio Rentals. Choose the Single Payment Discount Rental Plan. For the 19" Model 662, illustrated here, you make just one payment of £22.2.0, and nothing more for a full year. This includes

installation, darn good service – even if we say it ourselves – and insurance against fire and theft. Quite a package for so little money.

You'll be able to change from black-and-white to colour TV with every confidence, because of our years of research and practical experience. Our service staff have already learned colour techniques in our laboratories – so they won't have to learn in your home.

So why don't you give us a call now?

We have about 750 showrooms and about 7,000 trained staff waiting to switch you on to TV viewing the way it should be. Ring or drop in at your nearest showroom and ask for a no-cost trial in your own home. Most of our branches have 24-hour phone facilities. If you live in the London area, phone HUNter 5271 up to 10 p.m.

Go on. Do it now.

RELIABLE

RADIO RENTALS

Radio Rentals help out the new brides in 1967.

stony silence have passed. Apologise quickly and agree not to make the same mistake again. Support one another.

You are both going to need support to deal with everyday ups and downs. Be sympathetic and interested in your partner's bad day with the boss or terrible drive home from work. Tell your partner how proud you are when they do something well. Think twice before you give criticism and offer praise as much as possible.

Tell your partner you love them. It's amazing how people forget this most basic of communications. You can say 'I love you' in many different ways. A cuddle, a cup of tea at the end of a long day, a note left on the kitchen table or a phone call when you're apart, will all help you to express your love as well as simply saying the words.

Making the loving commitment of marriage is like starting a journey. When the wedding is over, it may feel as if you have just arrived at your destination, but you are in fact about to begin a new stage of travel together.

On the journey with your new husband or wife, you will need to make preparations. A willingness to develop your personal communication skills, and to offer support to each other in good and bad times, is vital. So is the ability to plan for difficult times by developing strategies in order to cope with tough decisions. On this marital journey, however, there are no maps, and you cannot know what lies ahead. You both need to build and maintain trust, so if the path in front looks hard to climb, you know you can rely on your partner to help you.

It's also important to enjoy the good times and laugh together. Shared fun is like money in the bank – it will support you when you feel less happy.

So now you're married and you've got your ticket – enjoy the journey.

Julia Cole is a Relate-trained Couple and Marital Counsellor, Psychosexual Therapist and Counselling Supervisor. She is the Problem Page Editor for Essentials *magazine and a freelance writer and broadcaster on relationship issues.*

Jeanette Loff and her dramatically dressed bridesmaids in
King of Jazz, 1930.

Anniversaries

Traditionally, each wedding anniversary is associated with some material, either to add to household necessities, or on a much more romantic scale altogether.

In the early years, requirements are quite simple: the first anniversary is cotton; second – paper; third – leather; fourth – fruit or flower. Nothing to stretch the purse yet.

But by now you might be requiring something more substantial. The fifth is wood, and the sixth iron. The seventh year is traditionally itchy, so more modest demands, in the form of wool, are made this year. But after this, the wife might become more demanding in her requirements: eight is bronze, or, probably for Americans, 'electrical appliance'. Happy electrical appliance anniversary, dear.

The ninth is pottery; tenth – tin; eleventh – steel; twelfth – silk or fine linen. Well, you've deserved it. Lace is the thirteenth; fourteenth is ivory; fifteenth is crystal. The twentieth is china, which probably needs replacing after bringing up clumsy children.

> 'He early on let her know who is the boss. He looked her right in the eye and clearly said, "You're the boss".'
>
> Anon

Silver is, of course, the twenty-fifth; thirty is pearl (guess who gets the pearls); thirty-five is coral – perhaps a holiday in a tropical paradise? The fortieth is ruby, and the fiftieth gold.

The fifty-fifth is emerald and the sixtieth diamond. But for those rare couples who make it to their seventy-fifth anniversary, there is the ultimate disappointment: oh no, not diamonds again...

Copyright Notices